Enthralled

The Enslaved Duet. Book One.

giana darling

Enthralled
Copyright 2018 Giana Darling
Published by Giana Darling

Edited by Jenny Sims
Cover Design by Najla Qamber
Cover Model Mariam Agredano
Cover Photographer Xavi Smoke
Formatting by Stacey at Champagne Book Design

To Serena.
Your friendship has changed my life. You are my fairy godmother, Yoda,
best friend and confidante. Thank you for everything you do for me.
#McDarling4Life

"I want to be inside your darkest everything."
—*Frida Kahlo.*

xoxo,

Diane Darling

Part One

SOLD

NON DECOR, DECO. I AM NOT LED, I LEAD

Chapter One

*I*t was the biggest day of my life.

I know most people say that about something joyous; a graduation, a wedding ceremony, the birth of their first child.

My situation was a little different.

Sure, it was my eighteenth birthday, but it was also the day I was sold.

And I don't mean sold metaphorically. As far as I was concerned, my soul was still intact although my father might have been selling his in return for the thousands of dollars he would receive for my body. He wasn't that worried about it. And honestly, neither was I. If Seamus Moore had a soul at one time, it had long ago dissolved into cinders and ash.

You're probably wondering why I went along with it. Even as I sat in the beaten-up red Fiat my twin brother, Sebastian, had just fixed for the fortieth time beside my potentially soulless father who was singing along to Umberto Tozzi as if it was a normal day, I was wondering the same thing. My eldest sister Elena was taking a free online ethics course, and even she didn't know the moral answer to the question my life had been reduced to—was exchanging one body worth the price of multiple person's happiness?

I didn't really care that she didn't have a response. To me, it was worth it.

"You remember what I told you, *carina?*" my father asked over the tinny swell of sound from the car speakers.

"*Sì.*"

"In English," he reprimanded gently with a crooked smile in my direction. It was as if I was just being a silly child and teasing him with my mini rebellion. I wanted to tease his skin with the edge of a cold blade, but I held my tongue between my teeth and bit down hard until the fantasy dissolved in pain.

"Tell me," he continued.

"No."

His hand found my slim thigh, and his steely fingers wound around it in a rough squeeze. I was used to his physicality, and it did not intimidate me, not now when I faced a potentially much more dangerous future. But I indulged him anyway.

"I am not to look his eyes—"

"*In* his eyes," he corrected.

"*In* his eyes. Or speak unless I am directly spoken to. I will obey him in all things and keep him in comfort. I understand, *papa*, it is like Italian marriage, but with a contract instead of vows." I was fluent in the language, but stress ate at my erudite mind like termites.

He grunted, unamused with my droll comparison. Even though Seamus was not Italian—his Irish accent, deep red hair, and ruddy complexion would always betray him as otherwise—he had assimilated himself into every facet of the culture until being Italian had become a kind of religion to him. And my father's version of a priest? Let's just say, you'd never want to meet Rocco Abruzzi, the man who ran a large gambling operation for the current Neapolitan *capo*, Salvatore Vitale. He was unassuming enough with flaccid features and brows that sagged over wet black eyes, but he had unusually large hands and he liked to use them to deal cards, diddle women, and pound in the faces of those who reneged on debts, those like my father.

Seamus drew a hand over the lingering bruises on the right side of his jaw with fingers that were scabby and missing their nails. There was only one reason, in his mind, that I was being sold. And that was to pay off his incredible debt to the underground leaders of Napoli. For years, I wished that they would just finish him off, slice him up and drop him into an alley somewhere for someone to find and kick at, too afraid to report the murder to the police. A few times, when he had been missing for long enough, I thought my fantasy had come true only for him to show up the next day, bright eyed and bushy tailed as if he had been at the spa, and not on the run from men with wet eyes and bloody hands.

"You must speak English with him, *carina*, in case he does not speak Italian."

I straightened at the information, not because I was uncomfortable speaking English. Seamus had made sure that all of us could speak it to some extent and I had studied rigorously for the past two years with Sebastian. If we were going to get out, English was going to be a thread in our lifeline. No, what had startled me was my own father's lack of knowledge about who was waiting for us in a villa inside Rome.

"You don't know who is buying me?" My grinding teeth made my words gravelly, but I knew he could still understand me.

My heart was in my stomach, and that was in my throat. I felt like one of Picasso's strange imaginings, my body twisted up with tension and fear so that I couldn't even recognize myself as human anymore. I was trying to focus on anything but the great and terrifying unknown of my future—the dust motes in our dirty car, the smell of alcohol leaking from my father's pores, or the way the hot southern Italian sun burned through the windows like flames.

"I hope you aren't going to question your new…" He paused. "…guardian like that, Cosima. Remember, respect. Have I taught you nothing?"

"Yes. You've taught me to distrust men, never blindly obey anyone, and to curse God for giving you the capacity to father children," I said blandly.

I could focus on the hatred of my father that blazed like a dying star in my belly instead of that awful fear threatening to overwhelm me.

Hatred was more powerful than fear. One was a shield and an armament I could utilize while the other could only be weaponised against me.

"Be grateful someone is willing to pay for you."

"How much?" I had refrained from asking so far, but my pride wouldn't allow me to go on unknowing. How much was I worth? How much money could be found in the flare of my hip and the divot of my collarbone, in the meat of my tits and the folds of my sex?

It was his turn to grind his teeth, but I wasn't surprised that he didn't answer me. Honestly, I didn't think even he knew. It was a perverted friend of a perverted friend of my father who had set up the interaction, some human trafficker that Seamus had played cards with one time when he was drunk enough to admit he needed money and give away the secret of his beautiful daughter, the virgin. His trump card, as he often, tenderly, referred to me as.

The news had gotten back to the Camorra, and the rest was history.

"For how long?" I asked, and it wasn't the first time I'd done so. "He can't possibly own me for the rest of my natural born life?"

"No," he conceded. "A period of five years was promised… with the possibility of renewing the contract again for double the price."

"And how much of this dirty money will Mama and my siblings see?" I demanded even as my mind whirred.

Five years.

Five.

I'd be twenty-three when all was said and done. If I was off the modelling track for that long, I would be too old to continue to any kind of fame and fortune. I could have done without both, but I wanted to be able to provide for my family until the end of their days.

If I were a twenty-three-year-old washed-up model without any education to speak of, I wouldn't be able to do that.

So, some of the windfall from my sale *had* to go to my family.

There wasn't any other option.

"Enough to cover my debts," he admitted, adjusting his sweaty hands on wheel. "Nothing more."

I closed my eyes and rested my forehead against the windowpane, bringing up the sepia toned snapshot of my childhood home in my mind's eye. A box of concrete pasted together by crumbling mortar and bandaged with planks of brittle wood my brother had cut himself. It was a small home on the outskirts of Naples in a part of town the tourists could never reach even if they became lost. My city was a place of dangers and illusions; webs cast between buildings and at the end of roads, catching you in their sticky fibers just as you reached for a promise behind the netting. No one could escape it, yet tourists came, and people stayed.

I didn't want my family to be condemned to those depths forever. There was no way I was going to sell my life away for anything less than security for my family.

Seamus shot me a concerned look. "I can feel you thinking, Cosi. Put a stop to it right now. You are in no position to ask for anything more."

"And you are in no position to tell me what to do or think," I retorted.

Just when I thought I had a lock on the anger, he had to do something to break those chains. I hated the taste of fury in my throat, and the metallic bite of it on my tongue. I wasn't a senseless, angry woman. I was passionate, but to a point.

Elena had taught me from a young age that if you could understand something, its motivation or context, you held power over it and over your reaction to it.

I tried to channel that now as I sat in a car with my father on the way to my new master with little to no assurances for the people I was even doing this for.

As the car pulled farther away from the spidery tendrils, I could feel the throbbing pulse of the city recede at my back. It wasn't beautiful like the rest of the country, though it rested on the ocean. The harbor was industrial, and though it was only an hour away from Roma, unemployment plagued Neapolitans like the Black Death, and it showed in the dirty faces of adolescent pickpockets and garbage strewn across the walkways in place of pretty flower boxes. People were tired in my hometown, and it showed. But I wondered how people couldn't find a certain beauty in that?

I didn't want to leave. It wasn't my choice, yet I had accepted the pain of its inevitability easily, my body absorbing the shock without consequence. My love for crumbling, beautiful Napoli was a drop in the bucket compared to my love for my crumbling, beautiful family. I was doing this, selling my body and maybe my soul, for them. I'd get them some of the money they were due or else the sale was dead in the water. The mafia would kill my father; we would still be haunted by the looming shadow of their influence, and we might never get out of that godforsaken city alive, but at least we'd be together.

I drew up their beloved faces in my mind's eyes, etching them into the black screens of my lids so that every time I blinked, I would be reminded of the reason for my sacrifice.

I knew all too well the realities of our situation. If Sebastian didn't leave soon, no matter our economic status, he would be forced into the Camorra, who had been nipping none too gently at his tender heels for the past two years. He was now eighteen, old for recruitment when the average age of youth inducement into the mafia was as young as eleven.

I squeezed my eyes shut to distort the vivid image of my male self with a gun in one hand, blood on the other, and money, stacks of it, in his mouth. Sebastian was smart and able, afflicted with a beauty so striking it often brought him unwanted attention. I hoped that he would use some of the money to leave, maybe for Roma, and use his beauty to pull himself out of the stinking hole of poverty we had been born into. Even though I knew he wouldn't—couldn't—bring himself to leave our sisters and mother alone, I chose to believe my fantasy.

Just as I hoped that the money would continue to go toward the education of my prodigal younger sister, Giselle, so gifted with a pencil or brush that she could render whole people on a page with their emotions and blood trapped beneath the surface of her painted strokes. I'd been practically living in Milano and Roma for the past year working any gig I could get in order to send back money for Giselle's education at *L'*École des Beaux-Arts in Paris. She was too talented to be held back by our poverty, and too pretty and soft at heart to deal with the shark-infested waters of Napoli. I knew last year when Elena's older boyfriend began to take undue notice of our shy sister that she had to leave.

Her education was funded on my ability to provide for it with my modelling, and now that I was being sold, I needed to assure she would have the means to continue without me.

Ideally, funds would be left over for my smartest sibling, Elena, so she could attend a real school and earn a real degree. For Mama, a new home with a kitchen well equipped to deal with her delicious fare. And for my father—the man who just then was driving me towards my future as a bought woman? Well, for Seamus Moore, I could only wish for the best his soul would buy him in this life. A quick death.

Nico, one of Abruzzi's men—not much older than me and the only man in the Camorra who I had any sort of good feelings toward—had shown up at the house last week with Rocco and some others. I was home from Milano for the week to celebrate Sebastian's and my eighteenth birthday, and I'd been hoping to avoid the Camorra. Mama had been at the market with my sisters, and Sebastian was working at the factory in town, so the men had been able to retreat inside for some *grappa*, and Nico had stayed outside. "To keep me company," he had explained, but I knew now it was to keep an eye on their investment.

I had continued to read, my hair falling between us to create a thick obsidian curtain, but the well-loved, well-worn book shook slightly in my hands. My heart seemed to balance on a wire that thrummed dangerously with a staccato beat.

"What's happening?" I finally asked, unable to maintain the pretense of reading when my body was so attuned to the finality in the air.

The house felt like grounds for a funeral, only I didn't know who had died.

When I turned to look at Nico sitting beside me on the front step, he was gazing down at me with warm brown eyes. I only allowed myself to like Nico a little because his eyes hadn't yet turned wet and very, very black.

He spoke in the Italian of Napoli, filled with slang and more Latin notes than other dialects. His voice was hoarse and warm, like the sound of a well-fired furnace, and when I think of my home, my native tongue, it's Nico's voice I hear.

"You are the most beautiful girl in Italy."

I wasn't supposed to roll my eyes, but growing up with beauty, I got away with more than most girls, and a lifetime of favour had taught me bad habits. I was lucky that Nico only smiled in response.

"I've heard that one before, Nicci."

He shrugged his hulking shoulders. "Doesn't make it less true."

"No," I agreed and collected my rippling mass of waves into my fists. "You know, one day I am going to cut it all off."

He shook his head, and I wondered if he knew I wouldn't, that it was my security blanket, that I slept with it draped over my arm like a child with a stuffed rabbit.

Instead, he said, "It wouldn't make a difference."

I looked across the street at the yellow grass and glaringly bright yellow house under the yellow sun. Yellow was my least favourite colour, and sometimes it seemed that Napoli was soaked in it. Not burnished in gold but drenched in something hotter, a shade with a stench, like urine.

"What are they talking about today? More debts?"

Nico was slow to shake his head, but then again, Nico was slow to most things. His stature made him the perfect thug, but the goodness in his heart and the methodical pace of his thoughts made him a less-than-ideal villain.

I sighed. "I don't understand why they don't just kill him."

Usually, he ignored me when I spoke with a mouthful of vinegar, but he continued to shake his head. "No, they have another plan, Cosi. And it involves you."

Immediately, I understood I was dead. Maybe not literally, but from the second Nico enunciated those words, I knew that my life was no longer my own. We had expected this, of course. Seamus could only play so many hands of cards before the only thing left was me, his trump. We all knew it—my twin brother, my sisters, Mama—but no one would talk to me about it, not even when I pressed.

And now that day was here, and I was alone on the steps with a man I hardly knew. It pretty neatly foreshadowed my fate.

"Tell me."

He hesitated. "They will."

I swung my knees around, knocking his thigh so I could look him in the eyes. He was startled when I took one of his huge hands in mine. "I'm asking you."

"Things are changing. Salvatore's new *consigliere* is ruthless and very smart. There is talk of him taking over the New York City outfit if his plans for Napoli work out." Nico spoke of the handsome mafia boss whose specialty was transporting weapons and bribing politicians. "Rocco is getting nervous about his position with the *capo*. He needs more money. It's time for those with debt to pay with money or…" His shrug was eloquent as the unspoken words *or whatever else of value they had, even if it was their life* hung in the air.

"And I'm the most valuable thing Seamus Moore has," I whispered, almost afraid to say it out loud.

It was late August, and the air was thick with warmth, but a shiver bit into my spine with tiny, pointed teeth and shook me until my bones rattled.

Nico nodded and then gave me the silence I needed.

"I offered to marry you."

I laughed. It was such a sweet, foolish sentiment especially from someone who knew better that I couldn't help the laughter that burst from the compression chamber of my lungs.

He wasn't offended. "We would have been good together. Pretty babies."

"Yes," I patted his broad knee but didn't allow myself to see that future. "Pretty babies. Instead, what, I am to be married to some mafia boss?"

"Not quite. Salvatore's *consigliere* has found someone who wants to…" He cleared his throat and looked down at my hand on his knee. He brushed a thick knuckle down my wrist and sighed. "He has found someone who wants to buy you."

My mouth opened to laugh, I think, but only hot air escaped, fleeing as my lungs collapsed.

"You are very beautiful, Cosima, a virgin and a good girl, despite your independent streak," he tried to explain, his voice heavy and low as if the weight of his tone would subdue me. "You cannot be so surprised."

"Sleep with me then." I knew he would never, not like this. Not even the most beautiful girl in Italy was worth dying over. "I'll run away."

"You won't." Rocco emerged from the small house, wiping his scarlet-dipped fingers on a scrap of grey linen that I was almost sure he had ripped from one of Mama's curtains.

I shot to my feet, but he froze me in place with those horrible eyes.

"You won't, beautiful girl, because if you do, your father…" Seamus appeared in the room behind him, and even in the low light, I could see the blood dripping from his hands, streaming

like tears across his face from an open gash in his forehead. "...
and your mother, your brother, and your sisters, they will all die.
I will string them up from that tree." He pointed at a massive
Cyprus tree, the only spot of pretty on the narrow block. "With
bells tied to their ankles so that their bodies sing when the wind
comes. Would you be so selfish, beautiful girl?"

My imagination prepared the image in less time than it took
for me to blink, yet I was shaking my head before he had even
finished. The sound of bells tickled my eardrums.

I sagged.

Rocco nodded and smiled almost kindly, but my gaze was
sunk deep in the mire of his morally corrupt gaze. "You will be
sold to a foreigner, a man who has agreed to pay a considerable
amount for you. Before you ask, I do not know the details, and I
do not want to. You will be whomever this man wants you to be
if you want your family to live and prosper. Do you understand?"

When I didn't move, he came closer, taking my chin in
his hands and tilting it up until my throat was closed and I was
perched on my toes to reduce the tension.

"Such golden eyes. Money eyes." He breathed into my open
mouth. "It is almost a shame to lose such beauty."

He let me go, and I struggled not to stumble as I dragged in
deep gulps of tepid air.

"What does Salvatore think of this plan?" I asked desperately.

The *capo* had a soft spot for me that I'd never understood
because it started before I'd hit puberty and every man began to
take note of me.

No, the great Salvatore had been watching for years, a benevolent guardian with more in common with a demon than an
angel.

I couldn't believe he would be happy to sell me off.

Rocco's meaty paw wrapped around my wrist and tugged

me closer. Strangely, there was no violence in his gesture. Instead, as I tipped my head back to look into his dark as tar eyes, all I saw was anxiety.

"Salvatore understands the currency of beauty and flesh. This is a man who just yesterday stabbed a Neapolitan official in the eye with a fork because he disrespected him over breakfast. It's almost sweet that you think *capo* would give a shit about a pretty, worthless little thing like you."

I hissed in pain as he twisted my wrist and leaned closer to whisper, "In fact, I remember exactly what your Salvatore said to me. 'She is a great beauty, and that is the worst luck any woman in our world can have. Too tempting to let roam free and too dangerous to keep in one place. Make sure you get a good price for her.'"

I squeezed my eyes shut because I could hear Salvatore's smooth as crushed velvet voice say those words. He'd said similar things to me before on his rare, but impactful visits, his eyes sharp and sad like a weapon he didn't want to use against me pressed tight to my throat.

Make sure you get a good price for her.

The words punctured themselves into my heart like a scar written in Braille.

"It's a good thing that your pretty Elena will remain here under my protection, and Giselle when she visits on school holiday. Otherwise, there would be no telling what might happen to them," he added casually.

My neck snapped as I shot my gaze back over to him, but Rocco ignored my desperate eyes to focus on a clump of dirt sticking to the side of his well-polished shoes.

"Don't you dare touch them," I said, part plea and part threat but totally ineffective.

Rocco grinned his pointy teeth at me. There was a rumor

within the Camorra that he had sharpened them with a metal file when he worked as an enforcer in his youth. Looking at those sharp white teeth now, it was hard to believe otherwise.

"I have no desire to touch them, but many other men do. Your sisters have that pretty red hair like their father. Redheads are very rare in Napoli, a delicacy if you will."

"You won't," I ground out. "If you want me to go willingly with this *stronzo*, then you will promise me never to let any of your men near my sisters."

Nico shifted uncomfortably, and I could tell that he wished I would keep quiet, accept my destiny, and be happy that Rocco was even speaking with me in a civilized manner. The situation might have seemed unjust to someone from the outside, but the reality was that I was skating on thin ice. The men putting the finishing touches on my father's bruised and bloody body wouldn't hesitate to brand me with a different kind of violence.

As if reading my thoughts, Rocco swung his stare my way, scraping over my curves like a serrated knife. I wasn't wearing anything revealing—to do so would have been begging for it—but I still had the sense that he knew my body well, that he had fantasized about it enough to accurately guess at the swell of my breasts and the incline of my waist. I was used to the descriptiveness of desire written across men's faces, but I hadn't yet learned how to translate it into power.

So when Rocco took another menacing step toward me, I lowered my chin to stare at the ground, my shoulders rolling in and my hands clasping submissively before my groin. It was natural, this position, this submission, but I was still hot with shame when his chuckle wafted warmly across my forehead.

"It's a shame we must keep you a virgin for your future owner," he said as a thick finger slid down my middle part and over the shell of my ear. It was a gentle touch, but it made me shudder almost violently in fear. "I could have sold it off too."

He laughed again, hard and strong into my downturned face before he twisted and walked to the red Ferrari parked partially on Mama's flower garden.

Nico came to me then, placing a large ineloquent hand on my shoulder. "People will miss you."

If he meant to be comforting, it had the opposite effect. Anger rushed up from my diaphragm like dragon's breath. Screw him and screw anyone who thought the weight of missing me would come anywhere near to the emptiness at my center. They might not have me, inconsequential me, but I wouldn't have them, this home, this city of dirty beauty and this family of sin-soaked angels. And into the emptiness a new man, *my owner*, would try to shove pieces of himself, his home, his city, his language... least of all, his cock. I was smart enough to know, even then, that the only reason I was worthy was for my beautiful veneer and the only reason someone would buy me was for sex.

I kept my head bowed, and Nico took it as the dismissal it was.

As soon as the thugs had left, I went to the front steps and picked up my book. It was in English, the first book my father had ever brought home from work at the university. A collection of mythologies by an American woman, Edith Hamilton. It wasn't something that had intrigued any of my siblings, and I had claimed it as my own almost the second Seamus had stepped through the doors holding it and a bottle of American Bourbon.

I flipped to the story of Persephone, the beautiful child goddess who had been abducted by Hades with the consent of her father and to the obliviousness of her mother. My thumb tore the corner of the page as I jerked it closed, my damp print catching on the cheap paper and bending it.

"Cosima."

Seamus stood in the doorway. Well, he leaned against it, his body colourful and deflated like a child's old party balloon. They had pulled out three fingernails on each of his hands and he held them tenderly to his chest, even though I could tell one shoulder was dislocated. Without a word, I climbed the three steps, grabbed hold of his torso, and popped his arm back in place. His breath hissed out from between his dry, cracked lips, but he didn't protest. After all, this wasn't our first time doing this.

"It's a good idea," he said.

His damp forehead glistened, and I couldn't resist the impulse to mop it with my shirtsleeve.

"It is," I agreed, but only because emotions were impossible.

Each heartbeat forced them from my blood, condensing them into a small box tucked behind my breastbone. If I reacted now…Well, someone would end up dead, and I didn't like the odds of it being me.

"You can't tell the family," he warned.

"No." It would be my family who would die then. Thrown in front of me like broken shell casings in my standoff against Rocco and his crew. I was doing this *for* them, and I wouldn't allow them to get in the way.

I'd leave a note on the kitchen table as I did when I had a sudden job come up in Roma or Milano. Explain that I had to be out of the country for work, and I didn't know how long it would be before I'd return.

They would be upset, of course, but they knew it was a necessary evil of our survival.

I was often gone.

So it would take them a while to realize I wasn't coming back at all.

"I'll take care of them." Seamus always did a good job of pretending to be a father. When he was home, he tucked us in, his alcoholic breath soothing as he sang Irish lullabies. He read to Elena, who still, much to her frustration, struggled with English, and he posed for Giselle, who loved his red hair and freckled face so much like her own. Only with Sebastian was he distant, and even then, it was due to my brother's lack of respect and his blatant disapproval of everything Seamus stood for. If Seamus was in the house, Sebastian, often, was not.

And then there was me, his favourite daughter. It wasn't saying much, Seamus didn't have the heart to truly favour someone, even Mama, and honestly, I was everyone's favourite. In a family of fractures, I was the pane of glass.

But being his favourite had taught me enough about Seamus Moore to know better than to believe a word he said. And as I smiled sharply into his molted face, I knew he was proud of me for seeing through his bullshit. It showed him that he had taught me well.

Chapter Two

*W*e were almost there.

The signage for Roma promised us a farther fifteen-minute drive, but I recognized the route well enough, even in the dark, to know we would be there in ten. After that, we would ascend the hill to Aventine, the exclusive neighborhood outside of the tourist scope, tucked among leaves and hedges like a hidden Eden. I had never been to that part of the city. My infrequent modelling career had given me no reason to stray outside of the *centro storico* unless I was craving my favourite slice of pizza from a small trattoria in the Jewish Quarter.

As we climbed the hill, the Fiat huffing inelegantly with effort, I twisted my hands in my lap and forced myself to take three deep breaths. I had my own plan, and it was about time that I set part one in motion.

"Papa."

Seamus looked over at me and smiled as he pulled into a small side street. "Yes, *carina?*"

"I have one condition for the sale."

One red eyebrow rose, and though I looked nothing like him, it was uncanny how similarly we expressed ourselves in the flowing movement of our hands and the elasticity of our features. I felt a hard pang in my chest and wondered if it was because I would miss him or because I so deeply hated him.

"I will disappear, right here, right now, unless you agree to my terms," I said.

"Well then." He waved his hand to go on before flicking the turn single and coasting to the front of a large wrought iron gate. He rolled down the window, but the gates opened before he could speak into the intercom.

I waited, taking in the sloping driveway bracketed by beautifully cut grass and spiraling trees. The house appeared almost immediately, large and traditional with a red clay roof and golden stucco walls. It was beautiful, certainly, but a fake, a very obvious modern reproduction of something the owner could have had authentically with perhaps a few less amenities.

"You need to leave," I said as I got out of the car quickly and reached into the back to snatch the small duffel bag I had hidden under my seat. "I packed your clothes, some money." Money that I had shamefully stolen from Sebastian's getaway fund. "Even your pipe is in here."

"How thoughtful," he said, rising out of the small car and staring at me from across the hot metal.

"I'm serious, Papa." My accent thickened noticeably as my anxiety spiked. We didn't have much time to linger in the driveway. I had already seen a curtain twitch. "I need you to swear to me that you will never go back there."

"They need me," he said, but it lacked conviction because even Seamus Moore wasn't a good enough liar to make that true.

"They really don't. You've only brought the family shame and misfortune. Until now, it was almost forgivable. You have a gambling problem and a silver tongue." I shrugged. "You were born like that. But now, you've gambled away your daughter. And I won't ever let you put Giselle or Elena in the same situation."

"Ah, I see. So you think this is a good trade? The golden

daughter martyred for the wicked father?" Seamus' eyes twinkled merrily. He delighted in my mind, in the games and trades he had imparted to me like wisdom. It wasn't wisdom, it was foolery, but if he wanted to believe otherwise, I didn't really care.

"No, I think they'll be better off without both of us. We attract too much attention," I said.

The redhead gambler involved with the mafia and the beautiful virgin they lusted after... it didn't make for a happy ending for anyone, but especially their loved ones.

"Arrogant."

I shrugged.

"Your sisters are beautiful, too. And your Sebastian."

My heart started, stuttered, and stopped at the mention of my brother, my other half. But I had thought this out carefully, and I knew the statistics and probabilities of their future more clearly than I could ever foresee my own.

"A handsome man is still a man. And with you gone, they'll actually have a chance of getting out," I pointed out.

"No one just 'gets out', Cosima." It was the first time my father's voice had changed from anything but pleasant. "Not without consequences."

"I know." I nodded, the finality of the movement like a hammer. "What do you call this?"

I tossed the bag back into the car and slammed the door shut before turning on my heel to head for the massive oak doors of the villa. A small portfolio containing the only things I cared about in this life was clutched under my arm like something precious and superfluous, like a football.

I waited until he stood beside me at the door to say, "Swear to me."

He hesitated. "I'll need some more money."

I almost smiled; so predictable. "If you're willing to steal mob money, I won't stop you."

He kicked at the door, his knuckles too raw to knock. It opened suddenly, as if someone had been waiting with his or her hand on the knob for us to arrive. A man stood before us, dressed in an expensive black and white suit that matched his salt and pepper hair which was thick and deeply parted, tidily combed, and slicked to one side. He was the least impressionable man I had ever seen in my life; entirely pale like only a Brit could be with bland, fleshy features. Without a word, he stepped aside to allow two men in black to pass through and frisk us.

I could tell Seamus wanted to say something, object or, more probably, make an inappropriate joke, but one haughty look from the butler stopped him. It was easy to ignore the hulking man who moved from behind the butler to pat me down, brushing his thick fingers over my breasts and groin; he was professional and barely paid my face a cursory glance. It was the first time a man had shown himself to be sexually unaffected by my audacious curves, and I was strangely aroused by it. He wore sunglasses even though he had emerged from the cool, dark interior and when he grasped my arm firmly to tug me into the house, I shivered slightly.

We were led through an immense red tiled foyer down a long hallway to a large closed door. They left us there, padding silently away with no indication of what we should do. So we waited in silence because it felt like sacrilege to speak in such a tomb.

"If I promised to change?" Seamus spoke so quietly, his mouth unmoving and slack that even though I was looking right at him, I couldn't be sure he had spoken.

"You won't."

"Do you think I don't want to, Cosima? That I like being me? Do you think I want to do this, sell my daughter, for Christ's sake? I love you." A shaky breath wavered in the air between us. "I love

Mama and our family. Don't take both of us away from them."

"I really think I'm doing you a favour," I said, and I did.

I was giving him an out. If he went back to Napoli, he would have to be crazy to think that the family would welcome him with open arms after what he had done. This way, he could leave knowing he had my blessing at least.

Seamus Moore was a lot of things, but crazy wasn't one of them.

"Fine," he said. "I promise."

It should have sickened me how easily he agreed, but I was too busy being relieved. I could feel its effects suffuse my face, my mouth parting on a sweet sigh, my eyes softening like melted butter. There wasn't enough time between the hush of the lock shifting and the faint breath of the door swinging open for me to rearrange my expression. I didn't know how I wanted to look like when I met the man who would soon own my body, but it definitely wasn't like this.

And I could tell immediately by the look in his eyes that he was taking advantage of my disorientation. Thick lashed silver eyes marked and catalogued my body with the efficiency and mild interest of a librarian with a stack of books and the Dewy decimal system. With superhuman senses, he noted the triangle of moles on the left side of my neck and the ripped cuticles around my long nails, the way my modest patterned dress floated around my thin calves. I could see the conclusions too, in those dark eyes: undernourished, stressed, and covered in the thin film of poverty. The familiar burn of shame forged a steely rod of rage in my gut that lodged itself in my throat and made me want to gag.

Blinking slowly, I pulled my eyes from the sticky depths of his gaze and studied the man before me. He had thick, luxurious hair the colour of burnished gold that brushed the collar of his suit jacket and skin that seemed edible like caramel stretched taut over his strong features. Surprisingly, he was almost a foot taller than my abnormal height, and the awesome width of his shoulders tapered into a narrow waist. I catalogued these physical attributes without qualm and easily too. Beauty was my profession, and even in my disorientated state, I could appreciate a gorgeous man.

When my eyes wandered along the square cut of his jaw up to those blade grey eyes again, they were lacquered with mild humour. I bristled, realizing that he had been indulging my curiosity, watching me as I studied his appearance and found him anything but wanting.

I glared at him in horror as I realized who he was.

"Not quite worth one million pounds, is she?" His husky voice was at odds with the crisp, obviously upper-class British accent, so it took me a moment to decipher his words.

I opened my mouth to snap at him, but Seamus quickly grinned and spoke first, "I think you will find that she cleans up very nicely."

"Before we get to that," I bit out, stepping slightly forward and to the side in front of my father to excluded him at least symbolically from this negotiation. "I need to renegotiate the fee."

"Do you?" he asked with the kind of bored ennui only the rich could affect so beautifully.

"I do," I affirmed, planting my fists on my hips and tipping my chin. "You will also need to provide either a lump sum of 300, 000 pounds or a monthly allowance totalling that amount over the course of my five-year contract. Payable to Caprice Marie Lombardi."

The man stared at me with hard eyes, as grey and intractable as stone. He didn't seem the type to discuss his decisions with others, let alone make concessions. There was arrogance sewn into the corners of his mouth, the creases beside his beautiful eyes, and the geometric line of his hard jaw.

"What, may I ask, do I get out of this increase in expenditure?"

I jutted my chin forward and narrowed my eyes at him. "Some may say you owe it to me."

My father shifted uncomfortably beside me, completely unaware that this stranger *did* owe me, for more than just the future use of my body.

Not so long ago, I'd helped him.

"You'll give me unencumbered access to your body and freedom without complaint," he added blandly.

"I can't promise to be completely docile to your wishes," I ground out.

"Irish." The Brit's eyes narrowed, but there was humour hidden in the fold of his full lips. "Not exactly a fine indication of her temperament. For 1.5 million quid, I expect a docile asset."

Seamus stepped slightly ahead of me to block my viciously bared teeth. "You are paying for her beauty. Her nature may change with time."

The door opening and closing behind us pulled our attention to an older man entering the room. He carried an expensive looking briefcase, and his hair glistened like a silver helmet.

"Are you ready to begin then?" he asked expectantly.

The blond man—my future owner—gestured dismissively toward me, which prompted the older man to step into my space.

I shied away. "Do we have a deal?"

He stared at me, his beautiful face entirely impassible. I could only guess at the inner workings of his thoughts behind the façade and pondering that unknown terrified me.

"We have a deal, though I'll have it known now that if you resist too much, I reserve the right to terminate our deal. Now," he ordered, "be still."

I was still. Not because I wanted to be, but because I was

used to obeying men, used to putting my safety before my pride.

"Be thorough, doctor. I don't want to drag her home to England only to find out that she isn't pure," the blond man clipped out in an accent like cool British steel.

I vibrated with fury, but still I stayed unmoving as the doctor rounded me once, twice, and stopped at my side the third time. He made a few quick notes on his clipboard before he tucked it under one arm. I tried not to flinch as he patted me down the way one might inspect a horse, perfunctory swipes down my sides, over the pert swell of my ass and down both sides of my thighs, inside and out. A hiss erupted from between my lips when his cold fingers swiped over my sex before plunging inside, a shallow thrust that poked at my intact hymen.

"Pure," the doctor stated, removing his fingers and wiping them on a kerchief he pulled out of his breast pocket. "Beautifully intact hymen."

"As I told you," Seamus said, smugly.

The blond man shot him a withering look. "Excuse me if I do not trust the word of a man who would sell his daughter to repay his gambling debts."

I choked back the slightly hysterical laughter that bubbled up my throat. Seamus scowled, but there was no rebuttal to such a statement of fact, so he remained quiet. I wondered how my owner knew the circumstances of our situation then decided that someone with enough money to pay a small fortune for a girl would have the means to find out anything they wanted.

"Now is the time to say your goodbyes. The doctor will need to take her to run some tests before we leave," he told my dad.

I noticed somewhat warily that he hadn't looked at me at all after his initial inspection. Why would an obviously gorgeous, wealthy man have to pay for sex?

Because it was obvious that was the reason I was being sold.

What else would anyone want with a beautiful woman? And then it became obvious to me why someone like him would need to buy a woman... because his tastes were too deviant for a free one.

I swallowed thickly and edged closer to my father even though I had long ago learned not to go to him for protection.

Seamus surprised me by wrapping an arm around my shoulders and tugging me closer. He rose to his full height, somewhere just over six feet, but even then, he was woefully shorter than the Brit.

"I need your assurances that she will be well kept," he surprised me again by saying.

The other man turned his head slowly toward us, his dark eyes pools of glossy ink before they've written words, totally blank.

"First, get your hands off her. I own her now, and no one but me will touch her," he said coolly. "Secondly, Mr. Moore, I will make no such assurance. I will do with her what I will as she is no longer a person, but *property*. You might assume that given the money I am investing in her, I won't do her too much harm, at least not enough to mar her beauty or kill her too quickly, but you neither deserve assurances nor warrant them through the contract so..." He took only one small step forward, but his powerful frame was coiled like a predator, taking the last step before devouring his prey. "Take your filthy hands off her and get out."

I wasn't sure if it was Seamus or me who shuddered, but after we had both recovered, he quickly dropped his arm from my shoulders and took a large step back.

Shame and anger burst over my tongue, bitter and thick like bile. What kind of father put his own safety before that of his child?

Seamus Moore.

He opened his mouth to say something, his eyes shifting

from me like polar magnets, but I beat him to the punch.

"I won't ever forgive you for this," I whispered painfully in Italian, each word squeezed past the iron fist wrapped around my throat. "My only consolation, Papa, is knowing that you won't stop the gambling or the drinking, and you'll probably get yourself killed in the next few years. If for some inexplicable reason that doesn't happen, if for some incredible reason, I survive this ordeal you've set for me and I see you again, I want you to know that I will kill you myself."

Seamus took a staggering step back, his grey eyes wide in his bruised face. A different kind of pain, something worse than the physical, made those eyes blur then shine with tears.

I remained unmoved.

The bastard was selling me as a sex slave to save his own ass.

It amused me to think about how I'd been so afraid of Sebastian joining the Camorra, of my sisters falling to one of their men, when I was the one pledging to kill a man.

My own father.

It was disgusting, but my words were true.

If I survived, if I saw him again, I'd string him up from a tree with bells tied to his ankles so he sang in the wind, just as Rocco had promised to do to the rest of my family.

"Cosima," Seamus started to say, stepping forward with his hands outstretched in benediction.

"Remember the promise you made to me. Now, get out."

Stupidly, my father looked at my owner who only crossed his arms over his chest and dipped his chin so he could glare at my father from a better angle.

Tears spilled over as Seamus looked back at me, but he nodded slowly, his shoulders sunken as he followed the butler out the door.

I didn't turn to watch him go.

Instead, I swivelled to fully face my new owner with my hands on my hips. "Now, you can tell me what the fuck you think you're doing. I saved your goddamn life!"

He only blinked at me in a way that was much more elegant than a shrug.

"So, this is how you repay me?" I snapped.

"I told you that day to take care where you stick your pretty little neck out. A hunter like me might find you too pretty a thing not to take a bite out of, or at least to use as bait."

Despite myself, his cruel expression scared me. Goose bumps ripped like torn Velcro across my flesh. "I didn't take you for a man who would resort to *buying* a woman like livestock."

A shift came over his face unlike anything I had ever seen before. His placid expression melted away to reveal the cold as stone heart of him.

I opened my mouth to say something but stopped when he took a massive step forward into my space. His fingers found my chin and held it in a firm grip so that I couldn't look away from his liquid black eyes.

Without thought, my lips curled into a snarl at his proximity.

"Irish and Italian," he scolded with a soft click of his tongue against his teeth. "I doubt you'll prove the stereotypes incorrect and prove to be an obedient, docile little slave."

"*Hai ragione*," I said, agreeing with him.

He surprised me by smiling sharply into my face, pressing a thumb over the middle of my closed lips so that I couldn't speak. "No problem, my beauty. I look forward to breaking you."

Then, before I could bite his thumb off the way I planned, a sharp, small pain erupted at the side of my neck, and I passed out.

Chapter Three

Four months earlier.

*O*utside, Milan was sweltering and bright. A baby cried somewhere in the street while another couple argued furiously in dialect Italian. The yellow light of a mid-spring dawn saturated the waiting room and made the multitudes of beautiful women lining the white plastic chairs blink sleepily. It was five am and no one had the right to be attractive at such an early hour but for these women, visible fatigue was not an option.

I sat in the corner in the small, stuffy room clutching my portfolio with both damp palms. It was abysmal really, next to the stacks of photos weighing heavily in the other models' laps but I couldn't afford to be pessimistic. There were sixty-seven girls vying for the same multimillion-dollar campaign, and each was more beautiful than the last. A gorgeous African woman with skin like polished bronze and a caramel kissed Afro sat next to me chatting with one of those rare Asian women who are both tall and curvy. Across from me, sat Cara Delavigne and the girls beside me were speaking quietly about Kate Upton's chances of being chosen. This kind of gig was a model's golden ticket and everyone in town wanted it.

The only edge I had against them was this; I *needed* it.

The money from a job like this could go beyond just paying

Giselle's art school tuition and using the meager remains to keep the rest of the family in Naples afloat. It could set up Elena in university, get Sebastian out of his dead-end factory job and put Mama in a house with working heat and plumbing. It would get the black-eyed mafia men circling our dying economy like carrion away from us for good.

I shifted the weight of the world on my shoulders so it settled more comfortably and reminded myself that if Atlas could hold up the world, I could withstand holding up my own.

The door to the interview room swung open and a ruffled blonde emerged. Her heels made a *tsk* sound as she hastily crossed the floor between us all and it reminded me of my mother, her finger wagging, tongue clacking as she chastised me.

"Cosima Lombardi."

My head snapped up and I took in the sight of the slim redhead who called my name. She had freckles and a pinched look that I could empathize with; it was obviously stressful catering to exacting businessmen and neurotic models. I smiled demurely at her as I moved passed her through the doorway she stood in, but she only blinked up at me and closed the door firmly behind us.

I took a deep breath to center myself, pulling every particle of confidence like a shield around myself, before I turned around to face the panel for the go-see.

Four people would be my judges. The first was perhaps my biggest challenge, Freida Liv. Arguably the most successful model in the world in the past ten years, she was heartrendingly beautiful. Her golden hair was cut short, she had been one of the first to adopt the radical page boy cute twelve years ago, and showcased a perfectly symmetrical face made striking with pale, luminous blue eyes. Despite her beauty, her expression was unattractive, pinched and distorted as if someone were pulling her apart. I guessed someone was, after all, since she was interviewing for her replacement.

The other was an older man, deeply tanned with eyes like the faded denim of his button-up shirt and brilliant white blonde hair. This was Jensen Brask, the infamous director of the St. Aubyn fashion house who often forced his models to commit heinous mental tasks before hiring them. Modelling might seem glamorous, he was once recorded saying, but it required true mental fortitude. I was surprised he was here, at the second casting call, when I knew this was only the intermediate step in the selection process. He watched me with a slight frown as I stepped before them, my arms at my sides, my face carefully devoid of emotion. It was always this way at go-sees, the inevitable staring contest while they judged you unashamedly on every physical asset they could reach with their eyes and imaginations. In my limited experience, it was best to stand still and take it.

Next to him sat Willa Percy, the CEO and founder of Looking Glass Models, one of the largest modelling agencies in the world. If I landed this job, not only would it secure me this massive, international campaign but also a place on Willa Percy's golden docket. She was a beautifully groomed African-American woman clad entirely in Chanel, but there was a look in her eyes that didn't speak of class but of ruthless, poverty-given ambition.

I knew that look because I'd seen it in my eyes often when I looked in the mirror.

The final critic was none other than the man I'd be modelling beside in the campaigns, Jace Galantine. In less than three years, he had appeared on the American model scene and without skipping a beat, he became one of the biggest names in the industry. Now, he had secured his place as the male face of the St. Aubyn brand, and he had the authority to veto whomever he wanted as his female accomplice. He was staring at me intently; his square cut facial features compressed as he studied me.

Boldly, I met his gaze and winked slowly at him.

He blinked before erupting into throaty laughter that was absurdly attractive. "Who is this, Renna?"

The redhead checked her clipboard. "Cosima Moore, 17 years old, Italian, Tivoli Models Roma."

The judges efficiently located my headshot amid their folders and spent a moment reading it over. It was a short portfolio, and I wrung my hands nervously when Freida Liv tossed it aside with a flick of her thin wrist.

"Your biggest campaign was in June with Mila Cosmetic," Willa Percy confirmed. "And most recently Intimissimi lingerie?"

"Yes, I was lucky enough to work with some of the most talented people in Italy." The memory of my time with Intimissimi warmed me, and I felt my usual confidence return, straightening my spine.

"Yes, well, this isn't a dinky little national campaign." Freida Liv stared at me with her glacier eyes. "Things are done differently here at St. Aubyn. You have some good runway experience…" She flipped carelessly through the photos of my runway walks for Dolce & Gabbana and Valentino. "But that isn't what St. Aubyn is looking for."

"What Freida means to say is"—Jensen shot his colleague a look that spoke volumes—"St. Aubyn is an international fashion house with a cosmetic line, ready to wear and fragrance. You will have to be as adaptive as a chameleon and as strong as a jungle cat. We want someone women envy, Miss Lombardi. We want St. Aubyn to transition from staid, formal wear to sophisticated sex."

"You'll need more than a new face to do that," I said before I could help it. My hand flew to my mouth, but I lowered it just as quickly. Not thinking before I spoke had always been one of my greatest flaws. They might as well know it before hiring me.

Jensen's white eyebrow rose in his caramel face. "True, it starts with the designers, the creative directors, and the company, but it will end with you, and that is all consumers care about."

I opened my mouth to ask another question but stopped myself. This was not the kind of environment when it was appropriate for a run of the mill model to make inquiries. Jace Galantine noticed my hesitation and nodded to prompt me.

"Why not hire an actress then? It's the standard now and I'm sure you've been approached by some of the best to represent your revamped brand."

Jace nodded like a professor pleased with his student even though Freida Liv glared at me viciously. "The new CEO wanted to go another way."

"It's a test really," Jensen explained gruffly, excitement flaring in his tired eyes. "Of the brand. Can we take a no-name beauty and propel her to stardom?" Freida scoffed delicately, but the two men ignored her. "If so, it would do more for the brand than an actor with an identity separate from the brand. Brooke Shields and Calvin Kline Jeans, Adriana Lima and Victoria Secret." He opened his palms. "A new image calls for a new face."

"Enough." Freida cut in, her eyes cold on my face. "Renna will take you to try on a few items."

I nodded, my heart beating heavily in my chest. My hands shook as Renna helped me pull on the assorted items, a white organza dress that moved over my body like sheets of luminous fog and a brilliant red suit made of individually cut lace panels cut in a sharp V to my belly button. This was the opportunity of a lifetime and I had no idea what to do in order to stand out. I thought of the beautiful women outside, just as capable as me if not more so, and of my family back in Napoli. Fierce determination flooded my blood, hot and vibrant. When I returned to the room in each outfit, I could feel the strength shine like gold lamé against my skin. When I entered wearing the white gown, even Willa Percy seemed impressed.

After three dresses and four separates, I once again faced my panel of judges, but somehow the atmosphere had changed, iced over, and they each stared at me apathetically. It took only a moment for me to discover why.

"*Ciao*, Cosima."

Landon Knox lounged in the doorway, his salt and pepper hair and beard melding with the shadows to creature the allusion of a man with no face. But I knew what he looked like in the sun, the shade, at night and noon. I knew because the agent who stood before me had been the reason I became a model in the first place.

A brutal shiver raked my spine. "Mr. Knox."

His smile was thin on his pretty face as he stepped forward into the light. "I should have known you'd be here, scratching your way up the ladder like a starved cat."

The contempt in his voice made me nauseated, but I tilted my chin. "I work hard."

"Oh, I know." He was close now, almost directly in front of me, and I glanced uneasily at my judges to see if they would interfere. Though the two men and Willa looked uncomfortable, Freya smiled prettily at me. "But you won't be here, not for St. Aubyn."

He leaned close and lowered his voice so that his breath passed over my face in a sickly hot wave. "I told you when you left me, you wouldn't work in Italy again."

I swallowed the sob that rose in my throat and glared up at Landon, a man I had not so long ago thought I desperately loved. "That's your loss then, Mr. Knox." I turned to my panel of judges and smiled demurely even though my eyes were hot with anger. "Thank you for your time, I won't waste any more of it."

With my head held high and my fists furled tightly at my sides, I left the room. It was only when I passed the dozens of beautiful faces in the outer room, when I was safely out on the anonymous streets of Milano that I leaned my head against the brick building and fought the urge to cry.

Sweat beaded on my forehead even though I stood concealed in the shade of the alley next to the building, but I was grateful for the familiar heat and constant cacophony of Milanese traffic at midday. I pressed the back of my head to the cool stone of the building I had just emerged so unsuccessfully from and fought the crushing sense of failure that threatened to rob me of breath. We needed the money that job could have brought. I was the primary breadwinner for my family of five, and though I had been modelling since I was fourteen, the blow of rejection still hit particularly hard.

I gritted my teeth at the thought of Landon ruining the go-see for me. He was an Englishman and an editor at Italian *Vogue*. His special interest in me when I was just a girl was the very reason I was a model now. Once, when I was young and impressionable, he had been more of a paternal figure than my own biological father. He wasn't that old, in his mid-forties now, but compared to a fourteen-year-old me, he seemed ancient and safe in his old age. In a sense, he was. He never tried to sexually manipulate me, but that is where the line was drawn in the sand.

It didn't stop him from dictating what I ate, how much I

slept, what I wore to go-sees and then even at home with my own family, and how I comported myself around others. I was always to defer to him.

It was a relationship doomed to fail from the start.

You see, I'd never been very deferential.

Our relationship ended seven months ago, the same day I'd been admitted to the hospital for complications from anorexia.

I pushed off from the wall and tugged at the hem of my slightly sheer blouse and smoothed a hand over my hair, ready to head to the metro and back to my tiny shared apartment on the outskirts of town. The only reason I noticed the person passing by was because his earphones had become unplugged from his iPod and the tin-like sound of his music made me look over as he walked up the alley toward me. He was a handsome boy, not much younger than myself, but it was the expression on those features that worried me. His eyes darted quickly between the cars crawling along the street and when a sleek black Town Car pulled up in front of the building, blocking the entrance to the alley, he shuffled almost excitedly from foot to foot.

Cautiously, I moved closer to him, wondering what he was so obviously waiting for. My eyes were on him, but I could see someone emerge from the car and move towards the building I had just left. The boy bounced on his toes—once, twice—and I recognized the giddy fear in his stance as he launched forward.

Before I could consciously debate the decision to do so, I was following him. I swallowed a second of terror when I saw the unmistakable gleam of a gun in his hand as he took three looping strides forward, his fingers white knuckled over the butt. He held it uneasily though, and I drew confidence and conclusion from his shaky grip.

Just as he was about to reach the unsuspecting man from the car, I caught up to him and took a firm grip on his shoulder.

I waited for the hesitation in his stride, when one leg was locked straight, and the other remained hovering in the air, remembering one of the defensive moves Sebastian had drilled me and my sisters on for hours as young girls. I held my breath for that instant and brought down my foot hard against the outside junction of his leg, where the kneecap connects the leg muscles. There was a sickening crunch followed by a gurgled scream as he fell to the ground. I looked up from where he lay, deeply disorientated, my heart pounding brutally against my chest, into grey eyes as varied and intense as a mid-summer stormy sky. For a moment, less than a second, those eyes were the center of my swirling world and gave me the confidence to take one deep, trembling breath.

In the span of that breath the two men from the car burst into motion, the driver practically diving out of the car to detain the would-be-attacker on the ground, a knee pressed into his spine as he wrenched the assailant's hands painfully behind his back. I watched as he produced a pair of zip ties from the inside of his expensive blazer and secured him.

Not a second later, the man with the grey eyes was on me.

My breath escaped my body in one hard whoosh as his colossal build slammed unforgivingly into mine, and my spine cracked then compressed against the brick wall behind me. I tried to inhale and choked on the shock as his thick forearm came up to press against my neck in a punishing hold.

His eyes were all I could see. Those huge irises like brushed steel framed by dark brown lashes under a heavy, furrowed brow. I could read the threat in each stroke of those pewter eyes, in every inch they scored over my face like a scalpel through soft flesh.

He was threatening me not because I was the original threat, but because he didn't know me. Even more, he didn't understand my motivation.

Why would a stranger compromise herself for some un-known man unless she had an agenda?

I tried to convey with my eyes—metallic too, but gold, warm where his were cold— that I had no agenda but to escape his clasp and flee the scene of a crime I hadn't even committed.

Still, I didn't struggle against him. Something base that lived in the pit of my gut like a primordial creature stuck forever in a dark cave told me that if I resisted him, he would put me down.

And not gently.

Because this threat was about even more than my circum-stance or the suspicious question mark I posed. This man simply *was* dangerous. It radiated from him like a gravitational field, an added pressure against my already bruised body.

There was death in his dark eyes the same way it was in the eyes of the many Made Men that had been vultures circling the carrion of my life since its inception.

"Who the fuck are you?"

The crisp edge of his British voice cut through the fog of my receding adrenaline, strong and clean like the snap of a whip.

He spoke in English, and I wondered if he couldn't speak Italian or if he'd momentarily forgotten where we were.

"The woman who just saved your life, *signore*," I replied breathily because his arm was still belted across my throat. "I think that should earn me the right to breathe?"

"I will repeat myself once," he clipped out. "Who the fuck are you?"

Constellations of white stars were bursting at the edge of my vision as I struggled to breathe so I gave the bastard what he wanted.

"Cosima Lombardi."

Commotion from the other side of the car drew my

attention, the brassy shouts of Italian police arriving on the scene and the low British accent of the driver who'd incapacitated the assaulter.

"Cosima." He tasted my name, rolling the vowels together the way Italians did. "What did you just do?"

"I saved your life," I repeated, my hands going up to grip his suit clad forearms.

His soft scoff blew his minty breath over my lips. "That may be a bit overdramatic. Riddick was standing by, there was security in the building, and I know how to defend myself."

"I saw the gun," I gritted out between my clenched teeth, irritated that I was on the defensive when I'd acted the good Samaritan. "It seemed like the only thing to do."

"Next time, beauty," he said, leaning in even closer so his firm, full lips tickled my cheek. "Consider this. If someone is under attack, maybe it's for a good reason. Maybe, they even deserve it."

"Deserve to be murdered? Are you kidding me?"

He leaned back enough so that his eyes caught mine in a hold as fierce as the one he had against my neck. "I am not a man who kids. I am a man whom, unlike yourself, understands the causality of nature. There is no effect without cause, no act without provocation."

"So... you deserved to be killed?"

A grin sliced through his left cheek like a weapon. "All animals, deserving or not, die eventually, but some are powerful enough to warrant a hunt. And you just interfered in such a hunt, *bella*. Do you know what happens when a predator is under attack?"

"He turns into a *stronzo*?" I asked, insulting him and struggling against his tight hold yet again to no avail.

"He turns feral and will attack anyone in the vicinity, even an innocent." He leaned closer as his scent swelled in the warm air between us, fresh and cool like damp forest air. I could see the pulse throb strongly in his tanned column of his throat and felt the odd animal compulsion to press my tongue there. "Be careful where your good heart may take you, for it may be straight into the arms of a predatory beast."

"Ragazzi," a police officer called, shattering the strange energy between myself and the stranger as he jumped over the hood of the car to reach the criminal and the bodyguard who held him.

The strange blond man pressed tightly into me as if imprinting himself into my skin, then stepped back abruptly and dropped my hands. The darkness in his features retreated like night creatures into the shadows, only the glow of his silver eyes giving away his wicked intentions.

"This is the last time I try to save a life," I muttered, smoothing my slightly trembling hands over my bodice.

"Oh, I should hope so," he parried even though he was already turning, his eyes on the policeman, his mask affixed. "Though I very much doubt it will be the last time you become involved in a situation you shouldn't. You have no preservation instincts, and such a failing will be the end of you."

I watched him greet the policeman, how the officer winced at the firmness of his handshake and the unconquerable power he wore like a mantle over his broad shoulders. In under thirty seconds, the Brit had established his dominance over the lawman. I remained preoccupied with him even when a man came to interview me about the crime. Even when I was released from questioning after giving up my contact information and an officer was leading me toward the metro.

He lingered like the thought of a monster under a bed, like a creature lurking in the dark of my dreams ready to corrupt them into nightmares, and when I looked over my shoulder before descending into the underground, he was watching me with hawkish intent that blistered my skin.

I knew in the same way I'd always known my father would be the end of my life as I knew that this wouldn't be the last time I would see the predator I'd so foolishly saved from slaughter.

Part Two

SLAVE

NON DECOR, DECO. I AM NOT LED, I LEAD

Chapter Four

My brain was too heavy and hot in the confines of my skull. It throbbed like a pendulum between my ears, setting off a series of raw nerves throughout my body so that I pulsed with pain all over. I couldn't open my eyes or drag enough air through my lungs. I was paralyzed, stuck in what felt like the fetal position on ground so hard it had to be stone. I wanted my sight back because without it, consumed by hurt and wretched with loneliness, it was all too easy for my imagination to conjure up my setting as the pit of Tartarus, the last circle of Hell.

I thought about karma and fate, kismet and destiny. The mythical constructs we created to explain away the unexplainable things that happened to us. The absurd notion that if something bad occurred, we were somehow deserving of it.

I was a good person, but not the best maybe. I was too busy focusing on my own family to be altruistic and too devoted to my career to eschew the necessary level of vanity it demanded. There was nothing I could have done in my short eighteen years in the pockmarked pit of Naples to deserve being sold into sexual slavery by my own father.

I didn't deserve this, but it was happening to me.

The lack of poeticism, of justice or even hope, weighed on my sore bones like dense gravity.

At one point, I felt cool fingers thread through my hair brushing it off my damp forehead and aching shoulders. A while later, a straw was placed between my lips and I sucked without thought, pulling the delicious, cold stream of water down my parched throat to my empty belly where it sloshed like a churning sea.

"My beauty," I heard dimly from deep within my submerged mind. "My sleeping beauty, it's time to wake up. It's time to play."

I wanted to obey that clinical, sharp-edged voice, but my eyes were hot stones in my skull, and my brain was waterlogged earth.

As if sensing my struggle, my willingness to concede to his demands, the voice hushed me softly, and the fingers retuned one last time to pass through my hair. Cold pressure parted my lips, an unwanted kiss from an unwanted prince.

"Why?" I asked, barely awake, but desperate to understand.

"The blood of my enemy, however innocent, is still my enemy," he whispered against my ear so that the words rooted deep into my wakefulness and my dreams. "You cannot hide in unconsciousness forever. I will be here when you wake."

And then he was gone, and I floated again for endless hours until a nightmare about Hades breaking through the crust of the earth's surface to grab me by the ankles and drag me down to hell woke me up with a gasp.

And my eyes opened.

The light spilling in through dozens of massive windows lining either side of the long room nearly blinded me; the reflection of the sun off the gleaming, waxed marble floors stabbed my corneas violently before I could look away.

I squeezed my eyes shut and focused on my breath and not the horrifying pain in my head, my breasts, and between my legs, then opened them again.

I was in a ballroom.

Or, at least, I guessed it was a ballroom thanks to its grand size and unabashed opulence.

Crystal chandeliers dripped from the domed, beautifully painted ceilings and gold foil accents curled and unfurled in elaborate detail atop marble pillars and across sconces like expensive moss over ancient tress.

I was naked, twisted in the fetal position on a floor of white and black checked marble, threads and knotted cords of gold running throughout. My eyes caught on a length of heavy metal chain wrapped around a steel spike nailed in the middle of the ballroom just beside where I sat. As I shifted slightly to look at it more clearly, the hissing slide of metal over marble hit my ears, and the weight of something around my left ankle made me pause.

Slowly, I righted my left leg and stared at the thick leather cuff shackled to my ankle and the short length of chain anchoring me to the floor.

Tears sprang to my eyes, molten and painful as they fell down my cheeks.

I was seated in the most beautiful room I'd ever seen or could have imagined even in my wildest dreams, but I wasn't there as a guest or even as a stranger.

I was ornamental as much as the gold foil, immobile as those titan marble pillars. A part of the furniture owned and collected by Lord Alexander Davenport.

I shifted painfully, groaning in pain as I rolled to my back and stared up at the massive ceiling, then wished desperately that I hadn't.

Because painted there in stark relief was a tableau of the Greek god Hades clothed in black on his iron chariot pulled by undead horses bursting through the earth to capture the Goddess of Spring, Persephone.

I wondered if somehow in my fog, I'd noticed the painting and translated it into my dreams, but either way, the reoccurrence of the myth did nothing to soothe my frazzled mind.

Trying to focus on something else, I decided to sit up and check out the pain in my breasts and between my thighs.

With a groan, I sat up and stared down at my chest.

There was a gold bar tipped on each end with diamonds locked through both of my dusky brown nipples.

Another, this one curved and placed vertically, pierced through the hood of my clit.

"*Porco Giuda!*" I cursed faintly at the obscene sight.

I was a virgin marked wantonly with sex, a promise my new Lord and Master had punched into my flesh.

My free will and my body were no longer mine to control.

They were his.

As if summoned by the scent of my turmoil, he arrived, a mere shadow in the doorway at the far edge of my gilded cage.

"Ah, she awakens," he said quietly, but in the stillness of the ballroom, his voice carried to me as intimately as if whispered in my ear.

I shuddered.

"Come closer," I called hoarsely, full of false bravado. "So I can look you in the eye when I curse you to hell."

A low, smoky chuckle. "Oh Cosima, do you doubt that we are already there?"

I stared at him, struggling to swallow the sobs of desperation that threatened to ravage my throat. He moved forward, his smart leather shoes clicking against the marble like the tick of a clock counting down to my demise.

When he was only a foot away, he pinched the fabric of his suit pants as he settled into a crouch so that we were almost eye level with each other.

He should have looked ridiculous—his big body folded like that, his forearms resting on his strong thighs, fingers of one hand dangling so that they could feather over the coil of my chain—but he didn't. Instead, he was formidable, compacted into a position that called to mind a predator settled in to observe his prey. He had all the time in the world to pounce, and he was confident in his ability to capture so he'd decided to play with his lunch.

To play with me.

"I thought to welcome you to your new home," he began. "For now, it consists of these four walls. This ballroom is all you will know until you earn the right to more. And do you know, my beauty, how to earn the right?"

I clenched my teeth, felt the grind of enamel and let the pain settle my anger so I could actually breathe. "I'm sure you'll be happy to tell me."

His smile was more a ghost of an expression haunting his face than an actual movement of his lips, but it was all the more sinister for it.

"Yes, I am happy to tell you. You earn privileges such as freedom from the room, water to drink, and food to eat by obeying me, your Master."

"My Master?" I croaked. "You have to be kidding me."

He cocked his head, his expression genuinely perplexed. "Tell me, Cosima, why else would a man buy a beautiful woman if not to use her for his own pleasure?"

"You mean to use me against my will?" I snapped.

"Ah." He nodded slowly, running a hand along the steepled

edge of his jaw as he considered me. "I see. You don't seem to grasp the nature of the deal I made with the Camorra and, through them, your father. I bought you to *own* you, yes, but you agreed to the conditions of this agreement the moment you entered my house in Rome willingly. When you saw your father brutalized at the hands of the mafia, when they threatened to string your beloved siblings up from the tree across the street with bells tied to their ankles and you could practically hear the chime in your ears." He paused, taking in my horror and shock with the quiet satisfaction of a man used to knowing more than others. "If you want to put your family at risk with the mafia, Cosima, you must know that you are free to leave at any time."

"How did you know that about the bells?" I asked, my brain stuck like a broken record on the idea. "How could you possibly know that?"

"Knowledge is power. Can you ask me that, knowing who I am?"

"I don't know who you are," I told him honestly. "Only that you seem to be all four horsemen of my apocalypse."

One golden brow rose, cutting lines into his forehead that had me wondering how old he was. Much older than my eighteen years, it was obvious.

"At least you are well educated, as a professor's daughter should be. It'll make this easier for you."

"Rebelling against you?" I retorted, hyper aware of my vulnerability as I sat before him, chained and stark naked.

Something dark passed over his placid features, the clouds mere shadows on the ground, alerting me to an impending storm.

"I am Alexander Davenport, Earl of Thornton, and you are playing my game now, Cosima. Be happy that I'm taking the time to teach you the rules instead of making you learn by taking punishments when you unwittingly break them."

I spat on the glossy marble floors at his feet, but I was too dehydrated to make much of a statement. "Go to hell, you beast!"

"This is how things will proceed from here on out, my beauty," Alexander informed me coolly. "Everything you need to survive is mine to give you. Water, food, the very air you breathe. I own it all. So I suggest you shelf the rebellious spirit and discover a more servile side."

I glared at him. No matter that I was tethered to a bolt in the floor by heavy, medieval chains in a gorgeous room made of marble and gold leaf without clothes or possessions, I was not his to own, to set aside when it pleased him or to train like a dog.

I was Cosima Lombardi and that had to *mean* something to someone, even if it was only to myself.

"I won't be kept shackled to a bolt in the floor in the middle of your ballroom like some wild exotic beast caged for your entertainment."

He stood slowly, unravelling the breadth of his torso and the long length of his muscular legs. There was thread and calculation in the exactment of his movements, in the way he kept his eyes locked on me as he loomed above my chained self.

I watched warily as his hand reached out and stroked softly over my hair.

"Exotic, yes," he agreed softly, fingering a lock of my inky hair. "Wild, I've yet to see, but I am very much looking forward to it."

"I suppose I should be thanking you for not raping me immediately?" I scoffed.

He dropped my lock of hair, his lips twisted into a disgusted sneer. "You may feel like an animal, but I don't fuck them. My cock will be inside you when you earn the right to a bath and no longer stink like livestock."

"Let me out of these chains, and I'm happy to take one," I returned because now that I'd been made aware of it, I could smell myself.

I must have been kept unconscious for more than a day for them to cart me all the way from Italy to wherever we were in England.

His smile was thin, creasing his stubble-shadowed cheeks into disgustingly attractive lines. "You will learn, my beauty, that this is a relationship of give and take."

He leaned forward, his hands lashing out to snag my nipples in a tight hold and then he tugged, straining my body forward to reduce the burning tension in my recently pierced breasts.

"You give," he whispered sinisterly, twisting my nipples until I whimpered. "And I take of your exquisite body. Then, and only then, will I reward you, and even then, I expect you to accept those gifts with overwhelming gratitude." He paused, his eyes so hot on my lips they felt scalded as if by hot tea. "I can only imagine the lovely sound of the words 'please, Master,' and 'thank you, Master,' coming from that lush mouth."

"Good because it will only happen in your imagination," I gritted out between my clenched teeth as I squirmed against his hold.

Alexander's smile deepened those creases in his face, making him appear both older and younger at once. "That's it, Cosima," he practically cooed. "Hand yourself over to me. Let me take you to the precipice of pain and over the edge into the kind of desire your virginal mind cannot even dream of."

"Never," I bit out, wrenching myself out of his hold and crying out at the pain as I fell backward to the floor in an ungainly sprawl.

When I looked up, Alexander was standing, his huge form clad in an entirely black suit that magnified his sinister charms.

He stared at me passively in my disgrace, naked and bound, rebelling with no hope of revolution.

"Have it your way, slave. We shall see how long you last."

Chapter Five

I'd been in the dark for over two weeks. My sense of time was warped without light or regular meals, without company or clocks. All I had were my own thoughts to pass the time and the savage cannibal sitting in the pit of my stomach eating away at the lining with pointed, poisonous teeth.

They fed me every two days. Bread and cold ham someone slapped onto a plate that appeared sporadically when I woke up. I'd never eaten so little or been so distressed by it, not even during my days battling an eating disorder.

There was water too. Dirty and warm poured into a porcelain bowl at the very edge of the circumference of space the chain allowed me. There was never enough, a shallow pool that barely slacked my wicked thirst.

It was clever.

I was restless from lack of movement, hungry to the point of constant pain, and near delirium.

They'd closed the shutters over the massive windows and turned down the heat so that I could see my breath cloud in the wintry air as I curled in on myself, shivering in misery and unable to sleep comfortably.

I had the use of a bucket as a toilet and, thank God for small mercies, it was regularly emptied whenever I managed to get a few hours of shut-eye.

Two weeks.

I wasn't sure if that was commendable or stupid. All I needed to do was give into my new reality, and I'd be free of this gilded chamber of horrors, free to eat real food and drink more than tepid water.

Free to be me again.

I was locked in the dark, but it was more than an absence of light. It was the blackness of my own solitude; the quantum hole at the center of my soul that was slowly sucking away at everything that made me *me*.

I tried to write an encyclopedia of Cosima facts to cement my sense of self in the chaos of night that had become my life.

Cosima Ruth Lombardi.

Born August 24th, 1998 in Napoli, Italia to Caprice Maria Lombardi and Seamus Patrick Moore.

My favourite colour was wine red, captured in a glass and held over rich, warm candlelight.

I loved poppies best, of all flowers, because they reminded me of me in a way that was narcissistic but true. They were bold as blood but stark against the softer colours of the traditional Italian countryside. They demanded notice and received it. But their beauty was short-lived and fragile as the thin silk of their petals fell to bits within a week and scattered on the wind.

I felt very much like one of those black-centered blooms, falling apart with every breath I took without even one witness to my dematerialization.

He wanted me like this.

Lost like decaying particles in a petri dish.

I didn't have to hear his British accent clipping the words into neat little explanations to understand why.

He wanted me broken.

A beautiful, hollow shell to break open and fuck into.

It wasn't enough to own my person and rape my body. He wanted to empty my soul so that the only thing I was filled with was his cock and his cum.

His words from days ago broke into the blackness of my world and shone blindingly bright.

"When I drive into that virgin cunt and smear your blood on my cock, you'll cry. Not because I'm hurting you, even though I am. No, you'll cry because you are going to be so *empty*, so useless that you'll beg and sob to be filled by something. And that something will be me, Cosima. My fingers in your asshole, my thick cock in your spasming cunt, my tongue in your mouth, and your soul crushed right under my heel as I fuck up into you and you cry out the name of your Master."

He visited me frequently, hovering in the doorway, a black smudge against the bright hope of light spilling in from the hall beyond. There was always silence while he observed me curled into varying positions like a hermit crab without its shell, pathetically naked and fundamentally vulnerable.

Then his voice would come, smooth as velvet but violent, a ribbon tied too tight around my throat.

"Are you ready to kneel and greet your Master?"

The words played throughout my head like an infinite echo long after I'd rejected him with spitting words or frozen silence.

They taunted me.

I didn't want to kneel for anyone, to rely on my beauty and my body to get me out of yet another bind, but my choices were non-existent, and my spirit was cracking right down the middle.

I never could have known absence—of light, of sound, of food and drink, but most of all, company— could be weaponised so savagely.

But I felt run through by the steel edge of my lonesomeness, and I knew the next time Alexander stood in the doorway, I would be ready, though unwilling, to kneel and greet my Master.

The next time he opened the door, I was standing.

It took energy I didn't have, and my legs shook, but I faced the door with my hands fisted on my hips and my chin squared.

It was a longer way to fall to my knees, but I had a point to prove.

I wasn't a mindless, soulless slave.

I was a human, a woman, and an Italian one at that. I had too much spine to crumple without a fight.

"My beauty," Alexander said, his accented voice quiet but carrying. "Are you ready to kneel and greet your Master?"

"I am. Though I'd like to discuss it first."

There was cool humour in his tone as he made his way across the long room. "Oh? I'm curious enough to allow it."

I bit my lip to keep from raging at him for his arrogance.

"I want to say first that I understand the bargain I entered into to keep my family safe. I won't do anything to jeopardize their safety, so yes, I'm willing to kneel and be the sick slave you need to slack your deviant tendencies." He was close enough then to see his eyes flash like lightning-filled storm clouds. "But I need you to know that I'm more than just your property or a hole for you to stick your cock into."

I pulled in a shaky deep breath and steeled my shoulders against the tsunami of sorrow crashing over my head. "Each time I touch you, I will be thinking about my hands braiding my sister's hair, tending to my brother's scrapes and bruises, and rolling semolina dough with my mama. Every time you ask me to kneel, I will think about sitting in a field of poppies on a Napoleon hillside and running my fingers over their silken edges. When you force me to take you inside my body, I will remember the tender dreams I had of love and romance as a girl before I knew better, and I will hide in those memories until you are done.

"You may own my body, Lord Thornton, but you will never own my mind, my spirit, or my heart."

I stood there with tears on my cheeks, my chest heaving as if I had just completed a race, and I stared at him in pure, joyous defiance.

The revolutionary had spoken.

There would be no rebellion, but it felt magnificent to give my anarchist a voice in the face of this tyrant.

Alexander blinked from where he had come to a stop not two feet before me. Slowly, he raised his hands, and for a second, I believed he would strike me down.

Instead, he clapped.

Slow, powerful smacks of sound that took my traumatized mind straight to spankings and red ass cheeks.

He was clapping for me.

"Well done, *topolina*, very well done."

I bristled at the Italian nickname. "Little mouse" didn't exactly denote strength against adversity.

"I commend your show of spirit," he praised, and I could see that praise in his eyes, heated and dark like banked embers.

A shiver ripped viciously down my spine, and instantaneous regret flooded through to my bones.

He liked my show of spirit because there was more challenge in the squashing of it.

I held my breath as he stepped even closer, the luxe fabric of his designer suit tickling the bare skin of my thighs, rasping across the sensitive peaks of my pierced breasts. His dark eyes were my entire world as he wrapped a big hand around my throat, curling each finger one by one against my pounding pulse point.

"To own this body is enough," he growled. "For now."

Then he leaned forward, his thick lashes fluttering closed as he nipped my chin firmly with his teeth and trailed his tongue along the path of a fallen tear over my cheek. His breath fanned over my cheek, his lips against my temple, and his hand even tighter around my neck as he whispered, "But one day, it won't be, and I'll come for it all. Your mind, your spirit, and your innocent heart."

He pulled back just enough to stare into my eyes the way an astrologer might into the star-filled sky. I felt catalogued by him, defined by words I didn't understand in a language that was dead to everyone but him.

I squeezed them shut and whispered, "I will hate you every day for the rest of my life."

"Love me or hate me if you will. Either way, I will always be on your mind," he reminded me. "Now, slave, kneel for me."

I didn't want to kneel. It felt too enormous a gesture when previously, I'd never given it much thought. But to be on my knees before such a man felt like readying for a beheading, the axe gleaming in his hands, my neck tender with exposure.

I hated that I had no choice, that I had been condemned to such a fate not by my own actions but by those of my feeble father.

He was not pleased by my hesitation.

Fingers bit into my shoulder, and he slowly forced me to the ground.

"Kneel and get comfortable; you will be spending a lot of time on your knees," he ordered, shifting his hand to the top of my head as soon as my knees crashed painfully to the marble floor.

I panted slightly, a combination of fear, resentment, and dying pride like two fists compressing my lungs.

"This will be our first training session together. I don't expect much from you, but I do anticipate complete obedience, is that understood?"

I shut my eyes and licked my dry lips, trying to transport myself to another place, one without a cold Brit trying to tell me what to do.

"You will keep your eyes on me at all times," he demanded. "Customarily, a slave never looks in their Master's eyes, so you should thank me for the privilege."

"Thank you for making me feel so special," I said, saccharine sweet.

"There is a reason for every single move I make in this life. This is yet another example of that. I want my slave to look me in the eye so she can watch as the animal inside me breaks free to ravage her. Without constraint. Without mercy. Because there is no leash powerful enough to contain it."

I swallowed thickly, unable to keep back the shiver that played my spine like piano keys. "Understood."

"Understood, *Master*," he corrected sharply.

"Yes, *Master*," I ground out between my teeth.

"Mmm, you think your bad attitude dissuades me, *bella*?" He paused after the question, then used his hand on the back of my head to press my temple against the granite length of his cock beneath his slacks. "It achieves quite the contrary, so misbehave all you desire."

I could feel the heat of him through the fabric, the pulse of him beat against my cheek like a drum roll heralding an invading force.

"Now, this is how you will present yourself to me," he coached coldly as he used one leather shoe to kick my knees farther apart.

The cold air bit teeth into the lips of my exposed sex and made me realize with shameful clarity that I was wet.

It was too much to hope that Alexander wouldn't notice.

He ran the toe of his loafer gently over my bare, pouting lips, then harder over my newly pierced clit hood.

"You look good in gold," he praised mildly, reaching down to twist one of the gold bars in my nipples. "Golden eyes and golden sex for my golden slave."

"Happily, you had no hand in giving me my eye colour," I muttered darkly, hating that the smooth toe of his shoe felt deliciously cool against my heating sex, that the pressure made something in my belly unfurl like a bloom.

"Not the colour perhaps, but the demons that lurk there I now possess just as surely as I do this," he said, stepping into his foot so that it pressed firmly but not painfully over my pubic bone.

I gasped as he fisted both hands in my hair and wrenched my gaze up to his. He pulled so tightly my eyes watered while his burned, smoking like banked coals with carefully supressed desire.

"I own you, little mouse," he told me. "But you do not seem to understand how possession works, so let us make it your first lesson. I am feeling uncharacteristically benevolent, so I will give you a choice. You may accept me in your mouth, take all of me into your throat despite your struggles, and drink down every drop of your Master's cum, or I can hold you down and beat your ass black and blue, then leave you here without a drop to eat or drink for two days. If the former, I will have the chef prepare you one of your favourite meals. *Pasta alla Genovese*, I believe?"

I hesitated as my mouth flooded with moisture at the thought of the rich, meaty pasta after days of bread and tepid water.

He capitalized on my weakness before I could fortify my mind against him. "And, my beauty, if you truly please me, I will even allow you a shower. I know how much you must long for one."

My spine tumbled over like children's building blocks as I slumped under the weight of his bribery.

I wanted a shower.

Cleanliness was next to godliness for Italians as it had been since Roman times, and I was desperate to rid my nose of my own stench.

It was even more tempting than the food.

I wanted to stay strong in the face of his crippling ownership, but I was too realistic not to realize that I was fighting a losing battle. The irrefutable fact was, this man already owned me. Money had exchanged hands, contracts had undoubtedly been signed, my own signature forged, and the deal was more than done.

I was his.

If I didn't start accepting that, I'd lose my sanity to the cold, dark solitude of the cavernous cage.

"That's my *dolce topolina*," Alexander murmured almost sweetly even as he continued to grip my hair too tight. "Now, open that lush mouth."

My head tipped back as he urged me with one hand while the other undid his trousers efficiently and pulled out his cock.

I was a virgin, but I had seen penises before in biology books and the smutty magazines the Made Men gave to Papa and even as bribes to my brother, Sebastian.

But I'd never seen or even conceived of something like what Alexander presented to me then.

It was more a weapon than an appendage.

Thicker by far than the circumference of my index finger and thumb with a head the colour and size of a ripe Italian plum, I couldn't imagine taking it in my hand, let alone between my lips.

But something about the tapestry of veins pulsing down its length made my mouth water and made my tongue itch to trace them like drips from an ice-cream cone all the way down his shaft.

I shook my head dazedly, trying to shake the deviant desire from between my ears like some kind of earwig to the floor.

I did not want to find the weapon of my own destruction appealing.

Yet a small voice in the darkest recesses of my brain whispered to me that I did.

Alexander wrapped his big hand around his dick and pumped it tight and slow to the end so a pearl of precum crested the tip.

With the hand on the back of my head, he brought me closer to draw the moisture over my parted lips like gloss.

Unbidden, my tongue shot out to trail the path and taste him.

Brine exploded on my taste buds, and my startled gaze shot up to his at the discovery.

His eyes blazed, so hot they turned the air to steam too thick to breath easily.

I panted.

"Yes," he acknowledged in his cold British tones, the only hint of his arousal the slight deepening of his voice. "It's good that you like the taste. It's the only meal you'll be getting with any kind of regularity until you learn your place. Now, clasp your hands behind your back, open wider, and take me inside."

Tension gathered every single muscle in my body and bunched them into a tangled cord that he manipulated with every tug of his hand in my hair. My shoulders hunched and burned with stress as I opened my mouth to the breaking point and felt the broad head of his cock smooth over my tongue straight to the back of my throat.

He exhaled in relief as I choked on him, then swallowed convulsively, unintentionally taking him past the boundary of my gag reflex deep into my throat. Impaled on his cock, I groaned in protest and struggle to pull myself free.

If his hiss of pleasure was any indication, my struggle only brought him further pleasure.

The flat of his shoe pulsed slightly against my pubic bone, then lowered slightly so that it slid over my wet sex. The pressure felt good against my clit, and I squirmed, trying to focus on that instead of the grotesque sensation of Alexander sunk so deep in my mouth.

Finally, just when spots had started to erupt at the corners of my vision, he pulled me by the hair slowly off his dick.

I gasped and spluttered, dragging huge breaths into my

deflated lungs.

"Nothing is worth accomplishing without difficulty first," he lectured me, some kind of flagrantly perverted prophet spouting wisdom while his cock dripped with my saliva. "Breathe through your nose when I'm in your throat if you don't want to suffocate on my dick."

I opened my mouth to protest, but he replaced my unspoken words with the slick slide of his erection pushing down into my throat again. Tears sprung to my eyes as I struggled against the intrusion, my throat working open and closed against him.

"Yes, *topolina*," he breathed, looking down at me like a deity. "Earn your reward. Worship your Master."

I rankled against his title. Hated that I was forced to my knees before him, enslaved to a man whose arrogance and entitlement knew no bounds.

But there was also something dark and curious peeking out from the depths of my soul, something more animal than spirit and not even close to human. It was intrigued by the dynamic between this godlike man and my prostrated person.

There was something deeply arousing about feeling wholly vulnerable and knowing your only power could be found in giving a stronger person pleasure.

Unbidden, a second pulse began to beat in my swollen clit being manipulated shamelessly by Alexander's expensive shoe.

His hands manipulated my movements faster, slamming his thick length in and out of my throat, uncaring of my inability to breath, my constant gagging and choking.

In fact, I think he enjoyed it.

"One day soon, you will come to love sucking me off so much that you'll orgasm with one touch to your clit after pleasuring me," he told me, nothing in his clinical voice giving away his desire even though I could feel his pulse beating hard against my tongue each time he slid down my throat.

He pulled out fully, his dick glistening obscenely as it bobbed angrily in front of my face. I spat some of the excess saliva in my mouth on the ground at his feet and glared up at him with tears in my burning eyes.

"*Vaffanculo a chi t'è morto,*" I cursed, telling him to go fuck his dead family members.

It was a horrific insult in Italian, one I didn't think translated well into English, but Alexander's face clenched with instant fury at my words, so clearly, he understood.

With his furious eyes burning into my own, he pulled me slowly, firmly back onto his cock, tunneling deep into the back of my throat and holding me tightly to his lightly furred groin. One hand slid from my head, down my cheek to rest over my throat where his thick length swelled. I gurgled in protest as his fingers wrapped tightly over my pulse, completely unable to breathe or move past the dual obstructions.

Without leaving my throat, he thrust in and out of my mouth, his grip tightening with each pump until he cursed viciously and came straight down my gullet. I couldn't taste the brine of him on my tongue, and for one horrifying second, I was disappointed by it.

He held me against him, his cock softening slowly until it lay half-turgid on my tongue. I was surprised and disconcerted when he began to pet my hair, but he continued with it long enough that I started to relax slightly with my cheek pressed to the inside of his thigh.

The moment I did, he wrapped cruel fingers in my hair and tipped my head back so that I could look up into his coldly furious eyes.

"If you mention my dead family ever again, *topolina*, I will chain you to the wall and flog you until your skin peels off in gold ribbons. Is that understood?"

I felt his threat in my bones. My nod was truncated by the flesh in my mouth, but he took it for the promise it was.

His hands disappeared from my skin, his cock pulled from my mouth so quickly that I nearly vomited on the floor at his feet.

I braced myself against the cold floor as I coughed and then looked up at Alexander with hatred and fear in my eyes like flashing neon signs.

"Why me?" I asked, wiping my wet mouth with the back of my hand. My throat burned from his disuse of it. "Why do this to me?"

I'd saved this man's life, and he was repaying me with sexual servitude?

It didn't make sense.

"Why you?" he asked on a callous hiss. "You have done nothing to deserve the answer to the question."

My skin flashed hot and cold in shame and fear, a potent concoction that disorientated me more than any drug. The situation was too surreal for me to understand. A month ago, I'd been a teenage girl living a poor but pleasant life with her family in Naples.

Now, I was a slave kneeling at the feet of her Master in a country I didn't know with nothing to my name but whatever he deemed to allot me.

Without another word, Alexander tucked himself back into his trousers and turned on his heel to walk to the door. Only when he reached it did he turn to look at me, my chin still wet and trembling, my knees tightly closed but their insides glistening with my own traitorous arousal, the same arousal that coated the toe of his left shoe.

"I will tell you this, Cosima Lombardi, *topolina*, my slave," he said, his words lugubrious. "Your assumption of this role is as vital to your life as it is to mine. Even a predator is prey to something, even me."

Chapter Six

J had the dream again, the one about Persephone being abducted by a cruelly handsome Hades who dragged her into the dank underworld and forced her to take the throne at his side. Only, this time, the Goddess of Spring and Queen of the Dead was not wholly reluctant. She marveled at the beauty of the dark world and found surprising enchantment in the power she'd been granted as its ruler. The only thing she couldn't find delight in was the cold, mysterious man at her side.

"Who are you?" she asked the dark god. "Who do you want me to be for you?"

When I woke up to the sound of rattling chains, those questions were burned in my psyche.

Who did Alexander Davenport want me to be for him?

It had to be about more than sexual deviancy. He was an Earl, for Christ's sake. Handsome, titled, and moneyed, I doubted he needed to resort to importing a poor girl from Italy in order to get his just delights. Unless his kink was debasing atavistic, Neapolitan teenage girls.

"Good morning, dear," a woman's voice greeted, softened at the edges with a British accent very different from Alexander's own brisk tones.

I whipped around, rolling uncomfortably over a coiled

length of chain to face the first new face I'd seen in my new life at this house.

She was a woman constructed of circles, apples in her cheeks, a robust bosom, and rounded hips like half-moons. Her spirals of pale blond hair framed a face that spoke of gentle, natural aging, and her faded denim blue eyes were entirely kind as they wrinkled into a smile at the sight of me.

"What are you doing in here?" I asked then immediately decided another query was more pressing. "Please, help me get out of here."

"Oh, don't fuss, darling girl. I'm to clean you and care for you this afternoon in preparation for dinner tonight. Lord Thornton would like you to join him in the dining room," she told me as if I was just a normal guest being tended to in times gone by.

I clambered to my feet, chains protesting loudly at my movement. "I would prefer to eat separately."

Her lips pursed, but the rest of her face remained obstinately cheerful. "Oh well, Lord Thornton can take some getting used to, but it will be good for you to get out of this drafty place. I would have preferred to take you to your room, but apparently, you haven't been well behaved enough for that boon to be granted quite yet." She clucked her tongue at me and then gestured to my right where an enormous copper freestanding tub had been placed, the top curling into ribbons of hot steam. "So I had the tub sent up. Let's get you bathed before it loses heat."

I wanted to protest the bath because I wanted to rebel against everything in my new existence, but I wasn't stupid enough to cut off my nose to spite my face.

"You are skin and bones, poor thing," the woman clucked again.

I peered down at myself, noticing the obscene swell of my large breasts against the concave slope of my belly and the tracks of bones protruding beneath my skin.

"I didn't have much to lose in the first place," I admitted softly, more distressed by the sight of my skinniness than I had been by the alien sight of Alexander's dick or the length of chain connecting me to the floor of an unknown house.

It reminded me vividly of the time in my life I loved myself the least, when I let another person control my body to the point of physical pain and mental ineptitude.

I could feel the cycle starting again, this time with a new man.

At least this one had the decency to outright label himself my Master.

Landon Knox had only ever masqueraded as my friend and mentor in order to use me for his own personal and financial gains.

So far, Alexander Davenport seemed to only want to fuck me.

They were both disgusting.

I wanted to damn all men to hell, but I clung to the goodness I knew was inlaid in Sebastian's heart. He was the most loving man I'd ever know. The bravest, the most loyal, and by far and away, the most beautiful inside and out.

The thought of my twin warmed my heart even as it crumbled at the edges, rotting through the core with neglect.

I didn't have a lot growing up, but I'd always had the love of my mother and siblings.

Now, I didn't even have that.

"Let me help you, bairn," the woman slid beside me, wrapping a warm arm around my waist as we walked toward the bathtub. "You'll catch your death as you are. I have a mind to take Master Alexander over my knee as I did when he was a wee one."

The idea of this short, soft older woman spanking a grown man let alone a sheer predator like Alexander was nearly outrageous enough to make me laugh. Instead, I allowed her to hold my hand while I placed one foot into the stinging heat of the bath water.

An aroma of hot ginger, vanilla, and musk surrounded me as I sank with a deep sigh into the hot, silky water. The oil-scented water went right up to my protruding clavicles, but it wasn't enough. Before my caretaker could protest, I dunked my head and floated near the bottom, my hair curling like ink in the liquid. Even the chain linked to my ankle felt diaphanous in the velvet depths. Submerged, I could squeeze my eyes tight and imagine I was being reborn, saved in the womb until the moment it was safe for me to begin life anew.

A life without greedy men who were all too willing to use women as pawns in their selfish games.

Two hands plunged into the water by my shoulders and pulled me into the air, a midwife wrenching me out of the womb too soon.

I burst through the water with a sob.

"Gentle yourself, sweet bairn," the older woman cooed in her thick accent as she stroked her hands down my hair and then settled it over the lip of the tub so it dripped to the floor. "There is nothing to worry yourself about now. Let Mrs. White take care of you."

It was good to have a name to put to her face, even if it was a little creepy that she referred to herself in the third person.

Everything about this place was creepy, though, so I resolved myself to get used to it.

Mrs. White lathered her hands in spicy scented shampoo

that almost perfectly matched the aroma of the bath water. Something nudged at the back of my mind, telling me that I should recognize the distinctive smell, but the pleasure of her hands sinking suddenly into my locks and rubbing firmly at my skull erased my unease.

"We haven't had a girl here in absolute ages," Mrs. White was saying when I clued in enough to understand the thick lilt in her speech. "It will be good to have some young blood in the house again to invigorate us."

"Us?" I asked innocently.

"The staff have been idle too long," she tutted as her strong thumbs rubbed the shampoo into wide circles over my scalp. "We used to be a great hub of society here at Pearl Hall, you know? Why, we've hosted every generation of the Royal Family since the days of Queen Elizabeth I. Of course, I don't blame Master Alexander for being away from home doing his duty to this family and their various enterprises. I'm grateful they've the means to run a full household when most great families these days have to turn their grand estates in gaudy hotels and wedding venues," she finished, aghast.

"How horrible," I sympathized, eager to develop a rapport with the loquacious woman.

"We are one of the few remaining private estates in the country," she told me proudly as she pushed me forward gently in the rub and used a pitcher of warm water to rinse out my hair. "Pearl Hall has been a jewel in the architectural crown of the United Kingdom since it's construction in the 1500s."

"And Lord Thornton?" I asked.

It shouldn't have made much of a difference, but I preferred to address him as Lord Thornton, a title that others were also forced to address him by, than as Master Alexander.

Mrs. White might have called him that too, but I had no

doubt it was for an entirely different reason than my own.

"Oh, well, he went to Eton with Prince Arthur, though he was a few years above the boy. It's the king, really, who has a soft spot for our Master Alexander. They hunt together every fall at the Royal estate in Scotland."

I stared at my bony knees, trying to understand how a man so close to the king of bloody England could be in a position to buy a woman for sex.

Why do it?

"You don't seem surprised that a man like Lord Thornton would keep a woman shackled to the floor of his ballroom like some beast he snared and dragged back from safari," I said demurely, my tone such a direct contrast to my accusation that it took a moment for the lovely Mrs. White to understand.

When she did, her round face froze and her right eye twitched.

"Yes, well..." She cleared her throat and pulled me back against the lip of the tub so she could run conditioner through my hair. "Sometimes it is better not to know the details, but to trust in the result. I've known Master Alexander since he was a wee one, and if he has you here, it is for reasons known only to him, but reasons still that I have trust in."

I twisted like an eel through her hands and snatched one of her wrists. "Listen to me, Mrs. White. You seem like a good woman. Whatever reasons Lord Thornton has me here for are *not* noble or good. He has already pushed me to near starvation, kept me senseless in a dark room, and used me for his sexual gratification. Those are not the actions of a man with a noble quest, but the crimes of a monster no longer masquerading as a man. Please," I begged, my eyes so wide with beseeching sincerity that I felt they would fall out of my head. "Please, help me."

"Help you how?" she asked, her voice suddenly sharp

against my skin as she wrenched my hand off her arm. "You made an agreement with Master Alexander. It is your choice to be here, and it is up to you how you decide to endure this servitude. If you want to go on being ungrateful, living in a dark and drafty ballroom when you could have access to a home most would call a palace, so be it. But do not pretend for one moment that your destiny is not still firmly planted in your own hands."

I stared as she stood and moved to a small vanity that had appeared sometime while I was asleep to retrieve a plush towel the colour of crushed poppies.

Her words rang in my ears.

Hadn't I resolved to make the most of this situation last night when I'd allowed the man to defile my mouth without knowing much more than his name and station?

Clearly, Mrs. White was a devout servant. There would be no luring her to my side of this story, so I needed to adjust my point of view.

I didn't have to be the victim.

I could endure, survive the way I'd been forced to for the past eighteen years by using my looks and my body to get by.

And each act against me I would add carefully to the heap of kindling growing in my soul until the inevitable day that Lord Thornton, Alexander Davenport, made a mistake, and after however long of learning his ways, of being his perfect little mouse and slave, I could exploit that to my own advantage and set his world on fire.

Then he would be the victim, and I the victor.

Mrs. White returned holding up the towel and I stepped out of the tub so she could dry me carefully with the soft fabric. She led me to the intricate vanity, sitting me in the chair so she could brush out my hair with a silver comb.

"Master Alexander expects you to be presentable when you

attend him at dinners. Bathed, made up, and wearing the outfit of his choosing," Mrs. White lectured me.

I stared at my reflection, taking in the strange golden ocher of my irises and their thick fringe, the way my full mouth tipped down uncharacteristically at the corners and how my skin was more pallid than I'd ever seen it.

I gritted my teeth, straightened my shoulders, and resolved that it would be Master Alexander falling to his feet at the sight of me that night in the dining room.

I hadn't seen Alexander all day. It was the tattooed bodyguard I remembered from the incident in Milan—Riddick—who appeared behind Mrs. White and me as she was putting the finishing touches on my hair and bent to unshackle me from my chains when it was time to descend to the dining room. A blindfold made of folded over black silk was secured over my eyes so that I couldn't see my surroundings as he led me firmly by the hand out of my cage and into the greater house beyond.

He clearly didn't realize what being in the dark had done to me the past few weeks. My ears ached with sensitivity, keen to the swish of my long dress on marble flooring, the faint whistle of wind beyond the glass of a hallway filled with windows, and the soft, staccato voices of other servants gossiping behind closed doors.

I could smell the citrus polish they used to wax the marble tiles, the particular kind of musk that came from antiques and centuries-old tapestries. There was the odor of Riddick himself, artificial and manly, a cologne with no familiar notes. Mrs. White was hyacinth and myrtle, clean linens, and unscented hand lotion. The complexities of my own fragrance, that spice heavy smell with its own heat, was both strange in my nose and familiar.

It wasn't much in terms of freedom, but every new assault on my usable senses felt like a boon, and every step I took unburdened by the awful weight of those medieval chains was pure glory.

I could have kept walking blindfold for the rest of the night relishing the liberty of simple movement, but although it was a colossal home, we eventually reached the dining room.

I knew this not only because I could detect the mouth-watering scent of garlic, tomatoes, and rich meat, but because the instant we stepped through the door, I felt his eyes on me.

They were as electric as a cattle prod against my flesh, burning his regard into every exposed inch of my skin as he evaluated me.

And there was a lot of skin bared by the evening dress he'd chosen for me to wear.

It was the same black silk as the blindfold wrapped around my head, the material spilling down my steep curves and skinny limbs like an oil slick. The two panels covering my breasts were narrow, exposing either side of their swells, and connected in a deep V just above my navel.

My nipples pebbled in the cool air of the drafty home and the contrasting searing gaze of my Master.

"Bring her closer." His voice carried across what sounded like an enormous room.

Riddick pushed me forward between the shoulder blades so hard that I tripped over the edge of a carpet and had to catch myself on the back of what felt like a chair.

"Careful with the merchandise, Riddick," Alexander ordered lazily, as if he didn't particularly care if I was hurt or not, but the idea of someone misusing his things was egregious.

"Yes, sir," Riddick grunted.

His hand found the exposed small of my back again, but this time, he urged me forward gently until we both stopped at what I assumed was the head of an enormous dining room table.

I sucked in a sharp breath when cold fingers touched the pulse thrumming violently in the right side of my neck. Slowly, I released it with a soft hiss as those fingers skated down my throat and over the slope of my chest to rest over the swell of my breast.

"I've been groomed for this since I was a boy," Alexander said softly as he pressed his palm flat over my heart. "But I never imagined how heady it would feel, owning something of such exquisite beauty."

"Groomed for this?" I questioned, trying to pull the shroud off the mysterious man before me to reveal the true lines and form of him.

His chuckle was merely a gentle exclamation. "Such a curious mind, *topolina*. Haven't we spoken about how much trouble that will get you into?"

"I don't think we've really spoken at all," I countered. "I don't know anything of value, at least. Why you've repaid me for saving your life by ruining mine? Why you've kept me locked in the dark with my demons like a mental patient?"

"Careful," he warned on a low growl that Riddick nor Mrs. White would hear. "I enjoy your spirit, but this game we are playing is about more than enjoyment. It is about survival for the both of us."

I gasped softly at both his words and his fingers as they tweaked my sensitive nipple, and sensation radiated like a targeted blast through my nerve endings.

"Now, kneel," he commanded, loud enough for his voice to echo through the hall and into the ears of anyone watching.

I shivered as it occurred to me that truly anyone might be viewing our exchange. My ears strained to pick up any ambient noise that might give away the presence of other diners.

"Kneel," Alexander ordered again.

I fell to my knees.

There was something I didn't understand about this dynamic between us. He'd been sinisterly mysterious when I had saved his life in the Milanese alleyway, but he hadn't seemed cruel or sadistic. That, combined with his enigmatic words about our mutual survival, threw into question his entire motivation for degrading me.

So I kneeled.

And I prayed, though God had never been particularly good to me or mine, for answers that would absolve me of my servitude.

"Leave," he ordered whomever else remained in the room.

I let out a soft sight of relief.

No matter how much I wanted to provide relief for my family by keeping the Camorra at a safe distance and giving them Alexander's extra allowance, I knew I didn't have it in me to be ridiculed in front of a dining room filled with people.

When the soft click of a door closing heralded their removal from the room, Alexander removed my blindfold.

I blinked up into the constellation of bright crystal chandeliers casting light throughout the room and tried to regain my sense.

Surprisingly, he let me.

The dining room was long and narrow with high vaulted ceilings, domed archways over the oversized doors, and so much gilt detailing that the entire space seemed to glow with captured sunlight even though the sky outside the windows was pitch dark.

"Welcome to the hall," Alexander murmured, reaching out to pinch my chin gently between his fingers and tilt it until my eyes met his. "This is where you will eat with me when I am in residence."

He must have read the surprise in my eyes because his lips twitched with humour. "Did you expect to be kept forever in the darkness of my ballroom, eating only ham and stale bread? I told you, *topolina*, what I take from your body will be rewarded with privileges. A good slave eats with her Master. Last night, you proved with this beautiful mouth that you can be a very good slave indeed."

My olive skin was too dusky to show the way my skin heated with a furious blush, and I'd never been so grateful for it. I was at once pleased and repulsed. The memory of taking him in my throat was one of invasion, a warrior's remembering of war, yet I felt triumph despite the horror because it was a battle I had won.

"Yes," Alexander said, answering my thoughts as if he owned those too. "You can hate me and still delight in pleasing me, my beauty."

My lips twisted to the left, capping the emotions that bubbled in my gut. I was so conflicted that I felt sick with it.

"Do you know what buyers look for in a future slave?" Alexander asked me as he reached for his glass of red wine and swirled it in the bowl.

My eyes caught on the colour, the light through the red shining like blood, and I watched hypnotized as he swirled and swirled the contents in his big hand.

"It isn't necessarily a docile nature. The best Masters enjoy a challenge. It's the duality of a strong mind and a submissive spirit, a fierce heart. Only with all three can a slave be truly re-markable. The strong mind tests a Master's nettle, the submis-sive spirit is his reward, but without the fierce heart, no slave would trust their Master enough to enjoy their play."

He leaned down over the arm of his throne-like chair, the glass of wine dangling precariously between his fingers just above my lips.

"Open," he commanded softly.

I parted my lips, my eyes on his even as I tipped my head back so that I could catch the full-bodied wine in my mouth.

His breathing was deeper, his face tight with arousal as he watched me drink from his glass.

"I want you to enjoy our play, *topolina*," he told me as I licked my lips, and he straightened in his seat. "I want to give you joy in your servitude."

"But you want to hurt me," I said, my voice breathier than I wanted because I'd never seen such beautiful eyes in all my life.

A grey so deep and clear they shone like the polished pew-ter dining set on the table.

He sipped the wine, his strong throat working, his lips slicked with red liquor before he swiped it away with a sweep of his tongue.

I squirmed as my gut heated and arousal flooded between my legs.

Such a simple gesture, sharing wine from the same glass and then watching him lick his firm mouth, but it had such a profound effect on me.

I wondered if I was conditioned already, weaker than I'd previously thought...or if he was just that gorgeous, I was only woman enough to respond.

"It doesn't matter if I wish to or not," he finally admitted. "I will hurt you because I must just as you must endure it because you have no choice."

"You don't like it?" I asked, shocked enough to scoff.

His eye flashed at my attitude. "Would you like to see just how much I like it, my beauty?" Before I could protest, my hand was in his and he was pressing it to the steel length of his cock beneath his suit pants. "The thought of your body painted in my bruises and your pretty face lacquered with tears makes me unspeakably hard."

We both gasped as I inexplicably squeezed his dick at his words.

"I like it, but that is the very last reason I am going to do it," he reminded me cryptically.

"What does that mean?"

He leaned down, pushed his hand into the hair at the nape of my neck and pulled me further between his spread legs. I gasped, and he took advantage by dipping his thumb between my lips.

"Trust me when I tell you, I may be the one wielding the whip, but I've got just as much riding on this as you do. If you want to survive this with your life, you'll do as I say without hesitation."

I stared up into his deadly serious face and felt the threat sink into my skin, writing itself in goosebumps across my flesh.

"And if you think being hung from a pretty tree with bells tied to your ankles is a poor way to die, you're better kept in the dark about how this danger would dispose of you."

I shivered brutally, my teeth biting down into the soft pad of his thumb.

The next instant, I was hauled up under my armpits and deposited on the table, my bottom cupped by the gilded plate at Alexander's place setting.

"Enough talk," he growled, wrapping his arms around my

legs so that his hands could splay my inner thighs apart. "I'm starving for some sweet Italian pussy."

Fear sluiced through me as he reached beside my thigh for the sharp steak knife and brought it to my neck. His gaze was just as sharp against the pulse pounding in my throat as the weapon was pressed against it.

My entire body trembled like a mouse held by the tail in the mouth of its hunter.

Then with a quick slash and the quiet gasp of ripping silk, Alexander drew the blade down the center of my chest through the fabric barely covering my torso and groin.

The black silk slithered over my curves and pooled to either side of my body.

"Exquisite," Alexander murmured, looming over me. He ran a wide palm over the center of my body, following the line the knife had taken. His hand stopped over my pubic bone, and his thumb flicked out over my clit hood piercing.

"Do you know why I did this?" he asked me rhetorically. "So that from the moment you woke in your new life, you would know that your body was mine to do with as I pleased."

I shivered, and I didn't know if it was from the cool air, lingering fear, or the possessive, greedy way Alexander looked at my body.

He sat back in his chair, wrapped his legs once more over my legs, and jerked me closer. I fell back on my elbows against the table, disturbing expensive dishware that fell with a clatter. The plate under my butt tipped, cutting into my thighs for a second before Alexander dragged me farther to the edge of the table, and it fell to the floor with a loud crash.

I stared at his bright golden head bent over my sex, his breath wafting over my sticky wet exposed flesh, and I thought he looked like a king bent to pray at the altar.

My altar.

Desire ignited in my belly and blazed to the very tips of my fingers and the ends of my toes. Flambéed with desire, I wondered what I tasted like down there as Alexander slowly dipped his mouth to my inner thigh and trailed his strong tongue over my bare cunt.

"Burnt sugar," he murmured against my skin, his fingers tightening until they felt like staples holding me open. "I was a boy the last time I had dessert for dinner."

Then his mouth was on my clit, and he was sucking, licking, fucking my pussy with his tongue, his teeth, his lips, and his nose. There was pressure and suction everywhere at once. My head fell back between my shoulders as I gasped, my thighs a quivering frame around his broad shoulders as he feasted on me.

"*Si, così lo voglio,*" I gasped in my mother tongue, unable to believe how amazing his mouth felt on my sex.

"When you beg, do it in the language of your Master," he said into my slick folds.

I tried to find traction, in reality, in the fact that the man bringing me such pleasure was not a good man nor one I liked, but the way his tongue flicked my new piercing back and forth over my clit dissolved all of my recalcitrance.

"I want to hear you," he growled, nipping at the hood of clit so that my hips jerked and sent a salt shaker spilling to the floor. "Tell me how much you love my mouth on your cunt, or I'll keep you here all night on the edge of climax."

A sob bubbled in my throat.

I wanted to give voice to the pleasure, to release a little of the helium desire filling me overfull until I felt I would burst.

But I didn't want to give in to his desires. I promised to obey him, but I had warned him I wouldn't be docile.

"I doubt you can get me there no matter how long you try,"

I panted out.

His shocked, rusty laugh bathed my hot sex in cool air.

"That is what we call topping from the bottom, *topolina*, and it will not work with me."

His mouth went back to work on my pussy, somehow even more intense this time. Then there was pressure at my entrance, and I tried to squirm away because I had never before been breached.

I'd had a strange relationship with my old agent Landon Knox, but it wasn't sexual, and even though I'd always been curious about sex, I shared a bedroom with my three sisters so exploration was simply not an option.

"Has anyone ever played with this sweet cunt before?"

I moaned as his thumb swirled harder and harder with each pass until it slid through my incredible slickness inside me a few inches.

He reared up out of his seat, his hand still on my cunt while the other used my hair as a lever to pull me up to meet his mouth. His lips swallowed my gasp as he continued to rotate his thumb inside the sensitive walls of my sex.

He tasted like lightly salted pasta water.

He tasted like me.

I groaned against his tongue, undone by the onslaught of feelings, so ready to orgasm for the first time in my life that I was willing to do anything he asked in exchange for an end to this climbing, swelling pleasure.

"One day soon, *topolina*, I'm going to bury my big cock in your pussy. You're going to struggle and writhe against me, beg me to have mercy on your painfully tight cunt. But I won't take mercy. I'll bury myself to the hilt inside you and use you until you are raw."

I gasped into his mouth, then moaned as his tongue traced

my lips before plunging back inside, rubbing against mine in sync with the rhythm of his fingers between my thighs. My poor, confused brain struggled to understand how his words could pour over me like kerosene, lighting the fire he was kindling between my legs into a full-blown blaze.

Was it possible to hate a man, but love the way he made your body feel?

It didn't seem possible, yet there I was, on the edge of my first orgasm given to me at the hands of my own personal Hades.

"I'll fuck you while you cry, and I'll keep fucking you until your sweet, sore cunt clenches around me when you finally come for your Master," he continued in a slightly roughened voice that gave away how aroused he truly was. "I'll train you to orgasm on command and, *topolina*, your first lesson begins now. You have thirty seconds to come for me, or I'll take a cane to your ass."

He pulled away enough to look into my eyes, his prominent cheekbones flushed with pink, his eyes entirely black with pleasure, and I thought *I did that*. I was satisfying some primal need in him, something dark and base that needed to pin me to the table and dominate me. Even as he gave me pleasure, I knew I was returning it threefold.

He needed this, needed me to get off.

It shouldn't have been so arousing to know that, and it shouldn't have made my chest warm with something more than lust, but it did.

I looked into his ferocious, bestial eyes, and in less than thirty seconds, I came all over his hand.

My body seemed to split along every seam, my molecules falling out over the table like stuffing from a doll. The world disappeared as my mind fractured, everything but those big, long lashed grey eyes that stared at me in fiery triumph as I pulsed around his thumb and gasped into his face.

"This is mine," he growled, slapping my pussy sharply so that I shuddered violently. "You are *mine*."

And for one brief second while I lay depleted and torn apart from desire on his dining room table, I agreed with him.

Chapter Seven

When I woke up the next morning, my inner thighs were slick with arousal, and a groan was lodged in my throat.

I'd been dreaming of Alexander.

Riddick was standing over me, his stern features entirely free of censure even though I was naked once more, and there was enough dim light filtering in through the windows to make the moisture on my thighs glisten.

Shame sluiced over me like a bucket of ice water extinguishing the lingering desire burning through my skin. Even then, I could still feel Alexander's mouth on my sex like a permanent brand, and I wondered anxiously if it was a mark I'd wear for the rest of my life.

I wanted to hate that such a cruel, nonsensical man had given me my first experience with mind-bending pleasure, but a small part of me wondered if that wasn't one of the reasons I'd loved it.

For so long, I'd been navigating the choppy waters of my family's future, struggling to keep the ship upright and airtight against all the odds.

It was oddly liberating to have someone else make the decisions for me.

"Lord Thornton requests your presence in his rooms,"

Riddick said, cutting through my thoughts.

I frowned, shaking my head to clear it before looking out the massive windows to the murky landscape beyond. It was the first time the shutters were open, a boon I gathered that I'd been granted because of my obedience last night in the dining room. There wasn't much to see in the tenebrous light, through the diaphanous plumes of fog rolling across what seemed to be gently rolling hills of green in the distance, but what I could decipher was beautiful.

It was also clearly much too early to be awake.

"What could he possibly want me for at this hour?" I demanded.

Riddick blinked at me, then when I didn't move, he repeated, "Lord Thornton requests your presence in his rooms."

I huffed and unwound my aching body from the unforgiving marble floor, planting my hands on my hips and rolling my eyes as if I wasn't chained to the floor stark naked.

"Take me to his Mighty Lord then," I acquiesced.

It could have been a trick of the light, but Riddick seemed to smile as he crouched down to unlock my shackle.

I followed him across the wide expanse of the ballroom, holding my breath when he unlocked the door and led me into the hallway without blindfolding me.

The corridor was long, lined again with nearly floor-to-ceiling windows on one side and enormous, exquisitely detailed portraits on the other that were clearly Davenport ancestors. A coat of arms was worked into the middle of the wall, sculpted and painted out of stucco so that it drew the eye from every angle of the hall. Framed by a fierce looking griffon and lion on either side, topped with a vicious hawk and footed by a phrase in Latin that I didn't fully understand, the shield represented pearls, thorns, and red blooming flowers. It was beautiful.

I wanted to burn it.

We moved through quickly, bypassing an opening that led down to a grand marble staircase at the base of which lay a two-story grand hall painted pale blue with elaborate swirls of plasterwork. I noted the front door and thought briefly of running away, the thought of freedom so tangible I could taste its earthen grassiness on my tongue.

But Alexander's words echoed in my head, *if you want to put your family at risk with the mafia, Cosima, you must know that you are free to leave at any time.*

It was excruciating to quell my inherent flight or fight response to the situation. I wanted to run out those doors and never look back. I wanted to shackle Lord Thornton to the ballroom floor and beat him until he was a black and blue smear on the shiny tiles.

I couldn't do either.

In fact, I had to do the opposite.

I had to allow him access to my body, give him control over my every action, and cede to his every rule.

The house itself was a work of art. I couldn't help but think of how much my artistic sister, Giselle, would love it here, and it made my heart pang like a lost echo.

I wanted desperately to check in with my family, to see what they had made of my sudden job offer and of Seamus's inexplicable disappearance. Sebastian would be furious with me for not saying goodbye, his anger masking his broken heart. My own organ felt lopsided in my chest, half of it still sitting behind my twin's breastbone where it belonged. I missed him with a ferocity that stole a piece of my every breath. Elena would be struggling to make a life for herself in a city she hated, and Mama would be busy as she always was trying to hold down the fort in a home of big personalities with very little space to move.

We continued down the other side of the hall and came to a stop at a massive set of double doors. Riddick knocked twice but didn't wait for permission before pushing the doors open, snagging my wrist, and dragging me into the room.

The room was dark blue, gold accents winking in the low light streaming through two narrow windows framing a colossal four-poster bed draped in heavy navy velvet tied back with thick gold rope. They revealed a slick duvet, silver sheets and pillows and propped up against them with the same shade of grey in his eyes and a golden disarray of hair was a man.

It was clear Alexander had just awoken by the slumberous cast to his gaze, the softness to his full mouth when it was usually pinched closed.

A fist squeezed around each of my lungs at the sight of him like that, bare chested and stripped of his usual tailored armour.

He looked like a man, not the cold, domineering god I'd come to know him as in my short weeks there.

"Thank you, Riddick," he said in a slightly sleep-roughened voice that reminded me of his lustful tone of the night before. "You may leave us."

I stood just inside the doorway and fought the urge to wring my hands together. I'd never been shy or awkward and being so now was not how I wanted to present myself to the arrogant Lord Thornton. But I couldn't help the girlish giddiness and embarrassment that stemmed from knowing that the man lounging like a king in the bed before me had had his mouth between my legs just hours ago.

A slow smile slide across his lips as if he knew exactly how he affected me. "Come here, my beauty."

Subtly, I sucked in a deep breath to settle the butterflies in my stomach and the confusion in my head and then I walked to the left side of his bed. His eyes followed me, sharp and intent as a hunter tracking his prey.

"You are beautiful even in your confusion and misery," he said softly, reaching out when I came to a stop beside him to run the back of his hand over my breast.

My nipple beaded instantly, mirroring the tightening in my belly.

"I need to feed you more." He frowned as his thumb passed over my ribs, visible protrusions under my skin. "Did you enjoy your meal last night?"

I blushed at the memory of the dinner we'd shared after he'd eaten my cum from between my legs and settled me in my kneeling position back beside his chair. Then, he'd proceeded to feed me from his heaping plate of *pasta alla Genovese,* deftly spinning the noodles into his spoon and then waiting until I parted my lips to place the twirled bite on my tongue.

It had been oddly erotic to look into his eyes as he fed me, to watch as he studied my lips closing, my throat swallowing. Fresh arousal had swelled in my pussy and leaked down my legs. It was only at the end of the meal, when we'd finished his goblet of wine and my favourite pasta, that Alexander had acknowledged his effect on me by ordering me to stand. He'd then cupped my weeping sex, our eyes locked fiercely, and drawn his hand away wet with my juices.

He offered me two of his damp fingers.

I stared at them for a long moment, my mouth watering shamefully.

"Taste how wet I make you, *topolina*," he encouraged lowly, smearing his index finger over my parted lips before sliding them over my tongue.

My mouth closed instinctively, and I sucked hard when he groaned at the sensation.

He pulled away from me too soon and placed his two other

fingers at his mouth, sucking them off with a long pull of his pale pink lips.

I was panting by the time his hand fell away.

"You were an excellent slave tonight," he'd praised. "Tomorrow, you'll get your reward."

I blinked away the memory and focused on him. "My mama's pasta is better."

Alexander blinked, and then his pursed lips smiled. "Defiant to the last, even when you're eager for me to touch you again."

I snorted, determined to regain my atavism. "I wouldn't hold your breath for that... actually, no, please do."

This time, I received a low, sinister chuckle. "Careful, *bella*. If I were to touch your sweet cunt right now, are you promising me it would not be soaking wet?"

I narrowed my eyes at him even though I could feel the heavy pulse of lust thrum at the base of my groin. "And here I thought I was the one who'd need help understanding English."

His eyes flashed in warning, but to my surprise, he didn't give in to my taunting. Instead, he threw back the covers, exposing every naked, carved marble inch of him.

My eyes felt as if they would fall out of my head at the sight.

He was clearly not an indolent lord who spent all of his time indoors drinking scotch, reading, and writing letters.

No, this man was an athlete, his long lines of strength individually striated under his golden hued skin so that I could've traced each boxed abdominal, every lean thigh muscle under my fingertip.

My mouth went dry.

Alexander moved to the edge of the bed beside me and stood so that suddenly I was dwarfed by his awesome height. He had to be at least six foot four by the way he towered over my own impressive height.

"I will not be drawn into your games like those silly, virginal Italian boys you dealt with in Naples, led around by their dicks and your beauty. I am a grown man and a seasoned Dominant; you'd do best to remember that and not continue to taunt me into conceding control. Is that understood?"

"If you're so damned controlled, I think you can withstand a little taunting from an inexperienced Italian girl," I retorted, stepping even closer so I was toe to toe with him.

Desire burned in his eyes, and I knew he wanted to punish me for my insolence.

A shiver nibbled at the base of my spine.

"I don't have time to show you just how utterly inexperienced you are at the moment because I have meetings this morning. You are here to commence what will be part of your daily chores."

My eyebrows shot into my hairline. "Being your sex slave isn't enough, now I have to *clean?*"

His lips twitched with humour before he could screw them shut. "You will begin each day by tending to me the way my valet, Murphy, would. He is currently on a much-needed vacation in Scotland with his family and so, the duty must fall to my slave."

He moved away from me, walking across the plush Persian rugs to opened double doors that seemed to lead into a walk-in closet.

"Come."

I cursed under my breath in Italian but followed him.

He continued to speak as he moved through the closet into the enormous marble bathroom beyond that had clearly been recently updated. I watched as he moved to the rain shower encased in glass and turned it on. "You will bathe me and dress me, then see me off every morning. When I return each night, you will be waiting in the great hall in your position, naked and waiting for me."

"And while you are gone? Will I be made to sit in the ballroom all day contemplating my servitude and shackles?"

I was going to crazy if I spent too much more time alone in that blackhole of a place.

Alexander studied me with a furrowed brow, and I noticed just how clear his grey eyes were, so dark a grey they were nearly black before arrowing near the pupils into a colour so clear it seemed crystal.

He was truly the most beautiful monster.

"You've pleased me relatively well in the past twenty-four hours, so I'll allow you run of the house while I'm away. The rooms that are unlocked are the only ones you have access to. Do not attempt to take advantage of my generosity by breaking in to forbidden places."

I pouted before I could stop myself, but to my complete shock, my expression made Alexander chuckle softly and gently pinch my chin between his fingers so he could better look at me.

"What a delight your youth is," he murmured, seemingly surprised by his enjoyment. "I cannot remember the last time someone stood up to my tyranny or pouted in the face of my rules. It's oddly endearing, *topolina*."

"At least you admit that you're a tyrant."

"Oh, a tyrant of the highest order. One who rules with absolute power," he assured me, his tone oddly playful even though his face was cold, almost vacant in its impassivity.

"And you are utterly confusing," I told him, slightly breathless because interacting with Lord Thornton was like what I imagined riding a roller coaster would feel like, a constant change of atmosphere.

Whatever softness had lurked in his eyes solidified even though his grasp on my chin remained gentle. "If you trust anything about me, trust this. I am your Master, and I will be hard on you. I will break you and reform you into my ideal slave because there is no other option for either of us. If you believe in anything, let it be my cruelty and have my occasional lapse in judgement where I might be kind, be something to enjoy and then discount."

"But why does it have to be this way?" I asked, an edge of desperation to my tone as I stepped close, my nipples brushing against his lower chest. "I just don't understand why you'd do this to me?"

"Sometimes we are in the wrong place at the wrong time. Sometimes we are born to bad people and live a bad life. There doesn't always have to be a reason for misfortune, Cosima."

"No," I agreed, feeling those words like a punch to the sternum. "But there is for this."

"There is."

"You said something when I was out of it about being your enemy. Please, explain it to me," I begged, my pride drowned in a tidal wave of hope-fueled curiosity.

"What have I told you? This is a give and take relationship, my beauty. You give, and I take. If you please me, I will reward you. You have not even begun to please me enough to earn the answer to the question of your slavery." His grip on my chin tightened painfully, and he dipped down to bite hard into my lower lip. "You can begin now by bathing me."

"Bathing you?" I asked incredulously as he stepped away and prowled over to the enormous walk-in shower to turn it on. "Only children need help bathing."

His face was set in stone when he turned to look at me. "Clearly, that's untrue as I am a grown man and I require your assistance. I'm surprised you forgot, I also promised you a shower. Two birds one stone, *bella*."

I watched as the grown man in question turned to enter the shower, revealing his perfectly sculpted behind topped with deep dimples at the base of his back.

My mouth watered as he stepped under the rain shower. I couldn't help but watch as the water turned his hair to tarnished gold and every inch of his lightly tanned skin to bronze.

"Slave," he called out. "Tend to me."

I shuddered as I fought back my animal desire for him.

I was no animal, and I would not give in to such base instincts even though I knew myself well enough to understand I'd always been too much of a hedonist to resist gorging myself on various delights for any length of time.

And Master Alexander's body was certainly a delight.

I pushed through the glass door into the quickly steaming shower. Without speaking, Alexander handed me a bar of soap that smelled of pine trees and presented me with the broad, muscle swathed expanse of his back.

I watched my hand lift to rub the soap over his skin, how it trembled as I moved in broad circles over the topography of his spine.

I had never washed a man before.

It was a silly observation. I was a woman and a virgin, so obviously, I'd never been in a similar situation before. But this intimacy seemed to extend beyond sexuality into the realm of real intimacy.

I could feel the satiny texture of his skin under my fingers, the strength of his muscles tensed beneath the flesh, and the heat of his body as he absorbed the temperature of the steamy shower. There was a triangle of small brown moles high on his left shoulder and a faint, nearly indecipherable collection of thin, criss-crossing scars in the valley below his shoulder blades. I traced their edges with my thumb and wondered who had done that to him.

His muscles bunched with tension, and I realized that I had spoken aloud.

"As I've told you, every predator is prey to someone."

"I can't imagine a beast more terrifying than you," I told him honestly.

It wasn't just that he was ruthless or crueler than a starving wolf. Something in his manner spoke of the colossal effort of his restraint, as if one wrong moment would unleash that ravenous beast chained to the floor of his soul on whomever was unwise enough to be in its path.

"Some monsters are made, and some are born. You could say that I'm the worst of both worlds," he said cryptically.

I chewed my lip as I puzzled over his words, aware that the mystery of Alexander Davenport was dangerous to a woman like me. A woman who enjoyed the riddles of the human brain, and the strange complexities of a single personality. I wanted to sit cross-legged on the ground and assemble the facets of Alexander's mind like a ten-thousand-piece puzzle.

In my experience, if you could understand someone, it was nearly impossible to hate them.

And truthfully, I didn't want to hate this man. Not because he deserved warmer feelings, but because that hatred was just as corrosive to my mental health as my two-week stint in the dark. I couldn't imagine hating someone with all my heart and seeing them every single day for the next five years.

What kind of person would I be at the end of that?

How could I go from half a decade of hatred to a future reunited with my family? How could I find love in my heart, how would I know how to express it?

The answer, I feared, was that I wouldn't be able to.

If I allowed the horrible unjustness of my situation to disband my ability to love, I'd lose an elemental facet of who I was and the very reason I was even doing this.

For the love of my family.

Alexander interrupted my thoughts to hand me a shampoo bottle.

I sucked in a deep breath and poured the gel into my hands before working it into the thick strands of his hair. His scent bloomed in the humid air, so that I felt he was surrounding me.

He turned to face me when I was done, tipping his head back into the steam of water so that bubbles went sliding down over his chiseled chest. His eyes popped open to stare at me as I popped a big bubble over his left nipple.

Caught like a little girl, I giggled before I could clamp my mouth shut with both hands.

His eyes blazed, but he didn't condemn me. Instead, his voice was silky when he said, "Get on your knees and clean me with your tongue."

"Soap would do a better job," I retorted, but my knees were already softening, melting me like butter to the ground at his feet.

He was already hard. The long, veined length of him pulsed in time with his heartbeat, hypnotizing me as I stared at it. It felt strange to find something so alien to me so utterly attractive, but I loved the thickness of him as I weighed him in my palm and the way his heavy balls were framed by his lean, strong thighs.

I tilted his erection down to my mouth and kept my eyes canted up to his when I licked the flat of my tongue over the crown of his shaft.

His eyes went black with arousal.

Something like a purr vibrated through my throat before I could swallow it back. There was something unbearably heady about having his most delicate organ in my hand, about bringing such a powerful man pleasure.

"Tell me what to do," I asked, playing my fingers over his shaft, his pubic bone, and inner thighs.

His body tensed with surprise before relaxing. One of his hands slid into the back of my hair and fisted.

"Suck and lick the water from my cock as a guide. Trace the veins with your tongue, take me as far into your throat as you can and breathe through your nose so I can feel how tight and wet your mouth is around me. Essentially, treat my cock like your very own ice-cream cone." His voice was husky again, and I knew that seeing me lap at the head of his cock like a kitten with cream was the reason for it.

I hummed with my lips pressed to him and then looked up at him to say, "If I make you come like this, I want to be allowed to write a letter to my family."

The hand in my hair twisted painfully, and the pleasure previously saturating his features calcified. "Are you trying to top from the bottom again, *topolina*?"

His voice was a menacing hiss that pierced fear through me like a needle with thread.

I didn't answer because it didn't feel prudent.

"Let me rephrase that for you. If you make me come hard enough with your inexperienced mouth, I won't tie you down and take a cat-o'-nine-tails to your tender arse."

I could feel my eyes like hot coals in my head as I glared up at him, but he was unperturbed by my animosity, and before I could protest, he jacked his hips forward to sink the tip of his dick past my parted lips.

Gone was the option to learn about his pleasure, to explore him the way a virgin might have the opportunity to study their lover. I'd lost that privilege and the glimpse of a man with some semblance of a tender soul due to my impudence, and now I was just a vessel for his cock.

A slave.

The degradation of being used like that burned in my bones and radiated heat through my entire body until I felt suffused with fire. Yet those flames were not made of shame. They coursed through my blood straight to the tips of my puckered breasts and the apex of my thighs where they raged like wildfires.

It turned me on. The sucking, wet noises I made around his hard flesh as he pumped into my throat, the way my jaw ached with the struggle to accommodate his girth, and the pain prickling over my scalp as he fisted my hair too tightly in both hands.

It was too much, everything too hot. The steamy air, the splatter of shower water and the man towering over me, using me ruthlessly for his own pleasure.

I felt lightheaded with desire and confusion.

How could I be enjoying this?

Before I could find the answer to that question, Alexander's hands tightened in my hair, and his legs shook as he started to come. Unlike the first time, he pulled out of my throat so that the first blast of his briny cum landed on my tongue. I swallowed around him, then gasped as he pulled out farther, fisting his angry red shaft in a big hand. I was stunned and mesmerized as he pulled at his flesh almost violently, his cum flying out to land on my cheek, my neck, and my lust swollen breasts.

Painted in sin and steeped in shameful lust, I kneeled before my Master feeling as newborn and vulnerable as a kitten. So I was pliant when he reached down to haul me to my feet and then press me against the cold shower tiles. It was only when he stamped the full length of his body to my own and one of his hands went unerringly between my legs to cup my drenched sex that I stirred from the oblivion of my mind.

"Soaking wet," he rasped into my ear as he dragged his nose down the column of my throat.

I squirmed as he sank his teeth into the flesh where my neck met my shoulder. His hand curled firmly over my pussy, two fingers sinking inside me to bump gently against the barrier of my virginity.

"My beauty likes to be used by her Master," he continued to say as he ground the palm of his hand into my clit.

Instantly, I was on the verge of orgasming. I panted and winced, trying to stave off the overwhelming heat and the need to grind into his hand for further friction.

"The slave with a spine of steel melts with one touch to her swollen cunt. I'll remember that next time you try to stand up to me."

I swallowed the ragged edge of a groan.

"But I will not let you come this morning." He smiled against my wet cheek when I whimpered in protest. "Be happy I am not punishing you for trying to manipulate me. I will not be wrapped around your little finger, slave. Remember that today each time your greedy cunt yearns for the press of my fingers and tongue."

He pulled away from me abruptly and stepped out of the shower without further ado. I watched slightly stupefied as he dried off and tied a towel around his lean hips.

"You have exactly ninety seconds to finish washing, and then I expect you to dress me. If you attempt to touch yourself, I will introduce you to the ancient stockade we keep in the backyard."

Immediately, my pussy still pulsing and my mind sitting eschew on my head like a crooked hat, I did as he bade.

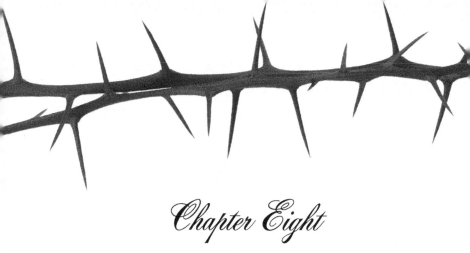

Chapter Eight

J spent hours walking the house after he left for the day. It was named Pearl Hall quite aptly as there were pearls inlaid in elaborate furnishings and scalloping the edge of sconces and doorframe plasterwork. There were priceless historical trappings everywhere I looked, from the centuries-old tapestries that covered the walls to the delicate draperies pulled back from every window. There was also surveillance everywhere. Cameras, sensors, and keypads beside some locked doors that seemed to call for fingerprints or retina scans.

I felt those technological eyes watching me as I lingered over paintings, and I hated that the only thing I'd been given to wear was one of Alexander's thin, cotton button-ups. Someone was tracking my every step through the manor and that knowledge made me feel like Alexander's "little mouse" even though he wasn't at the house to hunt me himself.

When I tried to open the front doors for some fresh air, Riddick appeared behind me, silent but heavy with censure. He would stop me, I knew, if I somehow found a way to get past the heavy lock. He appeared again when I lingered too long over a set of intricately carved wooden doors. He didn't touch me, but his presence was enough to have me scuttling forward like a scolded child.

Around midday, my stomach began to rumble, and I went in search of the kitchens, descending the grand staircase onto the main floor and then taking a smaller, darker one into the pit of the house.

Instantly, the eerie quiet permeating the upper levels was perforated with giggles and erratic chatter.

I wanted to be a part of the noise. I wanted to sit down with another woman and talk about the strange things happening to my body. My bizarre attraction to Alexander was even more confounding than puberty had been, and I yearned for someone to smooth the ragged edges of my panic with their wisdom.

What I really wanted was Mama to sit me down at the kitchen table with a simple task like rolling out pasta dough so that my anxious thoughts were steadied by a mundane task. Only then would she roll out her wisdom as calmly and proficiently as she kneaded the semolina under her fingers.

Even Elena would know what to say to me given her relationship with Christopher, a much older family friend who had been courting Elena since she was sixteen. They slept together even though she had never explicitly told me so. I could tell by the slashes of high colour on her cheekbones when she returned from his home, the way she smelled like him in secret places like behind her ears and in the hollow of her collarbones. She would break my attraction apart the way a mathematician would, into equations with logical outcomes.

It was the kind of advice I needed then, not Sebastian's empathy or Giselle's romanticism, but learned wisdom and defined logical. The why and how of my attraction to someone who was more monster than man.

I swept down the worn stone floor into a huge, airy kitchen that somehow maintained the feel of ancient grandeur while being completely modernized. There were a handful of servants working around the room and more sitting at a massive table off to the left, happily living out their day.

Until they saw me.

Instantly, they froze, and the chatter evaporated.

I swallowed back my nerves, hyper aware of the long length of my legs exposed by the shirt and the fact that they probably knew I'd been chained to the floor of the ballroom for the past few weeks.

"Hello," I said, then cleared my throat when my accent saturated the word. "Hello everyone, I am so sorry to bother. I was just exploring the, um, the house, and when I smelled something delicious, I followed my nose down here."

They continued to stare without deviation in expression or posture.

Um, okay.

"Excuse them," said a young man with flaming ginger hair and so many freckles he seemed like a walking constellation of golden stars. "They have no manners." He moved forward quickly to extend his hand. "I, on the other hand, *do*. Pleasure to meet you, Miss Lombardi. I am Douglas O'Shea, the chef of this illustrious household."

"So you are the wizard that made the *pasta alla Genovese* last night," I said, taking his calloused hand in my own. "Thank you for that, I cannot tell you how much I longed for a taste of home."

"Oh, the pleasure was mine. Usually I'm tasked with making the ordinary bland fare of my countrymen, so it was a delight to turn my skill to something different. Please, next time give me something truly challenging."

I laughed at his exuberance, my awkwardness washed away by his genuine kindness. The others watched us still, but I took no mind to them.

I'd been watched all my life but received little true kindness so I would focus on that.

"Come and have a spot of tea with me while I finish these finnicky little *petits forts*," Douglas encouraged me, turning our clasped hands so that he could lead me to a stool perched beside his workstation. "You look thin as a rake and in dire need of a cuppa."

I slid onto the chair and tugged down my shirt fruitlessly when one of the male servants went slack jawed at the sight of my legs.

Douglas rapped the servant in question over his knuckles with a wooden spoon. "Young Jeffery, out with you. I believe you have some work to do in the dining room before supper."

Jeffery blushed furious at being caught and scampered out of the kitchen along with the rest of the nonessential personnel.

"Don't mind them, ducky. It's been yonks since we had a proper young lady in the house and the lads are all a bit dense normally so your beauty don't help none," Douglas explained with a twinkle in his eye as he carefully began to pipe icing between small pink layers of cake.

"You'll forgive me if I don't believe you. Master Alexander hardly seems like the kind of man to abstain from female companionship," I retorted with a snort.

Douglas paused his piping to blink at me and then roared with laughter.

I couldn't help but laugh with him. It felt good to have some light-heartedness after so long in the pressurized company of Alexander or the vacuous chamber of my own solitude.

Douglas was young, closer to my age than I guessed Alexander's to be, and he possessed the kind of happy personality that was infectious.

"Oh, there were women before you, for both of the masters, but none quite like you," he prattled on, and I realized what a treasure trove of information he might be. "This is a man's household through and through. Or it has been since the passing of Lady Greythorn."

"Lady Greythorn?" I asked as a servant slid my way tentatively to offer me a cup of tea.

"Oh yes, the late Mistress of Pearl Hall. She passed, oh, nine years ago this May. A lovelier woman I've never known. Incredibly posh, but very down to earth with her household staff and family."

"What happened to her?" I asked even though I didn't fully understand who she could have been.

Wasn't Alexander titled Earl of Thornton, not Greythorn?

Douglas paused his activities and looked around the room guiltily as if he'd been caught in the act of blasphemy against his employers. I could see his reluctance to continue, but I was determined to unearth some of the mystery around this great empty house and its master.

I leaned forward to place a hand on Douglas's arm and looked up at him through my lashes with a pout curling my bottom lip just slightly. "I only ask because I recently lost my own father."

It wasn't a lie, not quite.

I had lost Seamus forever, just not to death.

Of course, the sadness was manufactured, but what was a little white lie between burgeoning friends?

My words had their intended effect. His face softened, and he patted a flour dusted hand over my own on his arm. "Poor thing, I'm so sorry for your loss. Well, it's not really the thing to talk about such matters, you understand? Here, try this." He shoved a gorgeously crafted little cake at me and waited until I'd taken a bite and moaned before continuing. "She died away from home while she was visiting... a family friend. Apparently, it was a tragic accident. She was drinking over dinner and wandered outside to the terrace for some fresh air. Next thing anyone knew, she was dead at the base of the building two stories down."

I cringed at the mental image. "And who was she to Alexander?"

Douglas frowned at me as if I was dense. "Why, his mother, ducky."

"Oh, and whatever happened to his father?"

Before he could answer me, the sharp clip of expensive shoes echoed down the hall, heralding the imminent arrival of a man who was most definitely not a servant.

He was exquisitely clothed in a charcoal suit, silk shirt, and matching tie with his dark blond hair brushed back from his broad forehead in a smooth wave that heralded back to the jazz age. It wasn't his expensive suit or formidable demeanor that gave away his clear status in the household, but his very obvious resemblance to Alexander.

"He is very much alive and well," the man in question said as he came to a stop in the entryway.

"Your lordship," Douglas addressed with a deferential tip of his head. "What a pleasure to have you visit us here. Is there something I can do for you?"

"I've come for the girl." He stared at me with dark, unerring eyes. "Miss Cosima Lombardi, we haven't yet had the pleasure to meet. I'm afraid my son has been remiss in this regard, so I've taken it upon myself to make the introductions. Come here so I may do so while I look at you."

I swallowed roughly and placed my delicate tea cup on the butcher block table in front of me before sliding off the stool, careful to hold down the edges of the shirt so I didn't flash my Master's father.

There was an instinctive kernel of fear in my belly, but

I couldn't be sure if the source was the heavy force of Lord Greythorn's personality radiating throughout the room or the simple fact that he was Alexander's father.

And if I thought Alexander was the spawn of Satan, maybe it was the devil himself I was then approaching.

When I stopped in front of him, he stepped close and tipped my chin with two of his furled fingers to study my face in the light streaming through the high windows.

"Golden eyes against inky hair," he murmured. "Like the summer sun against the night sky. A beautiful study in contrast."

"Thank you, Lord Greythorn," I said, because I'd learned from an early age how to take a compliment, however discomforted I was by it.

His broad face broke into a surprising smile, creasing his pale skin into pleasing fold. "Please, we will be closer than all that. Call me Noel."

I could tell by the sudden vibration in the air behind me that the servants were surprised by this allowance, and I didn't know what to make of it.

"Yes, of course, thank you, Noel."

"I've come to give you a proper tour of the house," he told me, dropping my chin and offering his arm up like a true gentleman. "If you will do me the honour."

I swallowed convulsively, fighting the instinct to look over my shoulder at Douglas for some indication of what the hell was going on. Instead, I placed my hand on Noel's arm.

"I know you walked the house this morning," he continued, clasping my hand over his arm in a way that felt just as final as the shackles I wore in the ballroom. I shivered as I realized that it might have been him behind the camera tracking my every move throughout the day. "But I thought I would show you the dungeon."

To my utter shock and uneasy delight, my afternoon with Noel was incredibly diverting, and while it did include a brief foray into the dungeon, it was only to peek at the ancient cells and torture equipment mounted like art on the stone walls. He took me through the hall of pictures that spanned the length of the house on the second story, telling me interesting anecdotes about the Davenport family and Pearl Hall. The house was first built in the 1600s but had been consequently added to and renovated throughout the ages so that now the interior resembled more of a French chateau than a typical British home. It was elegant even in its enormity, each of the over 250 rooms a marvel of colour coordination and detail. I learned that the first fork had been used in the dining hall in 1632, and that the extremely pious Bess Davenport, Duchess of Greythorn in the 18th century, had added a small, exquisite chapel to the left wing of the house. Each room was relatively overstuffed with furniture acquired across the centuries and busy with hand-painted wallpapers, gilt moldings, and elaborate plaster ceilings. It awed me to step over the worn stone steps, concave from the passing of many feet, to know that I was living in a home that had seen generations of royalty and important historical dealings. I'd never been a student of history, but by the end of the tour, I itched to read more about Pearl Hall and British culture.

We avoided speaking of Alexander, and even though it soothed me to pretend he didn't exist, it was impossible to remove him from my thoughts completely.

He was an apparition in my peripheral vision. A ghost's cool breath at my back. He haunted me as he had since the moment

I'd saved him in the alleyway in Milano, and I couldn't imagine a time, even years after this half-decade of servitude, that I wouldn't feel him in my thoughts or harbor him like a cancer in my cells.

"That concludes our tour, I'm afraid," Noel said as we descended the grand marble staircase into the pale blue great hall.

"We could go outside?" I said flippantly, as if my heart wasn't pounding in my throat at the idea.

Noel's smile thinned. "I think not; it's late and the damp doesn't agree with my old bones."

"You're hardly old," I teased.

Something darkened his pale grey eyes and then vanished too quickly to study. He stopped at the foot of the stairs and took both my hands in his to give them a gentle squeeze.

"You are too kind to me, my dear. I know you are probably bored of my company, but would you by chance join me before the fire for a game of chess?"

I wanted to say yes because I was sick and tired of being so alone. I was used to a matchbox house full of passionate Italians, not castles filled with dead air.

But I didn't know how to play chess.

I'd never even seen a chess set.

And I didn't want to tell Noel, a British fucking Lord who had probably attended the best schools in the country, that I hadn't even finished high school because I'd missed too many classes for modelling gigs.

He sensed my hesitation and bent his knees slightly to lower his great height in order to look in my eyes. "What's your name again, dear?"

"Cosima," I murmured, looking anywhere but in those eyes so like his son's only I'd never seen Alexander's warm with kindness.

His mouth twisted. "That's a difficult name to pronounce for an old Brit. Do you have any other given names?"

"Ruth," I told him with a cringe because each of my siblings had an English name from our Irish father, but mine was by far the ugliest. "Cosima Ruth."

"Ruthie," Noel said with a smile. "A new name for a new British woman."

A frown buckled my brow before I could help it. I wasn't British, and I didn't want to be called 'Ruthie'. It was an ugly name for a plain faced, meek girl.

I wanted to remain Cosima. Unique and beautiful, loving and vain. I didn't want to lose an iota of my personality, not even to the only man who'd ever shown me any kindness outside of my own family and an oddly watchful mafia boss back home.

Before I could open my mouth to protest, he was laughing lightly and turning away toward the second salon.

"Come," he said in a way that felt like a command even though his tone was light. "Come and I'll teach you."

I followed him through to the intimate den where a raging fire crackled in a fireplace big enough to comfortably fit a group of standing men. There was a small table set before the flames, the beautiful mahogany of the chessboard on top glowing in the warm light.

A servant appeared out of the shadows to pull the antique chair out for me, so I took a seat as Noel poured two fingers of scotch and sat himself.

"Now, there are many theories and philosophies about chess, dear girl," Noel began, running his fingers over the pieces on the board and straightening them with obsessive compulsion until they were perfectly aligned. "But one thing is simple, this is a game of survival, an example of mental Darwinism at its finest. The goal is not to be the smartest person on the board but the craftiest."

"That's good. I'm not particularly smart," I muttered, staring at the board in dread.

Noel stared at me, his eyes narrowed and his fingers stroking over his chin like a modern-day philosopher observing his subject. "Perhaps not, though, that's yet to be determined. Now, sit back and listen."

He explained for only a few moments, a quick rundown on the way each piece moved, that I had to go first because my pieces were white and his black, and that the winner of the game would receive a boon.

I had no idea what Noel could possibly want from me, but there were endless possibilities if I were to receive such a gift.

First and foremost, a phone call to my family.

I listened so hard to his instructions my ears strained and buzzed. My knee bounced with excess anxiety as I made my first move, pushing a pawn into the middle of the board. As we progressed through the game and Noel captured each and every one of my pawns, I felt a certain kinship to those limited, easily sacrificed pieces.

My life had been pawned my father, martyred in order to save the more important people in my life, the ones who could attain a better future than I ever would.

I just hoped, with every ounce of broken optimism in my heart, that my sacrifice would allow them to reach the other side of the board, to transform into any type of person they wanted despite the painful realities of their geneses.

I wondered idly, fruitlessly, what I may become at the end of this ordeal.

As I played with Noel, it was easy to imagine a different life, one with a father who would teach me chess as a young girl, who bought me lavish presents from his exotic travels just to spoil me, and one who would kiss me before bed each night with nothing but mint on his breath.

I wondered how different I would be; if the composition of my personality would have been arranged otherwise, and I'd be an altered woman.

Maybe one suited for the moniker 'Ruthie.'

"Check," Noel said, placing his rook in line with my king. "If you want to get out of it, you must sacrifice that last pawn."

I was attached to my last standing little solider, but I did as he taught.

He took my pawn with brisk, efficient fingers, glee so evident in the movement it seemed like they leapt across the board.

"Checkmate," he said again, this time using his bishop to hedge me into a corner. "You might take him with your knight, though I'll take that with my pawn."

I followed his logic bitterly, tasting the defeat on my tongue. My heart beat too fast, flooding my body with adrenaline that had nowhere to go.

I vibrated in my seat as he said, "Checkmate, again."

He was stalking me, hunting me across the board like a great cat playing with its food. It was a cruel and unusual trickery, especially when he had been so kind to me that afternoon.

Before I could question him, the half open door to the room slammed against the wall, and a tall, dark, and extraordinarily angry man appeared backlit in the doorway.

I had seen dangerous, scary men on countless occasions but never this close up and never with the considerable weight of their wrath focused so wholly on me.

It was clear Alexander was furious with me. His anger swelled in the air like static before the storm. Goosebumps raised on my flesh, and my already erratic heart began to canter through my chest.

"Alexander, good of you to join us," Noel said pleasantly.

My head turned on a swivel to gawk at his composure. Was I the only creature in the house with the instinct to run before the storm?

Alexander didn't speak. Instead, he took a few prowling steps forward, his gait a tight roll of tensed muscles. It was only when he stopped a few feet from the table that the light from the fire cast upon his face, and I could see the stark wrath in his features.

There was no fire in his fury, no geyser of shouted curses and passionate exclamations as there would have been with any one of my family members or limited friends.

Only coldness so absolute that it radiated from him like dry ice.

My panicked brain tried to search for a reason for his madness, if only so I could arm myself with a flimsy excuse, but I came up empty.

I was with the man's father playing chess.

Was it that I was having fun for the first time since I arrived? Was his kink thriving on my abject misery?

Or maybe it was that I wasn't where he thought I should be, chained up in the ballroom like a rabid beast.

I held my breath as his eyes tracked over every inch of my body in his line of sight before they cut to his father.

"We had an agreement." Each word was cut meticulously out of granite and shaped with deadly precision and control. I had the feeling if Noel or I made one wrong move, Alexander would unleash the violence I'd always sensed was coiled in his soul.

"Did we?" Noel asked, his bow crinkled in genuine confusion. "That I couldn't play chess in my own salon with a guest?"

"She is no guest of yours." He moved forward to stand beside the table, looming over his father. "She has absolutely nothing to do with you."

Noel leaned back in his chair casually, his fingertips dangling over the arm, his diamond cufflinks winking in the light. He was the picture of an indolent lord.

"That is where you are wrong. She has everything to do with you, and you are my son, my heir, and my protégé. Everything you do is a reflection on this house and my own ability to rule. Therefore, Miss Cosima has absolutely everything to do with me."

I jerked as Alexander's hand slammed against the chessboard, sending gorgeously carved wood pieces all over the floor. One of the pawns landed badly on the marble foot of the fireplace and broke its neck.

"If you touch one hair on her head, I will kill you," Alexander seethed. "I mean it, Noel. I will slaughter you where you stand."

Noel looked shocked, and I couldn't blame him.

"He's been kind to me," I found the audacity to say. My heart thrashed in the cage of my ribs, desperate to flee the ramifications of my actions.

Alexander turned his frozen stare to me and bared his teeth. "Excuse me?"

I cleared my throat twice before my voice found traction in my throat. "He has. He gave me a tour, and he's only teaching me to play chess."

His hand was around my throat before I could blink, squeezing hard enough for spots to explode across my vision. He leaned down to growl softly in my face, "No one teaches you anything except your Master. And who is your Master, *topolina*?"

"You," I said, more breath than voice as I struggled to suck in air around his punishing grip. "You are."

"Yes," he hissed, running his nose down my jawline so that he could speak against my lips. "I am the Master of this body, Captain of your fucking fate. I think it is past time you understood that."

I gasped as he sank a hand in my hair and twisted, dragging me away from the table by the force of his stride toward the door. My hands flew to his, trying to loosen his agonizing grip to no avail. Tears pricked my eyes, and I struggled even as I was forced to follow close behind him.

"I'll deal with you later," Alexander threatened over his shoulder to Noel as he tugged me out the door and slammed it shut.

I could barely keep up with his ground eating strides as he stalked up the staircase, heading back to my cage.

"Master, please," I begged as a headache stabbed into each temple. "Please, stop this. I didn't know…"

"You didn't know? Here I thought we were passably smart, *topolina*. You do not, under any circumstances, spend time alone with another man unless it is Riddick, and you especially do not allow any of them to touch you. Clearly, I made a mistake by allowing you to roam. It is an error I do not intend to make again."

I screamed as he pushed open the door to the ballroom and shoved me brutally inside. I tripped over my feet, crashing to the unforgiving floor on my elbows and knees so hard I thought for a second that they might shatter.

The clip of his shoes smacked against the marble like striking flints as he prowled after me.

I didn't want to know what might happen if he captured me.

The ballroom was huge, and at the other end, another set of double doors beckoned me. If I could reach them and get out to the kitchens, surely he wouldn't hurt me in front of his staff.

Painfully, I pushed up off the ground and raced toward the door.

Not one second later, the pace of his clicking shoes erupted like the ticking of a time bomb.

I was malnourished and not very athletic to begin with, but

my sheer desperation to get away from the man-turned-beast was insurmountable. To make it hard for him, I zigged and zagged across the marble, my breasts bouncing painfully, the soles of my feet slick with panicked sweat so that I almost skidded.

My heart felt near to bursting in my chest as I ran harder than I ever had before. By the time I was a yard away from the doors, my lungs were eviscerated by the strain, and I practically stumbled into the heavy oak frame. My slippery fingers slid off the ornate knob once, twice and then finally, they latched and pulled it open…

I screamed so loud I saw stars as Alexander's iron arms caged me against his chest and lifted me off the ground. I tried to kick out with my legs to leverage myself back down, but he was so much taller and broader that I only served to tire myself out.

"There is no escaping, *topolina*," he rasped in my ear as I yelled and yelled, cursing him in Italian and calling for help in English. "It is the law of nature. You are the mouse, and I the falcon. No one here is going to step in to save you now."

I turned my head and sank my teeth into his bared forearm, tasting blood as it bloomed on my tongue. He cursed viciously and tightened his hold around my chest so painfully, I could barely breathe.

With a grunt, he swung a leg forward to capture one of mine and bend it backward in order to take us both to the floor with his heavy body crushing mine. I squirmed and thrashed like the goddess Thetis in Peleus's hold but to no avail. Alexander was too strong, too indomitable to evade.

My screams of protest and yearning for aid drowned in a sudden flood of tears. I sobbed as he pulled my arms behind my back and pinned them there with one hand. As he fisted a hand in the back neck of the button-up I wore and wrenched it off my body with a single brutal tug.

"You're my possession to use as I please," Alexander ground out as he placed a knee over my captured hands in order to unzip and pull open his pants.

I was mindless, my gut instinct to fight and flee triggered so hard that there was no use for my thoughts, no bias in my heart. Only the sheer terror of being captured remained and so I struggled on, bucking my hips to dislodge him.

I failed.

Freed from his trousers, he laid his hot, heavy body against mine once more only this time, the steel length of his cock nestled between my buttocks.

He panted in my ear as he ground his hips into my ass. "I'm going to make you take every inch of my cock. You can pretend you don't want it. That you didn't know somewhere in the darkest corners of your mind that this moment was coming and that you were not secretly looking forward to it, but I know different. You've longed for it."

"You're a psychopath," I grunted as I tried to wriggle away from the increasingly delicious friction of his dick sliding over my sensitive skin.

"Whatever else I am, I am always your Master," he said as he canted his hips lower and spread his legs so they pushed mine farther apart. "You can scream, Cosima, and know that no one will come for you."

I opened my mouth to protest, but the air was punched from my chest as he thrust forward inside me.

Searing pain erupted through my core. It felt as if someone had ripped out the seams inside my body, and I fractured from the pain of it.

My virginity was gone. Crushed under Lord Thornton's expensive heel just as he'd foretold.

I sobbed against the cold floor, my tears pooling hot and

slick under my cheek. He was still inside me for one blessed minute, my flesh protesting around his girth and clamped tighter than a shaking fist around his length. I could feel his heavy breath, the low rumble in his throat as he slid out, paused, and then pushed back inside. My whole body shuddered at the alien feeling.

I wondered dazedly if this was the point when prey gave up to their predator, when they first drew blood with talons or teeth or cock and it seemed senseless to fight anymore.

Vaguely, I was aware of Alexander's harsh breath in my ear, the rough glide of him in and out of my torn pussy.

"I won't have you lie there like a broken doll so you can convince yourself that you don't love the feel of me inside you," Alexander gritted out before hauling me to my knees and then tipping my hips back against his own as he thrust.

I gasped, my head falling back onto his shoulder as one of his hands arrowed down to my clit and pinched it between his knuckles. In this position, the head of his dick pressed against something inside me, nudging and nudging until *click*. Something flared to life inside me, a heat that burned low and slow through my entire body.

"That's it," he said, sinking his teeth hard into the junction of my neck and shoulder, twisting his fingers over my clit, fucking me so hard it hurt. "Take your Master's cock."

God, but it hurt. It hurt like an aching muscle being painfully worked with strong fingers, an edge of pleasure to the pain that made my scalp prickle and my spine bow.

"I am the only one who will ever touch you," he growled into my sweat dampened nape as he thrust and thrust and thrust. "I am the only one who will ever hurt you."

His hands met at my breasts to ruthlessly twist my nipples. "Can you hear how wet you are around my thick cock? Sink into the pain, *topolina*, and you will find all the pleasure I have to give you."

I stuttered over my breath, my hips tipping farther to accommodate his girth between my legs. The mad slap of flesh rang out through the empty chamber, but the wet suck of my pussy grasping at his cock was more intimate. It was impossible not to agree with his ownership of me when he was deep within my body, cradled by the most intimate parts of my flesh.

The pain was transforming in my breasts, burning from a flash flare to a low-grade smolder that sent smoky tendrils of lust curling down my spine over my hips and into my sex.

I didn't understand the strange alchemy, how pain could evolve from plain hurt into golden desire. It set my teeth on edge even more than the sensation of being shackled to the floor like a dog.

"Bring your mind back to me," Alexander demanded, sucking deeply at the skin on the other side of my neck and punctuating it with firm biting kisses. "I am fucking *you*. Cosima Ruth Lombardi, loving sister, beloved daughter, and burgeoning model."

It felt as if he was reading my tombstone. The finality to his tone, to his words and the red evidence of the death of my innocence between my thighs where he churned and claimed were impossible to negate. I felt razed to the ground, the fire of my fight long extinguished by the wind so I lay as dust and ash on the floor, so easily conquerable I wasn't even worth the effort to conquer anymore.

But still, it wasn't enough for Master Alexander.

He gripped my chin, tilting it toward his mouth so he could claim mine. I moaned around his silky tongue as he plundered my mouth in tandem with his cock in my pussy. I could smell his cedar scent, his masculine musk, and the unique tang of our mingled sex. I could feel the roughness of his suit jacket against my back, his light stubble abrading my chin and cheeks as he kissed my breath away.

There was nothing to think or feel but him.

Nothing to be but his.

"Now, you're going to come for me, and it's going to hurt while you do it."

I was close enough to see the cold triumph in his eyes, the steam of passion as it collided with the heat of his constant fury.

I wanted to know why he was so furious with me, why he had to treat me so, but there was no voice in my sore throat and my thoughts were too diaphanous to grasp.

I felt as if I was losing myself to the intoxicating contrast of pain and pleasure, as if my very skin and bones had turned into an impossible oxymoron of sensation. Where were my ferocity and my independence?

His hand found the place we were joined, his fingers parting over the girth of his shaft as it tunneled inside me, his thumb rubbing slow, firm circles over my clit.

And suddenly, I could feel my spine.

It arched back into his thrusts, strong against his opposing momentum so that he hit harder at the knot of sensation deep inside me.

I could feel the ferocity unfurl in my belly, heat coiling and colliding into something so big it made my womb ache.

"That's it," Alexander ground out as he pounded into me, every component of his body playing mine ruthlessly.

Not just for his enjoyment now, but for my own.

He turned my body into a traitor as I recognized the beginnings of an orgasm taking form in my sparking blood.

"You're going to come for me just like this," he taunted me.

And God, I did.

My womb cramped so tightly I keened with pain, my pussy a vise around his cock so that he could barely pry himself out of my spasming folds. I screamed as he ripped me apart, and I screamed even when everything I was collapsed to the floor beneath him and still he pumped away.

Only when his shout of release joined my voice did I quiet, my mind preoccupied with the sting of his hot cum against my overly sensitive, abraded walls.

For a long moment, he stayed inside me, and his big hands moved slowly over my back, my buttocks and my thighs. It was oddly soothing, and the absurdness of his sudden tenderness made me want to cry again.

I didn't because he'd taken too much from me.

Finally, he pulled out, and I could feel the rush of our combined juices run out over my thighs. Alexander's wide palm cupped me there between my legs in a gesture that was somehow more possessive even than his taking of me. Gently but firmly, he smeared our cum from the front of my pussy over my clit to the end of my crack well beyond my asshole.

And as he claimed me like a primate, he told me in the elegant accent of a titled gentleman, "You are mine now, Cosima Lombardi. It is my cum between these pretty thighs, my ache in your womb, and my bruises beneath your skin. You will wear me like this every day for the next five years, and by the time your term is up, I promise you, you will beg me for another five."

Chapter Nine

I lay on the ground after he disappeared on the *click-click* of his expensive shoes, my sweat and blood and his cum cooling on my skin as my heartbeat slowed incrementally.

There were times in your life when it felt as if you were not really living it. I believed you were soulless at those moments, your spirit escaping your body through a puncture wound, some great trauma that your mind cannot endure, so it lets your essence escape for an all too brief reprieve.

I felt hollow as a broken relic as I lay there used, corrupted, and discarded, worshipped and warped by a heretic. There were no more tears at the backs of my eyes, but there was sorrow so deep in my bones I feared it would remain a part of me forever.

At some point, I might have slept because before I could comprehend the change, it was light outside the massive windows, and golden light was spilling across my body. I shivered at the warmth of it, then noticed how it highlighted the bloody smears on the floor, and the arrival of blackberry-coloured bruises on my hips.

Noel had told me the day before that the amount of floor-to-ceiling windows in Pearl Hall were an extravagance meant to highlight the family's wealth.

I hated them.

"It's time to get up and leave this place, dearie," Mrs. White's voice floated to me through my haze, and a moment later her soft, plump hands were smoothing back my hair.

I blinked into her face.

"Come, come," she urged. "Let me help you get clean."

"I don't think I'll ever be clean again," I told her in a hoarse whisper.

Her eyes shuttered briefly, but she turned her head before I could read the full extent of her expression. "You will, I swear it. Now, do as I tell you, and come with me."

My body ached so wickedly as I moved that I couldn't hold in the ragged moans as I gained my feet. I was a gutted building, my framework swaying in the wind.

Mrs. White wrapped her arm around my hips, cooing sweet nonsense as she led me slowly out of the ballroom.

I didn't ask where we were going because I didn't care.

The fire in my soul had gone out.

I was merely a body now, a vessel for Master Alexander's cock.

I shivered so hard it pinched a nerve in my spine, but still, I walked on down the hall into the opposite wing where we stopped before a large red door painted with gold leaf. The knob was delicate red blown glass shaped like a bloom, and I gasped softly at the beauty of it before Mrs. White's hand moved over it and opened the door.

The room inside was the colour of an oyster with gold cornices, sheer red draperies over the huge windows, and a bed covered in wine-toned satin coverlets and pillows. It was a room fit for a princess from the four-poster bed to the ornate gold vanity with its oval mirror.

My feet sank into the plush white, red, and pink rugs

layered over each other in a way that was artless and beautiful, and I couldn't resist the urge to wriggle my toes. When I looked up from doing so, Mrs. White was smiling softly at me.

"This is to be your room for the duration of your stay here at Pearl Hall," she told me as she went to the bed and pulled back the plush covers to reveal satin sheets.

"*Scusi?*"

She fluffed a pillow, stood back to survey the bed, and nodded contentedly. "Master Alexander had the room prepared for you. This is where you will sleep."

Tears bloomed in my throat, but I swallowed them down. "You mean I don't have to stay in the ballroom anymore?"

"Oh, darling girl," she cooed, rushing forward to take my hands even though I flinched away from her kindness.

Noel's kindness yesterday had only bought me pain.

"You won't believe me, but I do empathize with your plight. The Davenport men can be… mercurial at the best of times, and they are absolute demons once angered."

"I was with his father playing chess. I was hardly doing anything wrong," I muttered.

"So much is not what it seems. I would imagine a girl so oft judged like a book by its cover for her beauty would understand the deeper meaning of things."

I blinked and looked away from her, ashamed and confused by her words.

It was easy to judge Alexander, and I felt I'd been given more than a cover to do it by. I'd spent hours with the man now; I lived in his home and had taken him into my body.

Wasn't that enough?

But then, what did I really know about him?

He was an earl, heir to the Dukedom of Greythorn and the master of Pearl Hall, an estate that cost hundreds of thousands of dollars each year to run.

I knew the way he looked, admittedly well. His aristocratic feature crowned by the thick, silken gold of hair, overlong slightly at the top and pushed back from his broad forehead. There was age in the creases there and beside his eyes, bracketing his firm, masculine mouth that was only a few shades pinker than his golden skin. He was so symmetrical I could not find fault with any of his features, and each time I looked him in the face, I found I didn't want to.

His eyes up close were like twin moons, pale with silver star light but dark and cratered with mysteries I wanted to discover like an ancient astronomer.

He was abnormally tall, wide through the shoulders and narrow in the waist the way a swimmer was, with big hands that were elegant despite their breadth. I'd wondered what they might feel like on my body.

And now I knew.

No, I might have judged Alexander by the cover, but that didn't discount the horror of the monster depicted on it.

"I'll have one of the maids bring some supper for you. Master Alexander went to London, and we don't expect him back until late this evening so you can dine in your room. I imagine you'll want to rest early." Mrs. White clapped her hands and then stared at me as I wandered to the windows to look past the drapes.

The bedroom overlooked an immaculately laid out garden of sculpted hedgerows and brightly coloured flowerbeds. It was perfectly ordered with each wild thing put in its place. I thought wryly that it was a suitable view for a slave.

Beyond that, the land gently crested, then erupted into a thicket of dense trees like something out of a sinister fairy tale.

That, too, made sense.

"There's one more thing before I leave, Ruthie."

I jerked away from the window to look at Mrs. White, shocked that she would call me that.

"Excuse me?"

"Oh, Lord Greythorn has instructed the staff to call you by the name of Ruthie. He is excessively kind that way."

"Kind?"

"Yes, well, he knew some of us would find it hard to remember such a strange name, and he knew you would have a difficult enough time as it is assimilating to British culture. It's a wonderful remedy, really."

"I would prefer Cosima," I told her as my spine cooled and hardened with steel.

"Well, what's done is done." She ignored my statement with a wave of her hand and then clapped when someone knocked on the door. A moment later, a maid entered bearing a ridiculously ornate golden telephone and cradle. "Your second surprise is here, my dear. A telephone call home."

My previous irritation evaporated as I was struck down by her words.

Telephone call home.

Home.

I lunged for the phone and ripped it out of the maid's hands, feeling like a beggar faced with her first meal in weeks.

My finger was rotating the ancient dial before I had even taken a seat on the soft bed. Distantly, I heard Mrs. White usher the other woman out of the room before closing the door behind the both.

But I was preoccupied by the utterly melodic ringing of the phone in my ear.

My heart was suspended in my throat, blocking the passage of my breath, but I didn't care.

There was a pause in the ringing and then a brief click before, *"Pronto."*

A sob bubbled up through my lips before I could clamp my hand over my mouth to contain.

"Patatino, sono Cosi," I half hiccoughed into the phone. My heart seemed to break and reform against the familiar Italian of Sebastian's childhood nickname 'little potato.'

"Mia bella sorella," he said after a weighty pause. "My Cosima."

We breathed through the phone line for a long moment as we both digested the enormity of our feelings. I cradled the phone against my cheek and closed my eyes against the burn of tears that spilled beneath my lashes. It was too easy to picture Seb's handsome face, the strong bones in his face that hollowed out his cheeks and the square point of his chin contrasting the fullness of his mouth. I knew the exact shade of black in his hair and the thickness of the eyelashes cresting his cheek because I'd grown up staring into his face almost more than I had my own even as a model.

No sight in the world was as dear to me as my brother; not even my sisters, as treasured as they were in my heart.

There was a unity to twins that was impossible to explain to others. I felt a fundamental lack of ease if I was separated from him for too long even though I was all too used to it after the last year I'd spent mostly in Milano.

To simply breathe in tandem through a phone line was an intimacy we craved.

"How is everyone?" I asked finally, suddenly nervous Mrs. White would return to cut my conversation short.

"Missing you, always," he responded instantly. "Even when Salvatore came calling to wish me a happy birthday, he seemed miserable that you weren't in town."

I bit my lip at that because the Camorra *capo* was the one who signed the dotted line of my terms of sale.

"Did he ask where I was?"

"No, he only stayed to have another rousing fight with Mama and to give me a fine bottle of Tuscan wine as a birthday present."

"Seb, don't you think it's odd that he does that?" I asked.

I'd never put much thought to it before then. Salvatore's infrequent but influential presence in our lives had seemed ordinary in the smaller context of my life in Italy, but now that I was away and I'd learned the manipulation and games men played, I couldn't help to wonder what Salvatore's end game was.

Sebastian snorted. "I don't think mafia men are exactly known for doing the obvious sorts of things, Cosi. I think he's a man without children who discovered us through Seamus and took a shining to our family. He dotes on Mama just as much as he does us, when she lets him."

That was true, though Mama would sooner bite the hand that tried to feed her than accept what he was offering. To say she was not fond of the Made Man was putting it mildly.

Another puzzle I'd never thought to piece together.

"Anyway, his gift was the highlight of my day. So much for celebrating our birthday together."

I winced even though I'd known he would say as much. "It was too good an opportunity to pass up, but I am sorry I missed it. Sorrier than I can really say."

"You sound very unhappy," he noted.

In some ways, as happy as I was to hear my male voice echoed back at me, I wished it was one of my sisters or Mama who had answered.

"It's been grueling work," I admitted. "I'm not sleeping enough, and the man I'm working for is a monster."

"Well, if the money you are sending to Mama is any indication, it's worth your sacrifice. Cosima, we have more than we know what to do with," he said before gifting me his bold laugh.

"How much is it?" I asked before I could curb myself, hoping he wouldn't wonder why I didn't know if I was the one sending it. "I've had them set up a direct deposit, you see, and I'm curious it's everything I thought it would be."

"Five thousand pounds," he crowed, and I used the opportunity to let out a gusty sigh. The sum meant that Alexander was sending a monthly allowance that would amount to the three hundred thousand he has promised to send to them each year. "Honestly, Mama fainted when it appeared in her account the first month. When it was there the second time, she almost took out Elena when she fainted again."

Despite everything, I found myself smiling at the thought. "I'm glad. Now, tell me what you are putting the money toward."

"Giselle's tuition is paid through the year, and she has an allowance now that she informed me meant she could buy acrylics." We both laughed as we imagined her excitement about procuring the expensive paints. "Elena bought her own second-hand computer and has enrolled in online classes at Università di Bologna in law. We repaid the last of Seamus's debts with creditors in town and with the Camorra, but Cosima, you should know something. We haven't seen Seamus since August."

I closed my eyes again and silently let out a breath of relief that I hadn't known I was holding the past few weeks.

"*Grazie a Dio*," I said, thanking God. "We've been wishing him gone since the beginning of my memories. Please don't tell me that you're saddened by this."

"Don't be insulting. I spent too much on a bottle of grappa, and believe it or not, I shared it with Elena."

"You didn't," I said with a laugh, sinking back into the copious number of pillows lining the headboard of the bed.

Neither Seb nor Giselle got along very well with our eldest sister, and I couldn't exactly blame them. Elena was the type of woman who believed that elegance was more important than feeling, intelligence surpassed passion, and if you wanted to know what was in her heart, you had to earn it.

Sebastian and Giselle were more easily led by the beautiful hearts they wore on their sleeves.

Once, I'd been like them, but I had always understood Elena and her philosophies.

A woman should not be easy to know for mystery was half of her power.

"And Cosima, something else has happened."

"You published one of your stories?" I asked in the high voice of an excited young girl, but I didn't care.

My environment had disappeared, and even the imaginary shackles I wore seemed nearly non-existent. My mind was back home in Napoli with my family.

Sebastian laughed. "No, Cosi, but you know the play I've been doing in Roma?"

I bit my lip, trying to remember one of the many amateur productions my brother had been participating in before I left.

"You don't remember, and that's fine. The moral of the story is, a theatre company director from London was visiting, and he approached me after the play. It seems he runs Finborough Theatre. He wants me to move to London to pursue an acting career as a principle at his company."

My heart soared into my throat, and before I could stem it, I was squealing and jumping on the bed with joy even as I carefully kept the phone to my ear.

"Sebastian, you gifted man," I shouted through my happy

tears. "You beautiful, talented man! I could not be happier for you."

We laughed together as we talked about the particulars, and he recounted local gossip before handing me over to Mama and Elena who both nearly chatted my ear off with their own material.

I spoke with my family for well over an hour and only rung off when another maid entered the room with my dinner tray. When she took the phone away, I almost attacked her, but I held myself back on the thought that I might be rewarded the privilege again.

It seemed giving up my virginity granted me new living quarters and the connection to my family I so craved.

Later that evening, after I finished a supper I was sure Douglas had prepared because it was a delicious speciality from Napoli and after I'd showered away the remnants of sex from my body, I lay in the dark curled up beneath the most luxurious covers I had ever known more troubled than I had ever been.

I wasn't truly religious, but my parents were Catholic and a quote by Job from the Bible rattled around like a loose screw in my head.

"The Lord gave and the Lord hath taken away; blessed be the name of the Lord."

Only, I had no God in this new home of mine. My religion was servitude, and my lord was my Master. What he took from me, he rewarded me for, and in return for this unhealthy symbiosis, he expected me to worship him.

I didn't.

But the thing that kept me up late into the night when the brain was murky but thoughts were horrifyingly clear, was that I could imagine a time when I did. When the ritual of my everyday life of a slave wore me down as surely as the generations of feet against the stone steps in this house. When looking to him for orders was route and worshiping his body like a deity felt akin to taking prayers. What was faith if not the engrained instinctual and spiritual belief that there was a higher being out there looking over you?

After five years of serving Master Alexander, was there really any doubt I would revere him even if I feared him still?

Chapter Ten

"I want to teach you about obedience."

"I thought you were," I retorted drily as he led me up the third-floor staircase and turned us into the Hall of Mirrors.

I was a vain woman, so I'd spent some time here on my daily wanderings, staring at the money eyes that had gotten me into such trouble. I knew from my tour with Noel that it had been added after the fourth Earl had visited Versailles and fallen in love with the opulence. I'd never seen the French palace, but the gold gilt, floor-to-ceiling mirrors and the pink marble floor certainly seemed over the top enough for the French.

Alexander moved over to a red velvet ottoman and a small table set up in the middle of the space and beckoned me forward with a crook of his finger.

Each step felt like one inch closer to a tragic death by guillotine, only I knew it was my pride on the line and not my life.

Because even as I hated him for ripping my virginity out at the seams the day before, it seemed that he had emptied out my lining only to stuff me full of something else. Something velvety and dark, something with a scent like musk and honey, something that lived for sex.

I could feel my pulse settle between my thighs and beat like a gong.

"Your lessons will never cease, *topolina*. You are a submissive slave but not a weak one; therefore, my work will never be done. Come and stand before me."

I didn't stop until our toes were touching, a small act of defiance that made Alexander hum darkly. He moved back an inch, then clasped my chin firmly to lift my eyes to his.

"This is lesson two, *bella*. I am your Master, yes, but the game of Domination and submission is not the only one we play. We also play the one of life and death. If you cannot learn to obey me when you must, forces beyond my control will certainly kill you and probably me too."

"What kind of game is that?" I asked breathlessly.

He tightened his hold so that I had to strain on my tiptoes to keep my neck from snapping back. His mouth moved next to mine, his lips so close to my own I could feel the distance like a tangible thing, like a kiss itself.

"A game neither of us chose to play, but one both of us must win. So you'll learn." He pushed me gently away and picked up a frightening looking apparatus from the table. "Do you know what this is?"

I shook my head erratically.

"These are electric stimulation paddles. They are connected to this," he said, holding up his iPhone. "I am going to attach them to your body and give you a series of commands. If you do not react as you must, you will receive a small shock."

"Are you kidding me?" I asked, genuinely frightened. "What kind of monster *shocks* someone? I'm not some stray dog you are trying to break of bad habits."

"No," he said in that voice I was beginning to understand was the one of a Dominant. It was hushed but heavy, pressing in on me like a metal compressor, crunching my will into dust. "I am not kidding. I think we've established that I am not the kind of man who *kids*. And you are most certainly a stray, one I picked up on the streets of Napoli and dusted off, but one who needs to be trained. If you think the imagery is unflattering, I suggest you learn quickly to adapt."

"*Bestia*," I growled into his face as he lifted the mess of wires and attachments into the air.

"I am a beast, my beauty," he agreed with a feral grin. "But I am your beast."

He taped the small paddles to my breasts, the sensitive junction where my torso, pubis, and inner thighs met, and the upper and lower portions of my ass. I looked like some horribly deviant robot, delineated with black wires and tape. Alexander turned to grab something from the table and held it up for me to see before tossing it at me. I glared at him as I caught the soft piece of fabric, and he stared back, only raising one thick brow as if to ask whether I wanted to be disobedient before we'd even begun. With a gusty sigh, I dutifully stepped into the black satin corset that covered the paddles and kept them snug against my skin.

I could see myself in the many mirrors lining the four walls; countless reflections of my body and the way Alexander seemed to devour it with his eyes.

They burned when I turned from the reflection to look into their real-life iteration. They burned so bright he seemed almost manic with lust. It was such a contrast to the cold, hard set of his body, but it made me realize how much restraint he had to leash himself with around me.

He wanted to chase, capture, and fuck me like an animal, holding me down by the neck with his teeth as he rutted into me.

But he wouldn't because he was a gentleman, and he'd been raised on a steady diet of control and conservatism.

Instead, he would transform his animal aggression into deviant calculation, using whips, electro-shock paddles, his teeth, his hands, and his cock to dominate not just my body, spirit and temptations, but his own.

There was something thrilling in understanding that duality, and I felt a little piece of the Lord Thornton puzzle slide into place.

"Go to the door and stand there facing me," he commanded.

I could feel the dampness on the inside of my thighs with each step I took toward the door. By the time I turned to face him from across the room, I was panting slightly.

He had seated himself on the red ottoman, thick thighs spread, hands dangling between his knees with a short, black whip in one of them. His full lower lip was caught at the edge by one of his teeth as he stared at me with hooded eyes.

He didn't look like a lord or a businessman radiating power, but so at ease with it, he seemed casual. No, he looked like a god.

"Crawl to me."

I squeezed my eyes shut.

Was there anything more demeaning than that? I didn't think my knees would bend me to the floor or that my arms would carry me if I dared to try.

"I went to work today in London," he told me conversationally, completely throwing me off balance.

I'd been sure he was going to shock me.

"Meetings after meetings, my beauty, and do you know what I thought of through each and every one?" Quick as a flash, he snapped the whip in his hand through the air with a vicious *crack*. "You, crawling to me across this floor with mirrors all around us so that you could not escape how right you look doing that for me."

My pussy swelled, my clit like a diamond at its peak. I wanted him to get on his knees and mine me with his tongue.

But this wasn't about me or my desires.

It was about him.

"Crawl," he ordered again in a voice just like the lightning crack of the whip.

My body felt filled with lead as I tried to make it move against the objections of my heart. I stared at my trembling knees, but they would not bend.

Why was the act of crawling so difficult?

If I could understand it, I could do it. I knew I could.

But the answer to that question wasn't easy. It was buried in the cultural norms I'd had instilled in me since birth, and the tangle of Catholicism I'd forsaken as a girl never quite having figured it out.

I caught Alexander's dark eyes daring me from across the room and grasped that he took pleasure in my struggle.

Maybe it was easier to ask another question.

Why did my Master want me to crawl?

Those answers boiled to the surface of my brain from deep within my gut.

It was sexy. The slow slink of my body over the floor, the high crest of my ass in the air and the way gravity held my breasts in its hands. There was something about seeing a beautiful woman crawl toward you that would made a man feel like primeval lord.

It was power. He was above and I below, my limbs shackled to the ground by his words, my stubborn mind bent under the strong hands of his will. He would be hard beneath his suit trousers, harder maybe than he had ever been before knowing that our wills were at war in my mind and his was winning.

Of course, my Master would want to see me crawl.

I collapsed to the ground gracelessly, like a balloon punctured thanklessly by a child. I focused on my breath as I rolled onto my hands and knees, knowing that if I allowed myself time to reorient myself in my mind, to draw back my empathy from Alexander and root it once more in myself, I would stand up and fight back.

Fighting back was fruitless. Fighting back was for the dumb.

I wasn't stupid. I was a survivor. I would submit to Alexander's sexual games if it meant I could earn insight like this into his character. Insight that might get me home.

So I started to crawl.

There was nowhere safe to look save the veined marble floor, which made it impossible to tell where I was moving, but at least I didn't have to face the sight of me in the mirrors, or even worse, his eyes.

"Master says stop," Alexander drawled.

I took a moment to comprehend what he had ordered and didn't stop immediately.

Electricity bit into my skin at the site of my paddles on my breasts, hips, tummy, ass, and thighs. I curled my fingers and toes into the ground, gritted my teeth, and rode out the wave.

After the long pulse of sensation, it was over.

It didn't feel finished, though. My skin still buzzed as currents ran like tantalizing ribbons over my sensitive skin. My hips canted back instinctively, searching for friction.

I panted.

"Master says come," he said again, wicked humour in his voice as he perverted the child's game *Simone dice* or Simon says.

Even as I wanted to roll my eyes at his artifice, I admired the quirkiness of his mind.

Another shock surged through me, making me pause and pant through it.

I tossed my hair over my shoulder and looked up at him. "I didn't do anything wrong that time?"

"I will say whether or not you are obeying my orders," he said coldly. "Crawl."

I resumed my steady pace toward him.

"Take your breasts out," he ordered.

I used one shaking hand at a time to scoop my flesh out of the corset into the cool air of the hall. They weren't shaking with fear or fury but deep, bone-stirring arousal.

It was if the electric shock had tied my nipples too tightly in copper wire, so that each shock pierced brutally through the tender flesh.

I was moments away from orgasming. My pussy was a leaky faucet dripping down my thighs to pool in the backs of my knees as I crawled and crawled and crawled.

He stopped me again, commanding me to kneel and play with my hard clit for him. I shifted on my heels and let my fingers find that diamond of sensation. My head fell back on my shoulders as I felt it throb against my circling fingers.

"You don't like it soft. Pinch it. Pluck at it. Twist that pussy with your fingers until you want to come for me," he said, and his voice was even heavier, pressing on me like the absolute silence of a mid-summer desert.

My fingers plucked and pulled at my wet flesh, barely finding traction in the slippery folds. I gyrated softly back and forth before I could stop myself, grasping for something more, needing friction against my cunt.

"Stop," he said, and when I took too long, electricity stole through me like a full body sting.

My fingers pressed hard into my clit so I wouldn't come, and my breath stuttered out of my lungs like an old engine rattling under the hood of a car.

"Crawl."

I was going to cry.

The tears pushed at the backs of my eyes, creeping along the seam of my eyelids and finally, despite my efforts, they fell. The wetness was scorching against my cheeks. I could hear the splat of each drop fall to the floor in Alexander's compressing silence.

His utter stillness and calm only served to emphasise the riot of sensations raging through my body and the small sounds I made to release the pressure as they mounted inside me. I panted, cried, groaned, and whimpered. Alexander seemed to collect each confirmation of my arousal and pain like precious gems.

I had no doubt he wanted to polish them to a higher shine.

Finally, I reached him, stopping only when my cheek was pressed to the inside of his knee. My tears and sweat saturated the fabric. Alexander placed a hand on my head, and it centered my buzzing electrons like a lightning conductor.

My tears dried up with one last hiccough.

"Such a good little mouse," he praised.

If it wasn't for the thick erection pressing violently against his trousers beside my cheek, I wouldn't have known he was aroused at all.

A shiver zipped my spine straight vertebrae by vertebrae.

Why did I find his barely leashed restraint so alluring?

"Up here. Kneel over the back," he said as he stood up into my kneeling form, forcing his cock against my cheek and dragging it up my forehead as he reached his full height.

Suddenly, I wanted it out of his trousers and in my mouth.

Another shock, this one longer than the others so that I had to clench my teeth and bite my fingernails into my palms to keep from coming.

I stood when I could, aware of the slick of arousal cooling on my legs. Alexander dipped down and ran a finger through the dampness before bringing it to my lips.

They parted instinctively, and I sucked on his index finger as it slid over my tongue.

Clean, salty, and slightly sweet.

I watched the narrow rim of grey still fighting against his dilated pupils disappear as I swirled my tongue around him.

He tried to pull away, and I sucked harder. When he shot me an angry Dom look, I bit down with my teeth to keep him against my tongue.

I only released him on a yelp when he brought one huge hand around to slap against my backside.

"Down," he growled.

Triumph bloomed inside me at the telltale growl. His control was slipping, and it was game to crush it entirely.

I slinked up the ottoman and knelt over the short, raised back of it so that my spine arched in a steep slope from the high arch of my ass. I rested my forehead on my crossed forearms and tried to breathe steadily.

Alexander circled me once, twice, gently unpeeling the electric pads from my skin and then he stopped behind me for a long minute.

Crack.

The whip he'd held in one hand went snapping down against my exposed buttocks. My hips jerked forward instinctively, my hands jolting back to rub away the terrible burn.

"Resume your position," he barked.

"Please, Master," I tried, but his hand at my back shoved me face down into the back rest, and my plea was lost.

"Keep your hands away from you ass, *bella*. I don't want to hurt them with the whip. Now, I'm going to give you five strikes to each cheek, and then, if you beg very prettily, I'll fuck you until you can't come anymore."

I nodded into my hands, my eyes squeezed shut and my

breath regulated as if it would help cut the pain of the impending whiplash.

His hand slapped against the mark of the whip on my ass and then rubbed firmly so that the pain deepened and radiated through my pussy.

My whole body started to shake.

"Whenever I give you an order, I expect a 'yes, Master,' or 'thank you, Master.' Now, I want you to count each strike and thank me for them. Is that understood?"

"Yes, Master," I whispered.

The whipping that commenced should have shattered me. Each strike was short and hot like a branding iron against my skin, so painful and sharp it seared deep into my flesh to my very bones. My body was on fire, the flames licking away every inch of my skin and muscles and bones, leaving only my spirit exposed and quaking on the ottoman.

I had no voice, no thoughts or protests, just a deep need for my raw nerves to be contained before they split apart.

Alexander dropped the whip the moment I whispered, "Ten, Master, thank you."

The next moment, he was inside me, thrusting through my slippery cunt without one ounce of resistance. I groaned, my head listlessly between my shoulders as he set a punishing pace. The sound of his balls hitting my drenched pussy rang out through the room, cutting through the harsh pace of our combined breath.

One of his hands grasped my left ass check hard, reigniting the burn so that I whimpered and yelped. The other slid over my shoulder to grasp my chin.

"Look at us, *bella*," Alexander demanded as he forced my face up and locked eyes with me in the reflection of the mirror opposite. "Look how right it is for me to fuck you like this. For your sweet body to take my pain and my cock. Look how you blossom even more beautifully than you normally are."

It was true; my eyes were bright gold coins in my flushed, damp face, and my lips were so red they winked like rubies as I panted. Alexander's big body was curved over me, his abs tight and gleaming, damp gold hair falling into his furiously aroused face. He looked like a king fucking a servant girl because it was his right.

I squeezed my eyes shut as an orgasm gripped me by the throat and wrenched away my breath. My cum splashed out of his thrusting cock, wetting his thighs and the ottoman below us. The hand on my chin went into my hair and fisted it so that he could ride my orgasm out, fucking into me so hard that the one orgasm split into two, then fractured into four.

I submitted to it all, allowing Alexander to play my body and claim my mind as ruthlessly as he wished, and I was ultimately rewarded with a coarse shout that heralded his own climax.

He pumped wetly into my snug cunt, groaning at the feeling of my still clenching walls, and then he pulled out suddenly, letting our combined juices slide down my leg. I could see his face, ruddy with satisfaction and primal with male pride as he watched us sluice down my leg, and it made a mini orgasm quake through in the wake of them all.

"Mine," he growled, his civilized veneer crushed beneath the overwhelming power of the hungry, dominant beast at his core. "Fucking *mine*."

Chapter Eleven

It was strange to wake up in a bed. In fact, my back ached from the softness of the mattress, and I'd thrown off most of the covers in the night because I couldn't sleep with the heat of them compressing me. I didn't expect Alexander to be in bed beside me because he always left immediately after using me. Still, I couldn't help myself from seeking the scent of him on the pillow next to me, his forested fragrance woven into the silk fabric. It heated my blood instantly and ignited an itch between my thighs I knew nothing but his fingers or cock could gratify.

My entire body felt loose and warm with gratification after being thoroughly worked over hours earlier, but my brain felt sore and swollen between my ears as if I had an infection I didn't know how to treat. I'd loved the pleasure given to me and the erotic sight of such a strong man with his mouth on my most intimate place, bringing me to orgasm not because I needed it but simply because he wanted to. His controlling nature shouldn't have been so intoxicating, but I knew myself well enough to admit that I was in his thrall.

It was hard to fight against something I didn't understand and had no prior experience with. Desire was foreign to pre-sale Cosima. I'd never had a crush or felt attraction like a branding iron to my breasts and thighs, marking me with the scarlet letter of my unholy impulses.

I knew it now, all too well, and I had absolutely no defences to it.

Alexander was winning a game I didn't know the rules enough to play myself. It felt horribly unjust, and I found myself growing angrier and angrier as I washed myself in the shower and readied myself for the day.

Seeing the outfit laid out on my bed when I emerged from the bathroom only threw alcohol on the flames of my rage.

I was his doll to dress just as I was his flesh to use and his mouse to hunt.

I added this transgression to my list of hatred against him even as I rubbed the luxe fabric of the floral patterned wrap dress between my fingers.

It fit beautifully, just as the ludicrously expensive La Pearla lingerie in a shimmering gold fit too and magnified my curves. I knew he liked me in gold, not because it looked well on me, but because it cheapened me. It was a physical representation of the wealth he'd used to buy me like prized horse flesh.

For a moment, I considered ditching the outfit and walking around stark naked, but the idea of all those cameras and all those eyes on me was ultimately too much, even for someone as relatively immodest as I am.

There was no note on the bedside table and no instructions to follow, so with only a moment's hesitation, I tried to open the door to my chambers.

It was unlocked.

The sound of the mechanism moving into place heralded in my ears like a trumpet call. There were so few freedoms in this new life, each felt pathetically magnificent.

The waving hills outside the windows were silver with

heavy rain, and the pane was cold when I pressed my hand to it to peer at the elusive outside world. I wanted to run down the stairs, burst through the heavy front doors, and slip over the wet grass in my bare feet until they were brown with muck and I'd fallen to ground in a graceless heap. I wanted to spread my limbs in the cool blanket of green and watch the rain fall into my face.

"Am I ever to be outside again?" I asked myself, watching as my hot breath fogged the glass.

"You are." Alexander's voice startled me more than a gun held to my temple.

A moment later, the broad expanse of his body was pressed to mine so that I had the sunlight of his heat at my back and the cold eclipse of glass against my breasts. It was the very same duality I was coming to realize I'd always experience around my Master.

The hot kiss of unassailable desire and the cold slap of shame.

"You will be let out of this house and out of this life in due course, my beauty, especially if you behave as beautifully as you did last night." I shivered at the texture of his silken breath trailing down my throat, followed by the touch of his lips to my tripping pulse. "You fell apart for me just as you should for your Master. Tell me, do you feel reformed this morning?"

I did, and it broke my heart to bear the weight of that. It seemed each time he touched me that he tore me apart only to weave me back together with a sharp needle and the dark threads of his ownership. I was becoming accustomed to the pain, and that worried me.

Because that resignation was tinged with yearning.

I hissed as Alexander sank his teeth into the strong tendon on the side of my neck. He drew away with a soft hum of pleasure, and whispered, "I would fuck you against the window and use your cum to write my name on the glass if I didn't have a previous engagement."

My stomach cramped in an alarming show of disappointment, but I didn't let it show on my face when I turned around to scowl at him with my hands on my hips. Only, my indignation cooled into curiosity when I saw what he was wearing.

"What in heaven's name are you dressed in?"

Alexander smirked and dragged a hand through the thick wave of his golden hair. He looked so like a young, arrogant boy for a moment that I wanted to smile with him.

"I'm dressed in my fencing jacket and trousers."

I blinked. "I don't think I know what that is."

His grin widened, softer than I'd ever seen it, so gleeful that it even reached his eyes. "If you come, I'll show you."

Before I could protest, my hand was in his, and he was pulling me in the current of his wide stride down the hall.

"Fencing is an ancient sport first developed by your Italian kinsfolk, though it was popularized by the French. It's been a popular pastime of the Davenport men since the 19th century. I played varsity for a spell at Cambridge."

"Ah, *scherma*," I said, translating the word into Italian as I made the connection. "It doesn't surprise me that you play with weapons."

A short, startled laugh burst from his lips, and I noticed how full the bottom one was compared to the bowed top, and how pearlescent a pale pink they were.

"I am very skilled with tools and weapons, as you've begun to discover."

We descended the grand marble staircase into the great hall and the left wing of the house where we entered a large hall that had been turned into a kind of gymnasium. There was a long pool at the very end that seemed at odds with the elaborate décor and Grecian pillars, and modern exercise equipment arranged beside a wide length of mats.

A man stood in the center of those mats wearing a similar outfit to Alexander's only his was black. It took me a moment to recognize Riddick because his colourful tattoos were covered up, but when I did, I blanched.

Alexander, observant bastard that he was, noticed my surprise and smiled slightly.

"Riddick is trained in eight martial arts." I blinked at him, and he slid me a pleased look as he moved past me to shake Riddick's hand. "And I am trained in nine."

I stood mutely as I watched the two huge men shake hands and quietly discuss their workout. Alexander moved back to me as Riddick went to a sideboard and retrieved two large masks with perforated fronts.

"Sit over here and watch quietly."

"Why should I? Are my days not mine to do with as I please?" I retorted.

"They are unless I have need of you."

"And you need me to sit here and validate your prowess with a child's sword?"

My tyrant's eyes were dark, thrashing like storm clouds as he glared at me, but just as there was in a storm, electricity crackled in the air between us. My skin buzzed and raised into goose flesh.

"I need you to sit here and watch your Master. I need you to watch me move, witness the strength of my body and the discipline of my gait. I need you to watch as I attack and parry with calculation as easy as my next breath."

"Why?" I asked even though every time I'd asked such a question before, he'd mocked me with silence and enigmatic looks.

He quirked a brow and snapped forward to grab my hand, tugging me into his body so hard I fell against him. His torso was stiff with Kevlar, but I could still feel the heat of him against me and the way his erection pressed like its own weapon against my hip. "I fight the same way I fuck. Think of it as foreplay."

He let me go so abruptly, I stumbled a step forward before I could right myself. His soft chuckle burned like too close a flame against my cheeks, and I kept my hair curtained across my face as I moved over to the small set of stands opposite the mats to sit down.

By the time I was settled, both men were in crouched stances with their thin swords raised and one hand behind their backs.

"*En garde*," Riddick called out.

And the flurry began.

Their movements were quick as dragonfly wings, landed and parried with total calm and precision. I noticed a servant sat at a table off to the side and kept score on a digital screen. There was never more than a moment when Riddick was the one in the lead.

Alexander was right.

He was a Dominant in the bedroom just as much as he was on the court and in life. It awed me to watch the sheer breadth of his large body move with such speed and grace. Unbidden, thoughts of how he'd used his quilted arms to rain the flogger down on my heated skin roused to my mind, of how easy it had been for him to chase me across the ballroom on his thick thighs and quick feet then to hold me down with every carved inch of his frame when he fucked me into the floor.

They fenced three games, and Alexander won all three.

It didn't surprise me.

In fact, I felt an odd fluttering of pleasure in my chest that

Alexander had so soundly beaten Riddick.

Maybe it was that the man who had conquered me in so many ways had just proved himself capable of conquering another, someone even more capable of thwarting him than I could be, and still he'd lost.

Alexander was the king of this animal jungle, and it gave me a sense of relief to know I wasn't the only one forced to bend to his rule.

But there was the fear that it was something else entirely. That it wasn't mere schadenfreude. That I'd derived some primitive pleasure from the very masculine display of his power, two males fighting over their desire to fuck me, but the man who was rightfully mine declaring the victory.

That it was *pride* making my chest tight and my heart light. That if he was king of this animal kingdom, then maybe I could be the queen.

By the time they were finished, I was flushed, sweat beaded on my forehead like a crown of shame for Alexander to note as soon as he ripped off his mask and approached. There was that boyish, smug smile on his handsome face again.

I hated how it made my heart soften to him.

"I won't ask how you enjoyed the display," he said languidly, his usually clipped words elongated with mockery as he teased me. "If I was to put my hand between your thighs right now, you'd be wet."

Unconsciously, I squeezed my legs together.

"Unlike you, I am not constantly thinking of sex," I replied with a haughty tilt of my chin. "In fact, I was just thinking I'd like to ask Riddick if he might teach me fencing or some self defence while you're out working some days."

Alexander pushed back an errant lock of his sweat dampened hair and scowled at me. "There is no man of this planet who is allowed to touch you without my permission. And, it should be noted, there are none who would receive it."

"So permit him," I suggested, trying to ignore his delicious sweat-soaked scent of cedar and man wafting from him as he stood too close to me.

"Out of the question."

"Then teach me yourself," I dared even though it terrified me and thrilled me in equal measure to think of such a beast fighting against me.

I could feel arousal bloom like a rose between my thighs.

Something was wrong with me, some trigger he'd flipped in my psyche to make the thought of his flesh against my fists and his blood in my mouth arouse me.

Alexander clenched his teeth, a muscle popping in his jaw as he studied me. I watched as he reigned in his base excitement, filtering it through his gentlemanly upbringing and psychopathic calculation until it was polished and refined as a diamond.

My mouth went dry watching that, and for once, I didn't blame myself for the reaction.

Watching a man struggling to govern himself against the force of his attraction to you was a heady thing.

"Riddick," he called out even as his eyes remained latched on mine. "Get out."

"Yes, sir."

I didn't watch his bodyguard/man servant leave, but the banging of the door as it shut resounded like a starting gun through the chamber.

"You want to learn how to defend yourself against wicked men? Against me? Then get up."

He turned on his heel and stalked toward the center of the mats again, only this time he placed his rapier in a rack on the way and tossed his helmet to the side. It was only when he turned to face me that I realized I'd unconsciously followed him across the gym.

His dirty smile said *"good girl."*

My traitorous body shivered.

"You seemed able enough to defend yourself when a man was attacking me with a gun," he noted as he pulled off his light fencing armour, revealing his sweat slicked torso.

I watched a bead of moisture travel between his hard pecks and get trapped in the boxed hedgerows of his abs. My fingers literally itched to trace its path under the waistband of his trousers.

"My brother taught be dirty tricks so I could walk home from the train at night in Milan and feel relatively safe. I don't know how to subdue a real threat."

"No," he practically purred. "You don't."

"I find it hard to believe that you'd want to teach me," I admitted as he came at me on brisk, threatening strides. When he stopped before me, it was sudden as if he was a horse desperate to canter but reined in by his rider. I could feel the potential energy in his stillness like a promised threat of violence.

God, but I knew how much he wanted to hurt me.

Almost as much as I wanted it.

"There are times in this life I cannot be there to protect you. It's my duty to teach you how to help yourself, and I will teach you anything you need to know," he told me calmly even though I could see the pulse going in his throat and the strain of his erection against his white trousers. "Because I am the only man of influence in your life."

"You cannot be everything to me."

"Can't I?" he asked with a raised brow, looking every inch the haughty lord even half dressed as he was.

"I have a father, a brother, and friends. You are not the only man in my life of consequence."

"I am. Your father is dead to you, just as he should be. I did that. Your brother is benefiting from a placement in Finborough Theatre at London. Who do you think pulled those strings? You never had any friends outside your family; don't pretend otherwise. You were too pretty for the jealous village girls and too ripe for the boys to ignore as an object of lust." He stepped closer and looked down into my face from his awesome height. "I am your Master, Cosima. Not just of your flesh, but of everything you hold dear."

I wanted to cry for his kindness. I'd hated my father's selfish destruction. I loved my brother enough to thank God or him for any favours toward Sebastian.

But I always wanted to rip out his throat because even as he so obviously manipulated me, it was working.

"It's funny how people fight against the things they cannot change," Alexander noted cruelly as he watched my internal struggle. "Why don't you focus that lovely anger on defending yourself? At first, I want you to move on instinct, and then I will teach you some moves."

He attacked before the last word was gone from the air.

My breath whooshed out of my body as he slammed me to the ground and pinned me there with his weight. I wriggled just enough to pull my leg up between his, then I curled my toes hard into balls.

He huffed with pain, letting me go just enough that I could push off his shoulders and remove my torso out from under his. Using them as leverage, I dragged one leg out and kicked him hard in the face.

His nose crunched slightly, and a bead of blood rolled out of his nostril.

I howled like a beast in triumph.

Alexander took advantage of my gloating to flip me on to my stomach and crawl on top of me, pinning my legs and arms to the floor so solidly, I felt nailed to the ground.

"Never let passion rule," he advised against my damp neck. "It is cool minds that prevail."

He let me up even though I liked the hot press of him against me, and to my surprise, he began to teach me. I learned how to subdue my attacker if he grabbed me from behind, if he took me to the ground on my belly, and if he held a gun to my temple. We practiced for well over an hour until both of us were slicked with each other's sweat and our breaths worked through our lungs like billows.

"Come at me," I dared him finally, crouched low with my hands loose at my sides ready to fight him.

"Winner gets to fuck the other," Alexander parried.

He would win.

We both knew he would, and I doubted there would ever be a time—however often I practiced or proficient I became— that he wouldn't beat me in a wrestling match.

This bet wasn't about the impossibility of my victory. It was forcing me to acknowledge that I didn't want to win.

I wanted him to.

"Deal," I said, and then I pounced.

I swept one of his legs out from under him, then I went for his throat with a vicious punch. It was a cocky maneuver, which was why I decided to do it because I assumed Alexander would be looking for easier movements.

He was ready for anything.

I winced as he caught my fist and twisted, taking me to the floor with the pain, both of us on our knees, facing each other.

We blinked, suspended in the moment when a prey knew it was in the sights of its predator. And then he attacked.

I was pinned with my wrists to the ground and his heavy body straddling my belly in less than a heartbeat.

He'd taught me how to break such a hold, though, so I thrust my hips and jerked my arms down toward them, jerking him forward so sharply he nearly fell on his face.

Only, he was too quick and strong.

He caught me again by the ankle as I tried to crawl away, and then he dragged me kicking and yelling under his body. With a vicious yank, he broke the closure of my dress so that the colourful fabric spooled beneath us like crushed flowers. I gasped as he cupped my sex, then ripped the fabric there too, the expensive lingerie shredding to bits in his fingers.

His cock was suddenly in his fist, swollen and an angrier red than I'd ever seen it.

He thrusted inside me, parting my molten folds like a spear arrowing to the very depths of me.

"To the victor, the spoils," he growled into my ear as he pinned my wrists down in one hand and used the other to choke me lightly.

He set a punishing pace, angling his hips so that his thick head dragged against that knot of nerves on my front wall. The light stubble on his groin rasped against my aching clit, nudging the piercing back and forth so that my entire sex filled with static electricity.

I held him tight to my body even though he hurt me, because he hurt me.

I loved the way his teeth bit into the tender flesh of my neck and breasts, how violet bruises and ruddy poppies bloomed beneath my skin at his touch. The ache of him in my sex as he planted himself deep and finally came with a rough shout like a warrior claiming triumph over the death of a fallen foe.

I was fallen, sunk beneath the depths of his darkness, and so entrenched in the underworld, I knew there would never be any going back.

Five years might pass, the contract between us might dissolve into dust with time, but I would always be, elementally and crucially, Master Alexander's woman.

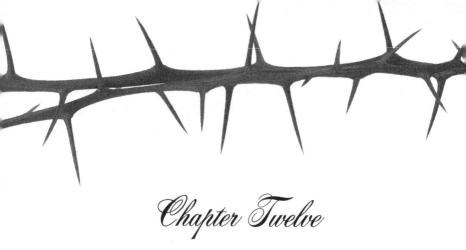

Chapter Twelve

*J*n the next two weeks, I was fucked so thoroughly, I couldn't walk without the echo of his cock between my legs. My body was sore to the bone, skin burst with bruises, and muscles burned from the constant stretch and pull of my limbs worked into wicked positions. I learned the difference between the wide spread heat of a flogging, the mounting burn of a paddling, and the excruciating, venomous bite of a whip. In fact, he used me so completely each day that there wasn't a single moment I was free from the reminder of sex. I wore it on my body and housed it in my mind. A moan of want or protest seemed lodged in my throat like a lozenge that wouldn't pass.

Every morning, I woke up wet and stayed that way as I bathed Alexander and dressed him for work. He used me in the shower, always, soothing me with his cock and almost cooing to me as he fucked me, promising to bring me relief with his cum and his special brand of agony.

He used me all around the house, everywhere but those rare locked doors and his own bedroom. He liked to fuck me in the greenhouse most. I think it made him feel like he was cornering, caging, and conquering a wild animal. I made sure to mark him with scratches and bite marks to add to the allusion.

And every night, he used me in my room, pulling out his black bag of devious toys and using them on me the way Dr. Frankenstein might have experimented on his monster. I became one—a monster, that is. One that lived on debauched displays of submission and constantly yearned for domination.

I spent my days learning to cook or hanging out in the kitchen with Douglas, who proved to be the joy of every day with his affable charm and easy manner. Sometimes, Mrs. White made us tea and regaled me with stories about a young Alexander that I convinced myself I didn't think were charming.

Still, cooking wasn't my passion, nor was working out in the gorgeous gymnasium as I'd taken to doing with the rest of my spare time.

It was Noel who kept me company in those moments when boredom threatened to overwhelm me, as if he knew just when I was susceptible to breaking my promise to Alexander. I knew it was forbidden to spend time with his father, though I had absolutely no idea why. To me, Noel was on the wrong side of middle age, clearly retired, but still fit enough to desire some mental sparring and interesting company.

At first, I worried the servants would tattle to my Master, but after a few days, I realized that even though Alexander clearly helmed the ship, his father owned it.

Besides, I enjoyed having a secret from the man who fancied himself as the most omnipotent and important person in my life.

We spent most afternoons on the chess table before the fire, as the grey world of England grew even darker and wetter with the coming winter. I learned how to move the pieces as if they were an extension of my mind and how to parry Noel's clever attacks, nearly always aggressive, with subtle defensive moves of my own. Mostly, I learned how to fight with my pawns—when to sacrifice them for the greater good and when to level one up to a more impressive piece.

One day, one of those white pawns went missing, and Noel was forced to bring out a spare. I didn't tell him I'd pocketed it, but I think he knew and didn't care.

He enjoyed my company, but I was a pawn as much as the one I'd stolen, and we both knew that.

I woke up on the first day of my third month in Pearl Hall without Alexander. He had ben in London for the night, though he Skyped to watch me use an enormous black dildo he'd given me on my tiny pussy. I was still wet that morning, and as he bade me, I didn't shower it away. Instead, I dutifully dressed in the outfit that was always laid out for me in the morning, some kind of expensive dress that allowed for easy movement but hugged my curves, and set out on my daily exploration of the home.

Only, that morning Noel was waiting for me in front of two double doors I knew very well were barred to me.

"Hello, my dear Ruthie," he greeted as he always did. "Today, I have a surprise for you."

Those doors were different from the other doors in the house, double wide and carved from a heavy ancient wood that was cracked and worn smooth in some places. They hadn't been replaced or painted in the clean, light colours of the rest of the residence.

I knew before Noel grasped both rough metal handles and pushed open the weighted doors that inside would be a library.

Whenever I walked past, I could smell the hint of vellum and cloth seeping beneath the thin wedge below the door. I wanted inside so badly, sometimes on my daily tour of the three-story mansion, I would stand outside and press my fingers to the pockmarks and whorls in the wood while I imagined what treasures lay inside.

I never could have guessed they would be so terrifically awe inspiring as this.

The enormous room was longer than it was wide and filled to the rafters with exquisitely carved wooden shelves painted white and trimmed in gold leaf. The ceiling was painted as many others in the house, but these images depicted Atlas with the entire, beautifully detailed world on his grotesquely muscled shoulders.

The parquet floor was glossed to a high shine where it showed beneath massive, faded Persian rugs, and at the very far end of the large room stood a marble hearth so enormous it could fit my entire Italian family comfortably.

I wanted to live out my days amid the books and die curled up in the deep-seated leather chairs in front of the hearth.

"You are taken with it," Noel said with a smile like a proud father. "I knew you would be."

"There are not enough words in English or Italian to say how very much I love it," I told him honestly as I ran my fingers over a large globe set in a wooden stand. My index finger trailed unerringly to the small spot on the map that read "Naples."

"You might be wondering why Alexander barricaded you." It wasn't a question, but I could feel the lure flashing in the light spilling through the warped glass windows.

He wanted to go fishing, and I was the prized trout he meant to catch.

"To be quite honest, Duke, I've come to realize wondering why Master Alexander does anything is a fruitless endeavour."

He chuckled and clasped his hands behind his back, cutting the perfect image of a well-bred English gentleman in his expensive suit.

"Be that as it may, let me pierce the shrouded veil for a moment."

I trailed him across the long length of the library to the chairs clustered around the fireplace and followed his gaze up to an oil painting that hung above it.

The woman depicted there was one of the most beautiful I had ever seen, but that wasn't what took my breath away.

No, it was the startlingly clear fact that she was Italian.

It was in her warm olive complexion, though her skin was fair from spending some time in England, and the almond set of her dark lashed eyes. She had the thick, black hair and brows of a Sicilian woman and the body too, high, pointed breasts and wide hips after a neatly tucked waist.

"My wife," Noel explained, his voice carefully devoid of all feeling. "Chiara passed away nine years ago. I believe I overheard Mr. O'Shea explain so in the kitchens when we first met."

I nodded, my voice trapped deep within my throat. There was a wealth of condolences and questions I wanted to gift him, but I didn't think they would be well received.

"I want to tell you a bit of the story myself, so you can better understand what you are doing here at Pearl Hall."

My mouth opened in shock, and my hand flew to cover it.

Noel was offering me answers to some of the many questions that had haunted me since my arrival, and I didn't want to say or do anything that might retract his generosity.

"Sit please," he told me, and then waited until I sank into one of the mahogany chairs before he too took one. I watched as he settled in, crossing one leg over the other and steepling his fingers as he prepared to tell his story.

"I met Chiara when I was doing my modern pilgrimage of the Grand Tour. She was this gorgeous thing I spotted leading a tour in the Roman Colosseum and being the young, arrogant lord I was, I marched right up to her and demanded she allow me to buy her a gelato." He smiled at the memory. "It was love from that first day."

My romantic heart sighed in my chest. I curled up my feet onto the seat and sank further into the soft cushions.

"When it was time to go home, I took her with me. She had no family back in Italy, and I was more than happy to provide for her as my wife. Over the years, she became one of the crown jewels of British society even if it took a while for her to smooth over her Latin edges." He smiled at me encouragingly, so I gave him a small laugh even though I quite liked my Latin edges.

"She had a… a friend, though, who was determined to visit over the years. I thought nothing of it at first, and this man, Amedeo, become like a brother to me, like an uncle to my children." I frowned at his use of the plural, and his lips thinned in response. "Yes, Cosima, I will get to it."

"You see, I trusted this man to care for my family. I thought nothing of it when my wife began to increase her visits back to Amedeo's home in Italy, but then my youngest son, Edward, began to follow her. They would spend long stretches of time there and return sullen, broken in spirit. I began to get worried, but they wouldn't tell me anything. Chiara and I had rather a row about it before her last trip there because I told her she was forbidden to go.

"Two days after she left with Edward, who was a strong, beautiful lad, four years younger than Alexander, Edward called home. It was Alexander who picked up, and it was Alexander who was first told his mother had been killed."

I gasped. "Killed? I thought she had an accident?"

He waved the words away. "That fabrication only came later. At first, Edward himself acknowledged that she has been killed, that he had heard her scream, and then a moment later, the sound of her death against the ground. The police got involved, but nothing was found. If someone pushed her, it had to have been someone in the house."

I blinked at him, imagining the scene, destroyed by the obvious truth. "You think it was Amedeo?"

"I know it was Amedeo," Noel confirmed. "But that is not all. You see, Edward never came home after that. He stayed in Italy with the murderer and pledged to the police that Amedeo had not pushed Chiara over the ledge. I begged him to come home, to speak to us and explain, at the very least, to attend the funeral, but he didn't, and he hasn't returned since." He turned from looking at the cold stone hearth into my eyes, and his were dark as empty coffins. "That is why we do not speak of the death of Duchess Greythorn and why the name of Edward Davenport has been scrubbed from our minds."

"But how? I mean, why in the world would Edward stand up for his uncle when it's so obvious he committed the crime?" I just couldn't wrap my mind around it. "You must be missing some details of the story."

"I am missing nothing, but Amedeo's confirmation of his crime. Since then, I've done research into the man with the help of some very powerful friends, and I've learned that he is a member of the *Camorra*."

Shock stoppered my breath.

"In fact, you might know Amedeo as *Capo* Salvatore. I see you know him," Noel said with a small, enigmatic smile. "I take it he has rather a powerful hold on Napoli and the surrounding regions."

"He does," I admitted as my stomach cramped and my heart stuttered.

I felt like a flailing engine.

"Haven't you wondered why Alexander chose you when he could have had any woman worth buying in the entire world?" Noel taunted.

"Yes," I whispered, my hand going up to massage the great stone mass suddenly obstructing my throat.

I had wondered and wondered, and now that I was faced with the ugly truth of it, I didn't want to know.

"He wants to use you to infiltrate the *Camorra*. To get close to Amedeo Salvatore and end him."

The words thrust through my mind like a bullet, tearing apart my brain and spewing everything I was across the beautiful library like lost grey matter.

How had Alexander known my connection to Salvatore? Had he known the day I saved his life and spoken my name aloud or even before that?

How could he expect an eighteen-year-old girl to infiltrate anything, let alone one of the most notorious mafia outfits in the entire world?

I'd been so curious, but now that Pandora's Box was spilled open at my feet, I wanted to stuff the answers inside because they only led to more questions.

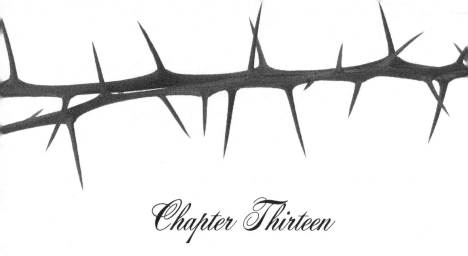

Chapter Thirteen

$\mathcal{I}$ woke up sometime in the night when the sky was at its darkest and everything felt too close, like ink spilled from the black bowl of the atmosphere and dropped between every crevice. It took me a moment to orient myself because it was immediately obvious I wasn't on the cold, hard ground of the ballroom as I'd grown accustomed to.

I shifted slightly, and my hands caught, jerking back against some invisible bonds. I pulled again and unwittingly kicked out my legs to find that they too were bound.

I was spread open and apart in a giant X across the bed, my limbs tied off at each post.

My mouth opened to scream, but a hand clamped down over my mouth before I could emit a sound.

"Hush, my beauty," Alexander's crisp words rustled like papers in the still air. "It's late and the whole house is sleeping."

I tried to protest behind his hand, but he kept it firmly banded over my lips.

His warm breath fanned over my cheek as he leaned closer to run his nose over my ear and whisper, "There is no need to struggle, *topolina*. I have you pinned like a butterfly to this bed, and I mean to treat you thusly. With reverence and tenderness, like the beautiful and fragile creature you are."

I moaned, and he seemed to perfectly translate the words I wasn't given permission to speak aloud.

"This isn't about what my father so wrongly told you this afternoon. It was not his place to unlock the doors and secrets in his house. We will talk about the lies he told later. This isn't an act of forgiveness for my roughness with you last night or the one before that. I will never ask your forgiveness for the things I do to your body." He shifted in the dark, a great looming monster of shadow like a demon summoned up from hell. The wet tip of his hard cock smeared over my hip as he straightened and reached for something on the bedside table. A shudder of rampant desire went through me at the knowledge that he was naked.

"This is about the other side of BDSM," he continued in the bland tones of a professor reciting a lecture to a group of inane students. "Our relationship is about control and submission. This means if I want to fuck you until it hurts, I will, and you will let me. It also means, if I want to eat the honey between your thighs for hours until you are an incoherent mass of quivering flesh barely able to think past the pleasure, I will. I do not need to hurt you or threaten you to own you. There is dominance in pleasure too."

"Does it matter that I don't want your touch right now? Do you care that I feel torn apart by what Noel told me? You... you want me to put my life in danger for you, and I barely know you, let alone like you!"

"Hush, my beauty," he coaxed, pressing a finger to my mouth. "I will make this deal with you. If you play with me now, I will answer your questions after."

"Why does it have to be like this? Why can't we just talk?" I asked, squirming against the cuffs.

"Because many times in our relationship, you will not want to do something, and I will. You must learn that the only person's desires that need be met are *mine*. Lesson three, *bella*. Now, do we have a deal?"

I wanted to fight him for the right to talk. To take my fists to him the way he was teaching me to do in our sparring sessions and make him bleed for being so pugnacious, but I was immobile and at his mercy, so I nodded tersely.

"Yes?" he prompted.

"Yes, Master," I hissed.

There was a laugh in his dark voice as he said, "Good little mouse."

I stayed quiet as he brought something soft as kitten fur against my chest and ran it down between my breasts and over my tummy to the apex of my thighs.

"As I was saying, this scene isn't about pain. It's about discovering all the delicious ways you can be made to come. I'm going to flog you, and then I'm going to do just that, settle between your thighs and feast until you orgasm on my tongue."

"That sounds painful," I whispered hoarsely around the instinctive fear in my throat. "Haven't you taken enough from me?"

"It will make your skin sing for me," he promised silkily as he ran the tendrils over my limbs in feather-light passes. "If you can stay quiet for me, I may let you have another phone call next week."

"Manipulation and orgasms won't endear me to you," I snapped at him even as my nipples pebbled with unfurling lust.

"That would be a first," he commented drily and then *smack*.

The flogger landed like hundreds of bee stings against my breasts.

I gasped like a woman possessed, and I felt it as he continued to bring the flogger down onto my flesh, as if a mindless spirit made for sin had overtaken my mind.

I loved it.

The soft swish of air as the leather came down on my skin and the gentle snap like the sound of sparklers as it set fire to my skin.

Before long, I was writhing, my mouth panting.

Every inch of my skin felt alive with sensation, and my mind felt bright in my head. If I hadn't been tied down, I would have floated off the bed.

"Look at all that gorgeous skin turning rose gold for me," Alexander murmured an interminable amount of time after he started.

There was a thump as he dropped the flogger to the ground and then one of his hands was pressing hard into my breast bone as the other hooked firmly inside my sex and unerringly found that knot of nerves on my front wall.

He curled his fingers hard into my flesh, and it felt like a key entering a lock.

I burst open, my cum crashing against his fingers, my spirit colliding with magnetic force to the potency of his hold over me, the pillar of strength he represented at that moment when every-thing else about me, around me, was lost.

His name was on my tongue and caught between my teeth, looped like a broken record in my voice box. I loved the taste of it, curling my lips over the vowels and biting hard into the con-sonances. It was as erotic and dangerous as Eve's forbidden fruit.

Even as I reeled with sensation, the rational part of my brain recognized that now I'd had a taste for such dark delights, there might not be any going back.

"Such a good slave," Alexander praised as he played his fin-gers in the wet pool between my thighs, the sucking, slippery sounds completely obscene in the midnight silence. "I'll give you a pass on speaking because you say my name so beautifully."

I panted softly as he ducked below my line of sight and

returned with something that glinted dully in the low light.

"This will hurt," he said and then his fingers were pinching my clit.

A growl of pain wedged itself into my throat as he clamped my swollen sex, already so sensitive from one orgasm. The flash of bright pain grew roots that curved around my inner thighs, arrowing into my sex and my buttocks where they throbbed and spasmed with constant life.

I wriggled and moaned against the cuffs, but they didn't yield.

"This is your fourth lesson, *topolina*," Alexander said over the rush of blood in my ears. "How to take your pleasure from the pain."

He stood, looming over me as he looped a shimmering strand of metal between his hands. "These are nipple clamps. Are you ready for them?"

"You sadistic bastard," I ground out.

A flash of light in the dark that was his wolfish grin. "I am a sadist. Just as you are a masochist."

"*A fanabla.*" I cursed him to hell, and the devil laughed like it was a blessing.

"If you come in less than five minutes with these vicious clamps on those sinful breasts, I will make a liar of you yet," he promised darkly.

I watched his shadowed head as he leaned over, biting at one nipple while his fingers plucked at the other as if it was a flower. When the tips of my breasts were red as poppies, he clamped those metal teeth over each point and kissed away my groans of pain.

He stepped away from the bed to survey his work, the soft pad of his bare feet against the floor my only indication that he had stepped away from the bed.

The lights flipped on and dimmed immediately.

I blinked away the spots in my vision, panting around the everblooming pleasure in my body and watched as he carried an ornate gold full length mirror to the bottom left side of the bed.

"There," he purred, angling it just so. "Now you can see my masterpiece, and I can watch your beautiful cunt as I make you come again and again for me."

He was right.

I could see the entire length of my body in the reflection. I looked obscene, my outrageous curves swollen red from the flogger, my skinny limbs pulled taut by the thick, leather cuffs securing me to the scarlet bed. My hair was a pool of ink beneath my glowing face, my lips parted and plump from his kisses.

I looked wanton, elemental, and deliciously wrong. Lilith, the first woman created by God, but too willful, too full of passions that sent her plummeting straight to hell.

The sight of myself like that, bound and at Alexander's mercy, shouldn't have run me through with longing, but it did.

I was tied down, but I was not helpless. I was following orders, but I was not meek.

There was power in the eyes of the woman staring back at me from the mirror.

I only had to shift my eyes to Alexander to know where the power stemmed from.

He seemed carved from marble, Michelangelo's *David* built to four times the scale. Every one of his muscles was clenched with longing and clamped off from movement by his ironclad willpower, but his eyes were savage. His pupil had blown them wide open so that the ferocity of his desire spilled forth, writing dirty words filled with his intentions across my red dyed skin.

"Please, Master," I said without deciding to. "Please, fuck me."

His entire big body shuddered, and then he was climbing

onto the bed, adjusting the cuffs on my ankles so that there was more slack between my feet and the posts. I shivered at the feeling of his rough hands sliding under my ass to tip it up into the air and then he ducked his head and clasped his lips around my swollen pussy.

I could see him feast on me from where I lay and also from looking over at the mirror. His proud shoulder bunched with strength as he held me aloft, his strong feet curled into the bed so that he could loom over me and drill down into me with his tongue.

He fucked me like that with his lips, his teeth against my clit in a way that hurt so beautifully it made my skin feel as if it was going to tear apart atom by atom. I humped against his mouth wantonly, senseless noises of pleasure streaming out of my mouth. He used two fingers to stretch me wide, working brutally in and out of my cunt until he could add a third and then, even though I screamed, a fourth.

I wanted to be filled to the brim by him, used until I had nothing left to give him. As if heeding my thoughts, he braced my thighs on his shoulders and used his other hand on my asshole, brushing his fingers around the sex dampened bud before twisting his thumb inside with a pain bright *pop*.

The light in my head exploded through my body like a super nova, drenching me in golden oblivion. I came so hard I only existed as burst particles, loosely held together in Alexander's exacting hands and by his talented mouth.

My mind was still floating, my pussy still spasming when he drove his thick cock straight to the end of my pussy. My dazed eyes spun in my head and then settled on the mirror over his shoulders.

I could see his buttocks, carved and full like perfect half-moons, flex as he thrust into me. I wished my hands were free so

I could cup him there and feel the strength and the suppleness of his golden skin under my touch.

He pushed me farther into the bed with his hips and spread my legs up and wide with palms on the insides of my thighs.

I was lewdly displayed in the mirror, and I realized that was his intent, so I could watch his ruddy sink into my glistening pink pussy with each and every hard kick of his hips.

I screamed as his tip nudged my womb, the bruising push of it spiraling my mind even further into outer space. My orgasm went on and on, softening slowly like the tide after a tsunami until I was limp but aware Alexander lay on top of me. Outside, my cunt grasped against nothing as his cock lay still hard on my thigh.

I wanted to protest that he hadn't cum because somehow that seemed vital to me. Was I good submissive if my Master didn't come?

But then I noticed he was stroking my hair.

I froze, my breath arrested in my lungs like amber.

My eyes scoured his face for answers to the tenderness, but all I found was the perfect symmetry of his aristocratic features, the plushness of his lower lip, and the bow of the top. There was stubble lining his strong jaw like flakes of pure gold, and his long eyelashes looked like spikes of precious metal over his storm cloud eyes.

I could read nothing in his face.

Unless he wanted it to be, there was nothing there ever.

I'd never seen a man with a face so much a mask.

Truth be told, it made my empathetic heart ache for him. What kind of life had he led that made him so removed, so callously reserved?

"I've never seen more inquisitive eyes," he murmured as he looked down on me. "A golden palimpsest of questions. What will you ask the hawk first, little mouse?"

"Why didn't you come for me?" I asked even though the question burned as it left my throat.

His smile spread slowly over his face, and he was close enough for me to watch how it changed his eyes from pewter to light grey and how it hooked from one side of his mouth and pulled through to the other.

God, but he was such a beautiful beast.

I had thought I'd known beauty before but never like his. Never a handsome so powerful it hurt the eyes, not a man so beautiful he could weaponise it.

"I didn't come for you because that is not always the purpose of our play. Sometimes, it's to teach you a lesson, sometimes to reward you for good behaviour, and sometimes, it will be about good old fashioned power dynamics. You just came like an eager little wanton while I was controlled enough to stave off. How does that make you feel?"

I knew the blush wouldn't show on my skin, but my cheeks burned with shame. "Like a whore."

"Mmm," he acknowledged with a very slight, smug grin. "Only ever for me."

"You seem to enjoy this, being cruel one moment and sweet the next. It's driving me even crazier than the isolation in the ballroom did," I admitted to him, staring at his fingers as they twirled a piece of my silky hair.

I watched as his eyes turned over from sun-shaded silver to the dark side of the moon, pocketed with craters and tortured mysteries. He stared as his fingers in my hair as if the strands held the answers to all of life's questions.

"I was raised to be a Lord and a Master. My father and his... friends trained me from a young boy to be ruthless in my perusal of pleasure and power, in dealings with money, society, and especially women. I'm not sure if I would have been born with the inclination to stripe a woman's ass with a cane, but isn't that the endless question of nature versus nurture?"

"I think you like it," I whispered, because this transparency between us was new, and I didn't want to tear the paper as I carefully traced his edges. "You like to hurt me."

"Yes," he agreed as his other hand slinked up my torso, between my breasts to collar my throat. "I love to see your body exposed and shaking under me like a stripped wire. I would do this to you even if I didn't have to."

"But you do have to. Tell me about Salvatore."

His sigh ruffled my hair as he shifted over me, tucking one of my thighs between his legs so that my entire body was plastered to his. I wanted to nuzzle under the right angle of his jaw, tip my nose against his pulse and feel him so strong and sure against me, better than any security blanket could be.

I shouldn't have felt so close to him or so safe in his arms, but I told myself it was the strange euphoric aftermath of submission that made me unduly needy and nearly weepy.

"When I held you in that alley, I knew who you were before you told me your name. I could see him in your eyes and in the cut of your jaw then when you spoke, you shared the same accent, the long, soft vowels of Neapolitan."

"What are you saying?" I asked, staring down the edge of cliff, my toes curling around the side for purchase.

I didn't want to fall, but momentum at my back was pushing me forward, and I knew the drop was inevitable.

Alexander's hand tightened around my neck so forcefully, I couldn't breathe. "Isn't it obvious? Amadeo Salvatore is your father."

I gasped, desperate to draw air and sense into my body, but Alexander wouldn't let me. His weight against my chest deepened, and his fingers throbbed over my throat in time with my pulse.

"Your mother had an affair with him over eighteen years ago when your father was held in prison for a time. I only know because Amedeo and my mother spoke of it sometimes over the years, when it was late and they thought little boys should be in bed. It resulted in twins, two babies so beautiful that even though he couldn't father them, he also couldn't let them go."

"Stop," I croaked as stars exploded in front of my eyes.

I didn't know if was from oxygen deprivation or the fact that my entire universe was rearranging itself to make sense of this news.

Salvatore wasn't my father.

He couldn't be.

Mama wasn't a zealot, but she was a devout Roman Catholic. It was one of the reasons she had never divorced Seamus even when she should have.

To have an affair with another man when she was married with two other babies at home… it just didn't compute.

Only, I could call up the haunted longing in Mama's eyes as she stared out the lone window in our small kitchen and how she would cry sometimes at night, holding her rosary beads and a book of prayer, mumbling about forgiveness and sin. I'd always assumed she was praying for Seamus, our family's penultimate sinner, but what if I was wrong?

I didn't look like Seamus or my sisters who had inherited only their golden complexions from Mama and otherwise were replicas of our father.

Sebastian and I were cut from dark cloth, constructed into strong angles and long lines that spoke of different genes.

Ones that harkened back to a *capo* I'd known my entire life, one that hovered over our small lives like a dark power. He was tall, strong, and swarthy with a smooth, rolling gait that reminded me suddenly of Sebastian's.

Alexander's smirk cut like a knife wound across his face. "You see it, don't you? I took you because your biological father killed my mother, and your faux father was stupid enough to use you to repay his debts. It seems both your fathers' sins have shackled you to your fate long before you realized it."

My breath wheezed through my throat like a poorly equipped air conditioning unit, my body hot and cold in strange turns.

"I thought about killing you," Alexander mused as he resumed stroking my hair, only this time, his touch wasn't tender; it was perfunctory. The way one might pet their prized hound after he'd passed his prime before he was sent to slaughter. "But that was before I met you and saw those prized money eyes Amedeo had always spoken about so poetically. What a better fate, I thought, to use you, to bend you to my will and then send you back to him. How much more poetic would it be if it was his own sacred daughter that led him to his demise?"

I want to scratch at his hand, desperate to peel his steel fingers away from my windpipe, but I was still tied to the bedposts, helpless as a starfish too high on the shoreline. My mind had lost its tether to my shattered reality and I was beginning to lose purchase on any semblance of my life as I knew it.

It was very possibly that he was killing me.

"It was such a good plan, you see, *topolina*, and I am loath to change it. Only now, things have changed irrevocably. I," he pulled in a deep breath and put his face even closer to mine so that his eyes swallowed my vision like a lunar eclipse, and his mouth was against my lips. "I find myself as much in your thrall as you are in mine. The taste of you lingers in my mouth, the echo of your giggle in my ears, and the feel of your satin skin haunts my fingers, so in strange moments, I feel I could manifest you in my hold from out of thin air.

"I don't wish to use you anymore to kill your father. I don't wish to be duplicitous about my motivations. I want you to desire to help me. Help me bring justice to a man who left you for poor and gone in the wasteland of Naples for years to fend for yourself until he finally sold you into sexual slavery. Help me send the man who killed my mother out of jealousy and rage to prison for his crimes. Please," he said with a stroke on his tongue over the top of my parted mouth. The word sat like a pearl on my tongue, a precious gift I wanted to swallow and keep safe in the shell of my belly for all time. "Please, when the time comes, help me."

I wasn't thinking rationally.

My whole world had changed that day for the zenith time in the short span of three months, and I needed time to think. Time to be away from a man who radiated a magnetic field to rival the earth's poles, who drew my eternal moral compass to him like a faulty true North.

I didn't take that time, and I didn't want to.

He had manipulated me too soundly. I was filled with anger that had been latent too long, with righteous indignation that needed some end and that end was being given to me.

Didn't arrogant, destructive Salvatore, who ruled the criminal underworld of Naples that had tormented my family for years, deserve to be punished?

He might have been my biological father, but that only meant I'd been seeded by the Italian devil. In truth, he had done just as much lasting damage as Seamus had, and hadn't I gotten rid of him?

What was one more wrong righted? Especially if riding Naples of Amedeo Salvatore meant my family could move forward unscathed.

My passionate mind and heart collided in unity, but it was my gut that churned up a response. "Yes, when the time comes, if it means you'll let me go back to my family, I'll help you bring him to justice."

Alexander's taciturn face broke open into a full-lipped smile that took my breath away. He'd removed his hand from my neck, sliding it up my neck so that he could cup my cheek and sink the tips of his fingers into the hair over my ear. His eyes were eloquent with pride, relief, and fierce triumph, but he didn't voice any of it. Instead, he slowly closed his mouth over mine and let me eat them off his tongue.

"You can't tell your family," he murmured. "They can't know."

I nodded because I didn't want them to know for my own reasons. I was the first line of defense for the Lombardi clan, so I certainly wasn't going to be the one to drop a grenade in their mist.

Besides, how could I be the pane of glass in a family of fractures if my entire life was a well-kept lie? Would Elena still confide in me, and Elle still allow me to support her? How would Mama answer for her sins and move on with me to a better place of understanding?

What would Seb do, knowing he was the spawn of the worst man he'd ever known?

No, it would be just one more secret I harbored like a cancer in my cells so that it didn't infect my family.

"Will you tell me about Edward?" I asked, desperate to take the pressure of my chest and focus on another mystery that had nothing to do with me.

Alexander rubbed his nose against mine. "No, my beauty. That was confession enough for tonight."

He pulled away his face shuttering until the light of his tenderness was gone and all that remained was the dark shadow of domination. My mouth went dry at the sight of his enormous cock saluting the ceiling as he walked on his knees, straddling my legs and hips, then settled his buttocks on my abdomen. He fisted his cock in one hand and used the other to plump up my breasts like cushions before pushing them together. I shivered as he spat on the steep valley of my cleavage and then slowly pushed his searing hot dick into their fold.

"Now," he said in a voice like a hand on my throat. "It's time for you to make your Master come."

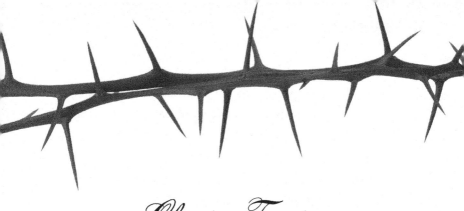

Chapter Fourteen

J was waiting for him.

My thighs were wet, the air around me perfumed with my honeyed scent.

I'd never been very patient, so the waiting shouldn't have worked on me as such a heady aphrodisiac, but each minute that ticked by struck my pussy like the beat of a gong, lust reverberating through my body from the source.

As much as my sex throbbed, my pulse was heavy, but even, my breathing long and slow. I felt centered by the weight at my core and my single-minded goal.

Wait for me by the door, naked, kneeling with your legs spread and hands behind your back.

When the waiting got too much, I thought of those orders in Alexander's clipped, unflappable tones, and they cooled me like an ice cube in hot tea, not noticeably enough and only briefly.

My shoulders ached from holding my hands behind my back, from tipping my breasts into the air, my nipples hard and pointed like arrows notched in a bow.

I wasn't comfortable in any sense of the word.

But my discomfort aroused me.

At that point, after nearly an hour of kneeling in the great hall, everything aroused me.

The cold, unforgiving kiss of marble on my shins, the weight of my entire body compressing my ankles, and the way the constant draft of the old manor whirred around my swollen sex like the whisper of a kiss.

If pressed, I honestly wasn't sure if I would state my name, date of birth, or prior place of residence.

I was just flesh, made pretty on a plate and waiting at the pass to be served hot to a high-paying guest or a severe critic.

He'd been gone for five days.

It shouldn't have been such an interminably long time.

In fact, it should have been a beloved reprieve from his constant sexual attentions.

At first, I'd rejoiced in the freedom. I took nearly every meal in the kitchen with Douglas who prepared Italian dishes that almost rivaled Mama's. I trained in the gym every morning, swimming in the lap pool, staring at the massive statue of Poseidon as I did the breast stroke. I spent every other spare moment in the library, reading first editions of the Bronte sisters and Byron, beautifully illustrated hard copies of fantasy novels like *The Lion, The Witch, and The Wardrobe*, and *The Hobbit*.

I thought endlessly about Salvatore. I no longer doubted he was my father. It made sense given his eccentric presence in our lives and how much we truly did look like him. Every time I let myself linger over it, I grew so angry I felt as if I would burst out of my skin. It was his face I imagined when I punched and kicked the hanging bag in the gym, his eyes I pretended to gouge when I fenced with Riddick, the only man sanctioned to do so while Alexander was gone.

Sometimes, late at night when the darkness and loneliness ate at my skin like so many crawling bugs, I let myself despair over the what-ifs. What if he'd stayed with Mama? What if he hadn't killed Chiara Davenport? And why? What kind of man did any of that unless he was just pure, straight-up evil?

To distract myself further, I gorged myself on food, exercise, and reading, but it did nothing to fill the bottomless well of longing that opened in the pit of my belly the minute Alexander had left for his travels.

My mind was erratic, flitting from interest to interest, unable to settle without the firm direction of Alexander's commands. I adapted slowly as if waking from a dream. By the fifth day, my mind was my own again but tuned to a station filled with static.

It was my body that suffered the most. I felt aching and restless, so listless at moments I wondered if I could get out of bed.

It was as if I was a depleted battery, and the only thing that could reanimate my ions was sex.

Apart from Douglas, Riddick was the only man I saw even though it was normal for me to cross paths with other male servants. It didn't take me long to realize they were being deliberately kept from me. Noel was gone with Alexander, so I didn't even have his chess games to fill the void.

Alexander had turned me into a sexual monster, but the only person he wanted me weaponised against was himself.

My sensitive ears picked up the telltale rumble of gravel churning under wheels even through the thick stone walls.

A car was pulling up.

We never had visitors, so it had to be him.

My Master.

My mouth flooded with salvia. I itched to catapult out of my pose so that the moment the door opened, my body would be on his, his hands catching my ass as I linked my long legs around him, and all would be right with my world at Pearl Hall.

It physically *hurt* to quell the impulse, but the ache when I clenched those mental muscles felt good. It felt good because I knew I'd be rewarded for my uncharacteristic patience.

When he saw it, he would know it was just another new trick in an arsenal of traits he was teaching me.

Heels clicked against the stone pavers on the steps. A low muffle of voices.

Then the heavy velvet against velvet sound of the door pushing open.

My breath left my body as I was filled to the brim with nervous, delicious anticipation.

My Master was home.

I didn't look up even as the shoes clicked twice, then paused for an endless moment in the doorframe, before they started up again, crossing the white and black checkered floor to me.

When his black Ferragamo loafers appeared in my line of vision, I could have cried.

He didn't speak as he stared down at me, not even when he finally placed a heavy hand on the top of my head and smoothed it over my hair. My breath stuttered from between my lips as he stepped closer and fiddled with his shirt.

His hand fell before my eyes holding a brilliant red tie.

I swallowed thickly.

He tied it briskly around my head, over my eyes, and though I tried, the fabric was too opaque for me to see anything.

The metallic gasp of his zipper, the rustle of parting fabric and then the hot press of his erection against my cheek.

He smelled so good there, deep musk and sinful man. My tongue flicked out to lick him, and I didn't care how depraved it made me seem.

I was empty, empty, empty, and I needed him to fill me up.

As if hearing my thoughts, he wove his fingers into the

back of my hair and slowly pressed me forward onto his length, impaling me.

I groaned, and tears sprang to my eyes.

I'd missed this, the swell of him between my lips and the struggle of him in my throat. My beauty had always been my only talent, but now I had another.

Pleasing my Master.

His hand spasmed in my hair, and the other joined it, threading through the locks to use them like reins. It delighted me to melt his usually ironclad control with my mouth.

I sucked on his shaft, squeezed my throat around his length, and lapped at the plump head like a kitten with milk.

He came all too quickly, both of us groaning as if in pain as his cum landed in lush spurts across my tongue.

Finally, he pulled my still eager mouth away from his length and stepped away, breathing hard.

As my submissive high abated, my gut began to clench with unease.

Alexander had never been a silent lover. He enjoyed taunting me as he used me, making me beg as he hurt me so well.

Why was he being so quiet?

I opened my mouth to question him when the hush of the well-oiled door whispered throughout the hall.

My spine snapped straighter, and I fought the urge to run.

I was naked, kneeling in the great hall like a statue meant for use instead of ornamentation, and there was another person there who was not my Master.

"What the fuck is this?" Alexander's voice boomed out across the hall, the echo sticking in the corners as if caught by spider's webs. "Get the bloody hell away from my property this minute."

I ripped off the blindfold just in time to see Alexander in the doorway, his body colossal with rage as he stared down the man standing before me.

The man who had just used me.

He was shorter and slimmer than Alexander, with mousy blond hair that curled floppishly around his ears. It was his cock that perturbed me most though, hanging half-turgid out of his opened trousers and still wet from my mouth.

Bile crashed against my esophagus, and I choked on it once before submitting to the urge to vomit over my shoulder into the massive oriental vase behind me.

From the corner of my eye, I watched as Alexander broke from his terrifying paralysis and stormed across the room, sweeping up the interloper in his cyclone wake. He took him off his feet with one hand fisted in his collar and the other at his shoulder.

I coughed and gasped, my hand over my raging heart as Alexander slammed him brutally into one of the walls. Two paintings plummeted to the ground beside them, the glass shattering into thousands of crystalline pieces at their feet.

Alexander didn't notice.

He was utterly consumed by his rage. I couldn't see his face as he pushed it close to my assaulter's, but I could see the fury in every line of his gladiator's form as he squeezed a large hand around the man's neck.

"You dare to touch what's mine, Lord Ashcroft?" Alexander seethed over the sound of the man choking for breath. "You dare to use the property of a Davenport man without my express permission? I will show you what is done to vile thieves in this house."

Summoned by the commotion, Riddick appeared in one of the many doorways to the circular room and took the man in a tight grip by the neck.

"Take him to the Iron Chair," Alexander ordered.

Lord Ashcroft whimpered. "Alexander, old chap, what the fuck is wrong with you? What's a little sharing between brothers of the Order?"

"I don't give a fuck about the Order. This is my home, and you stuck your miserable excuse for a cock in the mouth of *my* lovely slave. You've desecrated at my altar, and you will be punished as the heathens did, in a way that is so unmerciful, you will feel the consequences of your actions for the rest of your life."

Ashcroft wailed as Riddick turned on his heel and literally dragged him out of the room. I stared after them in mute horror.

I wasn't just traumatized by the assault of a strange man.

I was fractured by my willingness to submit. A healthy woman would have looked up into the eyes of the man she was going to pleasure; she would have demanded something in return or at the very least, not felt elevated to a spiritual plane the moment a cock was between her lips.

It was the realization that I was a slut that razed me to the ground at that horrible moment. So, when Alexander stalked over to me and bent down to tip my chin gently with his curled knuckles to look in my eyes and study my mental state, he found nothing.

No, courageous *topolina*, no atavistic Cosima.

Just a vacant shell.

"My beauty," he breathed, his voice vaporous as agony punched him in the gut. "My sweet, pure beauty. I am so sorry he defiled you."

Sorry from the lips of my Master.

It should have been a gift I spent overlong unwrapping,

smoothing the ribbons through my fingers, teasing the tape back with the edge of my thumb like a child on Christmas.

Instead, its prettiness felt foreign in my lap. A present I didn't deserve.

I should be the one to apologize for being such a floozy.

For allowing someone else to use me for their pleasure when it was only Alexander I wanted to serve.

He was horrible in ways I could recognize and understand. If there was a monster under my bed, I wanted it to be him because his was a cruelty I was familiar with.

The idea of being used and terrorized by another completely undid me.

"I will beat him to within an inch of his life," Alexander cooed to me as he gently used the edge of his sleeve to wipe the tears I hadn't known were spilling down my cheeks. "I will sit him in the Iron Chair and use the cat-o'-nine-tails on him until he is a bloody mass of stripped ribbons on the spiked throne. How does that sound, *topolina*? Do you think then he will understand that you were made for no one but me?"

Yes! my mind hissed. I could just imagine Alexander using his considerable force to flay the man for his transgressions, taunting him for his idiocy so that he could break his body and mind simultaneously.

Alexander was a champion at that.

I should know.

"Would you like to watch? Would that make you feel better?" he wondered, skirting gentle fingers along my hairline, trailing his thumb over my swollen mouth.

I could still taste Ashcroft, and it made me want to retch again. I could feel the shape of him like a phantom in my throat and the weight of his hands in my hair.

No, I didn't want to watch Alexander beat him.

I needed something else.

Something that my rational mind might consider even more abhorrent.

"I need you," I admitted on a broken breath.

I reached out to coil my fist in his shirt. He wasn't wearing a tie. I should have known the moment I saw that garish red tie that it wasn't Alexander seducing me. My Alexander never wore ties.

I leaned forward to press my nose to the hollow of his exposed throat, breathing deeply of his delicious cedar smell. "I need you," I repeated again, stronger this time. "I need you to take me and prove I'm yours and no one else's."

Alexander made a noise in his throat that was half agony, half purr, and his hand went up to fist brutally in the back of my hair, yanking it so I was forced to look up at him. His eyes scored the wet depths of my own, looking amid the broken fragments of my spirit to see how to make me whole again.

He found the answer he was looking for and groaned again as he angled my head and plundered my mouth with his own.

I used the minty, manly taste of his mouth to cleanse my palate and pressed closer, kneading my hands into his chest like a cat seeking affection.

He gave it to me.

We kissed until my mind spun like a top, until each breath felt wrung from my lungs and my heart was on the precipice of bursting.

There was one thought in my head that drummed out all else, *I need him, I need him, I need him.*

I gasped when his hands went under my armpits, and he lifted me up so that I was forced to wind my legs around his neck and sit my pussy flush against his face. My hands dove into the silken strands of his hair and pulled him tight to me so I could balance precariously with my ass seated in the wide bowl of his palms.

He ate at me ruthlessly, nibbling on my lips, sucking hard, smacking kisses against my clit, then tunneling his tongue deep inside me. It pulled my focus to the apex of my sex so that the wet slide of his mouth against my flooded entrance was all I could hear and all I could be was sensation.

Normally, when I came for him, I splintered apart, undone by his touch. This time was different.

As I climaxed, fire flooded over my jagged, broken edges, melding them back together, soothing the connections away until they were seamless, and I was whole in his arms again. I cried out at the oddity of the sensation, and the overwhelming rightness of the pleasure, my shouts magnified by the room until they echoed throughout the house.

I wanted them to hear.

I wanted the servants to know I was Alexander's so that they would stop their lecherous gazes. I wanted Ashcroft to know that even as he was impaled on a chair of spikes and beaten by Riddick's meaty fists that I was experiencing pleasure from my rightful owner, expunging his mark on me as easily as wiping a whiteboard clean.

When I finally came down from the height of my climax, I found myself slumped over Alexander, my fingers carding through his beautiful hair in a way that brought us both comfort. He pressed a kiss to the damp inside of my thigh but otherwise didn't move, letting me take my time to recover.

I realized that it was the gentle intimacy that I so loved about our sexual dynamic. Alexander could fold me in half, break me into weapon-sharp edges of pleasure with his scenes and his demands, but he always, always brought me back to earth with the gentle touch of his hands.

His tenderness was my undoing. Even realizing it, I knew nothing would change. He had been slowly unravelling the great length of me from the moment I'd arrived and even before that when he'd set his sights on me in Milano and grew determined to take me.

I was a goner before I even realized I'd gone.

I sighed heavily, and Alexander took it as the cue it was. He slumped slightly so that my legs slid off his shoulders, and I fell into his lap, his arms binding around me in sweet bondage.

"Who knew something so strong could be so heartbreakingly beautiful," he whispered as he studied my face and dragged his rough-edged thumb down the line of my jaw.

I wanted to duck my head and hide behind my hair because a compliment had never felt so profound before, but he wouldn't let me escape his scrutiny.

"He took nothing from you because he is worth nothing, do you understand?" he continued in the hushed voice he always used when dealing with me. As if he didn't even want the air between us to know our secrets.

My lip trembled, and he pressed it steady with the pad of his thumb.

"Say it to me," he demanded.

I sucked in a deep breath that burned down my throat and fortified me like strong brandy. "He took nothing from me because he is worth nothing."

"I am going to give you everything because you are worth everything," he said in a way that made it a vow, and to seal it, he closed his mouth over mine in a firm, hard kiss that felt like a wax seal stamped with his crest.

"I don't understand you," I told him shakily. "You want to destroy me one minute and worship me in the next."

He closed his eyes, looking so very tired for the first time since I'd met him. I didn't curb my impulse to reach up and smooth the lines in his puckered forehead with my fingers.

"You aren't English, and you aren't a peer, so how can you understand? I was born into something that I cannot change, and I must carry the burdens of my ancestors."

"Nothing is irrevocable," I told him, but the words felt like a lie as I sat in the cradle of his arms because I knew there was nothing changeable about the way he had altered the composition of my mind.

"Some things are. There are secrets with roots that stem back into the 1500s in a family as old as mine, and there are some that are as recent as my lifetime that are too egregious to ever lay down."

"And these secrets explain why you bought me?"

He pulled back to consider me, idly wrapping one of his fingers in a lock of my inky hair. "I think perhaps I would have acquired you even if I hadn't needed you. The moment you saved my life was the moment you unwittingly became mine."

"A strange way to repay a debt," I noted because even though I was soft from my orgasm, there were still thorns at the edges of my thoughts from the trauma of it all, each memory a prick of pain against my psyche.

He'd done that damage to me, directly and indirectly.

"It is. I hope one day to explain it all to you, but that day is not today, and it is not soon. Now, get up and go directly to your room. I want you to stay there while I deal with the bastard currently occupying my dungeon. Unless you want to watch?"

I thought it about it as I bit into my lower lip. There was no denying something would be satisfying about watching a man hurt for his transgressions against me. But I didn't think I wanted to be the kind of glutton who indulged in such a thing.

"I'll go upstairs."

"Good girl," he said with a small smile that didn't reach his eyes.

He pulled my chin forward to press a kiss on my mouth, then stood us both up easily.

"Oh good, you're organizing yourselves," a voice said from the entryway to the left wing of the house.

Noel stood there in something more formal than a tuxedo, his silver threaded golden hair pushed away from his face with pomade.

I made a noise in my throat and ducked slightly behind Alexander because I was tired of being undressed in front of fully clothed men.

"What the hell are you talking about?" Alexander demanded, crossing his arms over his chest and bracing his feet like a military man.

"The Order is coming."

Something dark permeated the room, and the light from the small windows at the top of the two-story space suddenly went out. Logically, I knew that the ever-present English clouds had covered the weak late autumn sun, but the omen felt too powerful to rationalize.

"And who the fuck invited them?" Alexander asked even though the answer was obvious.

Noel smiled sedately. "They inquired after the girl, as is their right. You hadn't done so; therefore, I gave them an update."

"An update that clearly required them to check up on us."

His father shrugged. "I am not the man in power. Take it up with Sherwood."

"Oh," Alexander said darkly. "I will. You and I will also be having words. Ashcroft arrived early and assaulted Cosima."

"Cosima?" He frowned, looking so much like a confused

older man that I felt the urge to go to him. "Oh, you mean Ruthie? What a terrible misunderstanding."

"There was no misunderstanding," Alexander ground out, his fist clenched at his sides. "You are the orchestrator of this madness, and it is *you* who should have to the bear the mark of it. Not Cosima."

Finally, an expression that was not calm or solicitous crossed Noel's face. It slithered beneath his skin, not quite there, a snake in the grass hoping to move by undetected. Reflexively, I recoiled. The man I'd spent my afternoons with had been wise, kind, and old enough to bring comfort to me because such a man didn't view young women like me as anything but delicate young ladies.

That look did not say all that had been conveyed that day.

"Do not call her by that name," he ordered Alexander. "She is Ruthie now."

I'd never seen anyone order Alexander, and true to my expectations, he took it as the insult it was.

"I will decide what to call her as she is *my slave*, Father. You forget yourself. Perhaps your senility is impairing your judgment."

"Perhaps your cock is impairing yours," Noel snapped, the tendons in his neck straining. "Do you forget the reason we do the things we must? Is it so easy to forget your own mother?"

The silence that stretched between them was dense and toxic like the aftermath of an atomic bomb. The two men stared at each other unmoving for so long that I began to feel uncomfortable.

"Go upstairs," Alexander bit out, clearly addressing me. "Go upstairs and ready yourself to be presented as my slave tonight."

My cold feet were fleet against the marble, and I was

halfway up the stairs before Alexander called out, "Oh, and *topolina*, if you don't follow my every instruction without hesitation, you will be who next sits in the Iron Chair."

Chapter Fifteen

I could hear the low murmur of male voices punctuated by the clamour of cutlery on fine china and the clink of crystal glasses filled over full with wine. My heart was in my throat as I waited outside the servant's door to the dining hall, my hands twisted like tangled twine in my angst.

Mrs. White had attended me as soon as I'd stepped through the doors to my bedchamber. I'd been bathed, buffed, and lotioned, combed, dried, and curled, then stuffed like a doll into a ridiculous frilled white frock that would have been better fit for a child since it barely covered my ass or breasts.

Finally, she'd secured a large pendant around my throat, the heavy carved ivory resting in the hollow of my neck. It depicted a red flower and a design that resembled a keyhole, as if the bloom was the key to unchaining some ancient sect's secrets. Combined with the dress, it made me look occultist, like a sacrificial virgin offered up to some mythological sea monster.

She'd stepped away from my face in the mirror, beaming like a proud mother at the way she'd gussied me up to be paraded in front of a dining hall filled with men.

Now, I was waiting like a good little slave for Master to summon me into the hall. I'd been waiting over an hour if the grandfather clock by the sideboard was to be believed.

It wasn't the waiting that bothered me, though I wasn't a particularly patient person. It was that I could not fully grasp how I felt about my life or even in my body.

I'd set out with the intention to understand Lord Thornton. If I could understand him, I could humanize him. Strip away the gentlemanly artifice, the cold mask of domination, and the clinical rules of ownership to truly understand beneath it all.

Only, I felt as if I'd fallen down a rabbit hole. Not only had I failed to master the mystery of Alexander Davenport, but I'd lost sense of myself.

If someone had asked me four months ago if I would ever love to kneel for a man, to take the pain he gave me and thank him for it as a worshipper thanks God, I would have laughed.

Even two months ago, when I'd first arrived and been stripped so thoroughly of my liberties, I would never have imagined I could find a drop of compassion for the man who owned me.

But I did.

I thought of the awfulness of his mother's death and the mystery that lay in its wake like an open, festering wound. I remembered the criss-cross of whip marks between his shoulder blades from an unknown incident that couldn't have been pleasant for a natural Dom to take. I knew that he worked ceaselessly to increase the family fortune, not for greed, but in order to preserve a house and history he felt he was the custodian of.

He could be kind and tender, as he had just proven after the vile Lord Ashcroft defiled me. Ruthless too, as was evident by the way he punished him, screams ringing throughout the house. Mercilessness was not normally a characteristic to admire in a man, I knew, but I also understood that we lived in a merciless world and only the truly ferocious could survive it.

I startled from my thoughts when the butler, Ainsworth, pushed through the side door and stopped before me.

His eyes were gentle in his big face as he studied me. "Lord Thornton will see you now."

Merda.

I straightened my shoulders but ducked my head to the proper respectful angle and then walked through the door Ainsworth held open for me.

Immediately, the cacophony of the dinner party fell flat.

I could feel dozens of eyes on me as I stepped through the door and waited to be called by my Master.

"Crawl to me," Alexander's hushed voice still resonated in the large, quite hall.

I sucked in a deep breath to steel my spine, to lock away my dignity into a very small box inside my soul, and then I melted to the ground.

Unlike the first time I had crawled for Alexander, I was not aroused. I could feel the strange eyes of many horrible men on my body, slipping and sliding over my curves until I felt covered in grease marks. There were a few whispers and dark chuckles as I made my way to the head of the table where Alexander sat, but they otherwise seemed committed to the ceremonial silence.

"Rise," Alexander ordered when I reached the left side of his chair.

I stood gracefully, my head still bent. I hoped I presented a picture of calm because I had the very awful feeling that these men were the predators that would dare to prey on a man like my Master, and I didn't want to toss either of us at their feet with the stupidity of my actions.

I tried to find subspace and failed. Instead, I took deep breaths, counting as I did to settle my mind.

Even that didn't work.

The entire dining room was filled with Britain's finest men dressed tight to the throat in designer finery, their spines starched with noble titles and lips pressed tight against the threat of their many dark secrets. I could feel their countless eyes on me as they looked at the head of the table to the man who hosted them there for this society gathering.

"Gentlemen," that man announced, standing up with all the authority of a born aristocrat, a learned man, a Master. "May I present slave Davenport."

I stepped forward at the same time I bent my knees, sinking into a kneel before I could finish moving in line beside Alexander. My head was ducked, my hair curled and tied loosely with a red ribbon down my back so that I couldn't hide behind the thick curtain of it, so that all the men could see the way my face was composed into careful, pretty blankness.

"A demonstration is in order, I think, Lord Thornton," a creaking old voice said from somewhere down the table.

"Yes, after the reports we've had and your little tantrum with Lord Ashcroft, I'm of the mind to take the slave away from you and transfer her into the care of another, more capable Master. Perhaps Mr. Landon Knox."

My head jerked up as my heart nearly flew out my throat.

Instantly, my eyes found his.

Landon Knox.

The man I'd known since I was a prepubescent teenager, the man who had launched my modelling career and driven me to anorexia was sitting at Alexander's table.

The clash of my two worlds meeting resounded like crashing symbols in my head. I swayed as I blinked hard, trying to process.

Alexander's stern voice severed our connection. "No one

will be taking her away from me. I own her. The papers were signed, her virginity was taken, and she bears my gold at her tits and clit. She is *mine*."

"Careful, Thornton, your caveman is showing," Landon drawled.

"And caution to you, Mr. Knox, your lack of pedigree is obvious," Alexander retorted.

"Gentlemen." A man with steel grey hair stood up, long and thin as a reed but with the bearing of a king. "There is one way to settle this. The girl must be put through her paces."

"I don't believe it should be Thornton who does it," Landon argued, his eyes over bright and overeager as he stared at me. "Let it be a new Master."

"Agreed," a voice said from the very end of the table.

I wouldn't have thought anything of it, but Alexander tensed beside me so viciously, I thought he was having a heart attack.

The man spoke again, his voice strong but oddly accented, a hop and a skip of something Latin in his tones. "If we are trying to prove whether the girl is being properly trained and if Thornton has neglected his duties because he is enamoured with her, we must separate them. Make him watch while one of us does the deed."

"You take things too far by letting that man into my bloody fucking house," Alexander said, each word sharp as a bullet casing tearing through the air. "Show yourself, Edward."

My heart tripped and then raced through my chest.

Edward, the long-lost son and brother?

The slowly, cringeworthy sound of a chair screeching against the parquet floor was the only sound in the ominously silent room.

I risked Alexander's wrath by lifting my chin to see the man

Noel and his son had excommunicated from their lives.

I didn't know what to expect from Edward Davenport.

My only knowledge consisted of his betrayal when he chose Salvatore over his own family. I'd never wondered what he would look like, how he would hold himself, or what I would feel if I ever met him.

I simply wasn't prepared.

Because if Alexander was a golden prince, King Arthur or Emperor Augustus, some shining example of leadership and male beauty, Edward was his rival.

They could have been two sides of the same coin, contrary though they were, they had the same colossal bodies packed with muscle, Edward's perhaps even more quilted, and broad faces so beautiful they made my eyes ache in their sockets.

Yet that was where the similarities ended. Edward was coloured not in precious metals like his brother, but in *shadows*, his hair as ink stained as my own, his eyes so deep a brown they seemed to swallow the light, and his skin tanned and polished to a glossy bronze. The bearing of his broad shoulders was not regal but forceful; his hands large and blunt tipped like some medieval weapons of torture.

He seemed more weapon than man.

His eyes slide to mine swiftly, and our gazes collided like two cars on an icy road. I felt the crash in my gut and shuddered as it passed through me.

I blinked, and his eyes were still there, watching me as though he knew me and even more, held some bizarre degree of familiarity and affection for me.

I gasped quietly when he had the audacity to throw me an almost imperceptible wink.

"How dare you show your face in this house after what you have done?" Alexander asked in his quiet voice filled with fury that boiled so hot and deep within his chest he seemed like a living volcano.

"He is a member of the Order of Dionysus, Thornton. He has a *right* to be here," Sherwood stated implacably.

"Whatever right he had was stripped along with his surname and inheritance the moment he joined sides with the villain who killed my mother." I had never seen Alexander so wholly still. He was on security lockdown, every vault spun shut, every door coated over in titanium so that not one of his vulnerabilities could escape or be plundered by the ruthless men in the room. "I hope you brought him to take responsibility for his actions."

"We brought him here to test you, if you must know," Landon drawled, his eyes wicked as they darted between Alexander and myself. "You will watch from the gallery as we put slave Davenport through her testing, and you will not intervene in anyway. Will you, Thornton?"

Alexander stood mutely for a moment, but despite his quiet stillness, it was evident he was struggling internally with a cyclone of emotion.

My Master might have been a cruel one, but he had never hurt me, not irreparably, not more than my body could stand or my mind couldn't translate into pleasure.

The other men of the Order, I knew, would have no such boundaries.

My skin went suddenly very cold.

"If we find you've developed feelings for the girl," Sherwood said coldly, peering at Alexander as if he was a turncoat of the highest order. "Not only will the girl be taken from you, but we will have to consider your punishment. You remember what happened to Baron Horst, do you not?"

"Crippled," a man sitting to Alexander's right leaned over

to sneer quietly at me. "Couldn't take the whipping like a real man."

"Of course, you're familiar with the Order's punishments. You were only twenty-two when you stood up for the Russian slave, weren't you?" Sherwood continued.

My mind immediately conjured up the thin white scars dissecting Alexander's otherwise flawless back. I kept my eyes focused on the ground as they burned with tears.

I didn't know who I was more sorrowful for. Myself for my upcoming ordeal, or Alexander for being raised and ruled by such a barbarian group of men.

The room hung in animated silence as they waited for Alexander's verdict, and even though I knew the impossibility of his decision, my heart still turned to ash in my chest when he spoke the words I knew he would say.

"Take her, beat her, flay her, and bring forth her tears. She's just a slave to me. It's only her body that brings me pleasure."

Chapter Sixteen

They set up in the gymnasium. It was clear orders had been given before dinner to arrange the space for their intended show because a strange apparatus shaped like a massive X was settled beside a wheeled table filled with sex toys and equipment. They had known Alexander would capitulate to their demands.

Alexander's cryptic threats about predators more powerful than himself suddenly made blood-curdling sense.

Two men carried me in.

Alexander was not one of them.

They had parted us immediately after he acquiesced to the demonstration, but I caught sight of him on the small set of bleachers, sandwiched between two stocky men who looked ready to rip his head off if he made one wrong move.

I swallowed thickly as the men dragged me over to the huge cross and bound my limbs to each branch of the X, facing away from the gathering crowd and the Master who would test me. The cuffs weren't leather as they usually were, but cold, sharp metal that bit into my skin too tightly. The man on my left laughed under his breath as I gave my wrists a little jerk and winced.

He liked me in pain.

They all did.

I was the lone masochist in a room full of cruel sadists with no one to temper their lust.

My mind buzzed and whirred as I tried to mentally prepare myself for the coming onslaught.

Then Landon stepped forward in all his finery with a long, thin whip coiled over his knuckles, and I knew no meditation or platitudes would prepare me for what was to come.

Landon had controlled me for years as a girl, flagellating my independent spirit for petty transgressions until I was as mentally submissive to him as I was now to Alexander.

If he was so well trained in Dominant mental warfare, I didn't want to even imagine how he might be at the physical act.

"This is a black snake," he explained to me as the two men attending to me melted away, their job done. "It's my preferred whip for punishing unruly subs. It makes this sound, you see, this slash through the air and then a cutting *crack* as it bites into the arse. Then the sound of the sub as they scream and beg through their tears for me to stop… well, it gets me so hard."

I wanted to rally against him. To spit in his face and tell him he was a coward, not a Master. A real Master shared trust with their slave. They promised to braid pleasure with the pain as it whipped against their skin, to reward them with praise or orgasms if they followed the rules of their game. I knew without having to know the particulars that Landon did no such things. He was a pathetic excuse of a man who hid behind BDSM to make him feel more of a man, to falsely prove his thesis that men were the better gender.

I closed my eyes as he pressed forward into my body, running his tongue along the edge of my jaw in a possessive move that made me shudder.

"If you were anyone else, I might be soft," he told me as he savagely bit my ear. "But you need to be punished for leaving me in Milano."

"Isn't my life now punishment enough?" I whispered.

He paused for such a moment, I thought maybe I'd reached some dusty corner of goodness in his head.

"In the Order, we believe in punishment by blood," he said, and then he thrust his erection against my ass and ground hard into me. "So I'm going to make you bleed."

"Mr. Knox will serve slave Davenport twenty-five lashes," the man named Lord Sherwood declared in his dry, professor tone. "If the girl has been trained in pain, she should be able to thank Mr. Knox for each one through to the very end. If, on the other hand, Lord Thornton has been too soft with the girl, and she breaks before then… Lord Thornton will be flogged and taxed for his inability to Master."

There was a murmuring of agreement.

I loathed that I could see what was happening behind me. It felt as if my naked body was prostrate before a gaggle of hyenas, yipping in sinister laughter at the idea of eating me through to my bones.

"Ready, slave?" Landon asked from a few feet away.

He didn't give me any time to answer or brace myself. There was the slicing whistle of the whip through the air and then a sound like a gunshot as the thin, braided leather connected across my upper back.

A scream tore from the fabric of my lungs, leaving the delicate tissues ripped and bloody in my aching chest. I cried out so loudly, I could feel the sound in my hair and my toes as I tried to use the noise to force out the devastating pain I felt reverberating in every inch of my body.

Somewhere, in the deepest pit of my psyche was a small chained and locked box of reasoning that rattled with a reminder.

I had to do something.

There was an order amid the hellfire of pain, something I had to do to avoid more of it. For myself and my Master.

"One," I said as my scream morphed into a shout. "Thank you, Mr. Knox."

"*Master*," he seethed. "Call me Master."

"I am within reason to protest that," Alexander's voice called clear and strong through the gym. I felt the cool, aristocratic syllables slide down my painfully hot skin like ice cubes. "Slave Davenport knows only one Master, and that is me."

"I'll allow it," Sherwood declared after a moment of thought. "The slave will address you as Mr. Knox."

It was a small boon, but every gift felt like a miracle.

I was strung up before a secret society of Britain's wealthiest, most tilted gentleman, being tested because they worried my cruel Master was being soft on me.

If it hadn't been so horrible, I could have laughed at the improbability of my own life.

I knew the next strike was coming, and that it would be harder than the last because Landon would be angry and jealous of Alexander's title, but the pain was still impossible to brace against.

It burst across my back and then sank spikes of skin-sizzling heat deep into my spine, impaling me with pain.

"Two, thank you, Mr. Knox," I gritted through my teeth.

On the tenth whiplash, I felt my skin part like butter under the knife of the leather whip. Blood trickled down my spine and pooled in the twin dimples over my ass, tempting Knox to thrash me harder, the colour inciting his bull-like wrath.

By the fifteenth score, I couldn't breathe through the mess of snot and tears clogging my nose and the air through my mouth was metallic with blood. At some point, I had bitten clean into my cheek and pink-tinged saliva slid out over my chin.

My mind wanted to break through its physical tethers to my body and float away into space, a balloon lost to the atmosphere. It would have been so easy to sever the ties, to evacuate my pain-riddled limbs and lose myself entirely, but I wouldn't do it.

There was something like losing in the thought of it.

I was tired of the loss I'd suffered.

My family was gone to me, my name taken and replaced by moniker's men had given me to mark me as their own. I had no skills, no job, no money of my own. My very future was shackled to the whims of others.

I'd lost so much already; I couldn't stand to lose myself.

So I tried to sink into the pain. Each lash brought a different type of agony, a different way to feel it.

The seventeenth strike was lightning striking the bloody swamplands between my shoulders.

The eighteenth, a thin wire cutting through warm clay, dissecting my flesh so painfully, so swiftly, it took away my breath.

I held it through the brutal bite of the next strike and the one after that, expelling a tiny swell of air punctuated by a, "Thank you, Mr. Knox," after each one.

By the twentieth, it was obvious that my tormentor's arm was growing weary. The whip hit my back strangely, the angle wrong so that the thin tip wrapped around the cross I was bound to and flicked over the tender underside of my breast. I felt the skin split open into red beads of moisture.

The next five had Landon's entire body weight behind them and lacked his original finesse. They were heavy, brutish blows that pounded me against the wooden beams like hammer strikes and blunt fists.

He finished, and my last thank you was only a wet breath of relief as my body sagged boneless in the cuffs. My wrists and ankles were wet where the cruel metal had abraded through layers of my skin, and I could feel the sticky blood from my back dripping down my bum and thighs.

Just as I became when I was with Master Alexander, I was only sensation.

It was my coping method and my salvation.

I was every ache, pain, and horrible cramp in the body of Cosima Lombardi. I had thoughts, however fractured, and a tall spine, however abused.

There was heavy silence as the men absorbed my resilience. Even in my painful oblivion, I could feel their surprise that I had preserved.

"You should have hit her harder, Knox," someone sneered.

"I'd like to have seen you do better, Wentworth," he snapped back.

"She passed," another voice said wearily. "Let the poor thing down. She looks less appetizing than a skinned rabbit, and she's spoiling my dinner."

The sound of shoes drew close, and I shuddered as a finger traced over a raw, opened wound. It felt as if someone had stuck a fork into my socket.

"I think," Sherwood mused from behind me. "It's time for Lord Edward to take his turn at her. What will it be, Edward? The quirt or the bull whip for another twenty-five."

I knew I wouldn't survive another *five* lashes, let alone twenty-five.

There was a moment of absolute silence and then an explosion of shouting and movement.

There was a quick, heavy tread of shoes bursting toward me and then a growl as someone fell to the ground close to me.

"Don't be a bloody fool," someone whispered harshly over grunts of effort.

"Get the fuck off me before I rip your head off your body,"

Alexander growled. "I'll deal you with later after I take care of these twats."

"You take this punishment for her, you're dead, and you fucking know it." I gasped softly as I recognized the other voice. The voice of Alexander's brother and rival, Edward. "They've been looking for reasons to end you since you beat out Stockbridge for the Olympic bid in 2012. You're unruly, selfish, and too fucking hard headed for these fucks to rule. Don't you see what's going on? Don't you ever fucking see?"

There was the sound of a tussle and then more men clustering around the two on the ground.

With all my remaining energy, I turned my head against the wood to view the spectacle.

It was Edward on top of Alexander, holding his hands over his head while some of the other brothers of the Order tried to pry him off.

"Please, Lord Thornton, explain your behaviour?" Sherwood asked silkily from where he loomed over Alexander.

"I want to take slave Davenport's punishment."

Alexander's steady words struck me with the force of the snake whip.

"You do?" Sherwood questioned with barely concealed glee. "Because you can't bear to see her hurt?"

"I submit to the Order's punishment. Though I haven't been soft on the slave, I did take my hands to another brother without first going through the Order. I believe a flagellation is the normal punishment for such a misdemeanor."

"You are correct," Sherwood mused. "Though it would have to be Lord Edward who wields the whip."

No, I wanted to scream. There was no way Alexander would take a beating from his own slanderous brother for me. I couldn't believe it, and more, I didn't want to.

It said too many things that shouldn't have been true for us.

"I submit to the Order's punishment," Alexander repeated regally, as if he was not being sentenced to a flogging.

"Very well. Prepare him."

I closed my eyes in sorrow and relief, tears searing through my lids and sliding down my cheeks.

Alexander was taking this punishment so I didn't have to.

He was going to be beaten by his traitorous brother for *me*.

My heart set to aching even more than my back.

I gasped as something warm and heavy was draped over my me.

"Hush, *bella*," Alexander whispered in my ear as they pressed him to me and shackled him to the contraption with thick, secure leather cuffs. "I'm here, my beauty."

The urge to cry grew like a thorny thicket in my throat.

"Oh, Xan," I whimpered as the men jerked loudly on Alexander's bounds to test their strength and then stepped away. "Why are you doing this?"

"No one hurts you but me," he claimed fiercely as he used the tip of his nose to wipe a tear from my cheek. "Knox nearly flayed you alive, and he will die for it, I swear to it, but for now, let me save you from this."

"Begin, Lord Edward," Sherwood snapped.

"This is the world I was brought up in," Alexander whispered quickly. "It's not an excuse, but context, Cosima. If I am a monster, these are my creators."

A slice and whistle then the sharp *crack* as the whip ripped across Alexander's back. His entire body tensed against mine, trying to keep himself off my tender back.

He didn't make a noise.

Edward beat him soundly, the thwack of the leather harsher to my ears than it was when Knox went at me, and I realized that because Alexander was a man, he was getting an even more thorough punishment.

After a while, he gave up trying to keep a small gap of separation between us and his sweat-slicked torso stuck to my back, stinging the open sores.

"I'm sorry," he muttered almost drunkenly.

Another apology from my Master, this one so much more potent than the last. It could have been in tribute to so many of his dastardly acts against me, but my brain was stripped of its ability to nuance and so those two small words seemed to encompass everything.

This Lord and Master, who submitted to no one for nothing, was taking a thrashing from a man he reviled for me.

I could feel his great warrior's body jerk and tremble against my own with each whipping, the jumpstart of his breath after each strike and the sweetness of his lips against my hair, and all I wanted to do was hug him.

I wanted to wrap my aching limbs around the aching limbs of my Master and hold him close enough to feel my heart beat from my chest to his. I wanted to pepper his beautiful face in kisses and cry for the tragedies of our lives.

Instead, I pushed my cheek back slightly against his, and I breathed, "I forgive you."

The twenty-fifth blow landed and then Alexander's gusty sigh cooled the sweat to my skin.

"Get them down," Sherwood ordered, his voice rife with dissatisfaction. "Ready the cars."

There was sharp strike of expensive shoes on wood, and then the muffled sound of them crossing the mats we stood on.

Then Sherwood was there, his face over both of ours as he hissed, "Prove you are repentant, Thornton. Bring the girl to The Hunt."

Chapter Seventeen

It was deep winter in Scotland, the air so crisp it seemed to shatter against my skin as I jumped up and down on my toes to keep warm. I should have been wearing a thick overcoat, scarf, and gloves, or at the very least pants and shoes, but I was not. Instead, I was dressed as the other twenty-six women surrounding me in the corral were in a simple, old fashioned white shift dress. I wasn't even wearing underwear. One of the girls had questioned a lord in the hall when we first congregated about how we were to keep warm. After he'd slapped her across the face for her impudence, he'd informed her running for her life should keep her warm enough.

I shifted my weight from foot to foot and cupped my hands together in a feeble attempt to warm them with my breath while I looked over the assembly of men, all finely dressed on horseback. It was easy to spot Alexander in the mix with his crown of golden hair glinting even in the twilight fog. He was also the only one wearing thick, elbow length gloves. I looked at the sky and saw his falcon, Astor, circling overhead. As if summoned by my thoughts, Alexander raised his forearm over his head and the bird went plummeting from the sky, pulling up to slow his flight just before he landed gracefully on his Master's limb.

It seemed Alexander was good at training all kinds of creatures.

All the men wore tweed coats and tight riding breeches in fawn and earthen colours but for the Master, the Earl of Sherwood, his huntsman servant, and the whippers-in who would do reconnaissance and control the hounds for the group. They wore traditional red coats and black hats to distinguish themselves from the lot.

They were the leaders of the annual hunt, but it wouldn't be the traditional fox they raced to capture.

No, it would be the women corralled together in a wooden pen.

This was the Order of Dionysus's greatest event, the highlight of their year.

Every man participating must have paid the cost of admission.

A young woman for the other men to hunt.

There were very few rules as far as Alexander had explained it to me this morning before he was called away for the General Assembly.

One, the men were not under any circumstance allowed to use weapons against each other or the girls. Fisticuffs were expected and even encouraged. Sexual assault was literally the name of the game. But no weapons.

As if that made this game civilized.

Two, The Hunt wasn't over until each and every woman was found and fucked. A man could claim as many women as he pleased, but every time one was captured, they had to be brought back to their captor's rooms at the hunting lodge before the hunter could go out for more.

Three, a special prize would be awarded to the man who caught the "Golden Fox", the woman deemed the most desirable by the vote of the men of the Order.

It was this we were waiting for in the brutal clasp of a darkening Scottish evening.

Master Sherwood was on a platform before his great stone hunting manor in the wild Highlands waiting for his manservant to tally the vote and name the girl.

I knew before he accepted the folded piece of paper that it would me because I was just that unlucky.

Whoever said beauty was a gift had clearly never experienced it for themselves because it was nothing but a prettily wrapped curse.

"Slave Davenport," he announced, and the gathered men let out a collective roar.

They were all sober of drink and drugs but so high on the coming thrill of the chase that the very air around them seemed to shimmer with energy.

A girl beside me with true Scottish colouring, pale freckled skin, and hair the colour of juiced carrots grasped my arm for a moment in empathy before I was ripped away by one of Lord Sherwood's men.

He tossed me over his shoulder, my dress flipping up to reveal my buttocks to the gathering. There was another cheer, this one tinged with dangerous fervour.

The manservant deposited me on the stage beside Lord Sherwood and stepped back.

I kept my gaze down because Alexander had stressed the importance of my submissiveness until the cows came home on the way to this highland retreat.

I saw the edge of Sherwood's shiny leather riding boots stop just inside my scope of sight, and then I felt the heaviness of his hand on my head. Instantly, I folded elegantly into a kneel, a human origami shaped just to his liking.

"My brothers, I give you the Golden Fox," he announced

boldly as he placed a cornet on my head I knew was made of golden thorns and ruby flowers.

It was ludicrously expensive, far more valuable to the Order than the woman wearing it. There was deliberate irony in the gesture that set my teeth on edge.

Women were nothing to these men.

They had been practicing The Hunt since they stole the idea from the Spanish Civil War practice during the White Terror, when wealthy landowners would hunt down and murder peasantry.

They wouldn't spill our blood today, unless it was between our thighs, but it was still unspeakably horrible.

I could only hope Alexander would be the one to find and capture me.

He would hurt me, but only to tame my wild spirit and bring me a calm I'd never before been free to experience.

I didn't want to think about what the others would do to me.

After the trauma of my previous experience with the Order, I didn't hold much hope that my mind would emerge unscathed if another Master claimed me.

A shiver rippled through me like a ghost as I thought of Landon and his cruel black snake whip. My back was barely healed from the ordeal, thin pink ribbons of sadism still bifurcated my flesh and twanged with pain when I moved the wrong way.

It had been two weeks since the Order of Dionysus swept into Pearl Hall and fundamentally changed the way of my world there.

Two weeks since Alexander had taken a beating for me.

Two weeks since he'd last touched me.

In fact, after the events of that horrible night, I'd barely seen him to speak to him, let alone continue my valet duties of dressing and bathing him, or my sexual duties of taking his cock whenever it suited him.

He gave me nothing but a cruel amount of space and time.

It was Mrs. White who tended to my split and scabbing back, Douglas who delivered my food, and surprise of all surprises, Riddick, who was also trained as a doctor, who sat by my bedside to check me for infection and rewrap my wounds.

Christmas had come and gone, and with it, New Year's Eve. Douglas invited me to the servant's dinner, but I didn't want them to feel strained, so I only had a dinner of turkey on a plate in my room. I'd been given licence to call my family, and I'd cried when I spoke to Sebastian, who had successfully moved to London, and Giselle, who seemed meek as ever but artistically thriving in Paris. Mama had made me laugh as she recounted neighborhood gossip and Elena had listened quietly, attentively as I told her my made-up stories of modelling gigs in Milano and London.

I was homesick and lonely without any true company.

No Alexander.

No Noel either, though I wasn't so sure that was a bad thing after his behaviour the night of the flogging. I hadn't looked too closely at his motivation for being kind to me previously because I'd been so starved for affection, so used to my prior life where a person was kind without needing a reason to be.

I was different now.

I knew the truth of the world.

No one did anything for anyone unless it benefited their agenda.

I didn't know what motivated Noel besides his obvious hatred of all things Amedeo Salvatore, but I knew he was playing me across a board I couldn't see, ready to sacrifice me like one of the pawns he had taught me so much about.

I lifted my chin as Sherwood bade me to rise and rejoin the other girls. My eyes snared on Alexander's broad frame, seated on a huge white horse that suited his rider's size and ferocity. My Master's eyes were on me and inside me, his jaw clenched as he tried to pry my thoughts out of my head across the space between us.

He'd been giving me that look a lot since the ordeal, whenever I caught him leaving early or returning late to the house.

I think he expected me to hate him.

I didn't.

But I did feel hurt that he had stripped away our rituals together after everything we'd gone through that night.

I was lonely. I missed eating dinner at his feet from his hands, washing his dense muscles and acres of gorgeous pale gold skin before dressing it well, buttoning him up like a present for myself that I knew I would unwrap later.

It was all gone, and it made my slavery feel worse, hollow and cracked like a broken tool.

The five-hour drive from Pearl Hall, which I'd learned was in England's Peak District, to Glencoe, Scotland, was the first time I had spent any real time with him.

Yet Alexander made me sit in the front with Riddick while he closed himself behind a soundproof partition in the back seat and worked. It was only after we'd arrived, and I was getting out of the car that he'd stopped me with a strong hand on my arm and whispered a few words of wisdom in my ear, including the rules of The Hunt. Before I could reply, he'd turned on his heel and marched inside the stone home, yelling a greeting to someone inside.

A servant began to drag me off the stage, and I shivered as a particularly icy gust of wind raised the hem of my shift. Alexander's jaw clenched with irritation before he wrenched his gaze away to a man who sat on horseback beside him.

"First time?" the girl with orange hair asked me as I rejoined the others in the corral.

I nodded, wrapping my thin arms around my torso for warmth.

"It's my third," she told me, lifting her chin so that I could look into her dead brown eyes. "I have a good hiding place; do you want to stick with me?"

"Gentlemen," Sherwood boomed. "Welcome to the 76th annual Hunt!"

There was a cacophony of shouts and hollers before a servant in red on horseback raised a horn to his lips and blew.

The trumpet echoed through the small clearing and stirred the dark trees at the edge of the forest.

"What happens now?" I asked the ginger-haired girl.

"Run."

The doors to the corral were thrust open, and a stampede of terrified women flooded out, nearly pushing me to the ground in their haste. I heard the muffled cry of someone fall behind me and then the crack of breaking bone, but I didn't turn around.

I ran.

Away from the barking hounds and agitated horses. Away from the predatory men who would spend the entire night chasing us down, one by one.

I ran and a small part of my brain wondered if I could run fast enough and long enough, then maybe I could run away from it all forever.

It was dark as tar and just as sticky, tendrils of night black low-hanging branches from trees ripped across my arms and face. I tasted blood on my lips, the metallic heat of bile at the back of my tongue as my lungs labored like overworked billows to keep my arms pumping and my legs churning. Running. My mind would waste my body away to nothing just to keep on running.

The lord had finally let me out of the manor, but my liberation was a trap I should have known better to have taken.

Why does any master let the fox out of its cage?

To hunt it down...

And I was being hunted, ruthlessly and ceaselessly through the late hours of the night by more than just my Master. I'd already dodged one man's hands as he'd ridden close by on his horse and kicked another in the teeth so hard I felt them break under my toes.

I'd been running through the dense cover of frost-coated pines for hours. My feet were ripped to bloody shreds by roots and rocks, so bloody and slimy from brackish puddles that I fell more often than I could afford to, cutting up my hands and my face.

Acid burned through my tired muscles, pulsing in time with my cantering heart until I felt I would burst apart at the seams any minute and die.

Still, I didn't stop.

I'd seen four girls taken by riders in the mist, heard their blood-curdling screams as they were raped against trees, taken in the mud, or flung like carcases over the saddle.

I didn't want to be them.

In a way, I was lucky because Alexander had been teaching me self-defence and given me free rein to use the gym, which I did nearly every day. My previously thin body ripe with soft curves now had lean lines of muscle running through it, muscles I was using to race and dodge through the thicket of trees as agilely as the fox I was named after.

The howl of hounds pierced the thick night air to my left. I went careening in the opposite direction, my feet tramping loudly over debris, my breath like gunshots in the silence as I burst into a small clearing.

"There you fucking are," a man crowed from the inky dark immediately in front and to the right of me.

I spun in the opposite direction and cried out as two strong arms banded around my hips. The man lifted me into the air as I kicked and screamed, my fingernails scratching at his arms until they bled.

"There you fucking well are," the first man crowed in delight as he appeared in front of me, highlighted silver in the moonlight.

It was Ashcroft, the same man who'd used my mouth in Pearl Hall.

My scream doubled over, exploding through my lungs like a train speeding off the rails.

"Shut your fucking mouth," the man holding me ordered as he fell into me, pushing us both to the ground.

I choked on the mulch, the earthy soil filling my mouth as I sucked in another lungful of air to scream.

The stranger wrapped his arms and legs around mine and flipped over like a beetle so that I was strapped down on top of him.

"Take her already," he jeered in my ear as Ashcroft undid his trousers.

"Should've shagged you when I had the chance."

"You take me, Alexander will find you and *murder you!*" I screamed.

God, was there ever any end to this madness? Was I to be ordered around, assaulted, and manipulated until my dying breath?

Ashcroft bent over to ruck up my muddy shift, and I spat in his eye.

"You fucking little bitch," he roared, going to one knee and roughly pulling out his cock.

There was a flash of movement in the dark behind him and then a bass thud. Ashcroft trembled slightly and then fell to the side, out cold.

"What the—" the man grunted as two hands reached out of the dark and wrapped tight around his neck.

I could feel the fight go out of him, his limbs loosening around mine until they fell off. Adrenaline flooded through me, and I shot to my feet before the other man could grab me.

"Cosima," a steady voice said into the wind.

The sound of my name warmed me like a velvet cloak.

I paused, tense and ready to spring forth.

"Cosima, settle, *tesoro*, I just want a word with you."

I recognized the skipping lilt of his muddled accent, the crisp cut of an upper crust English accent made lyrical by the sounds of my homeland.

"Edward."

There was a pause, then the soft, sucking tread of boots through the muck. I spun to face him with my hands raised and my legs bent, the muscles shaking with exhaustion.

His hard-cut face, so like Alexander's but darker and carved a tad more crudely, went soft as he looked at me.

"You look knackered."

I realized my breath was coming too fast, wheezing in and out of lungs like a billow. "What do you care?"

"I care very much." He raised his hands out to the sides, palms up in surrender. "You don't know me, but I care very much indeed."

"I don't believe you," I said wildly, my eyes searching for an exit as he moved closer. "Stay away, Edward!"

"*Pace*, Cosima," he murmured. "And please, I don't go by that name anymore. I haven't in a long while, and if I had it my way, I wouldn't again during my lifetime. My name is Dante."

My laugh burned through my ravaged throat. "Which circle of Hell is this, then?"

"The very worst," he agreed, pausing just out of arm's reach. "I'm so sorry you have to go through this. Your father is sorry too."

I blinked.

"If he could see you now," he murmured as his eyes tracked every cut, scrap and bruise painted and punched into my body. "He would cry. And Salvatore is not a man prone to tears."

"Who the fuck are you? What are you trying to do?"

"I'm trying to tell you that I am a friend. I'm sorry this had to happen to you, but—"

"None of this had to happen," I shouted, spittle flying through the air.

I felt rabid, a dog too long without food in a place too cold to bear it.

"None of this had to happen," I sobbed angrily, dashing at the blood, tears, and mud on my face. "If you are a friend of Salvatore as you say, tell my *papa puttaniere* to go fuck himself! None of this had to happen, and none of it would have happened if he'd stepped up once in all my life."

There was a rustle in the bushes, and the heavy rush of breath through the nose of a beast. Seconds later, a horse burst out of the trees into the clearing.

"*Minchia*," Edward Dante swore, swivelling to face the man. "Fucking *run*, Cosima."

I turned and ran, the sounds of hooves beating into the ground behind me like the drum of a funeral song.

There was a shout, and a huge splash behind me.

I took a moment to look over my shoulder and see Dante straddling the hunter in the shallows of a stream, beating his huge hand again and again into the dethroned rider's face. The horse stomped and whinnied restlessly, pawing at the air.

"Cosima, *run!*" Dante yelled as another rider appeared in the clearing.

I faced forward again and raced as fast as my legs could take me back into the densely woven trees.

The second rider wasn't deterred; he took the horse leaping over fallen logs, swerving around tight corners until I could feel the breath of the beast at my back and the vibration of its steps on the forest floor.

I was so tired, and I was going to lose.

Hands twisted in the back of my hair, then wrenched so hard, I flew into the air and went sailing over the pummel of the saddle.

A slap rained down against my rump as the rider howled into the night. "Right where you belong again."

I shivered at the sound of Landon's voice and wriggled enough to roll over, landing a kick to his shoulder that had the reins falling from his hands. The horse bucked slightly and sent us both falling hard to the root gnarled earth below.

The breath left my body as my head hit the base of a tree and pain exploded in white shards across my vision.

A hand grabbed my ankle and dragged me across the mud. I flipped onto my belly, scrambling with my hands to find purchase in the soft soil.

And I screamed.

I screamed and screamed like a symphony of terrors as Landon used his hand to pull me under him and rip my dress straight down the middle of my spine. He hissed with pleasure at the sight of his pink whip marks on my skin. I struggled, bucking and twisting against him as he took each mark between his teeth and bit down, tasting the symbols of pain he'd branded me with.

A stick was in my reach, the sharp, the pale end of it gleaming dimly in the mist-shrouded, moonlight murk. With an almighty shove, I reached forward enough to grasp it in my hand and then twisted my torso with a warrior's shout.

Then I slammed the branch into the nearest bit of flesh I could find.

It impaled Landon in the cheek.

He roared as he reeled off me and onto his knees, his hands clambering at the blood wet stem, desperate to remove it.

A high-pitched screech rent the air in two, and with a great flurry of black wings, a bird descended from the sky and reached his dagger-like talon for Landon's prone face.

I scrambled backward as Landon shouted in agony and tried to bat the falcon away. Frantically, I tried to look for a way to get around him easily and back into the night woods.

Only, there was a shifting of the darkness in the trees behind Landon, a parting of night as if Hades himself was breaching the veil from the underworld.

And then there was Alexander, walking calmly, silent as a spirit across the leaf laden turf.

There was a glint of something in his hand, something red flashed in his hand, silver at the bottom.

A ruby hilted knife.

I gasped, but Landon didn't hear me as the bird of prey finally unlatched with a sickening wet slide and took off into the night again. Free from his tormentor, Landon finally pried the stick out of his cheek with a moist *pop* and spat bloody saliva on the ground.

"You little whore, I am going to hurt you until you sing like a fucking bird," he promised me.

Alexander dropped to his knees behind him, so much taller that he loomed over the other man even like that. The knife went to his throat smoothly, his other hand hard in Landon's hair as he tugged his scalp back and jutted his neck into the blade.

"I am the only one that hurts her," Alexander stated as his falcon let out an almighty screech of primal victory from somewhere above us.

And then he slit his throat.

I watched like a camera lens devoid of bias as blood, black in the darkness, spilled like a silken shroud over Landon's front. He twitched as Alexander held him, and then moments later, his eyes rolled up then closed, and he was dead.

Alexander stood, hefted the body in his arms, and walked some ways away into the black until I heard a heavy splash that had to have been Landon's body sinking in the stream. My ears strained for the sounds of his boots in the mud, and I felt such an immense sense of relief when he returned, I almost dissolved into sobs. I looked at my muddy, torn up knees, my naked torso riddled with scratches, and tried to compose myself.

"Look at me, Cosima," he ordered in that hushed, Dominant voice I couldn't disobey.

A shiver wracked through me because I hadn't listened to those delicious, dulcet tones in weeks.

His eyes glowed brighter than the moonlit fragments filtering through the trees. I swallowed thickly at the way they owned me, the way *he* owned me even with one look, even five feet away.

"You're okay," he told me. "Hush, *bella*, I'm with you."

I realized I had been making a keening sound like a lost kitten and the moment he told me to *hush*, I stopped.

"You shouldn't have killed him," I said hoarsely. "You'll get in trouble again."

And then what would I do?

What would I do if I had to go to a new, crueler Master?

What would I do without *him*?

The moon disappeared behind a cloud, and Alexander's eyes

went dark.

"People die in The Hunt each year. We don't even look for the ones who don't return. We just cover up their deaths as if nothing's amiss. No one is taking you from me."

"*Grazie a Dio*," I whispered, thanking God.

I wanted to ask him to hold me because I was cold, and hurt, and defenceless, in need of comfort. But also, because he hadn't touched me in so long that I wore my ache for his touch like weights between my legs.

I couldn't put that into words. I didn't want to and given my current mental state, I couldn't even try.

But I reached a hand out into the blackness and I felt Alexander lean in to it from where he kneeled.

His stubble roughened jaw fit into my palm like a puzzle piece and something deep within me that only he could reach, clicked on.

I lunged for his mouth, my lips hitting his awkwardly, mostly on his chin, my tongue in the slight cleft there.

He held still, surprised.

I dragged myself forward with my hands at his neck and wrapped myself around him, moving my mouth to the strong pulse in his neck because it steadied me.

"Safe," I whispered to myself to soothe the wild terror still gnawing at the back of my mind.

"Safe," he echoed, his strong arms finally going around me in a tight cinch.

It was strange magic, a hug, especially a hug from that man.

It settled the demons at war inside me, sung them a lullaby and put them to bed. So when Alexander finally stroked his hand over my head and tangled it into the back of my hair to angle my face for his kiss, I was ready for it.

His plush mouth ate at mine as if we had all the time in the world, nibbling my lips with his teeth, rubbing his sinuous tongue against mine, and breathing his sweet mint breath against my cheek.

He seduced me with that kiss into trusting him and needing him. A low fire stoked in my center and flooded my chilled body with delicious heat.

"You're mine," he said against my lips, nipping them between his words until they felt tender as bruised petals. "You're mine to protect and comfort just as much as you are mine to play with and use. Say it, Cosima."

"I'm yours, Master," I whispered into his open mouth, planting my words like a decadent chocolate to melt on his tongue.

He savoured it, licking his lips as his eyes darkened. "Good, little mouse. Now, I won this pussy fair and square. Lie back and show me my prize."

Then the hand in my hair pulled tighter, manipulating my desire like a puppeteer with string. My need flared higher, and I whimpered into his mouth as his kiss turned cruel.

He pushed me down into the mud, but he didn't have to, my legs were already spread, the cold winter air biting into the honeyed folds of my sex. I wanted him to see me, to watch his eyes burn as his fingers trailed in the wetness, smearing my arousal across my entire pussy and inner thighs like some heathen worshipper.

My mouth watered as he shoved his riding pants down enough to free his thick cock and then as he fisted it roughly in his big hand. His face was savage in the dark and with desire as he planted a hand near my face and used the other to notch his dick at my entrance.

"You can scream all you'd like, *bella*, no one will come to your rescue," he promised, and then he plunged straight to the end of my cunt.

I screamed, but this time it braided the edges of my torn lungs smooth and felt like honey coating my throat.

I screamed as he rutted into me in the middle of a wintry Scottish night, our combined heat melting the frost on the pine needles overhead so that they dripped over our bodies like a cleansing rain.

I screamed as he bent his head to take my nipples in his teeth, the pain cracking like a nut between his molars into divine pleasure, and I screamed even harder as he used the hand at my sex to slide another finger into my cunt beside his cock, and I became stuffed, deliciously overfull.

I did not scream as I came like a flood over his dick and thighs, as everything inside me that was not beautiful and pure expunged from me in exodus.

Instead, I breathed his name on a sigh and let my terrorized mind find comfort in his discipline over my body.

Dimly, I was aware of the hot splash of his cum inside me as he climaxed, holding me close and tight so that I could feel the sharp tension of his arousal jerk then fall lax with satisfaction.

And then, I think, I passed out.

When I opened my eyes again, it was because Alexander was lifting me atop his horse. I blinked slowly when he didn't mount it himself, instead turning to walk into the near distance.

I blinked again when I saw something hanging there from a tree.

It was the orange flash that caught my eye and pulled my submerged mind into the clear.

I recognized the colour of that hair from the corral, from the poor girl who had offered to share her hiding place with me.

She hung from a tree by the torn and knotted together length of her shift dress, her milk white body glazed in moonlight and speckled with mud as it swung in the cold wind.

There was blood blackening the inside of her thighs, and I had no doubt she'd been used and thrown aside for the third time in as many Hunts.

The third strike had proven too much for the girl with the dead eyes, and she'd succumbed to her demons by taking her own life.

My heart twisted up, bloody and used like an old tissue as I watched Alexander cut her down from the tree and gently lay her to rest under an old rowan tree. He smoothed by that carroty hair, crossed her arms over her chest and then bent his head over her prone form in silent prayer.

"They're worse than beasts," I murmured through the fog of my exhaustion when Alexander swung up behind me on the horse. "Because they know better, and they still act this way."

"Yes," Alexander agreed, wrapping me up tight and taking the reins as we began to navigate through the forest.

Random shouts still echoed through the dark, but less now since most of the girls already had been captured hours earlier. I knew Astor was scouting ahead and would probably alert Alexander to any incoming hunters, so I allowed myself to relax slightly against his warm body.

"Why do you do this with them?" I asked.

I had to know; my heart was turning into two, one dark and one light, one-part Alexander's and one-part mine. I needed to know the intricacies of his atrocities before I could allow myself to sink deeper into the darkness.

"I told you, I was born into this and raised by their rules. It should be rote for me to be one of the Order's disciples just as so many other things in my life are my born obligations."

"Should be," I tested as I tucked my head under his chin and pulled the jacket he had placed at some point over my shoulder, closer around me. "But isn't."

"I thought for years I was destined to be my father's son, and I hated the idea of it. Then my mum died, and the man I'd always been unsure how to love when I hated his actions became the only person left in my family. It made the burden of being my father's son and heir even harder to untangle myself from."

"Maybe family isn't everything," I murmured, unaware of how my words could have applied to myself as I sank deeper into my exhaustion and began to fall asleep. "Maybe it isn't enough to make decisions based on them. After all, you have to live for yourself."

Chapter Eighteen

$\mathcal{I}$t was strange to return home to a place I had never seen from the outside but knew intimately from the interior. I'd spent so many of my early days at Pearl Hall wandering the halls aimlessly, my only distractions the many eccentricities of the architecture and design. I knew my reflection from the many angles of in the Mirror Gallery built by one of Prince Regent's many mistresses, the widowed daughter of the 6th Duke of Greythorn. The faces in the Long Gallery that reached from one end to the other of the second floor were more familiar to me than those of my long-ago friends in Napoli.

It was like falling in love with a man you'd never seen the face of even though you knew all his inner workings, how he ticked and the sound of tock and why he gave pause when he did.

We crested a hill on a little road carved out between thick trees of pine and cedar, rowan and ash and then a gatehouse appeared.

"Welcome to Pearl Hall," Alexander said from beside me, watching me take in my first sight of the estate.

The gatehouse was long and tall, more like a fortress wall with an archway carved out of the stone for us to pass through to the other side. I wanted to ask if it was manned, but I could see the security cameras winking in the low light and the man who waved to us as we passed through before he turned to close the massive iron gates.

"We get a lot of tourists fancying a tour of the grounds," Alexander explained. "As you know, this is a private estate, and it would be... dangerous for outsiders to wander about."

"Hmm," I said, biting back my smile. "Because of the herd of wild deer?"

"Those... and other predators," he responded drolly.

I didn't bother to hide my giggle, and when I shot him a side-long glance, he was staring at me in the way he had that wasn't a quite smile but somehow more intimate.

"You continually confound me, yet you refuse to explain yourself to me."

I tipped my chin at him and then moved my gaze out the windows again. "I may be a slave, but I am also a woman, and therefore I am under no obligation to make sense to you."

I wanted to talk to him about so many things. About Landon Knox and Edward Dante, about the future of his position in the Order now that he had caught the "Golden Fox" and Sherwood had reluctantly granted him a "boon." I wanted to ask if I'd already been through enough in the first six months of slavery to warrant setting me free before my five-year term was up at the same time that I wanted to ask him to keep me by his side forever.

I didn't, though, because he'd been moody and contemplative on the ride back from the Highlands, and I doubted he would answer my questions honestly.

We drove for another few minutes after that along the winding road until we descended into a valley that unfolded between the broad frame of forested hills to reveal the entire expanse of Pearl Hall.

It was breathtakingly lovely, the scope so large it seemed impossible that so many wonderful acres of land could belong to one family.

There was a temple on a small hill, a large pond that stretched in manmade perfection from one end of the grand house to the other beyond the studied maze in the back garden. A large fountain made of black marble burst from the center of the circular drive before the house, a chariot half submerged in the water with the great Greek god Poseidon at its helm.

The Davenports had a thing for Roman and Greek mythology, which wasn't surprising given their history, secret society connections, and predilection toward sexual assault.

It was the house itself, though, that brought tears to my eyes.

The three-story structure was a study in symmetry even though Noel had told me once it was a hodgepodge of Palladian and Baroque architecture. The roof was steeply gabled over the main house with a decorative and fantastical dome behind that like something I was used to seeing on Italian cathedrals.

A palace.

Every girl dreams of a palace at some point in her life, usually as a child, but I never had.

My dreams had been considerably more pedestrian.

A house without leaks in the wet season, with clean water and more space for four children to grow. I had no care for a father with a crown, just one that didn't drink himself half to death at least once a week or wile away what meager wealth we had over cards and horses.

I had no real dreams for myself, just those of my siblings.

But looking at that beautiful house, for the first time in my life, I felt my own dream take shape.

Deep in the secret recesses of my heart, I dreamt that I might one day be more than just a servant at Pearl Hall and a slave to its Master. I hoped beyond all reasoning that one day, I might be mistress of its halls and mistress of his heart.

It took precarious form and flight, too delicate to survive for long like a child's blown bubble, but that didn't make it any less beautiful to me.

The car pulled to a rolling stop in the limestone gravel drive, but I waited for Riddick to open the door for me before I alighted from the vehicle.

Servants were waiting in a neat row beside the front doors, Ainsworth at the head all the way through to a meek, young lad I recognized from watching him lay the fire in the library at night. They greeted their Master and he them in return; his face stern but not unfeeling.

I watched the pomp and circumstance with my arms wrapped around my belly. I still felt wrong in my skin after the Order had usurped our lives, and I didn't know how to center myself properly. Although I had a sinking suspicion that a scene with my Master would probably do the trick like nothing else could.

Riddick stopped a young manservant from taking the blacked-out cage where Astor was housed by gently slapping his wrist as he walked into the house with him. As the servants broke formation to grab our bags from the car and hurry back into the house, Alexander strode over to me. I watched as his thick thighs worked beneath the butter soft fabric of his trousers and how the dark grey dress shirt pulled just right over his pecs.

My pulse moved into my core.

When I looked back up at his face, his eyes danced with dark, sultry desire. He held out a hand and waited patiently for me to hesitate and then take it before he moved us away from the house around the side of the building.

"I have a present for you," he said. "Something beautiful and fierce enough to suit you and your bravery this weekend."

"I don't need a present," I told him honestly. "Other than the ability to talk to my family more frequently and... and you back in my life again."

His hand spasmed in mine as he led us down a beautifully landscaped path toward an outbuilding that looked distinctly like the stables.

"I'll have Riddick get you a phone with international texting. It will be monitored, so remember that when you converse with your family, but you can text them whenever you wish."

I tugged at his hand to stop him and then went on my tiptoes to press a light kiss to the edge of his jaw.

"Thank you, Xan," I said softly.

There was a growing tenderness around my heart that seemed to bloom just for him. It made me feel uncharacteristically shy and vulnerable even though it felt beautiful flowering in my chest.

He looked slightly stupefied by my voluntarily affection for a second, before his eyes smiled and he shook his head.

We continued up the gently sloping hill in silence. He pulled me through the huge barn doors and into the hay-sweetened air of the stables.

Immediately, the great black head of Alexander's horse, Charon, poked out from his stall so that he could whinny at his master.

Alexander chuckled and moved over to brush a firm hand down the horse's long nose.

"Do you like horses?" he asked me, reaching into a bag to produce a red apple that he fed to the happy beast.

I nodded, lifting my hand tentatively to stroke Charon's velvet snout. "I rode one a few times. A family friend, Christopher, used to take us to the vineyard for holidays, and we could ride the horses there."

Alexander made a clicking sound in his mouth and another head appeared over the stall beside Charon's. I gasped as I moved toward the gorgeous horse with my hands outstretched.

It was entirely gold. From the crown of its gorgeous, wavy mane to the very bottom of its hooves, the horse was a shimmering, pale metallic gold.

"She is the very same shade as your eyes are in the sunlight," Alexander explained. "She's a Golden Akhal Teke, a very rare breed from Turkmenistan."

"She looks like living sunlight," I told him as I stroked her nose. "I've never seen a creature so beautiful."

"Suitable then, that she's yours."

I blinked into the horse's golden eyes and then into Alexander's silver ones. "Excuse me?"

He shrugged one shoulder as if it was no small thing to buy me a rare and probably insanely expensive gift. A gift that would go on living well past the time I was determined to spend at Pearl Hall.

"You've been through a lot in the past few weeks. I wanted to bring you some joy again."

My heart clenched like a cramp, painful and so long I thought I might die.

"Why would you care about my joy?" I ventured quietly.

Alexander leaned against the wood wall and watched me from under low lids as I pet his horse. "Do you know why I call you *topolina*? Because you are a little mouse with no defence against me. I may experiment on you, hunt you down and feast on you or feed you to other beasts as easily as I please." I shuddered at his words and shot him an unhappy glare that made his lips twitch. "But there are a few fables where the little mouse turns out to be very clever indeed and dupes the cat or the elephant or the falcon into falling for their own tricks. You, my little mouse, are playing this game of ours so well, I'm not quite sure who is winning any longer."

I licked my dry lips and shrugged as I leaned in to smell my horse's warm, clean pelt. "I've learned that it's wise not to be taken in by the innocent airs of someone who has previously proven themselves to be dangerous."

Alexander's grin was wicked. "Smart girl."

"Not really," I whispered to my golden beauty, as if it was the horse I was giving my secret to.

"I have no skills," I admitted, and it felt as if the words were torn from the delicate fabric of my soul.

It was my biggest weakness and shame.

I was nothing but my packaging, pretty paper wrapped tidily around an empty box.

There was no reason to expose myself further to Alexander's absolute power over me, yet I felt an overwhelming need to.

It could have been a testament to his conditioning of me, but I thought it was something else.

I'd never met a man so like a maze. Around every corner lurked another shock, some horrific dangerous beast of a kind I could never begin to understand, but others softer, fair like summer Fae. Even his beautiful creatures were hazardous to my health, the seducers and destroyers working in tandem to eviscerate me to my very soul.

Alexander's heat pressed against my side a moment before he turned me into his arms and lifted my chin with his fingers. "Have I not given you some?"

I snorted. "Fine, I guess I'm a seasoned cocksucker now."

His frown was fierce. "I don't like that crude, filth from your lips. Yes, you please me in all the ways a woman can please a man, but I think you'll find, if you really look, you've learned other skills. Riddick says you nearly beat him at foils last week, you've learned how to play chess, some cookery from Douglas and some needlework from Mrs. White. You know self-defence, and you speak English now as beautifully as you do your mother tongue."

He dipped down to run his nose along the length of mine. "These are not the qualities of a stupid, talentless girl. These are the attributes of a queen who was made to think she was only a pawn."

My heart beat slow and hard in my chest, knocking against my ribs as if waiting for Alexander to answer the door and claim it for himself. A lifetime of insecurity had been neatly squashed under Alexander's expensive heel as if it were a mere cockroach. I felt the death of that shame in my psyche and sighed as its spirit drifted away.

"You know, *topolina*, I am very tempted to keep you here with me forever," he continued.

Sometimes I wondered if he was a telepath or if there was something symbiotic about our Master/slave relationship that gave him privileged access to my thoughts.

Hadn't I just been wishing for the very same thing?

"I know that won't be possible for a myriad of reasons, but I want to make sure that you will always remember you belong to me. You will remember when I am absent, and you will feel the loss of me in your cunt, mind, and chest. You will feel the phantom press of my hand against your throat like a necklace you can't take off. And, my beauty, you will wear the symbol of my bloodline on your skin for anyone who might dare get you naked to see as they bend you over to fuck you."

"What are you talking about?" I asked before Alexander's hands on me turned to shackles and he tugged me to the end of the stables where a brick hearth sat well away from the hay filled stalls, crackling with a small fire. Something roasted in those flames, an iron pole submerged in the depths.

Fear flooded through me, turning me on even though I was terrified because my conditioning had taught me that fear at the hands of Alexander could also bring pleasure.

He pushed me up against the bricks, placing my hands on either side of my head for me to lean into and then pulling out my hips, kicking my feet apart so I was displayed exactly to his liking. I shivered as he placed kisses and gentle bites to my neck while his deft fingers undid my wrap dress and let it fall to the ground beneath me. I kicked it to the side, which earned me a pleased hum and his tongue tracing the rim on my ear.

His rough hands moved over each cheek of my bare ass, pulling them apart and kneading them like dough.

"Such a sweet arse," he praised. "Tip it higher for me."

I canted my buttocks at a steeper angle for him and was rewarded with his finger tracing down my crack into the wet seeping from my pussy.

"You love being displayed for me like this," he confirmed, dipping one finger and then another just inside me so I could feel the teasing stretch.

My hips thrust back, seeking friction. He laughed cruelly and stepped to the side so that I could watch him slowly unbuckle his belt.

He watched my eyes flare and stopped. "I was going to take a crop to you, but it looks like my beauty is craving something a little harsher."

I squirmed against the wall, my lips parting as cool air kissed my swollen folds.

"Answer me." His voice whipped across the space and landed on my skin like an electric shock.

"Yes, Master. I want something harsher."

"I love to hear that lush mouth form the word *Master*," he admitted with a sexy groan. "Now,

"I'm going to give you fifteen lashes with my belt until your skin blooms redder than a rose, and then I'm going to fuck you against the wall like the beast you claim me to be," he told me in his silky, soft voice, his word binding me to his will. "Would you like that, *topolina?*"

He was hot in the way of nuclear blasts and raging wildfires that tore up the earth and razed it down to nothing. He was hot in a way that was elemental and truly, painfully dangerous to human health.

I decided then and there, as he looped his leather belt between his hands and snapped it taut in preparation, that I wouldn't mind a little heat.

"Yes, Master," I said as he stepped behind me with his hand raised.

The crack of the leather met my skin like a hot kiss in the next instant. My hips bucked forward trying to escape the pain as it tunneled from my skin into the muscles and through to my aching pussy.

"You move again, and I will still fuck you, but I won't let you come," he warned.

I gritted my teeth and presented my ass.

The next blow landed, and I hissed through my teeth at the strength of the swing. The belt was different from anything else I'd taken before. It carved a wide path of heat that flamed hotter the longer it settled into my skin.

As he continued spank me, my mind grew heavy and dark, melting into a place where there was no noise or chaos, no troubles or terrors, just pure velvety blackness and bright colour wheels of bliss each time a blow landed.

Unconsciously, my hips punched back toward each blow, inviting the pain because my body was well acquainted with how to twist it into mind-numbing pleasure.

I whimpered when I heard the belt drop, not because I was in pain but because I was greedy for more stimuli.

I felt like a faulty outlet, leaking electricity everywhere, desperate to be filled so that the currents would stop ravaging me.

Alexander knew just what I needed, but he didn't give it to me.

Instead, he teased his plump cock head at the slick entrance to my cunt.

"I can feel you drenching my dick," he said as he teased me, nudging against me and then sliding away. "Close your legs." I did, and he groaned as I trapped him between my sticky thighs. "I could fuck you just like this and come all over your belly. Would you like that?"

"No," I panted as he began to fuck through my wet thighs, the hot tip of his erection bumping with each thrust against my throbbing clit. "No, fuck me."

His hot breath wafted over my sweat dampened neck as he pressed into me and me into the wall. I gasped when the breadth of the hearth scraped over my sensitive nipples.

"Tell me exactly what you want, and I might just give it to you."

I moaned as he wrapped one hand over my hips and began to flick my clit piercing into my aching flesh. My legs began to shake, an orgasm on the horizon that I knew would raze me like a tsunami to the very ground.

"Please, Master, give me your hard cock and fuck me until I can't take it anymore," I begged.

"Good, *topolina*," Alexander said on a groan, and then he tipped his hips and sank his entire thick length deep inside me.

Alexander wrapped a hand around my throat to keep me steady and bucked up into me like the wild animal I knew lived at the heart of his civilized veneer.

Instantly, I came.

My entire body shook with the force of the orgasm, rattled

my teeth and my bones, jarring my thoughts inside my head until only two words remained.

I'm his.

"Mine," he seemed to echo as he planted himself at the end of me and let my fiercely clenching walls milk him dry.

I slumped against the wall, reeling from the way he could break me apart and put me back together better than I was before every time he touched me. I wondered idly if I'd been trained to respond to pain and control this way because of my conditioning or if it had always been in me to give, a dark seed at the heart of me that only had to be sown by the right hand in order to bear fruit.

Alexander was still inside me, but I felt him bend over close to the fire. I tried to turn my head to see what he was doing, but his hand went up to press my cheek gently against the wall, im-mobilising me.

"What are you—?" I screamed as something white hot kissed the bottom edge of my left ass cheek, searing so deeply into my almost sensitive nerves, white and black stars popped through my vision.

Alexander held me still with a firm hand and his hips for a long moment before taking the god-awful pain away.

Tears ran down my cheeks and into his fingers as he finally turned me to face him and cupped my face. I tried to move my hand back to touch the burning pain lodge on my butt, only he caught my hands and brought them between us so he could kiss each knuckle.

"What did you do?" I hiccoughed.

His dark blond brows knitted tightly over the cold burn of steel in his eyes. They branded into my gaze just as something had irrevocably been branded into my ass.

"I marked you with my coat of arms," he said, kissing then

biting my knuckles in a gentle, rhythmic way that lulled me like a hand over a kitten's back. "Now, no matter where you go or how far you get from me in this life, now or after our five years are up, everyone will know who you belong to."

I sniffed. "The Davenport family?"

"No," he snarled softly, biting hard into the fleshy pad of my thumb and then sucking it into his mouth. "You will only ever belong to me."

Chapter Nineteen

"You are an extension of myself tonight, my beauty, therefore I expect you to be a paradigm of submission and sensual power. Is that understood?"

I nodded from where I knelt on the floor, my hands behind my back and my head tipped down so that my face was curtained by my silken hair.

Alexander stood over me, having come into the room after readying himself in the bathroom of his London home in Mayfair. I'd been given instructions to bathe, dress in the complicated leather straps laid out for me, and then kneel for my Master to inspect me.

He was doing so now, circling me, taking in the way the lines of the harness curved around my hips, accentuated the shape of my large breasts and cut pleasingly into the underside of my plump ass. My hair was down, brushed out like a slick cloak of pure night around my shoulders and over my back, and my make-up was just as dramatic, highlighting the bright gold of my eyes and the exact shape of my full mouth.

I'd stared at myself in the mirror as I got ready, and I'd grown damp between my thighs. I looked like sex. Not something cheap and tawdry you could pick up on a street corner, but something classy and expensive as a down payment on a house.

It should have made me feel hollow the way my beauty often made me feel, but that night, barely dressed in something chosen for me by my Master, I felt like a goddess.

"You rival even Aphrodite's beauty tonight," Alexander told me, as usual on the same page in the dark novel of our life. "You put her to shame with your combination of purity and sin."

"Persephone then, Master," I offered as I stared at the high shine of his shoe and fought the urge to kiss it.

I was desperate for his touch and satisfaction. There was something about being dressed that way, trussed up for sex, that made me want to seduce him with every single one of my female wiles, my mouth and my hands, my cunt and my ass, my words and my sass.

I wanted to gorge myself on his beauty and his cum.

He stroked his hand down my head and back. "You're trembling. Do you want me very badly, my beauty?"

I licked my dry lips before I could respond. "Yes, Master, very badly."

"If I gave you permission to get off against the table leg, do you think you could?" he mused.

I eyed the bulbous curve of the table leg and nodded. "If I could also suck your cock at the same time."

His chuckle was a dark thread weaving my arousal tighter and tighter inside me. "Don't tempt me to keep you at home tonight. We have a mission."

We did.

I had to shake my head to clear the fog of arousal shrouding my rationality, but then I remembered all too clearly that there was a purpose to being in London.

We were going to Club Dionysus, the Order's exhibition space in London where slaves were taken to be presented like a debutante at court and displayed frequently by seasoned masters just for the fun of it. Alexander had been putting it off because he didn't like the idea of sharing me with the Order after everything that had happened six week ago, but Sherwood had sent a missive sealed in red wax and stamped with the official insignia. It had mentioned the disappearance of Landon Knox.

Alexander assured me it wasn't about the crime, that people died during The Hunt all the time and no one was ever turned in for murder. But we both agreed that there was something going on with the Order, something that pertained directly to him.

He hoped that he could uncover some things at the club when the brothers were deep in their cups and distracted by out-rageous displays of Domination and submission.

He tipped my chin up so I could look him in the eyes now, and he searched my face for any signs that I might be frightened of the night to come.

I was but not terribly.

Anyone who had witnessed the depravities and obscene violence of the Order would be wary of returning to their fold.

But I had Alexander, and he had proven more than once that he wouldn't let anything happen to me.

"If she wasn't a virgin goddess, I would suggest Athena," he said softly, rubbing his thumb over my lower lip. "Beautiful, intelligent and brave."

I sucked in a breath and flicked my tongue out to taste his thumb. He pulled away and straightened, buttoning the middle clasp of his black suit jacket and then offering me his hand to help me up.

I stumbled when he pulled me up too fast so that I went bending over the settee behind him.

"Stay down," he ordered when I went to right myself.

I shivered as his hand trailed down the edge of the strap covering my spine all the way to the place the leather held my ass cheeks up and apart. There was a snap of a bottle opening and then cool liquid pouring over my asshole and pussy.

"You're going to wear something for me tonight, *bella*, so that you are always aware of me."

His fingers circled my pussy, dipping in and out like it was a pot of ink as I grew wet beneath his touch. He dragged the sticky arousal over my lube damped asshole and rubbed his thumb over the tightly crinkled bud.

"We will have to perform a scene tonight as it's our first night in the club," he reminded me of something I already knew. "I've decided that I'm going to show everyone how quickly you enter subspace during a flogging and then I'm going to take your ass for the first time in front of an audience." I groaned long and low as his thumb slid into my ass and pulsed inside me. "Would you like that? For everyone to see how this tiny asshole opens up around my cock."

My hips wiggled as he took his thumb out and replaced it with his index and middle fingers. I panted as he scissored them inside me, stretching me and rubbing against my sensitive walls.

He smacked my ass cheek with his free hand. "Answer me, Cosima. Tonight is not the night to forget yourself."

"Sorry, Master. Yes, I would love that."

And the truth was, I would.

I was an admittedly vain creature, just as any model had to be in order to succeed, and as I thought about a group of men and women watching Alexander use me for his pleasure, lusting and envious of us, my pussy began to leak down my thigh.

His fingers disappeared even though I chased my hips back to keep them inside me. He chuckled at my eagerness and then something cold, smooth and *too big* was at my entrance.

"This is a stainless-steel butt plug capped with a large diamond," he explained factually as he slowly twisted the bulbous knob inside me.

I hissed with pain as it sank past the initial tight ring of muscle and slid inside me. I could feel myself closing around the narrow base, and I knew I would be able to keep it inside me, albeit uncomfortably, while I walked.

"When you kneel by my side in the club, everyone walking by will the see glint of the diamond snug between your sweet arse cheeks and the brand of my family crest on your skin, and they'll wish they owned you."

He patted my bottom and then helped me to stand, holding my arm, and I teetered trying to adjust to the cold, alien weight of it inside me.

"Okay?" he asked.

I nodded, "Yes, Master."

"Good girl," he praised, striding into the bathroom to wash his hands. "Tonight will be fun."

My hand was in Alexander's as I alighted from his Town Car just down the street from the club. I was wearing six-inch spiked black heels so my focus was on the ground as I stepped onto the curb, but something in the air made me pause and look up before I'd even finished moving.

Our eyes connected like two magnets.

He looked utterly, devastatingly beautiful. His obsidian waves were tamed and pushed in a perfect wave to the side of his golden forehead, his tall, leanly muscled frame was encased in an impeccably cut suit that made him look like the movie star I believed he should have been.

I'd seen my brother in many situations and forms of dress

over the years, but I'd never seen him as he was then.

I'd also never seen nor heard of the woman who was on his arm. She was a petite thing but elegant as a swan, the long line of her pale neck accentuated by the gently curled halo of her ashen hair. I could see the clarity of her blue eyes even from ten feet away, wide and bright as a child's crayon as they blinked at Sebastian for coming to an unduly halt.

There was a handsome man too, who wasn't frozen in action beside him like the woman, but who continued half a step and slightly in front of my brother, as if ready to protect him from some potential threat.

That threat, apparently, being me.

Of all the times to run into my brother in London, it was outside a secret society's sex club with the heavy weight of a plug in my ass and my Master at my side.

"Cosima," he said at the very same moment I breathed, "Sebastian."

Alexander tensed beside me and slid an arm around my waist to tuck me further into his side. His Alpha instincts ignited, his nostrils flaring and eyes snapping as Seb and his party unstuck and walked closer.

I tried to move out of the circle of his hold to meet Sebastian halfway as he somewhat woodenly greeted me with our customary three cheek kisses, but Alexander wouldn't budge an inch, so my brother was forced to get intimately close with him.

I could have sworn the man behind Seb growled at their proximity.

"What are you doing here?" we asked each other at the same time, our voices inflected and accented in the very same places.

I laughed airily. "I'm in town for two nights unexpectedly. A drama queen dropped out of a shoot, and I'm filling in."

"Why didn't you call?" he asked, his face crumpled with the

hurt he hid from his voice.

I bit my lips as I scrambled to find an answer.

"It was my fault, I'm afraid," Alexander stepped in to say with a small smile. "I never see Cosima anymore, and when our mutual friend told me she would be in town, I bagsied both nights."

When Seb frowned slightly, the man behind him offered, "Dibs, claimed, made her promise to see him both nights."

My brother accepted the translation with a broad smile aimed over his shoulder at his friend. I took a moment to sneak a peek at him and found him to be even more gorgeous than the silent woman with the swan's neck.

"We were, ah, just going to dinner too," Sebastian explained, suddenly remembering that he was in odd company too. "Would you like to join us?"

"No," Alexander said immediately. "We only have a short window for dinner before we're heading over to a party with some of my friends. Lovely of you to invite us, though, and it was good to meet you."

I squinted at the man over Seb's shoulder again and then gaped as the information clicked. "Is that Adam Meyers?"

To my absolute shock, my brother flushed. "Yes, well, Cosima, *mia bella sorella*," he continued in Italian so that we could speak privately.

He didn't know Alexander spoke Italian as well as we did.

"I will call you later," he promised. "Have a good night with your sugar daddy."

"I'll expect an answer when you telephone," I called lightly after him as he walked backward a few steps before casting a wave over his shoulder in farewell and ushering his friends down the sidewalk back whence they came.

"That was very awkward and very strange," I told Alexander as I blinked after my brother, my heart hurting that I knew so little about his life. I didn't even know who his friends were.

"They're clearly fucking," Alexander stated in his mater-of-fact British way as he ushered me down the steps and into the unassuming front door of the club.

I was so busy being outraged that I handed over my trench coat when Alexander held his hand out for it without batting an eye even though I was only wearing the ornamental leather harness beneath it.

"You think he's fucking the woman?"

"And the man," Alexander clarified as he handed our jackets to the doorman and adjusted his diamond cuffs before leading us down a dark corridor. "Both of them."

"Both!?" I squeaked, unable to imagine my brother with a man, let alone a man and a woman at the same time.

I winced as an image flashed across my mind, and I gripped my temples against the pain of it.

Alexander laughed. "Don't picture it, but it's true. The sexual tension between them was practically nuclear. I thought Adam would tear off my head for being so close to Sebastian."

"He really was Adam Meyers, the actor?" I asked, dazedly. "And that must have been his wife."

Alexander nodded, stopping us before a plain black door in the wall. He placed his hands on my shoulders and allowed me to watch his face turn firm with domination.

"Enough about that. Are you ready for tonight, my little mouse?"

As difficult as it was to push the awkward encounter and Alexander's explosive extrapolation out of my mind, I found myself naturally softening at the look of possession and dark control in his eyes.

"That's my girl," he said, and the praise settled like a crown of glory in my hair.

He turned us both and knocked on the door. A little window appeared in the center, opened from the other side.

"Purpose?"

"*Bacchanalia,*" Alexander responded, and a moment later, the door swung open and we were stepping inside.

Club Dionysus was exactly as I had imagined it, only even my imagination could not go to the lengths it needed to conjure up the scenes taking place on each of the three stages. It was darkly appointed in navy blues and blacks with silver accents and glowing ice blue lights under the bar and over the stages. Tables and chair were set up before each of the stages, but there were also booths in the middle, centered before the larger main stage where a huge bald man was whipping a young man strapped over a bench.

"Men?" I asked, because there hadn't been any men in The Hunt.

Alexander placed a hand on my hip and whispered in my ear. "There have been male slaves in the Order for decades, even before it was officially sanctioned, but they still aren't allowed in The Hunt. I think they believe it ruins the aesthetic."

I blinked at his droll comment and then giggled in shock when he winked at me.

We made to move forward when a scene on the stage to our left caught Alexander's eye and he stopped mid-step. My gaze followed his to witness a small woman around her mid-forties kneeling in the middle of the stage while her Master used her mouth. Her back was a brutal tapestry of red, white, and raised pink scars from old but savage whippings. I gasped at the ugly horror of it, turning into Alexander slightly for comfort.

Unwittingly, his hand cupped my hip and pulled me closer even as he didn't take his eyes off the woman.

"Who is she?" I asked.

"Yana," he whispered before he could check himself.

He looked down at me, blinking memories from his gaze like cobwebs and then his mouth pursed unhappily as he moved us forward again.

He led us to a free table near the front of the main stage, and as he took a chair, I folded to my knees at his side, widening my thighs to adjust to the thickness of the plug between my cheeks. He stroked my hair ideally as he perused the drinks list, but it wasn't long before a server came to take his order and not much longer after that for Sherwood to take the empty seat across from us.

"Good evening, Thornton," he greeted in his papery voice as his slave knelt beside him.

She was a woman not much older than me, though her body was aged with scars. Not for the first time, I was grateful Alexander had bought me and not some other more perverted Master.

"Benedict," Alexander said, rudely calling the head of the Order by his Christian name. "You summoned me and here I am."

I peeked through the curtain of my hair to see Sherwood's mouth thin and curl in distaste at the slight.

"I hardly summoned you. It was a friendly invitation. You hadn't brought your slave in the club yet, and I thought to remind you of that."

"Oh?" Alexander asked as he accepted his brandy from the server. "Then what was your rationale for mentioning poor old Knox?"

"It was just an inquiry, old chap. I'm sorry if you were offended," Sherwood intoned innocently.

I gritted my teeth against his saccharine lies.

"If we must speak business though, *brother*, there is something I'd say." Sherwood emphasized as he tossed the cherry from his drink onto the ground by his feet and his slave immediately leaned forward to eat it of the floor with her teeth like some kind of animal.

I looked away.

"By all means."

"Well, I've heard a rumor that you're hoping to acquire NF News. I wanted to talk to you about using Winston to sweeten the deal."

"No."

"Don't be so hasty. Mr. Winston might be a new affiliate of the Order, but he is still a brother, and as such, he gets priority in these kinds of situations."

"No," Alexander repeated coldly. "I've told you countless times before, and I am not a fan of repeating myself, Benedict. I will not pad my portfolio with dirty Order money and politics, I do quite well enough without them and I'd rather not have the headache."

"I don't care whether or not you 'don't want the headache,'" Sherwood seethed quietly. "You are a part of this Order and this is how things are done."

"If membership could be rescinded, you know I'd be gone."

There was a deep, ugly silence like a festering wound.

"Think about your priorities, Thornton," Sherwood advised in his silken tones that even I knew signified a threat. "You wouldn't want to end up like your dear old mum, dead before you time."

The air around the table turned electric, and I was sure, for one terrifying second, that Alexander would strike down the man where he stood.

Instead, his voice was dry ice as he said, "The next time you mention my mother or threaten me, make sure you have a gun in your hand to back it up with immediately because I'll come for you. And you won't like what happens when I catch you."

He stood back from his chair and offered me his hand so I could get to my feet in my towering heels.

"We're leaving," he growled softly just to me as we began to weave through the tables.

A few men called out to Alexander, but he ignored them.

I was happy to leave that place and particularly those people, but a small part of me was sad we wouldn't be able to have our scene.

"Don't worry, *topolina*," he whispered into my ear as he held the door open for me and then swatted my ass when I moved by. "I'll fuck your sweet arse the moment we get home."

I squeezed my hand firmly over the thick, veiny length of Alexander's cock until a pearl of precum beaded at the tip. It was my favourite game, teasing him and playing with his gorgeous cock using only my hands so that I could lick off every drop of moisture as it pooled at the head.

It tasted divine, communion from a sacred church.

"Hands behind your head."

Before I could even consciously compute the words, my hands were linked at the back of my scalp. Alexander slid his hands through the gaps in my bent arms and wove our fingers together in my hair.

Then he began to slowly, firmly fuck my throat.

He used me at his own pace, dragging the weight of his cock out of my throat and over my tongue so gradually I couldn't help but gag and swallow around him. On each inward thrust, he ground his hips into me, my nose against the coarse brown hairs over his pubic bone as he forced me to take him to the very root even though I could barely breathe.

It was methodical torture.

I never could have known how sensitive my mouth could be, how each rasp of his head over the crown of my mouth could feel sublime, and how every time he sank in my throat, I'd feel so resplendently full.

The place between my legs was a wetland.

I could feel how wet I was as I rubbed my thighs together, desperate for friction.

"Get that cock nice and wet and ready to take your arse," Alexander ordered in his perfect, upper-crust tones.

I sucked hard, desperate to hear him groan.

His hands tightened in my hair painfully in response, and he hissed as I flicked my tongue over him before he pulled completely out of my mouth.

His face was a mask of pure lust as he rubbed his thumb over my swollen, damp, and red lips. "Go to the window."

I was surprised because we were in the bedroom next to a colossal bed with posts only Alexander could find so many ways to utilize, but I followed his orders. The window was huge, stretching from one side of the wall another. It was one of the many modern architectural details in his other very traditional Mayfair home that made it incredibly beautiful.

"Press your hands to the glass and show me your bottom."

I did as he said.

"Wider."

I strained my legs even farther apart, teetering slightly on the high heels I still wore. My ass was clenched so tightly around the plug in this position, I wasn't sure he could get it out.

"I know you were disappointed that we couldn't preform tonight, *bella*," he practically purred as he moved behind me and ran his nose down my neck. "You would have been the envy of all the men in that room tonight."

I moaned softly as his tongue followed the path of his nose, licking up my carotid artery and then biting gently over my pulse.

"But this will have to do for tonight. I'm going to fuck you right here against the window so that anyone lucky enough to pass by will be able to see how gorgeous you look with a cock in your ass."

His fingers trailed feather-light down each notch in my spine over the curve of my tailbone, then deep between my legs where he gently tapped at the diamond imbedded plug in my ass.

"Does that feel good?" he asked me, nuzzling into my hair and tap, tapping at the plug.

I could feel every inch of my skin, every electron, proton and neutron in every atom of my DNA and they were all abuzz with electric pleasure.

"More, please, Master," I asked, trying to keep from whining.

"My greedy girl."

"Yes, Master."

He twisted the plug inside me like turning a valve, and it released some of the pressure inside me and replaced it with a yearning emptiness. I groaned, rolling my forehead against my hands and fogging the glass beneath them with my steamy pants.

His fingers delved into my ass, twisting one, then two, and then three until I was so full I couldn't move.

"Move against my fingers," he demanded, his other hand curling around my hip cruelly so that the edge of pain brought my mind to the moment, to the feel of him in my ass and the glass against my breasts. "Fuck yourself against me."

God, I groaned at my shamelessness as I rolled my hips back, tipped my pelvis so that his fingers dragged across every inch of sensitive flesh inside me. It felt so foreign, a pleasure that was heavy, striking chords inside me that resonated like a bass instead of tenor.

It wasn't enough. I kicked back my hips faster and faster, but the angle wasn't right, and I couldn't move fast enough. A noise of keening frustration rent the air, and I realized it was me making that sound.

"Hush, beauty," Alexander soothed me as he popped open a bottle of lube behind me and then used his slicked fingers to prep me. "I'll take care of that ache for you."

My breath stuttered when the wide crest of him caught at my hole and then slowly, irrevocably pushed inside. Something in my brain popped open like a champagne cork and everything turned fizzy, my blood popping with sensation as I was flooded with endorphins.

I tried to impale myself back on his cock, but he held me steady, slowly working his way inside until my hips were cupped in the bowl of his lap and I was seated to the root on his length. His hand moved over me, plucking my nipples until they sung bright arias, strumming my clit until it thrummed like a metronome, keeping time the escalading tempo of pleasure rising to a crescendo in my gut.

Then he started to move, and my entire body started to play its own harmony, manipulated by the shape and pull of Alexander's body into mine.

"You're going to come all over me, aren't you?" he taunted me as his rhythm changed, and he began to pound into me, ceaseless of my pain or pleasure, chasing his own climax because he was my Master and I was just a slave.

I groaned endlessly in response, so lost it was a wonder his voice could penetrate my lust drunk thoughts.

"You love my cock in your ass, in your pussy, in your mouth, and between your tits and thighs. You love it anywhere you can get it," he continued against my neck as he nipped at the flesh there.

"I'm, I, I'm going to…" I trailed off, losing my ability to speak in any language as my impending climax tightened every muscle in my body to the point of pain.

"Yes, Cosima, come for me," he said, and it was the sound of my name in his mouth, spoken in that sexy British voice that catapulted me over the edge of the most extreme orgasm I'd ever had.

Every circuit in my body lit up so that all I saw was light and all I felt was bright pleasure coursing through me from the point where his cock sank deep into my body. And then it became too much, and everything short circuited.

Seconds later, I passed out against the glass.

When I woke up, I was in bed with Alexander between my legs, cleaning me with a warm, damp cloth in the dark.

I tried to speak, but my speech was slurred nonsense.

Alexander looked up from his work to give me his small, slightly lopsided smile. "You passed out on me. I can't say I've had a sub do that to me before."

I frowned.

Alexander shook his head at me and tossed the facecloth to the floor before lying beside me and pulling over the covers. I sighed when he drew me against the hard lines of his body, my cheek against the inflexible swell of his pec and my fingers caught in the grooves between his abs.

"You have no need to be jealous of any one in my past. I had subs before you, but no slaves, and never anyone for longer than a few months. Even then it was casual because I had no need for a partner, only a warm, wet, and obedient woman."

"Nice," I mustered dryly.

His chuckle ruffled my hair. "Not everyone is looking for their future spouse."

"I can't imagine you married," I said as I yawned into his chest.

"Probably because I don't ever plan to be. I'd have to be out of my mind."

"You don't believe in it?"

He was quiet for a long moment as he contemplated my question. It occurred to me that it was only ever after a scene, when I was wrapped around him, that Alexander tenderized and conversed with me like a true lover.

I'd have to take better advantage of it.

"I believe it in it," he said at last. "I might be the pessimist, but I can't think of a single married couple who is happy for it."

I didn't know one either, so I didn't say anything.

"I have to believe if I ever felt moved to marry, it would be because I wanted my lover to have my name, my protection, and the promise of my love no matter what should happen in the future. I think it's a promise that should never die, even if the love is gone. One that says I will care for you, stand up for you, and be there for you no matter what."

I blinked into the darkness at the beauty of his words and the impossibility of them coming from such a man. But then I thought of other things he had said when his guard was down, how I was brave like the Goddess Athena and a queen who had been convinced she was a pawn.

It was the contradiction of his cold exactness and his warm soliloquies that seemed to crumble my defences before I knew they were even destroyed. It was impossible to stay on my toes around him because his behaviour was unpredictable, and his erratic moments of beauty were arresting.

Which reminded me of his strange behaviour upon seeing that submissive in the club.

"Who is Yana?"

His body stilled. "We won't speak of her."

"Okay, let's talk about what happened with Sherwood to-night. Why was he threatening you, and why shouldn't you be a little more concerned about it? I thought you said these men would kill you if you didn't do as they said?"

"They can try," he muttered darkly.

"Xan." I propped myself up on one hand so I could look into his face, and I watched his face soften at my nickname for him. "Please, tell me what happened tonight."

He sighed, an indulgent and vaguely irritated sound. "Fine, but lie down." As I settled, he tangled his fingers in my hair. "The Order isn't just about hedonism and women. It's also about keeping the elite men of Britain in the upper echelons of business, politics, wealth, and society. I own a media company that I inherited through my mother's family that I've made very lucrative. There are any number of people I should be supporting financially for mayor of London and Prime Minister, or hiring at my company because it is dictated by the Order. I refuse to do so."

"You always have?"

"Yes. I know it's hard to believe, given our current state, but I never approved of the Order even though I was groomed to be a leader of it by my father."

"How were you groomed?" I asked, drawing my fingers in soothing patterns over his chest in the hopes that it would distract him into staying open and pliant with me.

He hesitated. "My father always kept slaves. It was something I'm not sure if my mum knew about at the time of their marriage, but she certainly knew about it when I was a lad. Mostly, they were kept out of our sight in the servants' quarters or the dungeon, but when I was nine, my father decided I should begin my training as a sadist."

I stopped breathing.

"He took me to the dungeon and introduced me to the current slave Davenport. She was only eighteen and so pale and thin… I could see her veins and bones beneath her skin. Noel taught me how to train her like a dog, how to present for her Master and crawl and beg prettily for more. I had my first orgasm by her mouth and then on my tenth birthday, I lost my virginity to her."

"Oh, Xan," I breathed, flattening my hand over his heart as if I could reach inside and soothe the scars there.

"It was a few months after that Noel decided to teach me how to discipline her. I was a tall boy and strong from sport, so he felt I could properly employ a whip. First, he strung Yana up to the ceiling and 'put her through her paces.' By the time he was halfway done, her back had opened up and blood dripped like red rain to the floor. I couldn't stand it, so when my dad wouldn't stop at my screams, I tried to take the whip from him."

My hand flew to my mouth and tears gathered in my eyes as I understood where this was going.

"Noel took Yana down and let her weep in the corner while he strung me up and gave me the rest of her punishment. At some point, I passed out from the pain, which only made Noel angrier. Davenport men, especially the heir to the Dukedom of Greythorn, do not succumb to anything, even pain. He flayed me until my back was a bloody mess, and then he left me there on the floor. I was lucky one of the kitchen maid's sons had heard the screaming, and he came down to investigate. It was quite the ordeal, though it gave me Riddick."

"He was the maid's son?" I asked, shocked that the two had been together that long.

Alexander nodded, brushing the hair away from my face and rubbing the strands between his fingers. "There's more in my storied history with the Order, but that was my first taste of their beliefs, and I didn't like it."

"But you're a Dominant and a sadist now?" I ventured timidly because the terminology still confounded me sometimes, but I was fairly sure that was true.

"I am. I learned in time what my own boundaries were, and they were pretty much the same as any God-fearing man's. I don't take my pleasure from making you bleed or eat scraps off the floor like Sherwood's slave. I don't enjoy the thought of sharing you or watching you be raped. I'm just a simple man with a hankering for the sound of my sub's tears and the sight of the flesh after it has been reddened with a crop."

I laughed. "Yes, simple man indeed."

We were quiet for a moment thinking our own heavy thoughts before I whispered, "I'm sorry, Xan."

He squeezed me tightly and turned his mouth into my hair. "The woman I've bought and used poorly empathizes with me. What did I tell you about that tender heart?"

"I think I'm already in as much trouble as I can be," I muttered.

His shocked laugh vibrated through me.

"Xan," I asked because I'd always wanted to, and the air between us was fragrant with intimacy. "How old are you?"

"I'll be thirty-five on Friday."

"Seriously? We have to celebrate," I told him because it was a mandate in my family that birthdays had to be enjoyed.

I hadn't enjoyed my eighteenth birthday, and I wanted to make up for it by enjoying Alexander's with him.

"We have a ball to go to actually. We'll stay in London the next few nights and return to Pearl Hall after that. I've got you a dress already in the closet."

"Oh, well, I was thinking more like birthday cake and balloons, but I guess Lords do balls for birthdays," I mused.

He pressed his smile to my forehead and then replaced it with a kiss. "We can do birthday cake after the ball, how about that?"

"Deal."

We were quiet again for a time, and I almost drifted to sleep before I asked, "What are you going to do about the Order? What if they turn on you?"

He didn't answer for a long time, and when he did, I wasn't sure if I was already dreaming.

"It's what I'll do to the Order if they come for *you* that I'm worried about."

Chapter Twenty

*J*made Xan laugh eighteen times on his thirty-fifth birthday. My plan for the day had gone superbly with the help of Riddick, who actually made the calls and reservations for us, and Mrs. White, who had also travelled with us from Pearl Hall and helped me make the cake. We baked the Sicilian Cassata rum cake the morning before while Alexander was out on business, and I'd presented it to him in bed that morning when I woke him up.

This trip signaled my first time going to bed and waking up with him, and the new intimacy felt right given how my feelings had changed for him.

It felt even better when he'd eaten the icing off my nipples and between my legs until I came in his mouth and then claimed that I tasted better than the cake.

It was a silly plan, and I'd been nervous when I suggested spending the day together in London to celebrate, but Alexander had been surprisingly kind about my overenthusiasm. I think he'd even enjoyed going on the London Eye, although that was probably only because we had occupied our own pod and he'd played under my skirt in full view of the CCTV cameras until I'd come all over his hands.

I'd never seen Alexander as relaxed as he was with me that

day. He was still cold and aloof, unflappable, and difficult to impress, but there was a smile in his eyes that made them glow like multifaceted diamonds in the weak London light.

Experiencing him like that made me feel like a girl with a school crush, which was vaguely ridiculous as I'd never before been one. But the giddiness that rushed through me when he held my hand and led me through the crowds or pulled out my chair for me at high tea in Fortnum & Mason was enough to made me light-headed.

There was another, potential reason for my light-headedness, but I didn't want to dwell on it before I knew for sure.

When we'd returned to the Mayfair house to get ready for the ball, Alexander stopped me on the brick path before the door and took my face in both hands.

"I want to thank you," he said solemnly and vaguely uncomfortably, "for planning today. I haven't had much fun in my life and none since Chiara died and… Edward left. So this was splendid."

My heart was bright in my chest and even though that worried me just as my giddiness from earlier did, I allowed myself to feel happy because I hadn't had much of that lately either.

"You're very welcome."

He stared at me for another long moment, trying to translate the words he saw written in the line of my face and the gold of my eyes. I kept my features on lockdown, desperate to hold my secrets for just a while longer.

Then, his hands slid into my hair, and he tipped my head back so that he could give me a kiss so luxe it felt like satin against my tongue.

Now, I was sitting in the bathroom before the large mirror staring at Mrs. White as she fussed with my hair.

My make-up was done, a sultry cat eye that made me look like the Egyptian Cleopatra, and gold dust that shimmered on the ledge of my cheekbones and in the expanse of décolletage that was revealed by the low-cut sheer gold dress.

Mrs. White was braiding some pieces of my hair and crossing them over the top of my head so that they looked like dark crown. I watched, my leg bouncing with anxiety, as she threaded filaments of gold through the coils so that they caught in the light.

I looked like a queen, but I still felt like the pawn, especially after spending thirty minutes in the bathroom throwing up before Mrs. White appeared.

A pawn didn't have many choices that were not dictated by the other pieces on the board.

I couldn't even plan for my uncertain future without first trusting someone in my treacherous life to be my confidante.

"You are unusually flushed today, love," Mrs. White noticed as she spritzed my spicy perfume over my neck and hair. "Are you feeling quite right?

"I think something at tea didn't agree with me," I admitted, just in case she heard me vomiting earlier.

I needed to trust someone with my secret, but I was leaning toward Douglas or even Riddick instead of Mrs. White. There was no specific reason for my hesitation, but something in my gut told me to trust one of the other men with my explosive secret.

"Well, you look a treat, and Master Alexander will be knocked off his feet at the sight of you." She laughed delightedly and then peered at me in the reflection of the mirror as I leaned over to adjust my aching breasts in the cups of the dress. "He seems taken with you."

I rolled my eyes. "He's trained me well enough."

"No, dear, I've seen him with his fair share of women, and none have made him as… *intense* as you do."

"He laughed today," I told her to counteract her words. "Eighteen times."

Her lips pursed as I revealed my hands.

My throat burned as I ached to take back my telling words.

"Listen to Mrs. White, sweet," she advised me as she cupped my face in her plump, pale hands and looked at me in the mirror. "You are losing your lustre as knackered as you are. Let me tell you something, it is a quick end when the bloom falls off the rose…unless you have something else of value to give them"

"Give who?" I asked, confused by her speech.

"By the Davenport men. If you give them something they need, they'll keep you even after they've used you."

"Okay," I drew the word out slowly because something about her over bright eyes and cryptic words made my flesh drew tight with goosebumps. "What could I possibly have other than my body that is any value to two of the richest men in England?"

"A baby," Mrs. White said, and her words hit the bull's-eye so sharply, so neatly, I couldn't believe I hadn't seen it coming. "An heir or a spare."

I swallowed thickly, unable to find my voice at all, let alone the proper words to refute her enigmatic guess.

When I didn't answer fast enough, she smiled sweetly and pressed a kiss to the top of my head. "That's what I thought, love. That's what I thought."

Finally, my voice surged through my throat, and I stood, spinning around to face her with my mouth open to say, "Mrs. White—"

"Bloody hell," Alexander said from the doorway, where he stood resplendent in an entirely black tuxedo. "You look a vision, *bella*."

I placed a shaky hand on my lower abdomen and watched as Mrs. White winked at me, then scuttled out of the room, shutting the door behind her.

My eyes swung back to Alexander, and my heart stuttered as

he crossed the small space to stand in front of me. His hands went to my shoulders so that he could twist me back to face the mirror. One hand lingered over the column of my neck, his thumb brushing over my pulse as he studied me.

"I'm a wealthy man and a titled lord, so I own many things of incredible worth and beauty, items both inherited and bought. One of my most precious possessions is this," he explained as the other hand came out of his pocket to raise a glinting gold necklace constructed of stylized gold thorny stems and riddled with clusters of seed peals. There was a perfectly blood red ruby the size of a toddler's fists nestled at the heart of the necklace like a rose protected by its thorns.

It was one of the most awe-inspiring things of beauty I had ever seen.

Alexander raised it higher over my chest and then clutched the other end in his hand on my neck so that he could clasp it around me.

"I wanted to see what my most expensive heirloom would look like on my most treasured possession," he murmured as he clicked the necklace closed and smoothed it flat with his fingers.

I watched in the mirror as his hands settled over my collarbones, framing the gorgeous collar necklace that hung from my throat, and his ownership of me seemed complete.

"This is your collar tonight," he explained in a voice like drug smoke, the sound of it heady enough to make me high. "Everyone who sees it will know you are mine, and they will know how much you mean to me."

"Dangerous," I whispered through my dry mouth.

It was so dangerous for so many reasons. We couldn't afford to fall in love. Not the Master with his slave, not the avenger with the tool of his trade, and certainly not the man whose mother had been murdered by the girl's father.

There was no hope for us, and that was without outside forces interfering.

The Order and the Camorra.

Noel and Salvatore.

My baby.

I stared at the picture we made in the mirror, how well it lied to make it seem as if we were the perfect couple. We looked absolutely breathtaking together, regal and opposite but synergetic as if our differences fit together like puzzle pieces to complete the picture just right.

I sucked in a shuddering breath to control myself because Alexander's stare had turned sharp.

"When a Master collars a slave, Cosima, it is a very powerful thing. It means I believe you are worthy of praise, worthy to wear the weight of my powerful name around your throat. What do you say to that?"

"I say thank you, Master," I whispered thickly as I brought my hands to his, my fingertips over the cool necklace. "I hope I prove worthy of the gift."

The opulence was staggering. Light dripped from glittering chandeliers and thickly branched candelabras, reflecting off the multifaceted jewels adorning the ears, throats, and wrists of London's most elite persons all gathered in the ballroom at Mayfair's grand Grammar House. Gorgeous women floated across the glossy floor in lavish gowns while the men stood in groups drinking liquor and talking about politics and sport. The room itself was like the inside of a music box, so ornate in golds and reds and murals that it made me slightly dizzy even though I wasn't dancing with the multitudes of beautiful couples gracing the dance floor.

Instead, I stood by Alexander's side as he hobnobbed with some of the city's wealthiest and most prestigious men and women. I'd even heard someone say that the most scandalous second prince, Alasdair, was at the ball, though, I wouldn't have known him if I saw him.

No one talked to me very much, and there wasn't much to be said when they did. I had nothing in common with such people, and it showed the moment I opened my accented mouth.

Alexander kept me close, though, his hands eloquent on my hip or stroking across my back, platitudes for my boredom.

It was no wonder he enjoyed our celebration in London that day if this was how he usually spent his birthdays.

Finally, the older couple Alexander had been speaking to excused themselves, and I had him all to myself.

Instantly, I pouted.

His trademark small smile tipped the left side of his mouth and cut a crease into his cheek. "Poor bored little mouse. What am I going to do with you?"

"At this point, anything but another tedious conversation would do," I admitted.

His smile hitched higher.

"Why don't we dance," he said, instead of questioned, already leading me to the dance floor where couples were setting up for the next number.

"I don't know how," I hissed at him as he found space for us on the floor. "I don't even know the music."

"You don't need to," he informed as the first strains began, and he whisked me into his arms. "You just need to follow your Master."

After a few moments of stiff fingers curled into the fine fabric of his jacket and feet that clamoured helpless to move in the right direction, I relaxed enough to trust him.

"That's it, my beauty," he said, then drew my earlobe into his mouth. "Relax in my arms and show everyone what a lucky man I am tonight."

I melted further into his embrace, my body like wax against his as I molded to his shape and adapted to his steps. We spun across the marble hall as the London Orchestra played an elaborate piece of music that soared into the vaulted ceilings and swirled beneath my dress.

"Are you happy now?" Alexander asked me, and I got that sense he had meant to joke with me, but his tone arrived too somber.

"Do you care?" I asked, as I dipped my head back on my shoulders to see the colours of the mural above mix like an artist's palette as we revolved around the other couples.

When I looked back at Alexander, he was frowning at me as if I'd offended him.

"Yes," he admitted, "Yes, I do."

"Then, yes. I'm happy," I told him. "For now."

And now was all it would ever be.

"I have to use the toilet," I told him, wrenching out of his arms so quickly that he didn't have time to grab me. "I'll be back."

I picked up the slide train of my form-fitting dress and dashed as elegantly and quickly as I could through the crowds to the sweeping staircase where a manservant attended at the bottom.

I asked him for directions, and he led me to the powder room at the top of the stairs to the left. Instantly, I emptied my queasy stomach in the toilet, retching so hard tears came to my eyes. I rested my cheek across my arm over the porcelain for a moment to regain my breath as my tummy flipped then settled.

I wasn't sure if I was pregnant or not, but the sudden onslaught of nausea was reason enough to be worried. The same doctor who had administered my physical in Italy, attended me every three months at Pearl Hall to check on me and give me the birth control shot.

I should have been covered, my risk of pregnancy completely improbable.

But I wasn't sure about these things. I hadn't even been the one to choose the form of birth control.

My face was damp with nervous sweat when I looked at myself in the mirror, but otherwise my hair and make-up remained perfectly intact.

"Don't fall in love with him, Cosima Ruth Lombardi," I told my reflection sternly. "You're hormonal and crazy, and you are absolutely *not* falling in love with the man who bought you."

My pep talk completed, I splashed cold water on my wrists and pushed outside in the hall. The orchestra was playing something more rigorous now, something with a bite and snap like hounds nipping at the heels of a fox on the chase.

I paused at the top of the stairs to watch the colourful, diamond bright festivities for a moment, feeling homesickness for the urine yellow plainness of Napoli pang in my heart.

Unconsciously, my eyes searched the room for Alexander, and I found him already looking up at me, frowning as he peered across the long room.

I lifted my foot to begin my descent, preoccupied with thoughts of explaining my hasty departure to Alexander and how I was going to ask Mrs. White—now that she already suspected—to buy me a pregnancy test at the pharmacy.

So I was completely unprepared when two hands came from behind me and shoved me with brutal force down the two-story staircase.

There was no time to recover, to grab at the slick marble railing or steady myself on my towering heels.

I could only fall.

My body went limp after I struck the stairs the first time, the back of my head cracking against the stone so hard the sound echoed in my ears the entire way down the staircase, as I fell head over feet again and again until I finally reached the bottom.

There was a ringing in my ears, but I couldn't open my eyes to check if it was the orchestra still playing or the continued ricochet of my head impacting with the ground repeatedly. Something wet slid down my face, but I couldn't figure out how to make my hand work to feel if it was blood or tears.

Crippling pain snapped through my abdomen like cracking plastic, so excruciating that I curled my bruised body in on itself trying to lessen its severity.

Suddenly, there was the smell of cedar and pine in my nose and gentle pressure on the side of my head as someone tried to speak to me through the encroaching darkness of my mind.

"Xan," I thought I mumbled before I passed out. "Make sure you save our baby."

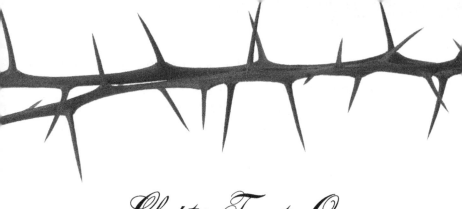

Chapter Twenty-One

When I woke up, someone was shouting.

The decibel slammed into my temples like stakes driven into the earth.

I tried to open my mouth to complain, but my voice died like a flailing butterfly in my throat.

And then the noise filtered through the fog of slumber and pain to truly penetrate.

It was Xan, and he was *screaming* at someone.

"Who the fuck put you up to it?"

With enormous effort, I peeled my eyes open and squinted through the bright light that assailed my vision even in the dark room.

Alexander was holding the middle-aged doctor, Farley, by the neck against the wall of our bedroom in the Mayfair house.

I watched as he slammed him into the wall again and then again, his face screwed up with vehement fury.

"I asked you a question," he roared, rearing back with one fist raised so that he could hammer it into the wall beside Farley's head.

Dry wall and dust exploded around Alexander's fist, and he punched it into the wall and then pull it back out.

"The next blow is to your face. Now, tell me who paid you

not to give her birth control?" Alexander repeated at a lower register, but his voice quaked with suppressed rage. "If you don't tell me now, I will drag you to Pearl Hall, string you up in the trees at the edge of the forest, and skin you alive like a felled deer."

"I, it's," Farley stammered, so wild-eyed his lids were peeled back into the crease of his eye sockets. "I'm sorry, but he's scarier than you are when it comes down to it."

An animal sound rumbled through Alexander's throat as he carted the man over to the door, wrenched it open, and threw him out into the hall.

Instantly, Riddick appeared, his redhead complexion gone scarlet with anger.

"He talks or he dies," Alexander ordered, before shutting the door with a clang and then leaning back against it.

He closed his eyes and rubbed a hand over his tired face. For the first time since I'd met him, he looked every minute of his thirty-five years.

"Xan?" I croaked once, the word falling like dead weight to the blankets tucked under my chin. "Alexander?"

Immediately, his eyes snapped open and locked with mine.

They were filled like crystal balls with a swirling torment on emotions I wasn't psychic enough to decipher.

I patted the bed weakly, too tired to speak to him from so far away.

He was at my side in a heartbeat, carefully peeling back the heavy blankets so that he could slide underneath and gently roll into my side so that he was leaning over me. His fingers went to my hair, pulling and twisting at a strand to soothe himself more than me.

He loved my hair and drew solace from it even more than I did.

"What a horrible end to your birthday," I ventured, letting my eyes drift shut for a moment as I absorbed the warmth and comfort of his body.

"Don't joke, Cosima." I opened my eyes at his use of my name and saw the sobriety of his features. "Did you know you were pregnant?"

I squeezed my eyes shut as a hollow remnant of pain panged through the empty walls of my womb.

"Not anymore," I whispered.

"No," he agreed, implacably. "Did you know?"

"I guessed. The past few days, I'd been overly emotional and nauseated."

I felt his fingers graze my neck, and I realized that I was still wearing the pearl and ruby collar. "Look at me, *bella*."

When my eyes opened, they were filled with the tears I didn't want him to see. One fell off the cliff of my lower lid and burned a path down my cheek. Alexander stopped it with one knuckle and brought the salty drop to his lips.

"I am sorry this happened to you," he said, filled with gravitas that pressed like a weight against my sore heart.

His anguish made mine all the more acute.

"I feel as though I'm always saying that," he admitted as he twirled my hair.

"You are," I agreed without malice.

I'd been through so much because of him.

But I'd grown so much too, just as I would grow from the ashes of this last tragedy like a phoenix.

"So heartrendingly beautiful, so savagely brave," he whispered.

"Mmm," I hummed, closing my eyes again because his handsome face combined with his beautiful words were too much for me to take even when I was at full strength. "My head feels wrong."

"You have a bad concussion, bruised ribs, a sprained ankle, and innumerable bruises. It was a nasty fall that honestly could have been much worse. When…" He sucked in a fortifying breath then let it out slowly. "When I saw you lying there, I thought at first that you had broken your neck."

"Someone pushed me," I murmured, remembering the distinctive imprint of two hands pressed to my back as if into wet concrete.

I knew I would always feel them there, a scar on my memory that was impacted on my flesh.

"I thought I saw a figure behind you, but I was too far away to make anything out. Do you have any thought of who it could be?"

I shook my head. There was no one at the ball that I'd even known.

"Did anyone else know about the baby?"

"I think Mrs. White guessed tonight while she was helping me get ready," I admitted. "But I doubt she would have been at the ball to push me down the stairs. She could have found a much more opportune time or way to get rid of me or the baby or both around here or at Pearl Hall."

Alexander's eyes narrowed into the distance as he narrowed down suspects in his mind.

"How did you know Dr. Farley wasn't giving me proper birth control?" I asked, shivering as a chill swept through me.

"You're cold," he noticed, gently scooping me into his arms and then carefully moving us both to the edge of the bed so he could stand up and carry me into the bathroom.

I stayed quiet, my hand linked behind his neck as he sat on the edge of the bath and turned on the faucets. Immediately, the bathroom began to fill with steam and the scent of my spicy bubble bath as he dumped half the bottle in the bottom of the tub.

Finally, he looked down at me in his arms, and a little of his outrageous anger dimmed at the sight.

"Riddick had been suspecting of the man for a while, and when he did some bloodwork after Landon flogged you, he thought something was off. It was a natural guess. When I called him here under the guise to attend to you, I confronted him, and he was easily rattled."

"But he didn't confess who asked him to do it."

"No." His jaw clenched as he undid the tie of my fluffy terry cloth robe and then stood me up to be rid of it before he helped me into the quickly filling tub.

The hot sting of the water felt like blissful agony against my sore muscles, the kind of duality I usually experience with my Master. I settled back into the bubbles and closed my eyes.

Moments later, there was a splash and I squeaked as Alexander swung his other leg into the water. He softly pushed me forward so that he could sink between the edge of the huge tub and my body, then he arranged me comfortably between his legs.

"What are you doing?" I asked as he opened the bottle of my shampoo and squirted the gel into his palms.

"Bathing you for a change. I think you deserve all the tenderness in the world after what you've been through tonight. Lean back again and let me care for you."

Reluctantly, I placed my head back on his chest. His sudsy hands worked across my scalp, massaging the lather into my aching head with just the right amount of strength.

"I thought you'd be angry," I confessed as I leaned into his touch.

"I am."

"At me, I mean," I clarified. "Because of the baby."

I hummed as his firm fingers kneaded down the length of my neck and then across my shoulders.

"It's not your fault."

"Still..."

"Have I proven myself to be irrational? I would never hold you responsible for something like that, even if you *had* been on birth control as you were supposed to be. Life is never what we want it to be; the trick is to make the most of it."

"So wise for a man who seems to do so many things he doesn't want to do."

"Touché," he conceded. "Though rarely are circumstances as complicated as these."

"For what it's worth," I purred as he turned on the hand-held faucet and directed the hot water over my hair, careful to keep the suds out of my eyes. "I've never met anyone more capable of directing their own life. I think you could get out of any trap and win any advantage you set your mind to."

He was quiet for a while, contentedly rinsing my hair and then soothingly rubbing a sponge along my skin, mindful of my many bruises.

"When you lose your mother to mindless violence and lack of reason, it changes you," he explained quietly. "Any kind of loss works to harden a person, but she was my ally in that house even more than Edward was. We were too different as children, and I was five years older, so I considered myself too old to play many games with him. He was still in nappies when I was being trained in the dungeon. My mum championed me with Noel and made sure my life of top marks, athletic endeavours, and social climbing had some free time for fun. She died, and that sliver of me that cared for levity and light died with her."

He pressed his nose to the hair over my ear and inhaled

deeply of my scent. "I know you feel you are only worth the price of your beauty, Cosima, but you underestimate the multifaceted nature of your loveliness. It's not just the geometry of your body and the wet between your thighs; it's not even the colour of your money eyes or the heavy weight of your hair. It's the way you make everyone around you feel beautiful about themselves. I am beginning to understand that I am addicted to the way I feel about myself when I'm with you. Like I'm the hero and not the villain."

My throat felt swollen under the weight of his collar, but I didn't cry because I knew once I did, I wouldn't stop. There was a hollow place in my soul that I'd carried around with me like an empty pocketbook for years, waiting for some currency to fill it with. Alexander's words slotted into place with the clink of coins and the crinkle of bank notes, giving monetary value to an asset I hadn't known I possessed.

Even if that was the only gift he ever gave me, it was enough to last a lifetime.

"I don't want the loss of this baby to turn you hard," he continued after letting me digest for a moment. "He or she could only have been a few weeks old and simply wasn't meant to be. You did nothing wrong to warrant what happen to you or the baby. If anyone is at fault, it is me and my host of enemies."

"I'm not without enemies," I reminded him, my words nasal with unshed tears. "You once called me your enemy."

"And how wrong I was," he muttered as he finished washing me. "Now, it's to understand who the real enemy is knocking on our gates so that I can kill him for hurting you."

"You would, wouldn't you?" I asked because even though he'd murdered Landon, that death had a surreal cast to it.

It felt more like a terrible nightmare than reality; a death that had broken the terror and brought us back to reality.

Plus, it was difficult for me to feel remorse for a man who had run roughshod over my mental health since I was a girl and then beat me bloody as a woman all just because he *could*.

"Yes," Alexander agreed easily, scooping me into his arms as he stood and the water sluiced off us.

He settled me on the bathmat and then retrieved a fluffy towel to gingerly dry my body. It felt surreal for him to take care of me so diligently when I was the one meant to cater to his every need, but there was also a strange rightness about his manner. If submission had taught me anything, it was that it was the submissive who was the most revered and the most vulnerable, and that it was that exact vulnerability that held the Dominants so much in their thrall.

To have a man or woman expose themselves to you so completely must be an intoxicating high, I thought, as Alexander bent his head to concentrate on drying my feet. Maybe nearly as enthralling as seeing a strong man bend the knee in order to do something as simple as dry me after a bath.

I placed a hand on his strong shoulder as he produced a plain pair of black lace full bottom underwear from the drawer under the sink and helped me into them. He barely dried himself before he moved us into the bedroom and plucked one of his undershirts from the open closet so that I could pull it over my head. Only when I was attired did he settle me in bed. I leaned back against the pillows with a sigh that drudged up all the wreckage in my soul and expunged it through my open mouth.

I was weary to my very bones, and I just wanted to sleep without nightmares.

Alexander returned and settled at the edge of the bed to drag a comb through my hair. I barely stirred as the methodical strokes lulled me further into relaxation and slumber. Dimly, I was aware of his thick fingers braiding my hair out of my face and then his hands softly lowering me back to the pillows.

I woke up again when he crawled into bed beside me and gathered me like tissue paper into the vacant space between his arms.

"I don't know what this changes," he admitted as he kissed the hollow behind my ear. "But it changes something."

Chapter Twenty-Two

I'd been in Britain for ten months, nearly a year of hard service under my belt and another four to follow it.

Only, it wasn't hard anymore, not in the weeks since the miscarriage. Alexander was attentive as a celebrant to his deity, bathing with me every morning and dressing me just as I dressed him. He ate dinner with me every night when he returned from work and continued to fuck me, in ways both hard and soft, as before.

But it was the way he looked at me sometimes with an edge of primal fear like a cornered predator even as he let me caress him or question him about his day that made me question his emotional landscape.

It was as if he feared my intimacy as much as he craved it.

My life at Pearl Hall was full in many other ways too. I enjoyed my time in the kitchens with Douglas as he taught me to make wonderful confections out of spun sugar and chocolate lacework. Mrs. White was determined to teach me the lady-like art of needlepoint even though the only thing I'd ever be close to stitching successfully was the word "sex" in shaky script. I improved every day in my fencing and martial arts training, whether it was with Riddick or Xan, and I'd taken to riding my beautiful golden stallion, Helios, over the extensive grounds.

For the first time in a long time, I felt a sense of joy in my everyday life, and England was beginning to feel like home.

My mother noticed my accent, how I'd clipped off the ends of vowels and stopped instinctively rolling my r's. I began to notice it too, how my English had ceased to skip and hop with the foreign lyricism of my homeland, how my vocabulary had swelled to include such British sayings as "scrummy," "botched," "chuffed," and "dodgy." When I commented on it to Alexander, he'd smiled his secret smile with his eyes half closed in pleasure and then fucked me so hard, he had me cursing in Italian.

He did that a lot, it seemed. Reading into my skin like a blind man with Braille, and the subtitles in my eyes like a deaf man with the news. As if his other senses could tell him my secrets more readily than his sight could.

Sometimes I wondered, after he'd worked over my body until I was crying out his name, what kinds of secrets he'd already divined under my skin.

The happier Alexander and I became, drawn together inexplicably by the loss of our child and the mystery of his or her death, the more agitated Noel seemed.

I would catch him pacing down the hall, muttering under his breath as his palm twitched, then smacked against his leg, and sometimes, at strange hours of the day, I would hear something like the wind howling through the walls of the house and wonder if Noel still kept a slave hidden somewhere on the grounds.

One day when I was on the way to the gym, I even witnessed a peculiar tableau. Mrs. White had been crying on her knees, her head tilted into Noel's thigh as he sat at the kitchen table below stairs and stroked her hair.

The image stirred a deep mistrust inside my soul, but I had no real reason to be suspicious of Mrs. White and only speculation and terrible history with his son to pin against Noel.

So I watched, but waited quietly until one morning when Alexander and I were cuddled in bed after a vigorous session tossing around the idea of him teaching me how to exercise his falcon, Astor.

The door to my bedroom flew open, and Noel stood in the frame, shaking a letter terminated in a familiar red seal in one hand.

A missive from the Order of Dionysus.

"They cut the bloody funding to my port project in Falmouth," he seethed as he stalked into the room and ripped the covers off us to reveal our naked, tangled limbs. "You fucking cock-up, this is not how men do business."

"As a more successful man than yourself," Alexander said haughtily, despite his lack of dress. He stood to get toe to toe with his combative father and stare down at him from his more advance height. "I dare to disagree."

"Fix this, boy," Noel demanded, shoving the thick card stock into Xan's chest. "Fix it now and stop being such a pussy. Your mother, your grandfather, and the entire Davenport clan are rolling over in their grave right now as they witness your idiocy and pigheadedness. Maybe if you weren't so tied up in that one's snatch, you'd remember what you brought her here to do."

My ears burned at Noel's crude language, but it was my chest that churned with rolling flames.

I hated Noel more at that moment for speaking to Alexander and relating to him the way he did than I'd ever hated anyone for myself.

Noel stormed out of the room, slamming the door behind him so forcibly that the painting rattled on the wall.

Alexander didn't move.

He stared down at the paper in his hand blindly.

"Xan," I asked softly, moving to the edge of the bed to place a hand on his shoulder. "Are you okay?"

"He has a point," he murmured. "I can't forget your purpose here."

A shiver of foreboding rocked through me.

"I can have more than one purpose. I am not just a utilitarian tool," I told him.

His eyes slid to mine, but they were some place deep inside his mind where the maze of his thoughts was at its darkest.

"Aren't you?"

I watched as he dropped the letter to the ground and marched from the room, naked yet utterly regal on his athletic, rolling gait.

He didn't return at all that day, and instead of eating dinner alone, I saddled up Helios with the help of the stable boy and took off.

Maybe I couldn't actually run away, but I could make it difficult to find me if he went looking.

A field beyond the left pastures at the back of Pearl Hall, snug between the forest at one end and the hedgerow maze at the other, was where the ground was covered in a thick carpet of poppies. The bold colour had drawn my eyes two weeks ago when I'd finally ventured far enough in my journeys with Helios to reach the forgotten corner of the estate, and I'd nearly cried at the beauty of my favourite flowers bowing steeply in the breeze.

I sat in their embrace that evening, splayed out over the broken stems and crushed petals beneath me while I played my fingers gentle in the silky filaments swaying into me with the wind.

The contrast of their bold appearance and secret fragility was all too easy to parallel to my own duality. It seemed I tried so hard to appear strong and resilient, but the moment something powerful slammed into my life, I was powerless to stand up against it.

I wanted to be strong enough to break through the last of Alexander's titanium shields and win the heart of my complicated Master, but the task seemed nearly insurmountable.

Dark grey clouds the colour of Alexander's eyes rolled across the sky, but I didn't move. I wanted the cold English rain to purify my muddied thoughts and leave an easy solution in its wake.

How did I untangle the knotted mess of lies my life had become and smooth out the threads so I could keep the good ones?

How could I keep Xan while still keeping my family and my independence?

The grey veil parted, and the rain rushed forth in a deluge. I propped myself up on an elbow to survey the sweep of water as it fell over the Greythorn estates, but something moving quickly from the stable caught my eyes.

Alexander on Charon, galloping across the rapidly dampening earth like Hades out of the underworld, determined to snatch the goddess Persephone from her field of flowers.

Only, I wanted him to snatch me away and make me queen of his dark domain.

I watched without moving as he cantered up the hill and swung out of Charon's saddle before he even came to a complete stop.

His face was immovable stone, threatening as the storm breaking through the air all around us.

"I thought you'd left," he fumed quietly as he fell to the muddy blanket of poppies at my feet and caught my ankle.

He dragged me forward under my hips slid up over his thighs and then he used the pocket knife he produced from him riding jacket to rend a hole in the center of my trousers. He fisted both hands in the fabric and tore it clean in two, so that the rain beat down on my white panties and turned them sheer.

"I thought you'd run away, but you have to know, *topolina*, I'd never let you go without saying goodbye," he promised huskily, and then his body was pressing me into the wet grass and blooms as he ravaged my mouth.

There was no finesse in the way he snapped my underwear with his fingers and pulled his breeches down just enough to free the angry length of his cock. There was only animal urgency and primal instinct to mate.

I clawed at his shoulder as he found my wet cunt and thrust inside, biting my neck hard as he pounded into me. I knew the mark he left would bloom red as the poppies trampled beneath us and just as soon gone.

I wanted him to plant poppies all over my skin with his hands and teeth so that I bloomed like the entire field of flowers, more alive than I'd ever been before.

And he did bite me, my neck, my shoulders, the exposed skin of my chest and even my thumb when I brought it to his lips. He fucked me hard like a barbarian claiming the spoils of war, and I loved every moment of his inflexible body driving mine into the dirt.

There was something mean in our sex, some edge of desperate cruelty that had been there even in the beginning.

He fucked me like I was his enemy and he wanted to impale me on his cock and paint me in the triumph of his cum.

"Take my cock, *topolina*," he commanded me, pinning my throat with a big hand as he rutted faster, deeper inside me. "Take it and thank me for it."

I came at the thought, spasming and thrashing against the marshy earth as my mouth formed the chant *thank you, Master*.

Seconds later, his cock kicked inside me, and his cum splashed against my womb. I held him tightly as I took his cock and his semen, committing the feel of his heavy limbs immobilising me and the smell of the rain in the flowers to my memory forever.

When my hazy brain finally cleared, he was still inside me, hard and thick as a steel pipe wedged between the tight pink walls of my aching sex. I could feel the hotness of his cum against the opening to my womb and the cool trickle of it sliding down my inner thighs into the crack of my ass. He was in me, his heavy weight on me, and his cruel, puppeteer's hands all around me, forcing me to dance to his dark, malicious tune.

I didn't want to like it.

The cold, calculating way he sliced me into pieces with the refined edge of his sexual commands until I was a pliable, passive mass of ribbons piled on the floor at his feet.

But after months of conditioning, of relying on him for the very food I ate and the water I drank, some primal part of my brain was programmed to like it. Some instinctual code in my DNA was prepared to lust after it.

There was no excuse, though, for what it did to my heart.

How it palpitated to the beat of his shoes striking the marble as he made his way down the corridor to my gilded cage.

How it twisted into vicious knots every time I displeased him and then collapsed back into shape, heavy with pride and elastic with satisfied submission when he praised me.

How I could feel his name etched into the bloody walls of my heart much the same way he'd branded it into the skin of my ass.

The last vestiges of my resistance lay crumbled around me as I held this fierce, brutal beast of a man against my skin and gave myself over to my heart's betrayal.

I loved him.

The cruel lord of this manor, the beastly man who owned

me and ruled my every whim.

And it was exactly at that moment of my capitulation that he destroyed me, as a shark sensing blood in the water.

"Tomorrow, you'll leave," he said, in that clipped accent that stripped emotion from every word. "And I'll finally be rid of him. And, thank heaven, of you."

My heart didn't break.

I'd heard about it enough times to imagine the sound of the shatter as it broke under the hammer fist of rejection like delicate glass.

That didn't happen.

Instead, I could feel the organ grow heavy and slow, the blood through it congealed with unsaid emotions, weighted with bone deep sorrow. It grew so heavy, it sank from my chest to the depths of my belly where it anchored in the mire there and ached dully with my pulse.

I knew in the same way I'd always known my father would be the end of my life as I knew it, that I'd never live again without the weight of my dead heart in my belly.

Alexander was sending me away to be the weapon of his revenge, and I know in my soul, I wouldn't return to him unscathed.

Part Three

SPY

NON DECOR, DECO. I AM NOT LED, I LEAD

Chapter Twenty-Three

*I*t felt strange to be back in Italy. The air was too hot against my pale skin, each ray of sunlight like a scalpel peeling back layers of my flesh until I burned red all over. My little family home felt too close, and I kept bumping into lamps and walls, tripping on uneven flagstones.

Other things were strange too, sitting at a table to eat dinner felt wrong after months of eating at Alexander's feet or in my bedroom with a tray of food over my lap. The cheap sheets over my twin bed in my shared room with Elena and Giselle abraded my sensitive skin and made it impossible to sleep.

I was also horny, bloated with repressed sexual longing that made my breasts swollen and tender, my sex heavy like a pendulum ticking away the time since it had last been touched.

I missed Alexander in a physical way that felt like the agony of detoxing from an addiction. Thoughts of him itched and raced under my skin, swirling through my mind so that a few times I even hallucinated his presence in bed beside me, in the kitchen watching me chop garlic, and in the shower as I dared to touch my aching pussy.

It wasn't easy to act normal around Mama and Elena. The first had given birth to me and could tell in the ways only a mother knows that I had been changed irrevocably over the past ten months. It was Elena, though, who questioned me tirelessly about my life during that time. Where I had eaten in Milano, who my friends were, what it was like to live in and work in London.

Lies fell easily from my lips. I'd learned from master manipulators in Pearl Hall, so I didn't seize up over the falsehoods or tangle them in my mind. Still, despite my ease, Elena peered at me often as if I was one of her ethics problems.

It worried me enough that after a few days, I had taken to avoiding one-on-one time with her.

I'd been home for over a week, and I still hadn't found a way to approach Salvatore. The truth was, I didn't want to lay eyes on the bad who had betrayed his own daughter by selling her into slavery. It didn't matter that I'd grown to love Alexander or that I'd been on a journey of discovery in the underworld and returned reborn, darker, and stronger than before.

He was still the villain in my life's tale.

There was nothing he could say or do that would earn my forgiveness because he had not only wronged me, but he had also wronged my family.

And that, as always, was where I drew the line between forgettable and unforgiveable.

Somehow, I would have to find a way to swallow my hatred and pretend I wanted to breach the void between us, reunite like some sweet story from a Bildungsroman novel. All so that he could be finally brought to justice for the wrongs against Alexander and me.

"You're so quiet these days," Elena noted, cutting through my distraction.

She was studying me as she taped a box of her books closed, and I took a moment to let myself love the look of her. She was the most Angelized of my siblings, her body long and lean, her skin white and her red hair so dark it shone like merlot in an artfully tousled mess of curls around her angular face. Seamus was etched in nearly every facet of her face and form, a fact she hated so thoroughly, and sometimes, I wondered if it tainted her entire perception of herself.

She had changed too since I'd been gone, her porcelain doll's face had lost its placidity to bitterness that tightened the edges of her eyes and mouth in a way that made her look cruel.

I wanted to ask her about her boyfriend, Christopher, but she wouldn't admit anything was wrong between them, even after he'd so clearly assaulted Giselle before she left for school two years ago.

Her silence on the matter perturbed me, but at least now I was certain she would never see him again. The promise of America shone on her future like a spotlight through the gloom of our pasts in Italy. If anyone could harness and tame the wild beast of the American Dream, it was my whip smart eldest sister.

"Cosi?" she asked again.

I shook my head slightly. "Sorry, jet lag."

"You know, that excuse has almost run its course." She raised an eyebrow and crossed her arms over her chest. "You can talk to me. I know you've done…things so that we can afford to move to America, but *cazzo*, Cosima, I'm your older sister. If I cannot be the one to make sacrifices for this family, at least let me shoulder some of your burden."

I stared at her, mute with longing. I'd always shared an incredible closeness with my family, but now I found myself too embroiled in the secrets of another bloodline to be able to converse freely with my own.

I realized with horror that I felt more like a Davenport than a Lombardi.

"It's nothing, Lena, I really am just adjusting to the time change."

"Two hours isn't much of a change, but fine." She sighed and pushed back an errant piece of hair beneath her black cloth headband. Then, having considered something internally, she moved swiftly across our small living room to where I was packing up Mama's fabrics, and she pulled me into a hug.

My sister didn't like physical affection. She had never been very demonstrative growing up, but her aloofness had only honed into a cold blade over the past few years, and now she barely allowed you to kiss her in the traditional Italian greeting.

So this hug was special, and it nearly worked to unlock the massive deadbolt I had across the chamber to my mess of emotions and web of secrets.

Nearly, but not quite.

I was a stronger woman than I had been, so I knew to take my pleasure when I could even if it was tinged with pain.

My arms banded around her small waist and pulled her even closer against me so that I could smell her perfume. It was Chanel Number 5, a scent she had lusted over for years even though we could only afford the samples found in the odd magazine. I bought it for her every year for her birthday since my first modelling check came in, and I loved smelling it on her.

"*Ti amo*," I whispered into her ear, hoping that she would wear the words there like precious gems even when I couldn't be with her.

She tightened her hold on me for a moment and then whispered the words back, her voice softer than I'd ever heard it before. "*Ti amo, Cosima, e grazie.*"

I love you, Cosima, and I thank you.

Tears pooled at the backs of my eyes, and I opened my mouth to give her something, a gift only Elena could fully cherish, one of knowledge, when the door to our little house burst open with a bang.

We sprung apart to face the intruders, but it was me who gasped when I recognized who it was.

Salvatore stood backlit by the flaming Italian sun, a great shadow of a beast with thick dark hair and beard that stained his strong, clenched jaw like ink.

"Why the drama?" Elena asked, fisting her hands on her hips as she interacted with a man she thought she knew well enough to be familiar with, a man who had been visiting us sporadically our entire lives. "You nearly broke down the door."

"Do not speak to *capo* that way," Rocco demanded as he stepped through the door at Salvatore's back, his thugs behind him. "You Lombardi women never respectful enough."

Mama appeared in the doorway to the bedroom, her face ashen as she took in the crowd of Made Men in our doorway. Her eyes darted to me then back to Salvatore, and she swallowed hard.

How had I never noticed her watchfulness and unease before when it seemed written in the air between us like subtitles.

"We are here for Cosima," Salvatore told Mama in his gravel rich voice.

Mama's hands fluttered through the air, touched on her heart, and then took flight again like frightened birds. "No, Tore, please..."

He ignored her, lifting a hand that signaled the men behind him to push forward into the house.

My conditioned flight or fight response flooded my body with heady adrenaline. Carefully, I pushed Elena farther out of the way and then faced the Camorra foot soldiers with a cutting grin.

"Let's see if you can catch me, boys," I taunted them.

The stupider of the two lunged for me. I hopped onto the low coffee table, landing on one leg while the over swung through the air with the leverage from my leap and crashed into the descending face of the mafia man.

He fell onto the couch with a groan.

"Don't be difficult," Rocco called out from the doorway. I tried to keep my eyes on the approaching man, but then the tinkle of bells tickled my ears and pulled my gaze over.

Rocco let the string of tiny bells dance in from his fingers, and he laughed at my look of horror. "I brought these for your Mama and sister, Cosima. Do you remember my promise to you if you fucked up that deal for us? I'm going to tie them up with bells stringed to their ankle so that they look like ornaments dangling from the cypress outside."

A sob ballooned in my throat and turned my voice to helium as the other man grabbed me, and I screamed as a hand caught my dress and pulled me into his arms.

"That is," Salvatore drawled, as if we were discussing the weather and his ex-paramour wasn't crying across the room while their bastard daughter was being assaulted, "unless you come with us now."

"Salvatore, no," Mama sobbed as she moved forward across the room to grip him by the shirt and mumble pleas in a string of rapid Neapolitan.

Rocco ripped her off and threw her savagely to the ground.

Elena and I made twin sounds of distress in our throats, and my sister immediately went to her.

I stopped struggling, hanging in my captor's arms.

"Fine," I said with my chin raised high. "I'll go with you. Just leave the house and my family alone."

Salvatore was already turning to leave when he said, "Bring her and make sure she does it screaming so the neighborhood knows what happens to those who go against the Camorra."

The man holding me wrapped a fist in my hair and half

dropped me to the ground so that he could pull me, kicking and yelling in pain, out the front door and down the steps to a waiting black sedan.

Mama and Elena hugged each other in the door, watching as I was thrown into the back of the car and the door was slammed shut in my face. I placed my fingers against my trembling lips and then against the hot, dirty glass in a distant kiss I hoped would bring them some minute degree of comfort.

The car started with a rumble and began to roll away from the house, but still I pressed my fingers to the glass until we were well out of sight.

"What a touching sight," a familiar voice said from beside me. I snapped around to see the long, broad length of Edward Dante Davenport lounging in the seat beside me. "Now, Cosima, are you ready to have that discussion I told you about?"

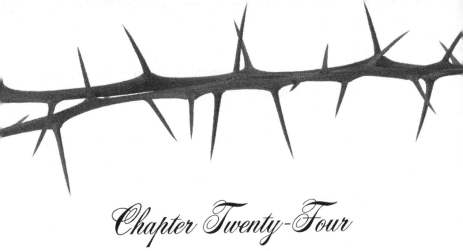

Chapter Twenty-Four

*D*ante lit a cigarette and placed it at the corner of his mouth as he waited for me to respond to his arcane question.

"At least open a window," I snapped at him, unable to move beyond the image of his insolence, lounging there without a care in the world while my life had once again turned topsy-turvy.

He grinned unapologetically and clicked the button to roll down the window.

"What the hell was all that back there?" I asked, realizing that perhaps the entire bizarre scenario had been staged. "Salvatore has never raised a voice or hand to me in all my life. Why did he order me dragged out of my home by my hair?"

"Fear is a powerful tool, Cosima," he told me, a curl of white smoke rolling sensuously between his full lips.

His mouth was redder than Alexander's, but the shape was the same.

The impulse to kiss him was shocking and disgusting, but I could feel it in my limbs like a drug.

Dante's smile was just as slow and curling as the cigarette smoke. "You of all people should know that. Living in the underworld, you learn to take every opportunity to strike fear into the hearts of your would-be enemies."

"I doubt ancient Signora Moretti or the Bianchi sisters are eager to start a gang to oppose your own," I said with an eye roll.

There was something about this man, something enough like Alexander to make my spirit buzz and something enough like *me* to put me at ease that made me feel reckless and brave.

He chuckled and took another drag. "No, I doubt it. Sometimes you have to look closer to home for your true enemies, though."

I caught the edge of his piercing look and deflected it by pulling through my tangled hair as if it fascinated me.

He was speaking of Pearl Hall, of his ex-brother and ex-father, of things he shouldn't know because he didn't live there.

"Rocco has been trying to outmaneuver Salvatore for years now. If he knew about your real relationship, it would not signal good things for Tore, or for you and Seb," he continued. "Personally, I thought the hair pulling was a nice theatrical addition."

"You're crazy."

Dante shrugged a shoulder. "Maybe. You're a product of your upbringing, as much as any of us try to hide it, and mine was crazy enough for most."

"I don't understand what the motivation is here. Why are you in this car talking to me? Why did you come to Pearl Hall after all these years and then save me from Ashcroft at The Hunt? What am I to you?" I asked.

I didn't have a good track record with getting my questions answered, but I was alone in a car with one of the many men who seemed to be pulling the strings of my life like a master puppeteer, and it wasn't like we had anything else to discuss.

Dante stared at me for a long moment with his undeniably gorgeous obsidian eyes, and then when he spoke, it was in a voice more British than he normally seemed to allow.

"Let me tell you a story. It takes place in a home that is like a castle, but it is not about a beautiful princess and her prince. Instead, it's about a man of great power who seduced a woman into marriage with false promises and then ruled like a tyrant over her for the entirety of her life. The only joy she ever had was her two sons, two boys she made a promise to herself would never turn out like their cruel father.

"She enlisted the help of her childhood best friend, a male influence to teach them about the difference between right and wrong, an important lesson they wouldn't learn in the world of power their father ruled from.

"For a time, everything was bearable, and then, the woman discovered an awful secret that changed her entire world. She vowed to take the boys and run away with the aid of her friend. Only, her husband found out, and before she could run, he killed her."

I blinked at him. "That doesn't sound like any childhood fairy tale I've ever heard before."

"It wouldn't."

"Listen, I understand that you think Noel is a cruel man. In my personal experience, I haven't seen much of that. He was kind to me when I lived at Pearl Hall. Alexander obviously has his own issues with his father, and in the end, we weren't allowed to spend time together, but I don't see him as this awful villain. And I do not believe he killed your mother. Not when she was at *Salvatore's* house with *you* when she died."

Dante's amiable façade vanished like the plume of smoke out the open window. His eyes went black as sin and his rough-hewn face went taut with rage.

"I was there, so I should know what really happened. Mum had taken me with her to Salvatore's to plan how we might get away from Noel. Alexander wasn't there because he was the heir, and Mum worried he felt too much of the family obligation and was already too much like him to understand how dangerous it was to stay at Pearl Hall. We weren't kids anymore. He was twenty-six, and I was twenty-one, so we didn't have to blindly follow anyone anymore. But I followed her, and Alexander stayed at home."

"Why did she decide to run after all those years?" I asked, invested in the story despite myself.

This was the great mystery. This was the reason Alexander had allied himself with a father he hated and was using the Order to find answers to his mother's death.

If I could find the answers for him, maybe everything would be different.

The car slowed, and I realized we were stopping. Outside my side window, a field of poppies stretched as far as the eye could see, and before us stood a huge stucco home the colour of daffodils.

The door opened for me, but I didn't get out because Dante was staring at me, his face so solemn I wondered if we were arriving at the place of my own death.

"She ran because she knew discovered what Noel had been doing all those years with the slave girls he took and didn't hide from her."

"What did he do?" I asked as Salvatore appeared at the opening to my door and stoically offered me his hand to help get out.

I didn't take it.

"He killed them," Dante said. "Just like he killed my mum."

After a brief reprieve to wash my face and gather my thoughts in a spare bedroom in Salvatore's home, I was led by a man with a gun strapped to his arm to a red flagstone patio off the back of the villa. Salvatore and Dante sat at a round wood table laden with a charcuterie feast and a huge flagon of red wine, talking animatedly in hushed voices. It was dark, the stars blazing in the velvet blue sky as they can only do in the countryside. The air had cooled enough to feel gentle against my skin, and the sweet scent of acacia blooms lingered on the breeze as it swept through the outdoor kitchen.

They both paused when they noticed me in the door, their eyes sweeping up and down my body simultaneously.

Dante's gaze was filled with male interest and admiration.

Salvatore's was harder to discern, but there was a slight smile on his lips that he couldn't quite suppress that made me think he liked to see me standing in his home.

I frowned and stalked forward, taking the seat the gunman pulled out for me and crossing my legs in a business-like manner.

"Well gentleman, the hour for explanations has arrived," I declared.

Dante didn't even try to curb the boyish delight in his smile, but Salvatore bit his grin back and nodded solemnly.

I pointed a finger at him. "Don't mock me. You may not have killed Chiara Davenport, but you abandoned my mother, brother, and me, then, to make matters worse, you *sold* me. So you are still the villain here."

Any humour or pleasure lingering in Salvatore's patrician face snuffed out, and when he leaned forward to speak to me, it was in the low, unspeakably powerful voice of an Italian mafia *capo*.

"Don't speak about something you know nothing about, girl. If you want to cast stones before you know the true story,

I'll send you back to your mother and you can return to England empty-handed."

I felt like a chastened child as I sat there struggling not to pout and glare in equal turn. Finally, I crossed my arms tightly over anxious chest and tilted my chin at him to go on.

Dante chuckled. "She looks just like you doing that."

We both shot him glares that made him hold up his hands in surrender even though his eyes danced.

Salvatore turned back to me, his eyes scouring my face like an artist ready to commit me to paper.

"I won't get into the backstory with Caprice. Your mother and I met when we were both very young. She already had two children by your father, but I was infatuated with her beauty and her mind. I wanted to take her and the girls away with me, but for many reasons, that wasn't to be. I didn't even know you and Seb were born until years after our tryst. I'd moved to Venice to join an outfit there, and I was moving up in the ranks when an old friend sent me a picture of you and Sebastian. You must have been only three years old, but you looked so much like me, I knew it the moment I set eyes on you."

"I can't believe Mama wouldn't have told you," I protested because the woman I knew was not duplicitous or immoral.

She went to church every Sunday and prayed before bed each night, sometimes so fervently I wondered what kind of conversations she held daily with her God.

"She didn't tell me because she knew what kind of man I was," Salvatore said, his voice raised with passion. "If I had known she was pregnant, I would have spirited her away where Seamus could never find us."

His fist hit the table with a clatter as he dislodged a plate filled with cheeses and bowl of olives shattered on the flagstones below us.

"When I found out, I flew back to Napoli, but Caprice refused to acknowledge my paternity, and it was obvious even Seamus had no idea. I moved back and tried to become as much a part of your lives as she and my job would let me."

"It wasn't enough," I said quietly.

I could read the tragedy in the set of his shoulder and the opaque helplessness in his eyes, but I only had so much sympathy for an adulterer, a mafia man, and the person who sold me.

"Caprice would only accept money when she didn't have enough to put food on the table for you kids." He shook his head in frustration, but there was a glimmer of pride in his smile. "She was always so stubborn. And I kept Seamus from being murdered time after time, so often that uncomfortable questions were raised about why I cared so much for him and his fate."

"Another black mark against you," I said. "We would have been better off if he was dead."

"That's not true. It was the only time your mother begged me for anything; the first time Seamus was brought before me to be killed. She showed up at my compound with your little hand in hers, and she promised I could visit sometimes if I promised to save her husband's life." His smile was self-depreciating. "I agreed on the spot."

"That doesn't explain why you allowed me to be sold for his gambling debts," I retorted.

I needed to latch on to something concrete as the world shifted beneath my feet like quicksand.

Dante grinned. "I think I can help with that one. You see, Alexander has been convinced that Tore killed Mum for years because Noel told him so. He's set Interpol, MI6, and *Polizia di Stato* on us like fucking leeches, and he's even tried to get people in our organization. For years, we've had an alert set up in case anyone searches your name or Sebastian's, and when he found out who you were last August, it was too good an opportunity to pass up."

"I don't understand," I breathed, my lungs two wrung out dishtowels in my chest.

Because I thought I did understand.

Alexander had bought me to infiltrate the Camorra.

But the Camorra had sold me to infiltrate Pearl Hall.

My mind spun, filled with dirty water circling a clogged drain.

"We sold you to Alexander so you could find out the Davenport secrets, and we could finally prove that Noel was the one to kill Chiara," Dante explained, so excited about his mastermind plan that he failed to note how pale I was.

"And what about Alexander? Do you want to implicate him in any crimes as well?"

"The entire fucked-up Order of Dionysus needs to be dismantled. They covered up Chiara's death, and the deaths of all the other poor women Noel and the brothers used as slaves." Finally, Dante hesitated, his eyes sharpening on my face. "Alexander is my brother, so I can understand your recalcitrance, but he might just have to go down with the ship."

"That's why you helped me in The Hunt and tried to step in at Pearl Hall," I said as the domino pieces began to fall into place. "You were protecting me even as you were using me."

"Exactly," Dante said with a bright smile before looking at Salvatore. "She's too smart to be your kid."

I ignored him.

I ignored everything but the sound of my blood rushing through my ears and the dangerous thrum of my racing heart.

"Cosima," Salvatore said firmly, catching my attention as he took my listless hand off the table and cupped it in his own. "I know this isn't easy, and it's a lot to digest. Stay here with us for a few days, a couple of weeks, and let's get to know each other before we make any decisions. I know it seems like I'm using you, and I'm sorry for that, but it's the nature of my job and the nature of fatherhood. I know I don't have the right to say this, but I truly am doing what I must to keep you safe."

"You have a decision to make," Dante said, solemn once more. He looked like Salvatore's sidekick sitting there, just as dark and powerful, utterly in sync with the older man's criminal thoughts and intentions. "You can help us take down a sect of terrible men, and we can help you and your family set up a new life in America, free of the past and of the Davenport influence. Or you can go back to Pearl Hall and the Master who will use you just as surely as we are, but toward a more bitter end."

Chapter Twenty-Five

Three weeks later.

"*Alexander, please come, I think he knows I'm here to spy on him.*"

The words of my earlier phone call echoed in my head as I paced around the small sitting room in my hotel suite in Roma.

I'd called Alexander in a panic, begging him to get me because I feared Salvatore and his men were onto me.

Alexander had answered his phone on the first ring, was barking orders to bring the car around to someone, probably Riddick, in the background before I could finish my first sentence, and the moment I stopped speaking, he promised he was on the next plane to Roma to bring me home safely.

Home.

Safely.

The two words were laughable.

My childhood home had never been safe with Seamus living there. Now it was no longer even ours because we had sold it, and Mama and Elena were just now settling in Brooklyn, USA in their new home. One I wouldn't be a part of, at least not for a long, long time.

Pearl Hall could never truly be my home although it was safe because I would never be anything more than a slave inside its walls.

Salvatore's Roman country villa might have been my home for the past three weeks, but I was by no means ready to call it my home and him my father.

It was one of the reasons I was doing this.

I jumped when I heard a loud banging against my door and then the sound of a key card sliding and clicking in the automatic lock.

My breath froze in my lungs as the door swung open to reveal Alexander.

His golden hair was a tousled mess from his anxious hands and a long plane ride, his handsome face creased with exhaustion, and his expensive suit wrinkled beyond what he would normally ever allow.

But it was his eyes I couldn't look away from.

They traced every inch of my body as I stood stock-still across from him, accounting for every new mark on my body or expression flickering across my eyes. It was the soulful search of a man who had been too long parted from a lover.

It was a look that made me want to cry.

He caught my expression, and his face turned fierce as he dropped his bag inside the door and stalked across the room for me, walking over the top of the coffee table to get to me faster.

The second he snagged me around the middle and carted me into his arms, the tears I'd been battling won out, and I burst into sobs.

Alexander squeezed me tightly for a moment and then used a hand in my hair to yank my head back. His eyes were darker than I'd ever seen them, pewter tarnished with regret and rusty with agony.

"Fuck," he rasped. "I missed you more than I could manage."

And then his mouth was sealed over mine, his tongue sliding against my own in a sensual glide that had me moaning and fisting my own hands in his hair.

"Don't ever make me leave again," I begged before I could remember that it wasn't part of the plan.

"Never," he swore, the word so filled with promise it felt as final as his brand against my ass. "Never again."

He kissed me again, so fiercely it bruised my lips, but I didn't care. I wanted to wear the blue of his passion and the purple of his possession on my mouth like lipstick.

"Where's your bag?" he muttered against my lips. "As much as I want to fuck you right here on the floor, I want to get you out of the godforsaken country even more."

"In the bedroom," I whispered, squeezing my eyes shut because this was where my plan could go very, very wrong.

And I really didn't want anyone to get hurt, least of all Alexander.

He gave me one final, bruising kiss and then moved beyond me into the bedroom. The second he disappeared from sight, Salvatore appeared in the open doorway from the hall and raised a gun in the air.

Seconds later, I screamed bloody murder, and Alexander appeared in the living room holding my bag and to my great surprise, his very own gun.

Salvatore's was currently pressed to my temple, the cold barrel biting into my skin.

"Put the gun down, Alexander," Salvatore ordered coldly, adjusting his chokehold so that it seemed even tighter against my airway. "We both know you won't risk her getting hurt."

"You're really so evil that you'd kill your own daughter?"

Alexander asked calmly, dropping my bag so that he could circle around slightly for a better angle at my biological father.

"You are such a fool. Your mother tried to teach you to think for yourself, but you remain brainwashed by your pernicious father and his precious Order. I did not kill Chiara. Why would I kill my best friend?"

"Why would you press your gun to the head of the daughter you abandoned at birth? Maybe you're a psychopath."

"When will you stop seeing the world in black and white. Your mother tried to teach you better," Salvatore tried again.

"Say my mother's name one more time and I'll put a bullet through your skull," Alexander said calmly, leveling the gun. "Now, let Cosima go."

I could feel the starch leech out of Salvatore's grip as he held me. Dante and I had both told him Alexander wouldn't be reasoned with unless there was cold hard proof, but Salvatore wanted to give it a chance before the next part of our plan went into action.

I made hard eye contact with Alexander and hoped that his strange ability to read my thoughts hadn't been transected by our time apart. Then, I tapped lightly on Salvatore's toe before I let out a battle cry and twisted in his arms. I used my momentum to spin us so that my back was to the door and my father's back was to Alexander and then... *bang*!

I watched as Salvatore's eyes widened in pained surprised as he was shot in the back. My throat worked hard to swallow back a sob as I pushed him off me onto the ground where he rolled over onto his stomach and lay still.

Alexander ran toward me, my bag in one arm and the smoking gun in the other. He wrapped an arm around me and leveraged me out the door.

"I think you killed him," I whispered thickly.

He barely spared a glance over his shoulder at the prone man before racing us both down the hall. A door to another hotel room opened down the hall as we pushed through the emergency exit and flew down the stairs.

There was a car waiting at the curb, and Riddick was in the driver's seat.

My eyes burned with unshed tears as Alexander threw me into the back and then slid in beside me, barking orders to Riddick that I didn't listen to.

I stared out the window as we screeched away from the hotel in the *Testaccio* district of Rome and headed toward the airport.

There was very little chance that Salvatore was seriously injured. The bullet had gone into his Kevlar coated back and probably only leave a bruise, but it surprised me how rattled I was by my own plan.

I'd needed Alexander to have closure even though I didn't believe Salvatore and Dante had killed Chiara. In fact, it was obvious that they loved her dearly and believed Noel had somehow been the one to kill her after she'd threatened to reveal his secrets.

Some of those being that he'd murdered his previous slaves.

I didn't know how much of that to believe given that I'd seen Yana, one of Noel's slaves, at Club Dionysus a few weeks ago, and he had been mostly kind to me during my stay at Pearl Hall.

All I knew for sure was that this blood feud was going to get them all killed in the end, and I didn't want that.

No, I couldn't *stand* that.

Not for Dante who I'd come to understand in my short weeks in Italy was opposite to his brother not just in looks but also temperament. He was more Latin, passionate, moody, and quick to temper, with a humour that could be cutting as the edge of a sword or hilarious enough to bring tears.

Not for Salvatore, who I remained unhappy with despite his explanations. He was a father. I didn't care if Mama ever took him back, he should have tried harder to make a positive difference in our lives. Despite my misgivings, my old hunger to have any kind of father figure stirred in my depths, and I found myself spending most of my three-week stay at his house helping him tend to his pet project of growing olives and listening to him speak of his plans to send Dante to America to take over the Camorra outfit there.

I think it was more so that Dante could watch over Mama and Elena, but I didn't press. Dante went by the last name of Salvatore in Naples, and it was obvious the two were bounded like father and son.

Mostly, though, I didn't want that kind of death or criminal end for Alexander. As much as I sat in the field of poppies on Salvatore's property and thought of the course my life had taken, I couldn't convince myself not to love the civilized man or the beast that lurked beneath his skin.

I wanted him to be free of his obligatory vendetta, free to fight his battles against the Order and his father so that he could live the kind of life he truly wanted.

And so, I cooked up my plan to stage Salvatore's death so that Alexander could move on from Chiara's murder. It gave Salvatore and Dante the space they needed from police scrutiny to transfer their resources and lives to America, while also allowing them to continue to look into Noel without his being aware they were still in action against him.

It was a perfect solution to that one problem.

Only the issue remained, what was I going to do now? It felt impossible that I should go back to slavery, lonely but for the moments of the day Alexander carved out to use my body like a vessel for his pleasure.

I craved more than his rare moments of affection and the title of slave.

I wanted to be allowed to love him.

"Are you okay?" Alexander asked, finally turning to me, his hands on my body searching for injuries.

I blinked a him. "Physically, yes, but I think you just killed my father, Xan."

His eyes flicked with a strange light. "And if I did? Are you going to judge me for finally avenging the death of my mother? I've been trying to bring that man down for years by legal means, but he was slipperier than an eel."

"Are you so sure he did kill her? I spent time with him while I was home, and he seemed convinced of his own innocence," I ventured. "I don't think he was a good man, but then again, neither are you."

"I've never killed an innocent woman, nor would I."

"No," I whispered. "But you bought one to use against her own father."

"I hadn't thought to kill him, only bring him to justice in whichever way I could. He destroyed my family."

"So your plan worked," I said with a tired, cynical smile that felt wrong on my face. "I was just the right bait to lure him out of hiding."

The last vestiges of triumph and adrenaline faded from his face and a battle-weary man sat beside me, fatigued by his demons and unsure of his own morality.

"I know it may be hard to believe after what happened, but I stopped caring about that a long time ago." He looked at his hands as if seeing blood there, and muttered mostly to himself. "I thought I would feel better once it was done."

"Yet you sent me to Italy."

He sighed, a sad sound like a toy deflating. "I didn't know how to deal with what I was feeling."

"What a classic male excuse," I said even though I knew nothing of classic male anything.

My experience was limited solely to Alexander, and I doubted anything was typical about his behaviour.

I just wanted to push him over the edge of his own expectations into a new place where he could shine a better light on his life and choices. It had taken me three weeks with Dante and Salvatore to understand that life was rarely as cut and dry as we tried to force it to be.

Alexander lifted his knee on to the seat between us so that he could better face me and sink a hand into my hair. He tilted my chin back just enough to make the angle awkward and my scalp sing with pain.

The small act of domination centered me as it centered him.

"No matter what happens, I'm never letting you go again. Do you understand me, *bella?*" he asked, his conviction hitting me like the strike of a gavel. "I want you... no, I need you to be mine in every single way you will have me."

I placed my hand over his wrist just to feel the strength of his pulse and use it as a metronome to set my own. "You have me already. You own me in body, spirit, and currency. I don't have anything left to give you."

"But you do," he insisted, his hand tightening until I whimpered, and my mouth bloomed open. He leaned close, licking at my upper lip, then biting softly into the pillowy bottom. "You can give me your name so I can replace it with my own."

I blinked at him, trying not to lose focus as he dragged his nose down my throat and bit the junction of my shoulder like an animal marking his mate.

"Xan, what are you talking about?"

"I want there to be no doubt in anyone's mind—not for the Order, Edward or even Noel—that we are bound together, and I will not allow us to be pried apart over anything. They can come for us if they want to, but when they do, we will be cemented together in the eyes of law as man and fucking wife."

Part Four

SPOUSE

NON DECOR, DECO. I AM NOT LED, I LEAD

Chapter Twenty-Six

J'd never imagined the day of my wedding. My sisters talked about it sometimes late in the night when we should have been sleeping instead of whispering about veils and tulle gowns, but I'd only ever listened, happy to imagine their settings and my place at their sides.

I had no dreams of my own, and a wedding felt like it should be a dream.

I felt as if I was living one as I woke up on my nineteenth birthday and prepared for my life to change again just as dramatically as it had the year before.

Mrs. White was already pulling the red velvet drapes open and directing the other maids to lay out my breakfast, air out the gown, and arrange the make-up just so on the vanity for when the hair and face girls came to do me up to the nines.

I didn't want to get out of bed.

My stomach knotted, bound in Shirbari knots as complicated as my feelings about my wedding day.

In one sense, a great one, I was more excited than I'd ever been. The secret wish I'd germinated in the fertile earth at the center of my soul was about to bear fruit.

I was going to transform like Cinderella from slave girl to aristocratic in only a number of hours. Pearl Hall would be my permanent home, and Alexander my forever Master.

It should have been pure euphoria coursing through my veins, but it was tainted with the lead poison of dread.

Alexander hadn't made any declarations of love or any further steps to ingratiate me into his life. He still kept his separate bedroom and only joined me when it suited him. He was still demonstrative after sex and careful with me whenever something reminded either of us of the baby, but otherwise, he remained oddly detached.

I worried he wasn't marrying me for the right reasons. That he wanted a war with the Order and a reason to fight with Noel, and I was the kindling and the flint.

Just another tool for him to use.

I was quiet after my shower as the group of servants fluttered around me, doing my hair, make-up, and nails while they tittered about the guests and the food and, of course, the handsome bridegroom.

"You're so lucky," the girl painting my lips a deep red told me. "He's the loveliest bloke I've ever laid eyes on."

"Not everything pretty is good," I told her somberly.

When she only blinked at me, I smiled to soften the blow, and she took my words to be a joke, laughing girlishly with her friends at my wit.

"You look beautiful, love," Mrs. White said, sniffing into a lace handkerchief as she stared at my finished complexion in the mirror.

I did.

In fact, I didn't think I'd ever looked lovelier than I did for my wedding.

My hair was curled in big, loose waves spilling to my waist, only one lock pulled back over my left ear and pinned with one of the poppies from my field. The dress had been chosen for me by Alexander, just as my entire wardrobe at Pearl Hall had been, and as with the rest of his choices, it suited me perfectly. It was Grecian style, clasped over the shoulders with golden closures shaped like thorns with a deep dip in the front and back that exposed huge swathes of my summer-kissed skin and the indecent swell of my breasts. It was the perfect dress to complement my thorny pearl and ruby collar, which glistened as regally as a crown at my throat.

I looked like a princess ready to walk down the aisle to her prince.

Tears surged to the service for what felt like the hundredth time already that day as I thought of the lie in that illusion.

I was no princess, and Xan, for all his titles and money, was no prince.

We were just two thoroughly fucked-up people who had found a little solace in each other.

And I was the idiot who had gone above and beyond that to fall in love with him.

"Jesus, marra," Douglas said, showing up in the doorway to my room with both hands clasped over his mouth. "Would you just look at your pretty face?"

I couldn't help but laugh at him as he came forward to brush a kiss against my cheek.

"I just had to sneak a peek atcha before the ceremony, so I dashed up from the kitchen. They're probably making a right mess of things, but this was worth it."

"Thank you, Douglas," I said, taking his hand in a squeeze before I could let him leave.

I wished desperately that any one of my siblings or Mama was here, but Douglas was the next best thing, and I wanted him to know that. Stupidly, tears filled my eyes as I looked at his chocolate brown gaze, and I couldn't properly voice the sentiments.

"I know, ducky," he told me softly, patting my hand. "I know. Listen, I'll be out to watch the ceremony before I chain myself to the kitchen for the feast. I'll be the one cheering inappropriately at the back."

I nodded, still overcome by tears, and then beamed when he ducked down to press a quick kiss to my cheek again before taking off.

"Are you ready, honey?" Mrs. White asked, checking the clock on the vanity. "It's time to go down to the chapel."

Each step I took toward the little chapel attached to the house tripped my heartbeat into a higher cadence.

What if he stood me up?

What if Sherwood came and put a stop to the proceedings?

What if I was making the best biggest mistake of my life?

But more, what if I wasn't?

What if every hard decision and bad moment in my life had led me to exactly this moment where I was supposed to be? What if Alexander was my reward for a short life hard lived?

What if this was my happily ever after?

I swallowed thickly as we reached the closed arched doors to the chapel, and Mrs. White helped me throw the lace veil over my head before giving me a delicate hug and then dashing into the room so she could watch the ceremony.

My hands fidgeted with my bouquet of poppies as I looked at the ceiling and tried to calm my racing breath.

"Are you sure about this?"

I froze and then slowly turned to face Dante, who was leaning languorously against a pillar behind me. There was a cigarette wedged into the corner of his mouth, and it curled the sweet scent of Italian tobacco into the air.

"God, don't cry," he demanded when he saw the tears rush to my eyes.

"I'm so happy you're here," I told him because I was emotional, and it was true.

Somehow, Dante had mired himself in my story as an improbable villain and a surprising white knight.

"Cosi, are you sure you want to marry him? You have options. Salvatore has a car waiting by the gates and we can spirit you away to America with Alexander none the wiser." Dante moved forward to run his fingers gently over my cheek through the veil. "It would be a shame to waste this once-in-a-lifetime beauty on someone who didn't deserve it."

Tears trembled in the overfull trough of my lower lids, but I valiantly fought to keep them from spilling over.

"I love him," I whispered brokenly even though the feel of it in my hair felt like glue, holding the dangerous and ill-fitted parts of my life and personality together in careful unity. "*Dio mio*, Dante, I love him."

He sighed and placed his heavy hands on my shoulders. "I can't say I'm surprised. You've been through a lot, and in some ways, he's pulled through for you. I even think, in his own fucked-up way, he loves you too."

"Maybe," I said, as if I wasn't hoping for the same thing with every breath in my body.

"I'll stick around until the end, just in case you need me," he promised before he leaned down to press a kiss to my cheek.

I wanted to believe I wouldn't need him, but my bad luck ran so deep I felt as if I was a black cat.

He stepped away from the door, the sound of his shoes fading as he moved down the hall.

A moment later, the swell of the wedding march sounded over the chapel's ancient organ, and the doors flew open to admit me.

There were pews filled with people. Villagers from the town

down the hill, people from Alexander's company who had travelled in from London, distant relatives, and a few hand-picked men from the Order. I recognized no one, but then again, I wasn't looking at the pews.

My eyes were locked on Alexander where he stood before the altar in a dark grey metallic suit that perfectly matched the shade of his irises. His hair was pushed back, his strong jaw clean shaved, and he had never looked so handsome, so like a king.

It was none of that which held me arrested, though.

I couldn't look away from the expression on his face as he watched me appear and then walk down the aisle toward him.

He looked like a dying man who had been sent an angel as a messenger from God to tell him of his future salvation.

That was how he looked at me as I moved steps closer to becoming his wife, as if I was his every prayer for goodness and hope for happiness on this earth.

As if I was everything good and pure he had ever laid eyes on.

When I reached the front by his side, he immediately took my bouquet from me and handed it off to Riddick who stood beside him, so that he could take both my hands in his.

"I've never seen anyone so beautiful as you," he whispered to me before the priest could even begin, and when he spoke his voice was rough with excess emotion like a white capped sea. "I've never felt so unworthy of a gift, but I promise to cherish you every day."

"May I begin?" the priest asked with dry British humour that had the whole room laughing.

Alexander tipped his chin imperviously, and said, "You may."

For the whole ceremony, he didn't take his eyes off me, not even when he was told to the kiss the bride and his lips closed over mine in a seal that felt more unbreakable than any legal paper or binding words could ever be.

The afterparty was in full swing, and I was finally enjoying myself. The champagne Alexander kept handing me made my blood feel as light as my heart as I tripped down the hall to the bathroom on the main floor. I was tipsy from wine, drunk on Alexander's salacious kisses, and more hopeful than I had ever dared to be before.

He might not have loved me yet, and he might not ever be capable of saying the words aloud, but there was no doubt in my mind after watching his awe during the ceremony that he *cherished* me.

For a poor girl from Naples with a broken, far-flung family, that was more than good enough for now.

I had just finished in the bathroom and was opening the door to the hall when a vicious hand shoved through the gap in the door and tangled in my hair. With a grunt, I tried to squeeze the offending limb out of the room, but whoever was behind it was too strong.

They burst through the door and were on me in a flash, one hand over my mouth to muffle my screams and the other in my hair so he could begin to drag me from the room.

"Daughter of mine," Noel said with a serene smile as he hauled me down the hall and then bumping down the steps to the servant's level. He abandoned his hand around my mouth because my struggles made it impossible for him to subdue me without the use of both. "I think it's about time we got to know each other a little better."

I screamed so loudly my eardrums quaked ominously and my throat felt on fire with agony, but still I screamed.

Alexander was nowhere in the house, but that didn't excuse

354 | giana darling

the nearly fifty odd servants that the Davenport's kept on staff.

None of them came for me.

Noel wrenched open the small, warped wooden door beside the kitchen entry that went to the dungeon and wrenched me by the hair so hard my screaming gave way to a whimper of pure hurt.

He didn't care about my pain, and he never had. The stolen moments where he'd tended to me had only been manipulation, a tool the Davenport men weaponised all too well.

Two hands pushed in the imprints already left on my back as I was pushed down the steep, narrow steps to the basement. I went tumbling down, this time bracing my arms over my neck so that I wouldn't hit my head.

I lay groaning in a pile at the base of the stairs as Noel closed and bolted the door before following me down.

"I'm so glad we can finally have some private time without anyone else watching," he told me in his gentile way. "I've been waiting so long to have his talk with you."

He gently lifted me by the hand so that I was half standing and then brutally punched down into my left side so that agony exploded in my kidney. I crumpled to the ground.

He repeated the maneuver twice more so that I was weak as a kitten when he finally pulled me by the armpits further into the room. I tried to knee him in the balls, and he backhanded me viciously across the face. I tried to scream again, and he kicked me in the calf so hard, I went down to one knee.

While I was down, he used the time to pull a pair of cuffs down from a length of chain attached to the ceiling. He secured them around my squirming wrists and then hit a lever so that I went catapulting into onto my tiptoes trying to ease the strain on my shoulders.

"Let's take you out of that pretty dress," Noel murmured

almost to himself, moving around me to the buttons along my spine.

I kicked out with my legs but cried out when the movement nearly wrenched my shoulders out of their sockets.

"Still," Noel ordered as he unclipped the last button, and my gorgeous wedding dress fell to the ground at my toes, leaving me only in lace white bra and panties.

He hummed a merry tune as he walked away to a wall covered with impact implements. After careful consideration, he chose one that was achingly familiar.

A black snake whip.

I whimpered as he moved back to stand in front of me.

"Why are you doing this? I just became your son's wife, for God's sake," I beseeched him.

"Such a fool to marry a nothing slave girl. At least his Italian bitch mother had money to her name. You have nothing but beauty, and that will fade. Trust me, it always does."

"He'll find out you've done this," I warned him. "He'll kill anyone else who hurts me."

"He won't find out because I cut the CCTVs. We'll blame it on a guest."

"I'll tell him."

"You won't," he said with a *tsk*. "You won't because you won't be here to do it. I'm going to beat you for your wicked enchantment over my pathetic firstborn, and then you are going to run far away from Pearl Hall and never come back."

"Why the fuck would I do that?" I asked, still struggling to slip my damp wrists through the tight bounds.

There was no way out. At least not physically. If I wanted to leave, I had to manipulate Noel into letting me go.

"If you don't leave, I'll kill him," Noel suggested simply.

I gaped at him, wondering how it was possible I had never

seen the psychopath lurking within him show his face before.

"Why would you kill your only heir?" I demanded.

The door at the top of the stairs pushed open, and Noel smiled.

"Perfect timing," he said over the sound of two descending pair of shoes. "Because I have a spare."

"You disowned Edward, and he would never agree to step in if you murdered his brother."

"Yes, yes, you're right of course." He waited a long beat, long enough for the two bodies to emerge from the shadow of the staircase and into the light.

My breath crystallized in my body, tiny shards piecing through my lungs and throat until they burned.

"Love," Mrs. White greeted me with a shaky but proud smile as she wrapped her hand around a boy of eight or nine and thrust him forward slightly. "I'd like you to meet our son, Rodger."

I blinked at them, my mind working furiously to process the information.

Mrs. White's cryptic words about making the most of a bad situation, her crying over Noel's lap, and finally, her mention of offering the Davenport men something of value when she knew I was pregnant with Alexander's baby.

Which meant, obviously, that it was her who had told Noel and who in turn had shown up at the Grammar ball to push me down the stairs so that I couldn't produce an heir to rival his own.

"I'll kill Alexander if you don't run off like a good little mouse," Noel sneered as he ran the whip lovingly through his hands. "Because I'm still young yet, at least young enough to train my third son in my image."

"He's a bastard," I pointed out, desperate to make sense of this horrible situation. My chest burned with the ache to scream even though I knew no one would hear me. "He won't be able to inherit."

"Well," he drawled as Mrs. White stepped forward to show me the simple gold band on her wedding finger. "You see that isn't actually true. Mary and I were married nine years ago this past May, a few weeks before Rodger was born."

The wheel turned with audible clicks and whirrs in my brain and then, I understood.

"You killed Chiara so you could marry Mrs. White and ensure you have another spare in case the first two failed you."

"Edward was already a lost cause, too much like his mother. I had high hopes for Alexander, especially after Chiara's death, but then you show up, and well… love makes fools out of everyone."

I shook with fury in my chains as Noel turned away from me and collect his young son, taking him to the wall so they could pick out his tool of punishment together.

They were both going to whip.

Just as Alexander had been forced by this father to whip Yana all those year ago when he was Rodger's age.

I looked at Mrs. White. "Please, please, don't let them do this to me. I truly thought we were friends."

She wrung her hands and bit her lip, her eyes trained down on the floor in such an obviously engrained show of submission, I was shocked I hadn't noticed it before.

"It's you or me, sweetheart," she admitted quietly. "And I've suffered enough."

"Ready, son?" Noel asked as he circled me behind me.

I felt the air stir with the lift of his hand and the backward moment of the whip.

"Let your father show you how it's done."

The leather landed like hell fire across my back, and I screamed.

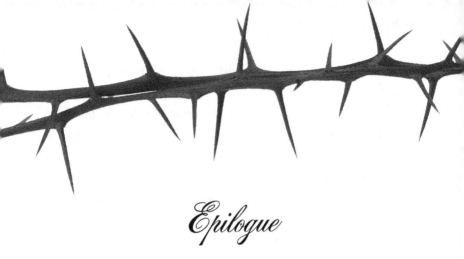

Epilogue

J found Alexander looking for me in the narrow corridor between the chapel and the main house. He hadn't seen me yet, so I fought to straighten the limping gait of my walk. I sucked in a deep breath to fill my hollow chest with air so that I might look similar to how I had before. Before Noel had carved out my heart with a serrated knife and beaten my back black and blue.

I'd found Dante first, lurking at the path to the gardens having a smoke while he flirted with a newer servant I recognized from the house.

He took one look at me and knew.

I'd made the excruciating journey up to my bedroom to fix my mascara-stained face and reapply my lipstick, to flatten the dark, tangled curls and clean up my torn back as best I could before I stepped back into my wedding dress.

Still, Dante saw me across the gravel and knew instantly that I'd been soundly defeated in body, spirit, and mind.

He crushed his cigarette beneath his heel and was at my side in a moment, gently holding my arms because he instinctively knew my back would be bloodied.

He urged me to leave immediately, but that wasn't why I'd taken such painstaking lengths to make myself presentable.

I'd only been married to him for two hours, but I wanted to say goodbye to my husband.

The sight of him peering into through the church doors then around the side of the building as he so obviously searched for me nearly brought me to my knees. It was nothing next to the crippling pain in my back.

It was like gasoline of the ragged hole in my chest where Noel had cut out my heart.

"Xan," I called, more breath than voice.

But he heard me, his head swiveling like a predator who's sensed his prey. His nostrils flared as his eyes pinned me to the wall where I stood, and then he was stalking toward me.

I was happy for the darkness under the awning of the passageway because it helped hide the dead in my eyes and shadow of a bruise already looming on my cheek.

He didn't stop before me.

Instead, he crashed me into the wall so that my sensitive back coursed with fire, but his mouth was over mine before I could scream, and so he ate at the noise in my throat until it was a moan.

His hand fisted in the veil I'd reattached to hide the damage that peeked out of the top back of my dress. He yanked my hair back at a brutal angle so that he could plunder my mouth exactly the way he loved to, with lush lips and clever teeth, until my legs shook and the only thing holding me up was that hand in my hair and his hips pinned to mine against the wall.

There was so much pain in my body, from the beating and the endless turmoil of my heart breaking, but I clung to the pleasure because I knew it was the last time I'd have it.

He feasted on my mouth as if he knew this was the last kiss we would ever have, as if he knew that at any minute I would leave him never to be seen again.

But he couldn't know because I hadn't planned to run. Not ever.

I was prepared to live out my days however they came as the new mistress of Pearl Hall and Master Alexander's eternal slave.

Only now the choice had been brutally ripped from my hands as so many other choices had.

I wondered wildly as I pushed harder into the kiss and sank further into the pain if I was strong enough to break my own heart in order to save his.

If he knew what I was planning, he would have flagellated me himself. He would never let me make the sacrifice I was making because he was arrogant enough to trust that he was invincible just because he believed himself to be.

If he knew, he wouldn't let be grinding his thick cock against my wedding dress covered center as if he could fuck me through the fabric.

No, if he knew my plans to abandon him, I would be right back where I started, shackled to the ballroom floor like the slave I'd tried for so long to pretend not to be.

But I would always be a slave.

I wore his brand on my ass, his metal in my flesh, and his name in the debris of my sunken heart.

"Lord Thornton," the manservant Dante had paid to interrupt us said from behind my husband.

My husband.

I would never even get to call him that.

"Lord Thornton," the young chap tried again, louder this time because Alexander only continued to fuck my mouth as thoroughly as he usually fucked my pussy. "Lord Thornton!"

Finally, he ripped his mouth from me like a wax stripe.

"What is it? Can you not see I'm kissing my beautiful wife?"

Wife.

A sob lodged in my throat like a giant splinter, cutting up my esophagus each time I tried to swallow it down.

"You're needed inside, milord, there's something urgent."

Alexander growled low in his throat, his hand tightening on my hip for a moment in a flare of pain.

I studied his handsome face desperately, eager to memorize every line in his handsome forehead, the way every strand of golden hair waved into the next. I needed the perfect description for the unique colour of his gorgeous eyes so that I would never forget what they looked like through mine.

But the moment was gone in a flash, and my mind was too traumatized to take a proper photo.

Alexander leaned forward to press a kiss like a flower between the pages of my lips, a promise for more later.

"Tonight, wife," he said as he pushed off the wall by my head and turned to follow the servant inside. "Be ready for me."

I waited until he rounded the corner to cave into my hollow chest and sob. There was no time to wallow, but I cupped my hands over my eyes to collect my tears for a long precious moment before I dropped them like rain filled clouds to the ground and ran.

I ran around the back of the building even though each jarring step threw my body into torment because I didn't want the guests to see the bride fleeing in her bloodstained white dress.

I ran down the gravel drive, the stones biting into my feet as I picked up speed on the decline and a car came into view at the gates. Dante stepped out of the running vehicle and waved.

I skidded to a miserable halt and caught my breath.

It felt like I was running constantly from the control of one man into the tyranny of another, and I was tired of the cycle.

It was at that moment of fleeing that I made a decision for the first time in my life that I should have been making the whole way through.

I decided this.

I was mine before I was anyone else's.

I was not my family's breadwinner.

Not Seamus's martyred trump card.

Or Sebastian's twin.

Not the mediator between my rival sisters.

Or Salvatore's bastard daughter and Dante's damsel in distress.

I wasn't even Alexander's anything.

I was just, quite simply and euphorically, my own.

And moving forward, away from the only dream I'd ever dreamed about a life at Pearl Hall, I vowed to only ever be mine again.

Enamoured (The Enslaved Duet, #2) is coming May 31st!

Playlist

"Intro"— The xx

"Ti amo"— Umberto Tozzi

"Prisoner"—The Weeknd, Lana Del Ray

"What Kind Of Man" — Florence + The Machine

"Waiting Game"— BANKS

"Pleasure This Pain"—Kwamie Liv, Angel Haze

"Paint it, Black" —Ciara

"Break It Apart"—Bonobo, Rhye

"Homesick"— Dua Lipa

"Transformation"—The Cinematic Orchestra

"No Control"— Anais

"All The King's Men" — The Rigs

"You Can Run" —Adam Jones

"Silent Running" — Hidden Citizens

"Love And the Hunter" —The Chamber Orchestra of London

"Heart Of The Darkness" — Tommee Profitt, Sam Tinnesz

"Are You Hurting The One You Love?" — Florence + The Machine

"The Limit To Your Love"— Feist

"Skinny Love" — Bon Ivor

"Solider" — Fleurie

"idontwannabeyouanymore" —Billie Eilish

"For You"— Tusks

"Promise"—Ben Howard

Preview of *The Affair*
(The Evolution of Sin Trilogy, Book 1)

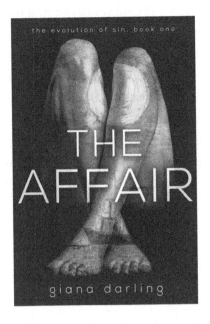

**Meet Cosima's sister, Giselle, and her Frenchman in
*The Affair!***

Is a week of passion enough to warrant changing their lives forever?

Italian born Giselle Moore is reinventing herself for the second time in her short twenty-four years of life, trading in her bohemian artist's life in Paris for the grit and glamour of New York City where the family she hasn't seen in years awaits her. But before beginning her new life, she travels to Cabo San Lucas, Mexico searching for a week of relaxation and reprieve before barreling into her turbulent future.

She never expected to meet the handsome and enigmatic Frenchman Sinclair on the plane and she certainly never would have imagined herself accepting his proposal for a weeklong, no-strings-attached affair. Giselle has never experienced anything as heady as Sinclair's controlled seduction and cool yet devastatingly erotic commands and she finds herself powerless to stop the ferocity of their passions, even when she discovers he has a partner back home. The last thing she needs in her life is another complication, yet as the week wears on, she finds it surprisingly easy to relinquish control to Sinclair, a man she knows nearly nothing about. And to her horror, the one thing she promised never to submit, her battered heart, is just as easily captured in the business mogul's unyielding hands.

CHAPTER ONE

Rain pounded against the steaming tarmac and the force of the wind slapped each drop against the oval window beside my head so that the grey of the runway, the rolling clouds and the Vancouver skyline blurred into one. The rain calmed my nerves, and I closed my eyes to better hear the tap and whistle of weather outside the tin machine that had—somewhat precariously—carried me from Paris to Vancouver in just fewer than seven and a half hours. We were deplaning a third of the passengers and then refueling to make the last leg of the journey to my final destination, Los Cabos, Mexico.

I took a deep breath and tried to focus on my happy place while the economy passengers filtered off the plane. The flight was necessary and after twenty-four years of travelling, I should have been used to the bump and grind of air travel.

In theory, I was. Before every flight I waited calmly in the endlessly snaking line to check my bags, greeted the attendant with a genuine smile and agreed that yes, I would have a pleasant flight. It wasn't until I was on the plane, secured in my seat by the tenuous hold of the belt, that the fear kicked into supercharge. I was intensely grateful to my younger brother Sebastian for loaning me the money for the first class flight. At least now, if the plane went down, I would have a bigger seat to cushion the fall.

"You still look a bit green, *cherie*." The middle-aged gentleman beside me leaned forward and offered me his unopened water bottle. "The worst is over, though. I hope someone is picking you up in Mexico, you are in no shape to drive after all of..." He waved politely at the remaining travel sickness bags the flight attendant had passed to me twenty minutes into our flight.

I managed a weak smile for Pierre. He was a fifty-year-old bachelor, quite distinguished really, with steel grey hair and cunning brown eyes. And maybe, under different circumstances, he would have propositioned me. As it was, he had offered to pay someone to switch seats with him when he discovered how sick I was. Failing that, he had settled in with relatively good grace and lectured me on the tricks of international trade law to distract me. Everything considered—I had managed to drool on his Hugo Boss blazer while I dozed between throwing up—I was grateful to him.

"No, but I'll catch a taxi to the resort." At the moment, I wasn't looking forward to my enforced vacation. All I wanted was to step off the plane back in my familiar Paris and slip into the small wrought iron bed in my studio apartment in *St-Germain-des-Prés*.

Pierre nodded, and shot me a sidelong look. "Are you going to be alright now?"

He was getting off now to visit his daughter and newborn grandson. He didn't like North America, and I got the feeling he was lingering just to eke out a few more words in his native tongue before switching to English.

I nodded meekly but before I could respond the deeper voice of someone behind us spoke, "If you will allow me, I think you are leaving her in capable hands."

I opened my eyes when Pierre nudged me indelicately with his elbow and cleared his throat. Immediately, I blinked.

The man who stood before us dominated the entire aisle. His dusky golden skin stretched taut over his strong features, almost brutally constructed of steeply angled cheekbones and a bladed nose. I had only the vague impression that he was tall and lean because his eyes, a deep and electric blue like the night sky during a lightning storm, held me arrested. The way he held himself, the power of his lean build, and the look in those eyes reminded me of a wolf, caged within the confines of civility but eternally savage.

"I'm sure she would be delighted." Pierre sent me a barely concealed look telling me to pull it together.

I smiled hesitantly at the gorgeous stranger, aware that I was a mess of clammy skin and melted make-up. "I'm fine really."

He nodded curtly, his eyes devoid of any real sympathy. "You will be."

Pierre hesitated, his eyes searching my face for reluctance. I smiled at him and took one of his hands between my clammy palms. "*Merci beaucoup pour tu m'aides. J'espere que tu passes un bon temps avec ta fille.*"

I was rewarded with broad grin before he hastily collected his things and moved towards the front of the plane. I watched him go instead of focusing on the stranger as he took Pierre's abandoned seat but after a few moments with his eyes hot on my face, I turned to him uneasily.

His thick hair was the colour of polished mahogany and curled, overlong, at the base of his neck. My fingers itched to run themselves through the silken mass but instead, I smiled.

"There really is no need to look after me, Monsieur," I continued in French. "I am quite well now."

I squirmed in my seat when he didn't immediately reply. "It's silly really, I've been afraid of planes since I was young."

"Oh?" He crossed his hands and I noticed that he didn't wear a watch, that his fingers were long and nimble. The freckles on the backs of those strong hands surprised me and I found them strangely appealing. I wanted badly to dig into the bag before my feet for my sketchpad.

Because I was uncomfortable, I nodded empathetically. "I was four when we moved to Puglia for a year and I don't remember the logistics of the move very well but I remember the plane." I looked at him from the corner of my eye and he nodded encouragingly, his hands steepled in front of his beautifully drawn lips. "It was with some budget airline and the plane itself was barely held together by rusty bolts. I think the captain might have been drunk because we dropped and dipped the whole way through."

"Which airline?" His voice was silky and cool, like the brush of a tie against my skin.

"I don't remember now." I frowned at him. "Why?"

He waved my question out of the air with those deeply blue eyes still intent on my face. "Tell me more."

Those are magic words to hear from a man, I think. It unfurls something hidden deep within a woman, something that is habitually scared and insecure. *Tell me more*. It was somehow intimate to hear those words, even from a stranger, *especially* from this stranger.

"My father was in debt so we were basically fleeing." I shrugged but the sharp ache of terror still resounded in my chest when I thought of my mother's despair, my brother's desolation. "Maybe I had caught the flu, or maybe I was scared, but I spent most of the flight losing the contents of my stomach. Needless to say, it wasn't a pleasant trip. Since then, I've travelled a lot, but the feeling never goes away."

"Ah, but flying is a pleasure." He did not smile, and I had the sense he rarely did, but his eyes grew dark with pleasure. "Close your eyes."

"Excuse me?"

"Close your eyes."

I pressed myself to the back of my chair when he leaned into me slightly in order to reach the button on my armrest. My chair tilted back and I found myself looking up into his lean face, his shoulder still warm against my front.

"Close your eyes," he repeated firmly.

I swallowed twice before doing so. I didn't know his name, where he came from, anything personal to mark him with. But somehow, it was thrilling. To be in the hands of a perfect stranger, to trust him enough to surrender my sight, to allow him to make even the simplest decision for me.

So, I hardly flinched when a blanket covered my chilled feet and was pulled up under my chin. His fingers, ridged with slight callous, brushed against the tender skin of my neck as he tucked me in.

"You are flying," he said quietly but it felt as though he spoke the words against my ear. "And if you relax, let every muscle loosen, and breathe deeply, there is nothing more soothing than being in the air."

Instead, the pit of my stomach coiled and I found myself wishing that I was another kind of person, someone who flirted with handsome strangers, who would lean into that firm mouth and take it without a qualm.

"We aren't in the air," I pointed out. "We are in a machine made out of metal that has no business being in the sky."

"Ah, it is the machine that frightens you." I wondered where he sat, if he remained leaning over me. "Let it be a bird then, a swan."

"Okay," I mumbled, suddenly exhausted. "But only because swans are mean."

I smiled at his husky chuckle but fell asleep before he could say anything else.

★ ★ ★

When I woke up, it was to the delicate tapping of rain against the window and the brisk click of fingers on a keyboard. Deeply rested and disorientated, I moaned and stretched myself across my seat before righting it. Blinking away sleep, I looked up and met the searing eyes of my stranger.

"You had a good rest," he noted, and for some reason, I flushed.

He was even more handsome than before, if that was possible. In the darkening night, his hair was mostly black, kissed red by the artificial overhead lights. He seemed like some creature of the night, something dark and too sexy to be true.

"Yes, thank you." We were speaking in English now and I couldn't remember if we had switched over before I fell asleep. His voice was smooth and cool, perfectly enunciated with just a hint of French charm.

"We land in twenty minutes." He watched my surprise and handed me a plastic cup of sparkling liquid. Our fingers brushed as he passed it off and a current of electricity made my grip on the cup shaky. Quickly, he righted it with his other hand and pressed both of my hands to the plastic. "You've got it?"

I nodded and flexed my fingers under his hold but he remained holding the cup, holding me, for a beat too long. He stared at me with a slight frown between his thick brows but I couldn't begin to discern if it was out of displeasure or surprise. I had never been so attracted to a man in my life, and I wondered if I was imagining the thickening tension between us. My tongue darted out to coat my dry lips and his eyes followed its path intently. Abruptly, his hands were gone and he was sitting back in his seat, his fingers flying on the keyboard of his Blackberry.

I blinked and slowly sank back into my chair. Obviously, I had misread the signs. I took a sip of the sparkling liquid and discovered with delight that it was Ginger Ale. Sipping it slowly to savour the sweet pop of bubbles on my tongue, I turned my attention to the early evening turning into twilight the colour of a bruise outside my window. The sparkling lights of Los Cabos could already be seen ahead of us and instead of wondering about the intrepid stranger beside me, I focused on my excitement. I had one week of paradise before I met with reality in New York City.

After five years in Paris and only a handful of visits in that time, I would finally be reunited with my family. The last time we had all lived under the same roof I had been nineteen years old. My twin siblings Cosima and Sebastian had been the first to leave, Cosima when she was seventeen in order to model in Milan and Sebastian months later to England, with Cosima's money in his pocket and a fierce determination to become an actor. I had lived with my mother and eldest sister Elena after that before journeying to Paris.

I squeezed my eyes shut and refused to think about those years. It had been nearly five now since I had left our small life in Napoli to attend *L'École des Beaux-Arts* in Paris. Though I was close to my family, it had been good for me to spend these years apart from them. I was returning home to them a better person than I had been when I had hastily fled and I was both excited and anxious for them to see that.

"What are you smiling at?"

His question was faintly brusque, as if he was irritated with me. When I turned to him though, his eyes were on the glowing screen of his phone.

"I haven't been home in a long time, I'm looking forward to seeing my family again."

"Your husband?" he asked tersely.

I laughed and it felt so delightful after hours of sickness and sleep that I laughed some more. He watched me with twisted lips, as if he wanted to smile but couldn't understand why. "Was that funny?"

"Oh, not really." I leaned forward conspiratorially. "But one needs a boyfriend to get married and I haven't had one of those in years."

"Now, that is funny." He put his phone back in his pocket and I felt a flash of triumph that he was once more focused on me. "It is incomprehensible to me that you would be single." His eyes sparkled as he leaned forward, and a lock of that over-long hair fell across his golden forehead. "Tell me, other than your obvious fear of flying, what's wrong with you?"

I laughed. "We're almost in Los Cabos, I don't have time to list all my flaws."

"I have a feeling there aren't many," he murmured, and stared at me in that way I was discovering he had, of looking through me and at me all at once. "But perhaps it's better that you don't tell me. A woman of mystery," his voice was low and smooth, so captivating I didn't register the pilot ready the plane for landing, "is a seductive thing."

"You had better tell me about yourself then." I leaned back in my seat as the plane began its steep descent into the city. "You're handsome enough already."

His loud chuckle surprised both of us. It was husky with disuse and his expression, though inherently beautiful, was almost pained. When the sound tapered off, it left him frowning. "What would you like to know?"

"Something repellent," I demanded cheerfully.

"Repellent? That's a tall order." Though normally I was uncomfortable under the eyes of another, those baby blues against my skin invigorated me and I beamed back at him. "When I look at you, I can only think of," his fingers found a lock of my auburn hair and he rubbed it between his fingers to release the scent, "Lavender and honey."

"Well." I cleared my throat. "Happily, we are talking about you."

His grin was wolfish as he leaned back in his seat again. "I make a very good living."

"Ah, you're one of those." His silver cuff links shone even in the dim light of the descending plane. "That helps, I'm more the starving artist type."

"Hardly starving." His eyes raked over my curves even though I wore a modest cotton shift.

Despite myself, I flushed. "No, but an artist all the same. Let me guess, you work with money."

"In a sense," he said, and his eyes danced. "Is this Twenty Questions?"

I laughed. "I haven't played that since I was a kid."

"Not so long ago."

"Long enough," I corrected and shot a look at him from the corner of my eye. "How old are you?"

"Thirty-one. I'm also 6'1 and I've broken my right arm three times." His small smile was a boyish contrast to his sharp, almost aggressively drawn features. I wanted desperately to trace the exaggerated line of his jaw and dip a finger into the slight hollow beneath his cheekbone.

"Twenty-four." I pulled the bulk of my wavy hair to one side in order to show him the tattoo behind my ear.

When I didn't explain its significance, he frowned. "What is it?"

"A mark," I said simply.

I jerked slightly when his fingers brushed over the swirled ink. "I like it."

"Thank you." My voice was breathy as I draped my hair once more over my shoulders.

"What brings you to Mexico? I take it your family doesn't

live here." A finger ran down my arm lightly, highlighting the paleness of my skin.

"My family is much more exotic than I am." I thought of Mama and the twins with a slight grimace; years of hero worship were hard to completely eradicate. "My best friend booked the trip but couldn't make it. I was only too happy to take her place."

He nodded, his eyes intense as he contemplated me. The connection between us thickened and hummed like the air during an electrical storm. Disturbed, I shifted away from him to look out the window as we swooped low over the ground above the runway. Strangely, I did not feel my usual apprehension as the plane tentatively brushed the tarmac once, twice, before smoothly landing.

We didn't speak as the pilot came on the overhead system announcing our arrival and it was only when we came to a slow stop at the terminal that I turned back to him. He faced forward, a furrow etched deeply between his brows and his mouth was firm with concentration. I wondered what he thought of me, of this strange meeting.

Sensing my gaze, he said, "I've been trying to decide if I should see you again."

"What makes you think I would want to?" His eyebrow arched and I gave into his silent reproach with a little shrug. "What's stopping you?"

The seat belt sign turned off and we both stood at the same time, suddenly almost touching, the slim space between us charged with electricity the colour of his eyes. He looked down at me, his deep chestnut hair softening the dangerous edge of his features. "I have never wanted someone the way I want you." His hand skimmed over my hip and sent a deep, throbbing shock through my system. "But I don't like the idea that you could very well change my life."

My heart clanged uncomfortably against my ribcage and though I desperately wanted to say something, I couldn't find the words to untangle the jumble of hormones and desires I had been reduced to. So instead, I watched a serious smile tilt one side of his closed lips as his eyes scraped over my face one last time and then, without a word still, he left.

Thanks Etc.

I first started writing about the Lombardi family when I was sixteen years old. The idea for Giselle and Sinclair's story (The Evolution of Sin) came to me like a lightning strike, quickly followed by the thunderous roll of a plot for Cosima.

But it's interesting how things develop over time. Not much changed about Giselle and Sin's story as I rewrote it years later, but Cosima and her story changed darkly and inexplicably as I wrote her side plot through their trilogy.

Originally, Cosima was a fashion model who became ensnared with a fashion house magnate. It involved infidelity and it was written in a much lighter tone.

Now, Cosima is still a model but she is slave to a completely different man. One who is cunning beyond understanding, ruthless to the point of cruelty and deeply defiant. Alexander Davenport crashed into the story and completely changed this narrative just as he completely changed Cosima's entire life and that of her family.

I love that the creative process is constantly growing and changing, hardly an ever-fixed mark on the horizon, but something elastic within each writer that grows and expands over time. Just as I can never fully finished exploring each writer I create, I can never fully understand the own mechanics of my creative brain, and I love that about this artistic expression.

Before I continue to the acknowledgments just a quick disclaimer, I do not in any way support human trafficking. This is a fictionalized version of a very scary and real problem that still faces our society. If you need to talk to someone about the realities of the social issue, please contact your national human trafficking center to learn more.

Now on to the good stuff, because thanking the people who make my dream job possible is like the icing on the cake of having published another novel.

As always, the first thank you goes to the woman I dedicated this book to, my PA and friend, Serena. I know I am an artistic mess as the worst of times and I cannot thank you enough for being patient with my process, my illnesses and my flakiness. You keep the ship on course even when I abandon it for a midnight swim with the sharks. There aren't words enough to express how much I love you, but I hope knowing I wrote this book with you constantly at the back of my mind if tribute enough.

Allaa, my twin and constant companion even though we live on different continents, I love you for your passion for my words. You inspire me to be a better writer every single day with your enthusiasm and love. I can't imagine a world where we don't nitpick over the perfect cover models and agonize over the right formatting for my paperbacks. You make my entire creative process even more fun, and I will always love for that.

To Ella, the Chanel to my Coco. Knowing you and speaking to you brings joy to my every day. It's so strange to think I've never held you in my arms yet I hold you so dear to my heart. I know these words will make you laugh uncomfortably, but I'm compulsively friendly and overly romantic as you know, so I had to do it ;)

To my #dirtysoulsister Michelle Clay. Before you, I never fully appreciated the meaning and beauty of sisterhood. You constantly provide a safe place for my ideas, personal sexy adventures and real-life pains. I could cry just thinking about the ways you're support has buoyed me in my hours of need. Love you forever.

Sarah from Musings of a Modern Book Belle, I love you so hard. I'm sorry I was a mess getting this book to you in time to beta, but I appreciate your every thought about my narratives and

I look forward to you beta reading again (for every single book in the future).

Jenny from Editing 4 Indies, you are my saviour. Thank you for polishing this manuscript from a diamond in the rough into a polished gem. I know put you in the pressure cooker with this release and I'm so grateful you put up with me because the finished product is perfect. I can't wait to work with you again.

Candi from Candi Kane PR, I finally found my guru and you're stuck with me. I loved working with you so much. You are one of the most genuine, fun, and hard working women in this industry and I think you're Wonder Woman.

Najla Qamber from Najla Qamber Designs, as always, deserves thanks for putting up with my last-minute demands for her gorgeous graphics and for making me the most stunning covers. I can't imagine working with anyone else and I wouldn't want to.

Stacey at Champagne Formatting is a genius and a wizard. Thank you for making my books so pretty and doing it so quickly on my tight schedule all the time. You rock.

I love thanking my gorgeous Master Alexander's Review Team for the amazing passion for my work and spreading the word about Alexander. I can't tell you how much it means to me that I have you ladies in my corner always cheering me on.

Giana's Darlings, you are the best reader's group on the planet and my safe, little happy place on the interweb. I love talking with you all about books, boys, and real-life problems. It's like having my own personal girl squad and that's pretty freaking cool.

I have to give a special thanks to two incredible women and authors who give me their invaluable time and advice whenever I ask for it (which is often because I'm still a novice). Leigh Shen and Sierra Simone, I love you both for your gorgeous stories, but even more for your enormous hearts.

I have so many friends in this amazing community that I

cannot possibly pay tribute to all of them, but quickly because I love you, thank you to: Lucia Franco, Charleigh Rose, Kennedy Ryan, Dylan Allen, Rebecca Scarlett, Fiona Cole, K Webster, Meagan Brandy, Amo Jones, Ker Dukey, QB Tyler, Cassie Chapman, Lylah James, Leigh Lennon, Skye Warren, Alessandra Torre, Shanora Edwards and Anne Malcom.

There are countless bloggers who made this release shine like the North Star in a sky filled with innumerable book release and I'm so grateful to each and every one of you. My most special thanks has to go to Jessica @peacelovebooksxo, Lisa @book_ish_life, @insanebooklover, @krysthereader and @kerilovesbooks for always sharing and supporting my posts.

To my sister Grace who wants to read every single book as soon as its written and who is probably prouder of me than I am of myself. You're the best sister a girl could ask for.

To my Armie. I have been forever changed by the beauty of our friendship. Every day without your laughter, beautiful face and positive energy is torture yet, I know that you could live in Antarctica or me the moon, we could be apart for decades, and the moment I saw you again everything would be just as it was between us. You are my soulmate best friend.

In all my wildest dreams and aspirations, I never imagined that I would be so happy as I've found myself this last year. It feels very rare and special to claim that two of my greatest dreams have come true in that time. One, is that I am making my living as a writer, something I have hoped to do since I was an eight-year-old girl. And the other, even more incredible dream, is being with the Love of My Love. I've known him since I was eleven and we developed childish crushes on each other, I've loved him since we were fifteen and our love felt too huge to comprehend, and I've fought for him every day since then because I know there was never anyone I would love as much as him. The path to true love is never easy, and my love story is no different. But that happily ever after you think only exists in romance books and fairy tales can come true. I'm living proof of that.

So, to the Love of My Life, thank you for holding me when I need to cry, for making me laugh every single day of our lives together, and for being proud of me even when I wasn't sure I should be proud of myself. There is no hero I could ever write who would be as perfect a man to me as you are. I will love you until the end of time.

About
giana darling

Giana Darling is a Top 40 Best Selling Canadian romance writer who specializes in the taboo and angsty side of love and romance. She currently lives in beautiful British Columbia where she spends time riding on the back of her man's bike, baking pies, and reading snuggled up with her cat Persephone.

Join my Reader's Group:
www.facebook.com/groups/819875051521137

Follow me on Twitter:
twitter.com/GianaDarling

Like me on Facebook:
www.facebook.com/gianadarling

Subscribe to my blog:
gianadarling.com

Follow me on Pinterest:
www.pinterest.com/gianadarling

Follow me on Goodreads:
www.goodreads.com/author/show/14901102.Giana_Darling

Newsletter:
eepurl.com/b0qnPr

IG:
www.instagram.com/gianadarlingauthor

Other Books by
giana darling

The Evolution of Sin Trology:

The Affair (The Evolution of Sin #1)
The Secret (The Evolution of Sin #2)
The Consequence (The Evolution of Sin #3)
The Evolution of Sin Trilogy Boxset

The Fallen Men Series:

Lessons in Corruption (The Fallen Men Series #1)
Welcome to the Dark Side (The Fallen Men Series #2)
Good Gone Bad (The Fallen Men Series #3)

Coming Soon:

Enamoured (The Enslaved Duet, Book 2)
Sloth (The Elite Seven Series, #7)
After the Fall (The Fallen Men Series #4)

Made in the USA
Middletown, DE
25 June 2019